"What if you discovered you could make your wishes real? When Jessie and Jared find that Angel Falls may grant them that power, they're forced to confront the effects their desires have on those they love. Teen and adult readers alike will be captivated, as I was, when mysteries of the past and secrets of the present collide in this eerie story of family, friendship, and the supernatural."

— Patricia Lillie, author of *The Cuckoo Girls*

"*Angel Falls* is a novel full of exquisite mysteries, tender magic, and family secrets. A generational saga that promises to heal the wounds of the past."

— Christopher Barzak, author of *Wonders of the Invisible World*

"Fast paced and compelling, *Angel Falls* is a page-turner with well-drawn characters and a terrific supernatural mystery propelling a story that is, at its core, about love, loss and the inevitability of change. I couldn't put it down."

—Lynda Rucker, author of *You'll Know When You Get There*

"What a lovely horror it is to enter Angel Falls where the air drips with fog, and the tender heart of human desire becomes a fetid root of loss. What a balm it is to go there and heal old wounds, without risk, through the gift of this well-told story!"

— M. Rickert author of *The Shipbuilder of Bellfairie* and *Lucky Girl, How I Became a Horror Writer: A Krampus Story*

Visit **www.angelfalls.org**

ANGEL FALLS

JULIA RUST
&
DAVID SURFACE

AN IMPRINT OF HAVERHILL HOUSE PUBLISHING LLC

Angel Falls © 2022 by Julia Rust & David Surface

978-1-949140-33-0 (Hardcover)
978-1-949140-34-7 (Trade Paperback)

Cover design & setup © 2022 Errick Nunnally

YAP Books is an imprint of Haverhill House Publishing LLC

For more information, address:
Haverhill House Publishing LLC
643 E Broadway
Haverhill MA 01830-2420

Visit us on the web at **www.HaverhillHouse.com**

ANGEL FALLS

"We are beset by a plague of angels or devils. God grant us the wisdom to discern one from the other."

> — from *A Compleat History of the Colonie of Angel Falls*

"The woods are lovely dark and deep"

> — Robert Frost, *Stopping By the Woods on a Snowy Evening*

Chapter 1

JESSIE

"Not much longer now," Jessie's father says. His good cheer sounds forced and grates on her nerves.

Looking through the windshield, she sees wipers barely clearing a semicircle before the rippling sheets of rain obscure the view. How can her father see to drive?

Jessie presses her forehead against the passenger window and stares out at the incessant splash of water. Beyond that, she can only see dull gray shapes, maybe trees, thinning out, becoming shorter, and then a sudden openness that could be a field or a lake. Other gray shapes, symmetrical with lights, buildings of some kind, fading back into a jagged line which might be a forest.

Now he's speaking again in the high-pitched, over-compensating tone he started using only two hours into the trip.

"Wait till you see the ocean, kitten. It's beautiful. Everywhere you go, water all around."

Jessie stares at the water pouring down her window but doesn't say anything.

The trip has been one long traffic jam from New York to the far side of Boston, but it isn't boredom or irritation Jessie feels. What she feels is fear. With every wet mile they put between themselves and home, she grows convinced she's made a terrible mistake.

"How can you even think of taking her there?" Her mother's voice was a harsh whisper that reached Jessie as she stood in the dark hallway. "That girl was Jessie's age!"

"It's not like I'm dropping her off at the edge of a forest. She'll be with me. What part of that seems so dangerous?"

"How can you keep an eye on her if you're meeting with realtors, contractors, whatever? Are you going to keep her with you every minute?"

"Oh, and that's what you've been doing all these years? You're just looking for an excuse to keep her."

Jessie squeezes her eyes closed against the memory. Their arguing had gotten worse, especially this past month.

"What was Mom talking about this morning?" she asks her dad now.

"What's that?"

"The girl my age? Mom was freaking out about it this morning. What happened?"

"Nothing," his answer sounds so quick and false that Jessie sputters out a laugh.

"Nothing?" she repeats.

Jessie sees his eyes flicker between the road and her face, measuring something. He goes on, "There was a girl who disappeared a few weeks ago. It was on the news this morning."

"From here?" The thought makes her shiver.

"Mmm-hmmm. She was last seen in the woods. You won't go there, of course. Nobody goes there."

"Of course," Jessie repeats, feeling its pull. Somebody goes there, or people wouldn't be scared of it. She looks at the wet blurry landscape speeding by.

"Do they think she's dead?"

He makes a strange sound in his throat before answering. "I don't know. You know everything I know."

Jessie leans her head against the window, thinking about how all this started.

"Your father's going to Beauport to take care of Cousin Dorothy's house," her mother had said. "He'll be a bachelor for the summer."

Jessie's mind had caught onto certain words; Beauport, summer, bachelor. *Her dad was leaving?*

She'd told her best friend, Dylan. "They're breaking up?" The sadness in Dylan's eyes made Jessie afraid it was true.

"I want to come with you," she told her dad that night, the instant joy in his face making her believe it was the right choice. She had to fix it. Fix them.

"Did you see the sign?"

Jessie jerks her head up and peers through the window. No sign, but there are buildings, nondescript angular blobs with lights in the windows even though it's late afternoon.

"Ten miles! Woohoo! We're almost there!"

"But you don't know anyone there," her mother had said. "Your father will be working most of the time. What will you do? Your life is here."

"I want to take care of Dad," Jessie said.

"That's not your job," her mother said, turning away, but Jessie could see the words hit home. *No. It's your job,* she thought.

"So come with us," Jessie blurted.

But her mother sighed. Her whole body moved with it. And Jessie knew the break was starting; she could feel it in her chest. She and her dad were leaving, and her mother wasn't coming with them.

"Second rotary! Which turn? Which turn?" Her dad's voice shocks her out of reverie, and she looks down for the line on the printed directions.

"Second right!" but he's already passed it; he's taking the third right, a minor road with a sign too small to read. Another car is right on their tail, and the road is narrow. So, they continue onward, looking for a place to turn around. The sound of a gunning engine and the lights behind them veer to the left. The car passes them, throwing water up and over the hood and windshield, blinding them.

Her father slows and peers through foggy glass. "Where are the houses?"

Jessie wipes off her window and peers into the gloom at the side of the road. It's like they fell off the map, all houses and shops vanished, and in their place, a wall of muddled dark shapes Jessie guesses are trees. The woods.

Finally, a side road appears, and her father stops the car to read a small wooden sign. It is black with wet, the faded letters barely legible.

Slowly as if he's having trouble reading the letters, her father reads, "Angel Falls."

The words sound mythic. A man with great wings, toppling out of the wet sky. She glances at her father, but he's squinting ahead at the dark path beyond the sign.

"Dad? Are we gonna sit here all night?" Jessie suddenly imagines a girl's body lying nearby beneath leaves and mud.

But her father doesn't answer. He stares into the dark for a few moments, then slowly pulls onto the road.

Jessie braces herself against the dashboard. "Wha...." Her voice catches in her throat, the way it feels in dreams when she tries to scream. "Dad! Stop! What are you doing?"

He stops the car, staring out at the looming dark for a few still moments. Then he puts the car in reverse and twists his body to look out the back. "Turning around, now." The car moves a few inches before the front tires spin in mud. "Damn," he says softly, takes his foot off the gas, puts it in drive, moves forward a few feet, and tries again. This time the car slithers to one side and then another before stopping, the sound of the spinning tires hurting her ears. It seems like the place is holding them here. Jessie's palms start to sweat. The gloom around the car seems to deepen and grow closer.

"It's okay, pumpkin. I'll get us out..." and again, forward a foot and backward, and again there's nothing but the high-pitched *wheeee* of spinning tires. She's afraid to look at her father, afraid to see worry there. She closes her eyes. This time, forward and back, and the tires grip and throw them onto the road. Her father shifts into drive, and they quickly return to the rotary.

They exit onto a well-lit road with signs indicating Beauport city limits, and relief pours through Jessie, the dead girl's image fading. She sees a raggedy-looking building full of lights, its parking lot overrun by cars. She reads the sign aloud.

"Rick's."

Her father almost shouts in delight, "Rick's is still open? That place makes the best chowder on earth. My grandpa brought us here. Oh, baby, are you in for a treat," and before she can object, he pulls into the parking lot and stops the car.

"Dad..." She isn't moving.

He is out and around the car, opening her door, umbrella in hand. "You've got to taste this. Come in. You must be hungry."

"Please. Can't we go to the house? I'm tired."

"How about I get it to go? You want to come inside?"

She declines and leans her head back. She watches him open the door; the light from inside highlights her father's face, happy, laughing, and then he's inside. The door shuts behind him, leaving the day darker, the rain

4

resuming harder than before. She can't make out the building or the other cars; she could be deep in the ocean. The image comes to her, a great tidal wave submerging the car, the café, and the eastern Massachusetts coastline. Her breath shortens, and the outside is completely gone until she realizes the windows have fogged. She rubs a face-sized circle in the glass and peers out.

A face peers in at her, inches from the glass, wild-eyed with a gap-toothed grin, and before she can hit the lock, the door flies open as she desperately hangs onto the handle and screams.

CHAPTER 2

JARED

Jared pedals as fast as he can. The rain that slashes his face is cold and feels sharp as knives, but he keeps going. It's ten minutes from school to Rick's, where he's due at 3:30 for the afternoon shift. On good days he's only a few minutes late, but today with the rain, the traffic is slow, so he stands up in the seat and pumps harder, whipping between slow cars, ignoring the blaring horns and the occasional angry shout.

When he turns into the gravel parking lot, he can see dozens of cars parked side-by-side with license plates from Massachusetts, Connecticut, New Hampshire, and even New York and New Jersey. Jared cuts behind the building and throws his bike against the cinderblock wall. He flies through the kitchen doorway and snatches his apron from a peg on the wall.

Jeff looks up from the steaming pot of chowder he's tending, his sweaty red face twisted into a smirk. "Late again, schoolboy?" Jared ignores him and ties the apron around his waist, hands moving fast, then takes his place at the sink.

Dirty plates and bowls, cups and saucers, glasses, forks, and knives keep coming in a steady stream. Jared washes them and sets them aside as fast as he can until the sink is almost empty, then Kate comes up behind him and dumps another load of dirty plates and cutlery with a loud clatter and splash.

Jared glances up at the clock on the kitchen wall—not even four o'clock yet, and he's already tired. At six a.m., he was here helping Rick unload the fish, shrimp, and scallops for the day from Gus's truck. Then he'd mopped the floor, wiped down the tables, peeled and diced enough potatoes and carrots for an army. When the four large vats of chowder were bubbling on the range, he'd stripped off his apron, jumped on his bike, and rode three miles back to town for summer school, where he sat in the back of the classroom and listened to Mr. Delany explain the difference between a simile and a metaphor. Then back to the restaurant to tie on his apron again.

Standing at the sink with his arms elbow-deep in greasy, soapy hot water, Jared runs through the numbers in his head. Twenty minutes to ride home, maybe thirty in this rain. He needs to get home before his dad wakes up. He knows nothing can happen while his dad's asleep, but he's never sure how long that will be. Six o'clock? Five o'clock?

Jared's halfway through the latest load of dishes when Rick pokes his head around the corner. "Jared—need you up front." Jared heads out to the counter full of regulars nursing their giant bowls of chowder, and right behind them, a sea of looming faces. Kate gives him a grateful-but-exhausted look and points toward where the line is building up and almost out the door.

Grabbing a pad and pencil, Jared starts taking orders. After two or three, he turns on his heel and clips them to the wire, facing into the kitchen so Manuel can read them. He turns back to take the next order like a ballplayer making a tag. Every time he turns around, he sees the clock on the kitchen wall. The little hand is on the five, the big hand creeping closer and closer to the six, just like he knows his dad is getting closer and closer to waking up in their little upstairs apartment on Plymouth Street, alone and in the dark.

"Excuse me," a loud voice cuts through Jared's thoughts. Jared sees a tall man wearing wire-rim glasses and a big, hopeful smile. The smile flickers as the man looks down at a couple standing next to him at the counter. "I'm sorry, did I cut in front of you?" He looks back up at Jared, eyes wide and questioning behind his lenses. "I'm sorry. Is it my turn?"

"What can I get you?" Jared asks. The man's smile blooms, and his eyes dart above Jared's head at the menu and around the room.

"Wow, this is great. This place hasn't changed a bit."

"Sir."

"Oh, oh yeah, sorry," the man says, flustered but still smiling. "I'll take ... we'll take two bowls of chowder to go, please."

"Anything to drink?"

"Oh." the man looks startled, glances over his shoulder at the parking lot, then turns back and fishes a cell phone out of his pocket. "'Sorry, just a minute." The couple behind him starts glaring. Oblivious to all this, the man looks worriedly out the window, pressing the cell phone to his ear. "Sorry," he mutters distractedly. "She's not ...."

"Jared!" Rick's voice booms out from the kitchen behind him. "Run this garbage out." Jared turns and points at the waiting crowd with a what-the-hell look on his face. "Kate's got it," Rick says. "*Now*, please." Jared turns and goes back to the kitchen, leaving the tall man still mumbling to himself and pushing buttons on his cell phone.

Outside, rain is pounding the gravel, stinging his neck and shoulders, plastering his hair to his head, and running into his eyes. As he moves through the rain toward the garbage bin, he hears a muffled electronic ringing—a cell phone, probably inside one of these cars.

From the corner of his eye, Jared sees someone standing at the corner of the parking lot, not running to get inside, simply standing in the pounding rain. Before he can make out the figure, he knows who it is.

"Pete," he yells. "Yo, Pete. Get inside, buddy."

The shadowy form starts to shuffle aimlessly, not toward the restaurant but along the row of cars parked by the fence. Poor old Pete, drunk again. Jared throws the bags into the rusty bin, then looks for Pete and sees him slumped against one of the cars, fumbling at the door handle. The door swings open, and Jared hears a girl's wailing voice.

Jared runs as fast as possible to where Pete is still trying to open the car door in a tug-of-war with someone inside trying to pull it shut. He puts his hands on Pete's shoulders from behind and pulls him away from the car, not too hard but firmly. "Pete," he says it loud so he can be heard over the roar of the rain, "Come on back inside." Pete straightens up, and the car door slams shut, but not before Jared glimpses a long white forearm, a hand with slim fingers and nails painted sky blue.

Jared turns Pete away from the car and walks him back toward the restaurant. The old guy's shoulders feel so boney and sharp; Jared feels like he's walking with a skeleton. He pushes the old man inside, then runs back through the rain toward the green car where he'd heard the girl's voice wailing.

The car's doors are shut, and the windows are fogged over, so he can't see inside. There's a round smudge on the glass where someone inside has tried to rub the glass clear. Through it, he sees a pair of eyes, large and pale blue, staring up at him.

"You okay?" he yells. At first, he's not sure if he's been heard, then the window rolls down a couple of inches at first, then a few more. A young girl, probably about his age, is staring up at him. Her hair is long and dull blond, her face is plain, but her eyes are huge, the biggest he's ever seen, wide open and afraid.

"Don't worry about him," he says. "Pete's harmless. He probably thought this was his sister's car. Are you okay?" The girl nods and looks like she's about to speak when he hears that ringing again, this time loud and clear, coming from inside the car. He watches her staring down at the ringing cell phone on the seat next to her, an annoyed look on her face, and suddenly he knows who she is.

"Your dad wants to know if you want something to drink," he says.

She looks up at him, startled. "What?"

He can see the rain is getting her wet, too, the drops make little dark spots on her shirt, but she doesn't notice.

"So," he says again, "you want something to drink or not?"

"No. Thank you." Her voice is shaky, still afraid.

"Okay then," he says. Her hair is getting wetter in the rain, the water weighing it down into dark tendrils framing her troubled face. "Better roll up your window," he says and walks back through the rain to the restaurant. *And answer your damn phone next time.*

Chapter 3

The House

"Don't worry, sweetheart, we're almost there." Jessie's dad says. He steers the car slowly through the narrow, twisting streets, peering through the rain-swept window at the small houses huddled together in the dark. Jessie doesn't answer. She's still shaking from her encounter with the crazy man. Her skin burns with humiliation. The boy saw her scared.

He heard her scream.

Her dad presses the brake, and she lurches forward from the sudden stop. "That's it," her dad says, "That's the one." Jessie looks through the rainy window and can barely make out the shape of a house, with no light in any of its windows. Jessie and her dad run from the car across steppingstones to a dark doorway. It takes her father a few tries with a couple of keys before he gets the door open, and they both rush in out of the rain.

A burst of old woman smell fills her nose. Dust, a faint scent of lavender, furniture polish, maybe? And something sour that, to Jessie, seems to accompany old people.

The outside gloom seems to follow them through the door, and even when her father switches on the ceiling light, it barely cuts through.

Here deep shadows line the walls. There are lamps on low tables, which he quickly lights, their dim bulbs making little headway in the evening murk. It's past six but could be ten or midnight, with no light coming through the faded curtains.

The word *mistake* sings in her ears.

Her father lets out a low whistle. "This place hasn't changed."

"Where's the bathroom?"

"I'm sorry. Of course, first things first," he says, but as he looks wide-eyed around the dusty room, it's clear he doesn't know. Jessie moves toward a dark hallway where she finds two closed doors directly in front of her and something she can't make out at the end of the hall. She feels for a light switch on the wall, finding a raised velvet pattern in the wallpaper. She finds and clicks the switch, another dim lightbulb comes on, and she can see a toilet through an open door at the end of the hallway.

Inside the bathroom with the door closed, Jessie bites her lip hard, but tears come anyway. The longing to be home is so intense it bends her double, and she hugs herself hard, willing the tears away. This is where she'll be spending the summer. The entire summer! Eight long weeks with only her dad. What was she thinking?

She washes her face, staring at her eyes in the mirror. It's like they belong to someone else—someone who knows what she is doing.

When she returns to the living room, she finds her father bending over a sideboard, staring intently at something. He looks up as she moves into the room.

"Come here. I want to show you something."

She moves next to him and sees an old-fashioned toy farm: barn door, silo, trees, and sky painted on the wood backing. There's a paddock with metal figures, paint peeling: a tiny pig, cow, goose, water trough, and farmer in overalls. Nearby a miniature farmhouse stands with its door ajar. "She had this when I was a boy. I used to beg her to let me play with it."

Jessie stares at the tiny man, his face almost devoid of paint. He looks sad. There is no farm woman. No children. Even the animals look sad.

Jessie shivers and feels a pang of hunger. She thinks the prized chowder must be cold by now.

"Can we eat?" It sounds more plaintive than she feels.

"Oh, sweetie!" her dad exclaims, "Yes, well, I'm sure..." he steps up to an area of the room with a round table, a bowl of dusty fruit taking up space in the center. He puts down the bag from the restaurant and then disappears through a dark doorway.

Doors open and close, and her father is muttering. He needs her help. Jessie the finder. She goes through the doorway and into a kitchen.

Here it smells of older things, old cooking, old spices. The stove is small, white enamel with rounded corners. Under the burners, there are black marks, scratches, or burnt food; Jessie can't tell. The fridge is also small, white, and ancient. It makes her think of ads she's seen on brittle yellow paper in the antique shop by her school. The cabinets are of painted wood, some doors hanging crooked on their hinges. And her father is still muttering.

"Need help?" Jessie doesn't wait for his answer. She opens the cupboard nearest the fridge and pulls out two plain white bowls and two glasses.

"Who needs GPS when I've got you?" Her father gives her a squeeze, taking the bowls from her and rummaging through drawers. Jessie opens the drawer nearest her, and something skitters out of the sudden light to the back of the drawer. Jessie jumps back, covering her mouth with her hand.

"What?" her father says, seeing where she's staring. "Creepy crawly?" He hands her the bowls. "You take these out to the dining room. I'll take care of this." And she's glad to leave, not to see whatever it was. She sits down and listens as something slams against the counter, and her father's voice, "Gotcha!" followed by a door opening. Her kind dad, letting the bug outside. As if it would be grateful in all this rain.

He comes back out with glasses of water and spoons. He removes two containers from the bag. Steam rises when the plastic lid is lifted, and an aroma thick with ocean and onion and cream fills Jessie's nose and mouth, and her stomach grumbles. Her father opens a bag of oyster crackers and fills the bowls with the thick, lumpy soup. They dig in, silent but for her father's soft moan of pleasure.

The chowder tastes rich, sweet, and salty, the potatoes burning her tongue, but she doesn't stop, slurping it up with handfuls of crackers and emptying the bowl in no time at all. She looks up to see her father's grin.

"Not bad, eh? Tell me it's the best thing you've ever had. Go on, tell me," he says, and he pokes her in the ribs.

"Okay, okay, the best, now stop... please..." she's laughing now.

When the laughter fades away, a silence falls, so complete it's eerie. Slowly, Jessie becomes aware of rain dripping on the roof, the ticking of a clock somewhere. They are in a dead woman's house—*Cousin Dorothy*. Jessie is alone with her dad.

"The groceries!" Her dad jumps up. "Damn, sorry kitten, I'll bring in the cooler. Take the dishes to the kitchen, please, then call your mom." And before she can say anything, he's out the front door.

Jessie carries the bowls with spoons jangling into the kitchen. She enters more slowly than before, her eyes darting everywhere, the fear of finding something with too many legs, something that makes that noise. Nothing moves, so she approaches the sink slowly and peers in, holding her breath. It's empty, so she places the bowls there. She turns on the water to a great thumping of pipes, a sudden sputter. The white bowls fill with brown water, and Jessie feels panic rising, but the water clears after running for a few moments. She fills the bowls with hot water and goes back to the living room.

The room seems lighter now. Not light, not by a long shot, but less dark. Or maybe it is the outside dark growing deeper. She thinks of calling her mother, but something holds her back, a sore spot she feels in her chest now. *She should be here,* Jessie thinks. *She should be here with us.*

She wanders around the living room, examining objects. There is a layer of dust on every surface. Jessie imagines vines growing up through the floor, covering the furniture, working through the plaster on the wall. If she and her dad hadn't come here, would that have happened? A bookshelf lines part of one wall, and she scans the spines, looking for something familiar. She reads *Fort Clarke* and *The Other Cape* and *Beauport, Then and Now.* One of the volumes is tilted, hastily stowed, and slightly less dusty. Its spine is blank, so she pulls it out, cobwebs trailing, and wipes it off.

A Compleat History of the Colonie of Angel Falls.

She flashes on the faded sign next to the bleak road where their car was stuck in the mud. *People lived there?*

She opens the book to find thin, brittle pages and carefully flips through to the first full page of text.

> *In 1641, Englishmen led by Captain Gilroy Clarke landed on the Cape near the area later to become Beauport township. They were encouraged to settle inland after skirmishes with local Indian tribes made it impossible to settle along the coastal areas. The colonie was originally named Fort Clarke, but colonists adopted the name Angel Falls after a bereaved mother claimed to have seen an Angel holding her child in its arms and standing at the peak of a local waterfall.*

Her phone rings. She pulls it out and sees a picture of her mother filling the screen, all eyes and teeth.

She puts down the book, wipes her hands, and presses *Accept.* "Hi Mom," she says.

"Hey you. I've been waiting and waiting."

"I know, I'm sorry. We just got here."

"Was there a lot of traffic?"

"I guess."

"How are you? What do you think of the place? Is it raining there?"

"I'm okay. Yeah, it's pretty wet still."

"Here too. Have you eaten anything?"

Jessie can't help herself; it makes her smile. "Yes, Mother." Her mom laughs. "How was rehearsal?"

"Okay, I guess, you know, early days." Her mother's voice is sing-song. Jessie does know. She remembers watching as Jessie's mom and cast members meander around a bare rehearsal space, books in hand. So hard to see a play in all the stops and starts. Her mother says, "I could use help with my lines."

It's the closest thing she's said to *'I miss you.'* Jessie feels the pull of the unspoken words. She begs her silently, *don't ask me to come home.* She can hear her dad at the door, fumbling with the knob. "I gotta help Dad with the groceries." She opens the front door and takes a bag precariously perched on the cooler. "Say hi to Mom." She pokes the phone close to her dad's face.

"Hi Cynthia," he obliges, then puts down the cooler and the other bags and wipes his feet on the doormat.

"I should go," Jessie says, sensing her mother's wish for her to come home in the silence that follows. *Please, don't say it,* she begs silently.

"All right then. Enjoy. I'll talk to you tomorrow. Mwah!"

"Mwah," Jessie replies, and her mother's gone.

And she hadn't said it. She hadn't said *Come home.* And Jessie's stomach flips; her eyes burn. She looks around the strange room, cobwebs along the tops of picture frames holding the faces of strangers, so many of them, everywhere she looks.

A dead woman's house. Jessie shivers.

Why am I here?

CHAPTER 4

PLYMOUTH STREET

It's almost six-thirty when Jared turns his bike off of Route 63 and starts the steep climb up Plymouth Street, pedaling hard until his thighs are burning. The rain lets up, enough to help him make good time, but not good enough––he knows his dad will be awake by now.

He speeds past all the plain white clapboard row houses until he reaches 474. Jared leaps off his bike before it comes to a stop, heaves it onto his shoulder by the top tube, and runs up the stairs, the keys already in his hand.

Inside the dark hallway, there's the sour smell of mildew and a trace of fishy ocean air. Jared can smell the heavy, smoky aroma of fried food, but he knows it's coming from his clothes and his skin—even the rain can't wash it off.

He carries his bike up the two flights of stairs, the rotten boards creaking under his weight. Jared pushes the key into the lock and then hesitates, frozen by the fear of what he might find on the other side. The same fear that stops him every time.

Jared turns the key and pushes the door open slowly. His dad is standing in the kitchen in front of one of the large canvasses nailed to the wall. His jeans and shirt are spattered with the same colors covering the canvas, black and dark gold and pale blue. His hair hangs around his face in stiff dirty strands, and drops of blue paint cling to his beard. He's staring at the canvas, and for a moment, Jared catches a glimpse of the blank, haunted face he's seen before, the one that frightened him when he was a child.

"Hey, Dad," Jared says. His dad looks at him, and his easy, familiar smile slowly replaces the vacant look. The tension in Jared's gut eases a little.

"Hey, buddy," his dad finally says, louder and cheerier than necessary. "How was school?"

"Good," Jared says, leaning his bike against the wall by the door. Jared glances at the paintings tacked to the kitchen walls, large dark bruises of stormy colors running down the canvas in harsh streaks and smears.

"You like it?"

Jared turns to see his dad looking at him with an expression that's so shy and unconfident it nearly breaks his heart.

"Yeah," Jared answers instantly, "Yeah, I do." Jared keeps his voice cheerful. He doesn't understand why his dad stopped painting the beach scenes he was famous for, the big paintings of sailboats and lighthouses wealthy tourists from New York and Boston used to buy.

The air is heavy with linseed oil and turpentine, smells Jared has known all his life. What he doesn't smell is food—nothing cooking on the stovetop, nothing in the oven.

For a moment, Jared can see his dad in the kitchen of their old house on Decatur Street, slicing onions and dicing garlic on Thursday nights. It's one of Jared's oldest memories—the sharp sizzle and pop of hot olive oil and the delicious aroma of homemade marinara sauce. His dad, smiling and laughing, letting him hold the big knife to help chop the herbs. His dad's strong hand on top of his, guiding him. *That's right, buddy. That's the way.*

That was before his mother left—before he'd moved with his dad into this tiny apartment. Before his dad had dragged all his paints and canvasses into the kitchen and started working there.

"You want me to go down to Sal's and get us some subs?" Jared offers. His dad doesn't answer. He's still staring at the canvas. Jared goes over to the coffee can on the counter, pulls out a five, three singles, and then starts counting out coins—three dollars in quarters, sixty cents in dimes. With the paper money, that's a little over ten dollars. Just enough for two subs. Good thing he gets paid tomorrow.

On his way out the door, Jared stops to look at his dad, who has stopped painting and is staring at the canvas, the blank, haunted look on his face again. Jared tries to estimate how long it'll take him to walk to Sal's, order the subs, and get back. Ten minutes? Maybe fifteen. *He'll be okay,* Jared thinks. *It's only fifteen minutes.*

"I'll be back in a minute, Dad," Jared says. "You okay?"

For a moment, Jared believes his dad hasn't heard him. Then the expression flickers across his face again, and he shows his familiar smile. "Sure. Why?"

"No reason," Jared shrugs. He looks at his dad's painting on the wall, and there, inside a shimmering, melting field of black and gold that reminds him of rain running down a window, he sees two pale blue orbs. They remind him of something, but he can't remember what.

Jared feels a stab of hunger, so he steps out into the hallway, takes one last look at his dad, then closes the door behind him. He slowly descends the stairs, but as soon as his feet touch the sidewalk, he runs as fast as he can.

CHAPTER 5

WHALE WATCH

Jessie wakes to the sound of rain. She hears it before opening her eyes in a dim room she doesn't recognize. The faded flower wallpaper and the dark wooden beams overhead look strange until she remembers where she is.

She swings her legs over the bed and walks to the window. Lifting the curtain, she peers out at the same wet blur of grey she's woken up to every day. Dad tried to put a happy face on things, promising her that the rain would stop soon. That was four days ago.

Jessie usually likes the sound of rain, the soft whispering noise that relaxes her and helps her go to sleep. Not this rain. This rain knocks and bangs on the eaves and the gutters like angry people trying to get in, making it impossible to sleep. After three days of this, she's exhausted and wants to go back to bed, but she knows the rain won't let her.

She opens her door and enters the hallway. The smell of coffee hits her, strong and reassuring; a smell she's known every morning of her life. Dad's up.

She wanders into the kitchen, where her dad lifts his mug in salute.

"Morning, kitten."

"Morning," she ducks under his free arm for a hug, then moves away and opens the fridge, pulling out a bottle of orange juice.

"Sorry about the rain. It's supposed to clear up later in the day."

Sure it will, she thinks. But instead of saying what's on her mind, she forces a smile because she knows it's what he wants to see. Why should he be unhappy too?

Jessie has spent the last three days trapped inside this dusty old house, helping her dad organize Cousin Dorothy's papers: copies of bills, letters, legal documents. Some were stuffed in the drawers and cubbies of an old wooden desk. Her dad said there should be more papers, so they'd looked and found them in the bedroom closet, stuffed in cardboard boxes of various vintages, dozens of them, stacked three deep and chest high. Her dad sighed when he saw them.

She'd helped him for as long as she could, carrying the dusty cardboard boxes out to the kitchen table, which was now her dad's office, moving the boxes back to the closet when he was finished with them, then bringing him more. The oldest boxes smelled like dead leaves and felt like they might come apart in her hands. She knows her dad doesn't want her to feel left out or ignored, but after three days, he's running out of things for her to do. She can tell from the nervous, distracted way he speaks to her when he looks up from the piles of old papers and notices her watching him.

"So, Dad...do you need any help?" she asks because she feels like she has to and because there's nothing else to do.

"Uh, thanks, kitten. I..." His eyes dart from the papers in front of him, to her face, then back down again. "I, uh ...." He looks so guilty that if he could tear himself right down the middle and leave half at this table, she thinks he would. She can't stand to watch him. A loud hammering racket starts somewhere over their heads—water overflowing a gutter.

"That's okay," Jessie says, "I'll just see if I can text Dylan or something."

"Sure, kitten. That sounds fine." The relief on her dad's face causes pain somewhere in her chest, and she turns and leaves the kitchen before he can see it.

The wash of water blurs the view outside her bedroom window. Her window looks melted, the figures beyond blurred with no edges. Jessie's eyes shift their focus to the faint smudges on the pane of glass, traces of oil from her finger from days of drawing in the foggy condensation. She draws a happy face on the glass, then crosses it with a big 'X.'

She's barely texted the words *Still raining,* when Dylan's photo fills the screen, lips pursed, blowing a kiss. Jessie presses the green circle *Accept.*

"You don't want to be here now," Dylan says, not waiting for Jessie to say hello. "I get soaked everywhere I go. You *know* what this weather does to my hair!"

"Yeah, makes it even more amazing." She can see her friend twist the thick red curls into a bun where it stays without pins. The longing to be with her makes her ache.

"Makes it crr-azy. Oh my god, did I tell you I'm taking guitar?"

"Guitar? Really? Since when?" Jessie feels a disconnect. Dylan doesn't have a guitar.

"Karen started last month and sounds so good, you wouldn't believe it, so I asked her about it, and she told me she's taking from Glen Browning. I had my first lesson today."

"Who?"

"Glen Browning, he's a senior. You know, the tall one always in black? Come on, you know! He's gorgeous! Anyway, he's a really good player, and I'm learning so much." Jessie doesn't remember him, but she can imagine her friend bending over a guitar while a tall, handsome almost-man sits nearby, leaning close to adjust her fingers.

"If he's gorgeous, how do you focus?"

Dylan laughs, not happy exactly, but *knowing,* and suddenly, Dylan isn't only 250 miles away; she's in a new world. Jessie thinks of this guy touching Dylan, maybe reaching around her from behind, his arms behind hers, showing her where to put her hands, his chest pressed against her back. The image bothers her, and she wants to be told that's not how it is.

Jessie says quickly, "Did you ask your parents when you can come?"

"Yeah, still August, I think. Maybe. Mom's gonna talk to your mom."

This should make her happy, but Jessie has no idea what her mom will say if she'll put her off the same way she's been putting off Jessie. *August is so far off.*

Jessie has nothing more to say. Her life is rain and dusty boxes, so she mumbles, "Gotta go, later 'gator," and presses the red circle to disconnect. She stands and steps in a puddle, her sock soaking up the cold liquid. It takes her several minutes before realizing it's coming from the ceiling.

"Dad!" she calls out.

He comes running into the room, saying, "What is it?" in a high voice.

"Water's coming in!" She points up. He follows her gaze and then down at their feet.

"Okay. Not too bad. You get a towel. I'll get something to catch it."

When she's back from the bathroom, towel in hand, her father's there with a stool in one hand and a dishpan in the other. "We'll put it like this..." he places the stool directly under the dripping ceiling and puts the dishpan on top. Instantly there's a *splat* as the water drips in. "Maybe we should check all the rooms?"

They find another leak in the hallway by the bathroom door. "See if you can find a big bowl, honey. I'll get the other stool." They watch the water gather in a seam of the ceiling. It fattens slowly, then separates into one large drop, which falls into the bowl with a sharp *ping.*

That night, like every night, she lies on her back in the dark, trying not to hear the pounding, rattling noises of the rain. But she is surprised by sleep and finds herself moving through a dark, dense wood. She has someplace to be, someone to meet, but she is lost, and the trees barely allow space for her to walk. Wet leaves slap her cheeks, covering her face so she can't breathe. She tries to scream, but the leaves fill her mouth.

With a soft moan, she wakes up and instantly realizes the light is different. Her room is full of light, the furnishings and pictures a soft gold hue. She pulls the curtains back; the glass is clear. The rain has stopped.

Outside her window is a small patch of grass facing the weathered clapboard siding of the house next door. Above its roof, the sky is brilliant blue, cloudless. She gets up and goes to the living room to look out front. Cars are moving in a slow, steady stream, and across the road, beyond a line of short fishing shacks, there is only the sky.

She opens the door, and the smell of the ocean slaps her in the face. And there, between the buildings, Jessie has her first glimpse of the harbor. Shale and sand glimmer in the sun, the smooth beach pocked with pebbles and strewn with brown seaweed. Boats rock gently against their moorings, and out beyond, she can see fishing boats setting out to sea. By the time she turns around, her father's there, drinking in the sunlight, the view, grinning so broadly, his eyes disappear. *He looks twelve years old*, Jessie thinks, putting her hand in his and smiling.

"Isn't this beautiful?" He's beaming at her, but she can see something. A bit of pleading, *Tell me it's beautiful.* She nods.

As they walk around the harbor, Jessie realizes how good it feels to stretch her legs, to walk with swinging arms, and the sun on her skin. Sunlight, sparkling water, and her father's joy are infectious.

"So, where are we going?" Jessie asks.

"You'll see," he grins. He'd promised her a surprise, a special treat to celebrate their first day of good weather. *Probably ice cream,* she guesses. Then she sees a long line of people gathered at the edge of a wooden dock, a big blue-and-white wooden sign with a cartoon figure of a smiling whale spouting water: **WHALE WATCH TOURS.**

She looks at him, her mouth wide open with amazement.

"Surprised?" her dad smiles. Before she can stop herself, she throws her arms around him and squeezes him as tightly as she can, wondering if other people are looking at her, not caring.

Standing in line to board, she notices a boy her age ahead of them, looking as unhappy as she's been over the past few days. "There's one of your kind," her father says.

"Dad!" She glares at him, checking to see if the boy heard and if he's noticed her. But he's wearing earbuds, a scowl on his face, and doesn't move when the people in front begin to board. A man standing beside him puts his hand on the boy's shoulder. The boy shrugs him off and shuffles forward.

Once they hit the main deck, Jessie says, "Can we go up top?" When he nods, she moves quickly to the stairs at the rear. She leans over the rail, feeling the engine's vibration through her feet. The shore is pulling away from her as the PA blares a welcome and describes a private castle off to their right–*Starboard,* Jessie says to herself, craning to see it.

Her father points down the coast to some tall buildings floating in a blue haze near the horizon and says, "Boston!" A place Jessie's never been. She nods and smiles at him, turning back and squinting at the sparkling sea. An island appears with two tall, thin lighthouses, one at either end, strange and lovely.

They ride for a while in silence. She starts to ask *how long before we get there?* but stops. The words sound whiny and complaining.

"Too bad Mom isn't here. She'd love this," Jessie says, then wonders if it's true.

Would she love this?

Her father doesn't say anything, and when she looks at him, he's frowning slightly.

She can't tell if he looks sad or just befuddled. She regrets her comment.

"We were on a whale watch when you were a baby." Jessie listens, attention sharp, her ears straining to make out every word. "We left you with your aunt Libby and had a mini-vacation on Cape Cod." He is silent for a long time.

"What happened? Did she like it?"

His face is suddenly blank. She can't tell if the memory is good or bad. "I think she got a little sea-sick," he grins. "But when we got out to the whales... well, you'll see."

"What? Tell me."

His face softens as he looks at her and smiles. "She loved it. Who wouldn't? Just you wait and see."

He turns to watch the ocean, and she joins him. Jessie imagines her mother, face perfectly made-up and hair in a scarf, laughing with her father at the rail, holding his hand. She can see it as if it's happening now, as if she were with them today on this boat, yet the image isn't clear. She can't think of a time when her parents held hands.

Jessie leans against her father, and his arm comes around her instantly.

"There!" he shouts, and she follows his pointing finger but sees nothing. The engine slows and stops, the crew member announcing, "Off the port side, watch for spouting." There is a sudden silence, the boat rocking from side to side as the passengers move to the left side to look. Someone shouts, "There! Look!" and Jessie sees what looks like a rolling wave, dark and smooth, barely breaking the surface of the sea before it disappears.

Her father says, "Keep watching." When nothing happens, she scans the water around them.

"Over there!" To the right are more spouts, and the boat shifts as everyone moves over, crowding the rails. Jessie notices other boats, some larger, some smaller, all rocking in the same waves as theirs. And then she sees a dark shape breaking the surface, black and shiny. The PA blasts, "This is a humpback, possibly Sherry, we'll know if she breaches." The whale curves up partway out of the water before sliding back in, and the tail rises, slowly, water dripping and sparkling as it twists before disappearing in the water.

Jessie's lips, dry from salt, scrape her teeth, and she realizes she's smiling hard. Whales! Another one arches out of the water, breeches, tail waving. And again. They take her breath, five, six, she's lost count.

"I told you so," her father says, eyes bright.

"You told me so what?" she says.

"I told you, you'd love the ocean."

And she does, and her summer, like a light switch being flipped, looks completely different. Her mother will come to Beauport. She will love it here. They'll be together on a boat. She can see it. She can see her mother looking at her father with new eyes. Loving him. Happy. Jessie closes her eyes and wishes for it so hard her nails dig into her palms, her breathing stops.

"Open your eyes, open your eyes!" Her father is shaking her, and right there, a few feet from the boat, a whale is gliding by on the water's surface, one fin raised in a regal wave.

CHAPTER 6

DELANY

When the buzzing alarm cuts through the fog in Jared's brain, he knows he overslept before he opens his eyes. He can feel it in the heaviness of his limbs, the way his body feels like it's melted overnight into the mattress beneath him. He turns his head and tries to focus on the clock and its red-lit numbers: 8:35. *Shit.*

Jared drags himself out of bed, finds his clothes on the floor, and gets dressed quickly. He walks carefully through the kitchen where his dad is asleep in a chair, his head resting in his arms on the kitchen table, which is now more of a painter's palette, broad pools of Windsor Blue and Burnt Umber drying on the linoleum next to tin foil wrappers and crusts of last night's sandwiches. Jared waits until he's sure he sees his dad's chest moving up and down. Then he picks up his bike, one hand on the tire so the wheel won't click, goes out into the hallway, and locks the door behind him.

The morning air is cold on his skin, even though it's summer. At the top of Plymouth Street, he stops pedaling and lets gravity do the work, enjoying the swooping sensation in the pit of his stomach as the bike rolls faster and faster down the hill.

By the time he gets to school, it's already nine o'clock. He chains his bike to the stand next to all the others, runs to the door, and shoves it open, breathing the school smell of chalk dust and disinfectant. He hurries down the hallway past all the posters of smiling basketball and football players and the banner with the big yellow words,

SCHOOL IS FOR WINNERS.

When he gets to room 109, Jared can hear the sleepy, sarcastic sound of Mr. Delany's voice coming from inside. He leans against the wall to catch his breath. He doesn't want to go in. He knows what will happen. *So, Jared...you decided to grace us with your presence?* Jared glances at the clock in the hall, takes a deep breath, and walks through the door.

Like the rest of the school in summer, this classroom looks strangely deserted, just five boys and three girls spread out like they're trying to keep as far away from each other as they can. Always more boys than girls. And one less girl than before. Karen Holcomb, who's been missing for three weeks, her desk looking emptier than the others. Jared remembers police cars in the school parking lot, how they appeared one day and then were gone. He glances at an empty desk, feels something cold in his gut, then looks away.

Delany is doing his slow-walk back and forth in front of the windows, one hand scratching the back of his neck. He doesn't look up, but Jared knows he's been seen.

Jared takes a seat at a desk near the door, folds his hands in front of him and looks up. Delany's face looks haggard as usual with what looks like a three-day growth of stubble on his jaw. Eyes bloodshot and heavy-lidded.

"So, *Jared,*" Delany says, not looking at him, "We were just discussing the difference between a simile and a metaphor...." Delany grabs a book from his desk, flips it open, and begins to read aloud.

"My love is like a red red rose that's lately sprung in June. My love is like a melody that's sweetly played in tune..."

A laugh builds up inside Jared but he holds it back until other voices start to chuckle around him. He lets the laugh come out a little, but it's enough for Delany to pause, snap the book shut, and look up with his tired, bloodshot brown eyes.

"You find Mr. Burns funny, Jared?"

As usual, Jared feels that little buzz of danger. Generally, it's safe to joke around with Delany, but you never know. One day he'll seem to enjoy sparring back and forth with his students, the next day he'll react to laughter or a smart-ass remark with an anger that's scary because it's so unexpected.

"So, Jared," Delany says. "Simile or metaphor?"

"You mean...the poem?"

Delany fixes him with a deadly glare; his voice drips with sarcasm when he speaks. "Yes, I mean *the poem!* Simile or a metaphor?"

"It's a simile."

"Why"

"Because...he says his love is *like* a red rose."

"Good..." Delany turns and walks away, flipping through the pages, a scowl of concentration on his face.

Jared catches a sympathetic eyeroll from Lucy Milano, along with a sigh of relief. *Better you than me.* Being called on in class by Delany can be nerve-wracking—it's a spot nobody wants to be in.

Delany tosses the book on his desk, strolls over to the bookcase, pulls another one from his shelf, thumbs through it, then reads:

> *"Whose woods these are I think I know.*
> *His house is in the village though;*
> *He will not see me stopping here*
> *To watch his woods fill up with snow..."*

Delany strolls closer and closer to Jared's desk as he reads. When he gets to the final line, he thrusts the open book at Jared. "Here...you read the rest."

Jared takes the book, not wanting to show any fear or nervousness. He remembers the first time Delany called on him to read in class, the cold grip of fear around his throat, the way the letters shifted and swarmed on the page under his eyes. Then, a year of afternoons in Delany's office, the two of them, working slowly, step by step, learning how to make the words slow down so he could catch up with them.

Jared looks down at the print on the page, waiting for the words to stop moving.

When they do, he reads the first line through in his mind, the way Delany showed him.

Then he begins.

"My little horse must think it queer..."

Jared hears Johnson snickering behind him. Delany's response is swift and brutal.

"Really, Johnson? You think that's funny? What are you, ten years old?" Then, "Go on, Jared. Take your time."

Jared goes back to the marks on the page and waits for them to stop rearranging themselves. When they finally come to rest, he takes a breath and begins.

> *"...To stop without a farmhouse near*
> *Between the woods and frozen lake*
> *The darkest evening of the year."*

The words continue to shift and swim, but Jared stays with them, pushing his way through the poem, line by line. He can see the end coming—he's almost done.

> *"The woods are lovely dark and deep,*
> *But I have promises to keep,*
> *And miles to go before I sleep,*
> *And miles to go before I sleep."*

He looks up from the page into Delany's haggard face, where he thinks he can see a flicker of a smile.

"So," Delany says. "Simile or metaphor?"

Jared starts to answer, but the poem has planted pictures in his mind, of blinding white, thickly falling snow...

"It's a metaphor," Johnson offers hesitantly.

"That's right, Johnson," Delany snaps. "You had a fifty-fifty chance of getting it right, and you lucked out." Delany turns back to Jared. "Now...what's the metaphor?"

Jared knows the answer but can't speak. He's far from the classroom, under tall, dark trees that go on and on forever.

"It's ... it's the woods."

"The woods," Delany repeats, peering closely at Jared. "Why the woods?"

"They're ... they're a metaphor for sleep. He wants to sleep. He's really tired and he wants to sleep. But he can't. He's got too much to do. He wants to go deeper into the woods, the same way he wants to go to sleep. He just wants to get away from everything and rest. He wishes he could. But he can't."

Delany keeps looking at Jared for a moment, then a ghost of a smile appears at the corner of his mouth. "See, Jared? I knew you had it in you."

Jared hears a few quiet laughs from the desks around him, but he doesn't care. For a moment, this one moment, he isn't embarrassed or self-conscious. He's not even angry at Delany for turning the spotlight on him one more time. He feels the thrill of making it to the finish line, of stepping out over a ledge into space and not falling. The bell rings, and Jared realizes—those same woods, the ones he just saw in his mind—he knows where to find them. And he's going there now.

CHAPTER 7

ANGEL FALLS

The day had started out with sun. Jessie had been happy and hopeful right up until breakfast.

"So, what's on the agenda today?" she'd asked. "Can we go to the beach?"

She was busy getting the cereal and milk in her bowl, so she didn't notice his silence. When she looked up, she was alarmed at the look of guilt on his face; chin tucked, eyes peering at her over his glasses.

"I, uh... the roofer is coming today. And I've got to find some insurance documents," he gestured to a pile of papers on the table. "I should be done sometime this afternoon. Can you wait for me?"

Jessie was conscious of his concerned stare. She didn't want to show her disappointment, but it was hard not to frown a little.

She lifted her chin, tossed her hair back, and smiled. "No big. Is it okay if I go?"

He was also struggling not to show something; she thought it was relief. *We're all actors.* The thought unsettled her. "Are you sure? You won't be lonely?"

"Nah," and she bent to eat cereal that tasted like nothing.

The beach roads are narrow and crowded with cars. Jessie has to stop repeatedly and walk her bike up rocky shoulders around the SUVs and massive trucks waiting to get into the beach parking lots, or past the folks waiting. She forgot it was Saturday. If it's this crowded on the road, what's the beach going to be like? A mass of bodies, noise, children kicking sand as they run by.

The traffic in the other direction is sparse so she slips between stopped cars and turns around. *Exploring,* she tells herself, trying to stay positive. Even while other words inch their way into her mind, *killing time.*

She takes a road away from the shore, uphill, through pretty neighborhoods, up steeper hills till even the lowest gear won't work, and she has to get off and walk. When she stops to rest, she turns and gasps. The harbor spreads out before her like one of the old photographs in Cousin Dorothy's house. The great circular bay with an island in the center and a squat lighthouse there. Rocky Neck jutting into the water, studded with docks. Another lighthouse and breakwater on the outermost rim of land. *And beyond that, Ireland,* she says to herself, smiling. Her mother would say, "Oh look. Jessie's got that moue again," and her smile disappears. She misses her mother; she wants her here. She wants to show her around. This view, whales, the diorama in the house. She shakes off the longing. *I'll call her tonight, ask about her show,* she promises and gets back on her bike.

When the road begins to flatten, she mounts her bike and pedals fast, the roads wider, traffic light, till she hits a traffic circle. She enters it cautiously and exits at a familiar-looking road. Once away from the circle, the road narrows and begins a slight uphill incline, making Jessie work hard. There are no other vehicles of any kind. The houses thin out and disappear, woods rising in their place. Soon the asphalt changes to gravel, the gravel to dirt, and she sees an old, crooked sign, *Angel Falls.*

It happened in the woods; she remembers her father's words when she asked him about the lost girl. *Nobody goes there,* and she finds herself shivering. She starts to turn around, but something holds her there. After the long climb on her bike, the shade feels delicious, and a light breeze is drying her sweat. She turns slowly back and peers down the gravel path. Maybe these aren't the same woods her father meant.

She pedals down the path, which is short and opens up into a parking lot, complete with picnic tables, a trailhead sign and map. Looped a couple of times around posts on either side of the road, making an ineffective barrier is a torn yellow tape with large black letters: *Police Line Do Not Cross.*

So, there it is. The girl disappearing. Maybe something worse. Jessie knows she should leave now.

She rides past the police tape and stops at the bulletin board. It is weathered, the paper under the plexiglass torn and water stained. Graffiti covers a large portion, but she can make out some of the words, a history; the area had been settled and slowly abandoned, the map marking known homesteads and buildings, long gone, and something about great pieces of granite in strange and beautiful formations. The box for maps is rusted, and the lid won't budge. *Probably full of spiders*, she thinks and sees the trail snaking through the trees. It looks better tended than the parking lot. It looks like a crooked finger. Beckoning.

The sounds of birds and wind high in the trees lull her. "Just for a second," she says out loud. "And then I'll leave." And she leans her bike against a tree and walks out along the trail.

At first, the trees are tall and well-spaced, giving room for extended branches with deep green leaves, lightly fluttering. But soon they grow closer together, moving closer to the trail, bending over it, obliterating the sun. Ahead she sees light, and it's this light that keeps her going, moving forward as the forest around her grows more dense.

The drop in temperature is striking, and goosebumps rise on her arms and legs, her sweat evaporated. Leaves rustle as birds take off or land, but she can't see what they are. A squirrel chitters at her from a low branch and a chipmunk darts across the path and stops on a fallen tree. *If I hold still, you can't see me.*

She walks for a while, never making it to an opening, the light always just beyond a turn in the path. Finally, she sees the opening, more light, more sky, and she moves towards it, eagerly, with curiosity. As she expects, the path opens up into a field, but what she doesn't expect are the boulders that lie before her, massive and countless, strewn haphazardly across an open plain.

"It's a moraine."

The voice is deep, male, and pierces her like a bullet between her shoulder blades. She freezes, actual cold creeping through her veins despite the pounding sun. She knows she has to turn, to assess the danger, but her limbs are immobile, the only freedom in her eyes, which strain sideways as far as possible.

"Left by a glacier," the voice continues, casual and knowing, and a boy appears in her peripheral vision, a boy, not a man, and her paralysis eases. She turns to face him. It is the boy from the chowder place. An image of the old man's face in the car window rises in her mind, and she shivers.

He says, "You're trespassing. This part of the park is closed."

Jessie becomes aware of her heart racing. "Who are you, the park ranger or something?" she snaps, irritated to be caught frightened. Strangely he laughs. "I saw the police tape, but I thought I'd be okay; no one was in the parking lot."

"Which parking lot?" He kicks at a loose stone, sends it flying on the boulder field.

"Aren't you trespassing too?"

He studies her and looks at the field of boulders. He's quiet so long she's not sure if he's weighing his answer or ignoring her. She studies his profile, the forehead high, nose straight, lips full. He turns to look at her, his face a cipher, and she's tempted to leave, get away from this strangely quiet boy, but she can't pull her eyes from his face. She remembers the first thing he said.

"Moraine? What's on the other side? Can you walk on it?"

The boy raises his brows and gives her a half-grin. "Only one way to find out," and he's running toward the rocks, leaping onto the first few and teetering, small bits breaking free and skittering down between boulders.

Jessie can't help it, she's running too, jumping from rock to rock, feeling the sharp points digging into the soles of her sneakers, noticing the deeper cracks between boulders that could pin her foot if she missed a step. The boy is ahead of her balancing and leaping and she knows she can't stop. He pulls ahead, pauses, then makes a long leap. By the time she gets there, he's standing across a wide gap, grinning wildly at her. She knows he expects her to leave, but she doesn't. She backs a little and takes a running leap, watching his eyes widen and his hands rise as if they could stop her, but she's flying towards him fast, landing hard but solid on the same rock.

Instantly, he's off, running and balancing until he disappears behind a boulder far ahead of her. He's trying to lose Jessie, and this makes her determined. She runs, leaps, and slips a little on the final boulder before reaching the trail on the other side.

He looks surprised, annoyed, but then he's grinning at her, his eyes a little wild. She wonders if she should be scared. She's not. She's happy; exhilarated. He shoulders off a backpack and removes a water bottle. He offers it to her.

Jessie sips from the bottle, the water warm but feels good against her tongue and throat, and hands the bottle back. She watches him tip his head back, bottle to lips, his Adam's apple bobbing till the bottle starts to collapse. She is still staring at his throat when he rights his head and brings the bottle down. She looks down.

She says, "So, where are the falls?" and dares a look at his face. A frown sits uneasily on his brow, but she can see a crease there, something etched over time, as if he's been worrying for a while.

"Falls? Oh, yeah." His face relaxes. They're hard to find. Believe me, I tried." He peers through the woods in front of them, then says, "Wanna see something?" And he's off, down a path before she can respond. She follows, and after a few minutes, he stops and steps aside, holding back some of the taller weeds so she can see past. All she sees is a slight depression in the earth.

"What?"

"It's a cellar hole of one of the inhabitants of Angel Falls. This crazy evil guy. They say he died here, in the hole, long after the house was burned to the ground."

Now Jessie can make out the shape of the depression, it is almost square, and she can see it's deeper than at first glance. She moves forward, close to the edge. "How long ago? What happened?"

"No one knows exactly," the boy's voice grows soft. "But long after everyone else had moved away, this one man stayed on, sleeping in this cellar hole by day, trapping any camper or traveler who dared come around."

The image of a man, dirty in ragged clothes rising from the leaves takes hold of her for a moment. She knows he's trying to scare her.

"What's down there?" she says, peering into the shadows. All she can see is a layer of old dried leaves.

"Nothing. Except the bones of his victims and the bear traps he used to catch them."

She thinks he looks smug. "Have you been down there?" When he slowly shakes his head, she jumps into the hole. She slips on the leaves, falling to one knee, fist into the ground. It reminds her of something. "Thor!" she shouts, laughing, and sees the boy peering over the edge of the hole, his face tight and angry.

"You shouldn't be in there."

"Why not?"

He reaches and grabs her arm. "Get off!" She jerks free of his grip. "Leave me alone! What's your problem?"

"Okay. Fine." His face disappears and she hears his footsteps rapidly crunching gravel, growing fainter, and then silence.

The sky through the trees has changed to a deep blue, and the light is a little less. She isn't frightened by his story. She doesn't believe in ghosts, and he hadn't said the place was haunted anyway. *Evil* was a word he'd used. The man was evil. But, Jessie thinks, long dead. She brushes leaves and dirt from her palms and looks at the ground. Beneath the surface of dry leaves she imagines the jaws of a bear trap, open, with sharp rusty teeth, and can almost hear the snap, feel the pain as it closes on her leg. She would call for help with no answer. The hole is cold, ice cold. Jessie starts to shiver.

She scrambles up the side, her foot taking hold briefly as she throws her torso at the edge before the dirt beneath her foot gives way and she slides back down. She tries several times, moving to different parts of the hole, but the dirt's too soft. She can't get out.

Panic looms, but she manages to control the terror and calls out, "Hey! Hey you! Come back! Help me out of here!" Her voice sounds low in her ears, muffled by the earth around her. Where did he go? Can he hear her? She listens closely to the silence, hoping it will be broken, but there is nothing but the faraway rustling of leaves. An evil face appears in her imagination and panic comes like two hands squeezing her skull.

"Hey! Come back! Please! Hey you, boy! Someone!"

She hears footsteps pounding fast towards her, and then a scrambling noise at the edge of the hole. Head and arms appear silhouetted against the sky, she can't see the face before strong arms wrap around hers. She jerks away but they hold her firmly and now she sees it's the boy. He looks worried and embarrassed, so she stops resisting, puts her foot against the side and lets him lift her up and out.

The minute she clears the edge, she shakes off his arms and punches him in the chest with the heel of her palm. "Why did you leave me?" The push of tears behind her eyes makes her angry, and she slaps his arm.

"Ow! Hey! Cut it out. I'm sorry, okay? I came back, didn't I. Ow!" He grabs her wrists until she stops flailing. "Are you crying?"

She sniffs hard, blinking, and walks blindly back in the direction they'd come.

"Wait. Where'd you leave your bike?"

She stops, without turning. "In the parking lot. I told you."

"There are *four* lots. Which one?"

"I don't know. I came from that way," she wipes her eyes, looking around. Nothing looks familiar.

"How'd you get there? Route 28? Rockland Road?"

She can't recall any names and feels more stupid by the second. "I came from the harbor, straight up by that old white church, then past a traffic circle... is that 28?"

"Yeah. I know where you are. I'll walk you back."

"No. I can manage," her jaw is clenched, she wants him to disappear.

"Yeah? And how were you planning on getting there? Back over the moraine?"

She glares at him, unable to speak.

"Look, the paths aren't marked, and people get lost here all the time." He studies her face for a moment and then says, more softly, "Let me show you out of here."

Jessie thinks of walking back alone, of being lost, the terror of being stuck in the cellar hole still with her. The joy of running on the rocks is long gone. This boy has seen her panicked, in tears, and now lost. "Just go away."

"Look, I'm sorry. There's a shortcut..." and he walks away down a new trail, not waiting for her. She's angry, but she wants out of here. She hurries to follow.

They walk in silence for a while, and the bird sounds, whispering of leaves high in the trees begin to calm her.

"You know where I can get a map of this place?"

The boy stops in his tracks and stares at her a moment, then starts walking, faster than before. "You *can't* come back here. I told you, it's closed."

She stiffens, "*You* come here."

"It's not the same."

"Why, because you're special?"

He's quiet for a while and she looks at him, but he's studying the path, looking unfazed. "It's dangerous unless you know your way around. Just don't come back."

"You can't tell me what to do."

"I just did." He stops and points down the path. "Is that your bike?" She sees it leaning up against the tree exactly as she left it, and nods.

"Well. Goodbye then." And he starts jogging back the way they came.

"I'll be back," she calls after him, the words ring childishly in her ears. Then, "Thanks," and after another minute, watching his back recede, "Hey!" but he doesn't stop.

"You can't tell me what to do," she says as his back disappears. Then adds, "Boy."

CHAPTER 8

THE GIRL RAN

Jared glances up at the clock on the classroom wall. He's surprised and a little annoyed to see that the minute hand has barely moved since the last time he looked. The paper on the desk in front of him is still nearly empty except for two lines written in careful blue ink.

Thunder rumbled like an earthquake.
The man stood still as a statue.

Jared isn't sure about the second line. Can you say "as" instead of "like"? Does that still make it a simile? Or something else?

Looking around from the corner of his eye, Jared notices he's not the only one having trouble with the assignment. To his left, Bill Destino has given up and is resting his head in his arms to cover up his blank paper, while to his right, Mary DeMarco is staring out the window like she thinks she might find a simile out there.

Jared looks up at the clock again. It still hasn't moved. It seems like it's waiting for him to make a move first. He picks up his blue pen and writes.

The girl ran.

She could run. That's for sure. Run and climb. He doesn't think he's ever seen a girl who can run and climb like that. He did his best to lose her. But every time he'd leapt onto another boulder and looked over his shoulder, she was right there behind him, her face flushed and her blue eyes blazing with a determined joy.

Not like her face when she'd first turned around and found him right behind her. He can still see her eyes. Pale blue, wide, and frightened. He was startled too when he first spotted her standing there at the edge of the moraine, looking at the big rocks like she was trying to figure them out. He wasn't used to finding other people in Angel Falls. A few older teenagers, maybe, who'd go far enough into the woods to drink and get high, but never that far, especially after the Holcomb girl disappeared and the yellow police tape went up at all the marked entrances. To go that far into Angel Falls, you had to really want to.

She wasn't from around here; he knew that much. Her shoes, that bike, both cost more than he makes in a week. And her voice, the way she said words like *moraine* and *falls*. She had New York City written all over her. Besides, if she was from around here, she never would have gone that far into Angel Falls. Not alone.

Jared looks at the clock again and sees the minute hand has moved from the two to the five. He looks down at the paper in front of him.

The girl ran...

She was stubborn. Smart girls have a chip on their shoulder and act like they have something to prove. Even the quiet ones. He saw it when he'd told her not to come back by herself. That spark in her eyes. The one that said *You can't tell me what to do.*

She'd wanted to know why she couldn't go there by herself when he could. She threw the question right in his face. *Why? Because you're special?*

That stopped him because he knew the answer was *Yes*. And because he had no way to explain it to her.

Angel Falls has been part of Jared for as long as he can remember. Its giant trees and tangled vines, the old stones and dappled sunlight flickering on the ground are all imprinted on his brain, as much as his parents' faces and voices.

Jared's earliest memories of Angel Falls were with his dad, following him deep into the woods, helping him set up his easel and paints, then climbing and playing on the old stones while his dad painted. Some memories are less clear than others, and some are strange as dreams. Like the day he slipped away from his dad and followed the trail of boulders down into a ravine. It was hottest summer, but the air suddenly felt cool and damp on his skin. He can remember how quiet it got, and the sense of someone watching him.

That was when he saw the woman standing at the top of the rise across from him, so motionless that at first, he thought it was a tree. Then she turned her head toward him, and he saw her face. It looked blurred and indistinct. At first he thought it was because of the light and the distance. As he watched, he saw her slowly open her arms to him, like his mother used to do. He started walking toward her. As he got closer, he realized that the pale blurred thing he saw was her face, something not quite solid, forming itself into something else. Before he could cry out or make a sound, his father's strong hand seized his arm from behind, lifted him up into the air, then they were running, trees and sunlight flashing past, his father's loud, ragged breathing in his ear.

Later, when he asked his dad who it was he'd seen standing on that hill, his dad had told him there was no one there, that he'd dreamed it.

That was the day they stopped going to Angel Falls. His father told him to never go there again. But Jared never stopped going. Even when the place began to change, when fear and neglect made the briars and brambles grow and choke the trails, even after the police tape and warning signs went up, Jared never stopped going. It was his place, and nothing or no one could keep him out. It was his, and his alone.

Until he'd found the girl.

He knows she isn't fearless. He saw the fear in her eyes when he came back to help her out of that hole where he'd left her. Why did he do that? He was angry at her, but why? For not doing what he'd told her? For invading his place? So he'd left her there and made her cry. That just about killed him.

He was surprised by how strong she was when she'd hit him in the chest. He'd never been hit by a girl before, so he had nothing to compare it to. He can still feel it, right in the center of his ribcage—he reaches up and touches that place through his shirt.

And that's when he knows. She'll be back. With or without him. And whatever happens then will be his fault.

What can he do to stop her? He doesn't know where she lives, or who she is. He doesn't even know her name.

He looks at the clock again; strangely, the minute hand has moved to the eleven.

Five minutes till the bell. He looks down at the paper in front of him.

The girl ran...

He tries not to picture it, then pictures it anyway—the high ledges with bone breaking rocks at the bottom. The deep dark places where anyone or anything could be hiding. Her face in the newspaper...

The girl ran...

He'd tried to lose her, but he couldn't. She wasn't easy to lose. She'd shown him that.

As the bell rings, Jared picks up the blue pen and writes as quickly as he can:

The girl ran like a boy.

Chapter 9

Please Come Home

"Where have you been?" Her father jumps up from the dining room table holding his cell phone, face pinched and red, anger sitting uncomfortably behind the round rimmed glasses.

"I said I'd be back by 5…"

"It's 6:45! You said you were going to the beach. I went looking for you… Did you lose your god-damned phone?"

6:45? "It's here, it's right here," Jessie fumbles in her backpack.

"I've been going crazy. You disappear, go God knows where, don't answer your phone…"

With relief her fingers find the hard edges of her phone and she pulls it out. The screen is black. "It's dead. I'm sorry."

"Where were you? Don't you know it isn't s—" He stops and Jessie watches as he bites the word back, the word *safe*. This is about the girl, she thinks. The one who disappeared.

"I'm sorry. I'm okay. Nothing happened." She knows it's a lie. The terror of being left alone in that hole still clings to her. She prays it doesn't show on her face.

"You scared me to death. I ought to ground you."

"Ground me?" It stuns her, then anger seeps in. "Like keep me home from the prom? No sleepovers with my friends? How can you ground me?"

The anger drops from his face, and his eyes grow shiny. She thinks he might cry. And it's her fault. He pulls her to him roughly, squeezes her hard. "I'm sorry," his voice is hoarse. "I should have known better. I shouldn't have brought you here. I should never have taken you from your friends."

She goes cold with fear. Is he going to send her back? Who'll take care of him?

How will she convince her mom to come here?

"I want to stay here, Daddy, with you." The *Daddy* slips out, the old endearment, and she hopes it doesn't sound false. "I'll keep an eye on the time in future, I promise."

He's still holding her so she can't see his face. She feels his chest rise and fall in a sigh. He kisses the top of her head. "You sure?" And when she nods, he sighs again.

"I want you here too, kitten."

She lets him hold her for a while, then pulls away. "I'm gonna wash up, then how about I make you dinner?"

"I didn't make it to the grocery. What do you want? Rick's? Pizza?"

"Pizza," she says quickly. The thought of seeing that boy again makes her queasy. She cried in front of him. He saw her scared. She punches in the numbers and orders.

At the pizza place Jessie jumps out of the car saying, "I'll get it," taking the folded bill he offers. The pizza place is frigid, and she holds her bare arms tightly as she gives her name. They hand her a box so hot, she can barely hold it, and she exits into the warm night.

Jessie's father's voice is loud enough to reach through the closed windows of the car, and she stops. He's talking to her mom. "I said, she told me she wants to stay here. What part of that don't you understand?"

Did he tell her about today? The pizza box is burning her fingers, but she doesn't move.

He sees her, reaches across the seat with his free hand and opens the door.

"Jessie's here with our dinner. I've got to go." He smiles but she finds it ghastly.

"Yes, paper food. Listen, I cook for her plenty." This time he mugs at Jessie, his head wags from side to side, *you know your silly mother.* But Jessie can hear her mother through the phone, not the words, but the tone, and it's not silly. Not at all.

"Mmm-hmmm. Yeah. Okay," her father repeats a few times before he is able to end the call with, "I'll have her call you later. Bye."

He lifts and rolls his shoulders back, straightening his neck and breathing deeply. "That smells amazing!" He puts down his phone and starts the engine. "Your mother wants you to call her." The casual tone sounds forced.

Jessie leans all the way back, pressing her back and head into the seat as if it could swallow her up, make her disappear. "Yeah, I got that."

Her father reaches over with one hand and touches her head. "Sorry about that."

"I want to stay." She watches as her father takes this in, how much she's overheard. Then she gulps some air and blows it out slowly. "I want to stay here and eat paper food with you." He laughs at this and the pain in her gut eases a little.

After they eat, Jessie takes her phone into her room and pauses with her finger over her home number. She doesn't want to hear it: *don't you think you'd be better off here? Why don't you come home? It's got to be lonely...* Praying for voicemail, she presses the number.

"Enchantee, mes amis. Leave a message after the tone, s'il vous plait," Jessie exhales sharp relief and starts to leave a message, when her mom's voice breaks in:

"Jessica, sweetheart, how's my favorite daughter?"

She hesitates before supplying the usual, "I'm your only daughter."

Laughter like ice in a glass, then, "Jess, I'm worried about you. Aren't you lonely out there?" And there it is.

She doesn't like lying, but she hasn't figured out how telling the truth will get her what she wants. She is lonely, she does miss her mom, her friends. But she says, "Not at all. There's so much to do, so many people around. Ask Dad, I can't get any reading done."

"You read too much. You know you do. You need to get out more, be with people. What about dance? Don't you miss it?"

"No. I mean, yeah, a little, but I'll be back in the fall."

"And Dylan. What's she up to? Don't you miss her?"

"She's coming here," her throat seizing at the breadth of this lie. Nothing's been decided or planned. "Maybe," she qualifies, "If her folks agree. In August. It'll be great."

And, knowing it's risky, adds, "Maybe you can bring her up when you come."

The silence is so long, Jessie looks at her phone to see if they're still connected.

Then her mom is saying in a voice pitched higher than before, "What a lovely idea. Maybe that's what we'll do," and Jessie knows two things; her mother is lying, and the plans for the summer have already changed.

"You are coming in August, aren't you?"

A shorter silence, then, "Of course, of course. August... it seems so far away..." and her mother's voice is far away too, and something in Jessie's head clicks off.

A dullness sets in, and Jessie says quietly, "I can't wait. Love you. Gotta go." Before her mom can say anything, Jessie cuts off the call, falls back onto her bed and stares up at the old, water-stained ceiling. With a sharp pang in her chest, Jessie realizes two things—that her mother is never coming there, and that the distance between Beauport and New York, between her mother and her father, just grew farther than ever.

CHAPTER 10

RICK'S

"Jared," Rick barks, "Up front."

Jared looks up from the kitchen sink at the crowd of people lined up at the counter. The place is packed, even for a rainy Friday. Jared dries his hands, grabs a pad and pen, and heads out front where the crowd is standing three deep on the other side of the counter. Kate gives him a look that says *it's about damn time,* and he starts taking orders.

A few minutes later, he looks up and his heart stops for a moment. The face looking at him across the counter is one he's seen before. For a split-second he can't remember where. Then he knows. It's the girl he'd met at Angel Falls. She's standing right there, looking at him with those wide blue eyes, although he's sure he looks more surprised than she does.

"Hi," he says, because he doesn't know what else to say.

"Hi," she says, casting those blue eyes down. He's suddenly self-conscious of the stained apron he's wearing, the pen and pad in his hand.

"So ..." he starts but can't finish it. He can't say, 'May I take your order?' or 'What can I get you?' That would make him feel even more ridiculous than he already feels.

"Oh, yeah." She looks startled like she is waking up. "Can I get two orders of chowder to go, please?"

He feels foolish. She didn't come here to see him. Why would she? Why would he even think that?

The girl clears her throat and looks down at the ground. "Uh, listen, I'm sorry. For the way I acted the other day." He has to think for a moment. Then he can feel again how hard she hit him, the light bruise that's still there at the center of his chest.

"It's alright," he says. "Don't worry about it."

"No," she says, "I mean, I'm not like that." He can read the deep embarrassment on her face, the undercurrent of anger, and suddenly he understands. She's not talking about hitting him. She's talking about crying. In front of him.

"It's alright," he says again, knowing he's repeating himself. She's looking at him like she's waiting for something, like it's his turn now. "Listen... I'm sorry I ran off on you like that. I shouldn't have done that."

She doesn't speak but looks at him solemnly and nods, like *Yeah, that's right. You shouldn't have done that.*

"Jared!" Kate calls out, "Stop talking with your girlfriend there and take some orders!"

Jared feels his face burn. He turns to glare at Kate but she's busy with other customers. He can't even look at the girl now.

"Sorry," he mutters, "I'll get you two chowders. One of each, okay? Just wait here."

Jared turns to place the order, his face still burning hot. Freaking Kate...why did she have to say that? Like this New York girl would ever have anything to do with him.

He takes the two Styrofoam containers Manuel has handed to him, puts them in a paper bag and hands it to the girl who's been waiting quietly.

"Thanks," she says, "And ... thanks for showing me that place. Angel Falls. It's really cool."

"Yeah. It is." And suddenly he knows he was right. She is going back. Alone. Maybe not today, or tomorrow. But soon.

Why should he care if she goes back or not? Why should he feel responsible? What if he'd never run into her? What if she'd come on a different day, or they'd just missed each other? Maybe she'd still be determined to go back, and it would have nothing to do with him. But even as he's telling himself all of this, he knows that's not what happened. He was there. He's part of what happened. And he's part of whatever might happen to her next.

"Listen," he says, "If you ever want to go there again, I can show you around some more."

She looks at him suspiciously. "That's okay..." she says.

"I mean ... going there by yourself ... that's not really a good idea."

"Why not?" He can see the resentment and defiance building in her eyes, so he backs off a little.

"I don't know. I mean, people get lost there sometimes." She's still eyeing him suspiciously, so he tries a different tactic. "Actually...I was kind of thinking of going there tomorrow. Maybe I could show you around some more. I mean, I kind of owe it to you, right?"

He can see her thinking it over.

"Okay," she finally says. "So, where should I meet you?"

"Same place—the moraine. What time?"

"Ten."

"Okay. See you there. At ten."

He watches her walk out and get into a green Toyota with an older guy he figures must be her dad.

"So. Jared," Kate says, her voice mocking singsong and musical, "When are you gonna introduce us to your girlfriend?"

"Jesus, Kate. She's not my girlfriend."

Kate grins and swats him on the shoulder with her order pad as she brushes past him on her way back to the kitchen. "Yeah? Says you."

Jared watches the green Toyota with the girl inside pause at the edge of the parking lot, then make a left turn into the traffic and disappear.

Maybe I could show you around. I kind of owe it to you. Why the hell did he say that? He doesn't owe her anything. He doesn't even like her.

For a moment he considers not going, not meeting her like he promised. He's already responsible for two lives, his and his dad's. He doesn't need another.

Chapter 11

The Deer

When Jessie arrives at the moraine, she sees him standing still as a post, stiller than the trees which sway in a light wind. The boy, Jared—she remembers hearing his name at Rick's—is wearing jeans that must have been black once, but are gray, thin, and stained, pocked with holes and nearly an inch too short, over equally faded, stained sneakers. His t-shirt, also black, hangs loose on his thin frame, a faded picture of a devil with long extended tongue, the name of a band, *Do It Till You Die* arching between its horns. She is filled with dismay. Why had she come?

"I thought you weren't coming." He shifts his eyes from her face to some spot over her head.

She feels a prick of insult. Thought or hoped? But she keeps silent as she locks her bike to a skinny tree.

"Or lost," he says. She remembers what he said, *people get lost here.* When she looks at him again, she can see past his shoes, his clothes and into his face. It's a nice face, despite the frown line between his brows, the cautious look in his eyes.

She tries a smile. "Sorry. So where are we going? To the vampire's lair? You have a black lagoon? The witches' circle thingy?"

And then he laughs, and Jessie feels some tension drain away.

"There's no lagoon, although we have a swamp. C'mon." And with that he's off walking parallel to the moraine, not pausing to see if she follows.

She runs to catch up and notices him increasing his pace a little when she does. The woods grow thicker as they walk, and soon they've left the moraine behind. At first there are noisy birds flittering in and out of the greenery above them, but as they move further in, a silence descends.

"It feels like anything could happen here," she says, her voice loud and strange and she instantly regrets it.

The boy stops, looking at her with surprise. "You feel it?"

She nods, looking up at the trees, finding the smallest bits of blue sky between leaves.

The boy starts walking again. "There used to be three different towns here. Fort... something. Then The Commons. Then Angel Falls." He points to a short pile of rocks, "Here's the wall." She sees rocks that snake around the bigger, older trees in a line that disappears as the land dips. In spots, small trees have broken through, tumbling the rocks around.

"What happened to them? The towns." He's already disappearing around a bend, so she crosses through a break in the wall and starts to run.

He calls back to her, "The settlers disappeared, or died, or left. The last ones were here in the early 1900's." She slows down as she reaches him. He continues:

"People in town called them gypsies or hobos. The 'unwanted'."

The word makes her cold. Then she thinks about New York. "It's like homeless people in the city. I walk by the same guy every day on my way to school, all bundled up, even on hot days. No sign, no cup. He just sits there, rocking." Jared is looking at her in a way she doesn't like.

"The city? Let me guess. New York, right?" His voice is dark, and she feels she's disappointed him somehow.

"Yes." And she's suddenly tired. Why should she care what he thinks? "Are you from here?"

He makes a sound a little like a laugh but looks grim. "Yeah. Me and the unwanted are like this," he crosses his fingers. Then, his expression softens. "Sorry. We get tourists from everywhere, but the ones from New York..." he rubs his jaw and gives her strange look she can't interpret.

"Maybe I'm not a tourist," she says, her jaw begin to clench. "Maybe I'm a long-lost returnee to Beauport. How would you know?"

He's silent a long time. "Maybe," he says, slowly, "you're a Martian."

He looks so serious it takes a few moments to realize what he said. She starts to smile, "Like Bugs Bunny!"

"Looney Tunes!"

"Take me to your leader," she says in a monotone and they both laugh, the tension in the center of her chest starts to ease.

"Did you grow up in Beauport?" Suddenly, she wants to know. "Did you come here a lot?"

He doesn't answer right away, and she can almost see different answers as they occur to him and are rejected, till finally he says, "Yes. I come here all the time," and then he runs ahead. "C'mon!"

She wishes he'd stop trying to leave her behind, but once she's running, she enjoys the stretch of her legs, the wind on her face. They break out into a clearing, and he stops to let her take it in. They are in a lane of boulders; each one at least double their height.

"Who did this?" she whispers.

"Boulders were here. The settlers cleared around them."

Jessie walks down the path and sees how the boulders are spaced irregularly, the cleared land implying order. "This one's got writing!" Jessie struggles to read the faded letters.

"They all do." She looks at him in disbelief. He is leaning against one of the boulders, arms crossed, face as close to a smile as it can get without lips curling.

She turns back to the first boulder. "*The devil*," she reads, "something... something. Does that say *tremble*?" She reaches a hand up, rises on her toes and can just trace the lowest engraving.

"This one's easier," he runs down the clearing and points to a boulder whose profile looks like a hawk-nosed man. "*They sacrificed unto devils.*"

She walks to where he stands, looking at each boulder in turn. "Cheery guys."

They walk down the open area, stopping to read each boulder as they pass.

Let us slay him and cast him into some pit. Jessie flashes on being trapped in the cellar hole, the crazed face she'd imagined peering over the edge.

Resist the devil, and he will flee from you.

I send an Angel before thee, to keep thee in the way.

Above the boulder she notices how the trees crowd out the sky, making an almost impenetrable barrier. Maybe these trees grew later, she thinks. Maybe there was more sky back when the words were chiseled on the stone.

When she looks down, she sees the boy's back as he lopes ahead down the trail.

A memory tickles her brain, her mother on a similar wooded trail, where was it? Catskills? Berkshires? Jessie doesn't remember, but her mother was ahead, her long legs making the distance between them increase. Jessie couldn't keep up. *Was she crying?* And then her mother slowed, her beautiful face turning to look at them, laughing, *C'mon slowpokes.*

"C'mon," the boy calls, and waves her along. "There's more." As they wend their way through deeper woods, a narrower path, Jessie loses all sense of direction. More rocks loom over them. He takes a side path and they walk for a while before another boulder appears.

"What's that?" Up high she sees something etched deep and uneven, more picture than words.

He takes a run at the boulder, leaps up higher than she would have thought possible, smacks the rock below the writing and lands next to her. "That," he says, slightly out of breath, "was here before any of the others. No one knows who did it or what the symbols mean."

"Were there Indians here?"

He nods, "Algonquin." He steps back and studies the symbol.

She looks up and tilts her head. "Looks like a boat, with people in it."

Jared squints and tilts his head, "Maybe. The early settlers killed them. Wiped them out."

"The Indians?"

He nods.

"We did that a lot," she says, surprised by her sadness.

"We?" Jared says.

"You know, the white man, Europeans," she points to her chest, "Us."

"So, the *city girl* wants to make it right," he takes off his backpack, offers her a water bottle.

"No thanks," she mutters, stung at *city girl*. She shirks off her own pack. "My dad says we can't change anything until we accept blame."

"Change? What, are you gonna give your city home to the Lenape?"

"That's not what I...."

"Do you know where the name Manhattan came from?"

"Yes! Manna- hatta. It means...."

"After the name of a fish. Menhaden. Do you know the only thing that fish is good for?" he interrupts again. His words are like hammers, making her feel attacked. "Fertilizer."

"You're making that up."

He shrugs. "Google it."

She pulls a water bottle out of her pack and takes a drink. She walks away from the boy to sit on one of the low boulders, then digs inside her pack for the lunch she's made. She'll eat, and then she'll leave. And she won't ever have to see this boy again.

"I made egg salad. Are you hungry?" It's grudging, but she pulls out the packet neatly wrapped in waxed paper and extends it to him.

The wary look changes, and she understands that he didn't bring food. Knows he's hungry. She waves the sandwich at him, "Take it."

"Thanks," he says, swallowing the word like it cost him something.

She digs again, pulling out a bag of grapes and a package of Hostess Cupcakes. "My weakness," she says.

He sits beside her, opening the sandwich with care. The stone is cool against the skin of her legs and surprisingly comfortable. Across from them are trees, thick and dark, only the smallest amount of sun making it through the dense leaves to the forest floor. She sees something move but can't make it out. It is all silent. She looks sideways at Jared.

He holds the cut half of sandwich in two hands and takes a small bite. It makes her think of something and before she can stop herself, she says, "You don't eat like the boys in my school."

He frowns at her. She closes her eyes. Idiot! When she opens her eyes, he's still looking at her. Waiting.

"They eat like wolves," she says finally, hoping he'll understand. "You eat—" she stops herself before saying *delicately*.

He chews carefully and swallows, wipes a piece of egg from the corner of his mouth. "This is really good."

They finish the rest of the food in silence. Then she says, "I almost forgot. We're supposed to look for the Falls."

Jared snorts, then stands and stretches. "Good luck with that."

"I thought you knew everything about this place."

His eyebrows shoot up, "I never said that. Nope. No idea. And I've looked."

A mystery! "It has to be here, doesn't it? No falls in Angel Falls?" The urge to find it is so great she almost starts marching off on her own. When she looks for a trail, all she can see are unmarked spaces between trees. They could be anywhere.

"I told you," he says. "I've looked. Followed all the different streams. I've been coming here since I was a kid..." then he looks at his watch. "Whoa."

"What?"

"It's a little after twelve. I have to check on my... I have to leave soon."

"Me too. I told my dad no later than one. Last time I left here, I got home late, and he went ballistic."

"Last time?" He looks alarmed. "When was that?"

"The last time, when I met you."

He's frowning at her, serious. "Promise you won't come here alone. It's dangerous. People get lost. Disappear."

Getting lost doesn't frighten her. She's never lost. But the word 'disappear' makes her feel strange. She shivers. "You mean that girl? Did you know her?"

"Not really. She's in my class. Was in my class." He's silent, and then, "Promise me you won't come here."

The fear on his face is real, and she doesn't like it. Her sense of safety crumbles and all she wants now is to leave. "How far is it to the parking lot?"

"Shouldn't take more than thirty minutes."

She stands, puts on her pack, thinking of the worry on her dad's face. It killed her when he looked that way. They should hurry. She looks up to find Jared studying her.

"I know what that's like," he says, "worrying about your dad."

Did he read her mind? She wants to say, *no you don't*, but looking in his face, seeing how deep the line is between his brows, she realizes maybe he does. Maybe his family is breaking up too, and she wants to ask him about it, about his dad, but tears well in her eyes and she looks away.

A flash of golden brown moves near the path ahead of them, and it's suddenly on the path; a deer. It stops and looks at them. Something's wrong with its hind leg. It looks as if it's been broken and healed badly; the angle is wrong and she feels the hurt in her chest explode and rise up into her throat. "Oh... She's hurt!"

The deer turns and tries to leap away but stumbles. Jessie sees a jagged white scar cutting diagonally across one flank. The doe disappears in the brush slowly, half dragging the malformed limb behind her.

"Best not to think about it." Jared's words are cold, his voice neutral.

"What?" she blurts, trying in vain to stop the sudden flow of tears. "It was probably a stupid, stupid car!" She starts walking fast down the path, stumbling, her arms strafed by branches.

"Wait. Hey! Stop." She feels Jared's hand on her arm and a calmness takes her by surprise, cool clear liquid in her veins.

"I wish," she starts, "I wish she wasn't hurt." And then she starts to tremble, and the trembling takes over her whole body.

When the shaking subsides, Jessie sees that Jared is staring at his hand, the one that had been on her arm. She feels outside herself, looking at the two of them from a distance and has the odd desire to comfort him.

"What was that?" he says, still staring at his hand.

"I made a wish," she says slowly, looking back where the deer had been. The feeling of disconnect—not unpleasant—keeps embarrassment at bay. "It's okay now." Not, *I'm okay*, she realizes. *It*.

She notices her face is wet. She rubs her eyes hard. "Sorry... I hate crying. Pretend you didn't see it."

He pauses before saying, "See what?" Then, "Let's head out."

They move down the path in silence, and for the first time Jared stays beside her.

He says, "It's this place."

"What is?"

"I dunno. The feelings that come up. Don't take it personally."

They step through the gap in the nearly buried wall. "Ladies and Gentlemen, you are now leaving Angel Falls," Jared intones into cupped hands.

It gives Jessie a mixture of relief and longing. Right away she wants to know when she's coming back. Whatever fear she felt before has vanished.

"I want to find those falls."

He looks at her. "I told you, you can't-"

She cuts him off, "come here alone. Yeah, I got that." She starts walking faster.

He catches up quickly. "Meet me Tuesday, 3pm, the usual spot."

She stops, catching a surprised look on his face, as if he hadn't meant to say it. But the words 'usual spot' give her comfort, as if they've been coming here for years. "Okay," she says, and they start walking again.

The calls of birds filter down through the trees, as well as a rustling of leaves. It sounds loud after all the silence.

"You called me Jared, back there," he says after a while.

"Isn't that your name?" Did she get it wrong?

"Yeah, but I don't remember telling you."

She breathes out sharply. Then, "I heard someone calling you at Rick's." He nods slowly but doesn't look satisfied.

"If you worked at a smelly clam shack like Rick's," he begins, "which you're much too classy to do..." She's not sure if it's a compliment, but he continues. "And I heard someone—"

"Jessie," she interrupts him. She feels light on her face, the trees are moving in a breeze. "My name is Jessie."

"Jesse?" He looks pleased. "Like Jesse James?"

She draws imaginary pistols and fires them at him, "Pshoo, pshoo." She blows pretend smoke from her fingertips. "Short for Jessica."

"Pleased to meet you, Jessica." Something rustles in the brush and they both turn.

A deer leaps easily across the path. They stare in silence.

Jared laughs. "For a moment I thought..."

Jessie says, "Yeah, me too." Her laugh coming out shaky.

The deer stops and stares at them, before turning and leaping away into the brush. And that's when Jessie sees it and points, turning in time to see the blood drain from Jared's face as he sees it too. The same single white slash on the deer's flank, both hind legs even and whole.

CHAPTER 12

AN AMAZING THING

Jared's racing, standing on the pedals of his bike and weaving between the cars blocking his way. He's late for school, but he's thinking about the deer, the way it stepped out of the trees and across the trail, unharmed. He can still see the girl's face, full of disbelief and awe.

It can't be the same one. All he knows is that something happened, something he doesn't understand and can't explain.

When Jared gets to the classroom, Delany is walking back and forth in front of the windows, rubbing one hand slowly over and over the bristly short hair on his scalp.

"So, Jared," Delany says, slowing the words down the way he always does when he's moving in for the kill, "We were just discussing the human brain."

Jared takes his seat quickly and sits up straight, waiting for whatever Delany is about to throw at him.

"The human brain is an amazing thing, wouldn't you say, Jared?"

Jared doesn't answer for a moment—he's trying to figure out what kind of trap Delany might be laying for him to walk into. But he knows that not answering a question quickly enough can be dangerous.

"Yeah."

"Yeah," Delany repeats the word slowly, like he's tasting it. He rolls his red rimmed eyes at the ceiling like he's looking for something up there. "So, you agree that the human brain is an amazing thing. Tell us why it's so amazing."

Jared's mind goes into overdrive, but he's not worried—putting his thoughts on paper may be a problem but putting them out in the air is easy.

"Well ..." Jared begins, "It holds a lot of information. Like memories. Facts. Not just facts, but how to do stuff too. You know, like how to tie your shoe or how to play guitar or drive a car..."

"It holds a lot of information," Delany repeats, his eyes narrowing. "Is that all it does?"

Jared takes a deep breath. Other teachers may settle for his first answer, but Delany keeps digging. It's what he does. It's what Jared expects.

"It controls our body," Jared continues, "Makes our heart beat. Tells our hair to grow..." Jared hears laughter from someone behind him. He's worried that Delany will think he's being a smart ass. Delany breaks his gaze with Jared, walks back over to the window and stares out at the green leaves.

"Ever hear the expression, like a chicken with its head cut off?" More laughter now from the back of the room. This time Delany reacts. "Johnson," he snaps. "Why don't you explain that to us—what does that mean?" Silence. Jared doesn't turn around to see the trapped look on Johnson's face. He's seen it before. Delany turns back to face the rest of the class.

"Mike, the Headless Chicken," Delany announces in a loud voice. "Colorado. 1945. Lived for eighteen months after his head was chopped off." Delany pauses for a moment to let this sink in. "If we chopped your head off, Johnson, how long do you think you'd live?" A ripple of nervous laughter goes through the room and dies. Jared looks toward the back of the room and sees Delany standing over Johnson's desk, glaring down at him, waiting for an answer. Johnson's face, which is always red, turns redder.

"I don't know," Johnson mumbles.

"I'd give you five seconds," Delany says, then walks back to the front of the class, ignoring the embarrassed, angry look on Johnson's face.

"Computers store information," Delany says. "Your iPhones and iPads all store information. Is that all your brain can do, Jared?" The spotlight is on Jared again. "Can your brain only do what an iPhone does? It can store facts. But can it change the facts?"

Jared thinks for a moment, then shakes his head. "No."

"That's right," Delany says, then turns away and walks back toward his desk. Jared relaxes a little. "Computers can only record reality and play it back," Delany is saying. "They can't make reality."

An itch begins in the back of Jared's mind, a hunger he can't ignore. "You're saying that the brain can take something that's not real and make it real?" Jared asks, no longer because he has to, but because he wants to. His thoughts are racing—*what would that be like? What would I do with a power like that?*

Delany looks up at the ceiling again, squinting, like the answer to Jared's question is hiding up there and he's trying to see it. Then he digs deep into the pocket of his jeans and pulls out a crumpled pack of cigarettes. Jared watches in amazement as Delany puts a cigarette between his lips and lights it.

Jared hears a few nervous whispers and smells the burning tobacco and the sulphur from the burnt match. Delany holds the burning cigarette up in the air, smoke curling from the tip. "See this?" Delany says. "I know—hard to believe, right? Mr. Delany...smoking in school. Probably freaks some of you out, right? What do people say when something freaks them out? I can't believe it. It's like if they don't believe it hard enough, they can make it disappear."

Jared wants to look around the classroom to see what the other kids are doing but he can't look away from Delany. There's a dead silence in the room like before a storm, and the same feeling of electricity building up in the air. Delany locks eyes with Jared again.

"And sometimes," Delany says, walking slowly closer to Jared, "Sometimes if a person believes something, really believes it, they can make it come true. What do you think, Jared? You think that's possible?"

Jared starts to answer, then Delany is lunging toward him, stabbing the tip of the cigarette into the flesh of his right arm. The burning, searing pain makes Jared cry out. "Shit! What the hell." Clutching his arm, he looks up at Delany in disbelief, hears the other kids babbling in shock. Delany is smiling at him, smiling... Then Delany holds up the cigarette, flipped around at the last second, so Jared can see it was the cold, unlit end that touched him. Jared takes his hand away and looks at the place where he felt the burn; his skin is unmarked and smooth.

"Now what do you say, Jared?" Delany smiles.

For a moment Jared has the urge to get up out of his seat and knock Delany to the floor. The urge is so strong that he has to dig his fingers into his desk until it passes. By the time it does, Delany is walking back to the window where he flicks the cigarette out onto the grass outside.

At the same moment, the bell over the door jangles. Delany walks to the door, throws it open and disappears into the hallway beginning to throng with kids. Chairs scrape backwards and feet slap the floor while Jared sits at his desk, unable to move. The place on his arm where Delany touched him is still burning and tingling, but when he looks again, nothing is there.

"Oh my God, are you okay?" It's Lucy Milano, staring down at him, wide-eyed.

Other kids surround him, whispering and muttering, *Oh my God...what the hell... Jesus, I thought he really did it...*

Jared stands up, not meeting any of the eyes that surround him. "Fine...I'm fine..." His head is spinning, but he keeps moving toward the door with the other kids still following him. *"Jesus...what an asshole...what are you going to do...you should tell someone...*

"No. It's fine...I'm fine..." Jared repeats, and as the last few kids lose interest and drift away, he stops in the doorway, unable to believe what Delany did. *Why?* No mark on his arm, but he can still feel it burning.

CHAPTER 13

COUSIN DOROTHY

Jessie's phone blips and she sees a text from her mom. *Skype at 6, K? Surprise 4 u!* And instantly she misses her. It hits her in the stomach. She misses her gingery perfume, the softness of her clothes. It seems to Jessie that everything her mother wears is soft.

The screen opens and her mom's face fills the picture, all smiles. At first Jessie thinks she's pulled her hair back tight, but then she notices the ends, different lengths and curled, framing her face perfectly.

"Oh my god, Mom, you cut your hair?" She thinks of the rich brown heft of it, her mother's hands pushing it off her face, making soft French braids, or twisting it into a bun. She can't remember her mother any other way. She stares into the screen, recognizing how good the haircut is, how good it looks, hating it anyway.

"Yes, do you like?" Her mother turns her head from side to side, then stands, her body filling the screen and moves away so she can turn around, give Jessie a view of the back. What Jessie sees is a neck, naked and vulnerable, a mole she didn't know existed close to the hairline. A stranger.

"You look... different." Jessie knows her mother wants a compliment, and it is true that she looks beautiful, younger somehow, her eyes suddenly enormous. But to Jessie it all seems strange.

"Yes! That's the point. I just couldn't see my character with long hair, and Gary agreed." It takes Jessie a minute to remember who Gary is. Her director. Yes, that's it.

"You could have gotten a wig."

"Not one that fit over all that," her hands gesture around her scalp, "And you know how much work it was. I was tired of it."

"But it was beautiful."

"Don't you like it this way? Gregor says it takes off 15 years."

"Why would you want to do that? You're not old! Besides, I liked your hair." She wonders what would have happened if she had stayed in New York. Would they have gone to the salon together? Could she have changed her mother's mind?

"I still have hair. Let's stop talking about me. Tell me, what were you doing while I was getting my hair chopped?"

What has she been doing? Jessie wonders what her mom would say if she told her the truth—hanging out in the woods with a boy. Oh, and there are giant rocks with creepy sayings engraved on them, and a magic deer. Jessie can still see the shock on Jared's face. It wasn't the same one, was it? It couldn't have been.

No. She can't tell her mom about the deer, the boy, Angel Falls. None of it. "We go to the beach in the morning, then I ride my bike around; it's a great place to bike. Lots of hills," she pauses, then, "Dad and I went kayaking yesterday. That was cool."

Her mother nods, smiling. "I forgot. He loved kayaking. We nearly bought one when you were a tiny thing, but storage was too expensive."

"There's space here," Jessie says, realizing for the first time this house, Cousin Dorothy, has been here all her life, and she never knew it. "You could have stored it in the yard."

Her mother chuckles but her eyes are serious, "Cousin Dorothy wanted nothing to do with us."

Jessie hates the way she says it, *Cousin Dorothy*, emphasis on the first word, as if 'cousin' was a curse.

"If she felt that way, why did she leave the house to Dad?"

"Who knows? It was a surprise to both of us."

Jessie looks at the photograph over her bed, a close shot of a young woman, barely older than Jessie herself, and a young man who looks like her father, younger, with slicked back hair and old-fashioned clothes. Facing the camera, the woman, is it Cousin Dorothy? looking out at the viewer with a fierce stare, one hand on the man's arm. The man looks at the woman, and Jessie can't decide if the look is loving or worried. Dorothy looks nothing like an old woman here, handsome rather than pretty, her look the gaze of a conqueror.

"What did she have against Dad?"

Her mother shrugs and looks away for a moment, then leans out of the screen. She leans back in holding up a framed picture. "Because he looks like his father." It is a photo of her grandfather, and Jessie realizes the man in the photo with Dorothy is the same man.

"So why did she hate my grandfather?" The word so formal. Grandfather. Dylan has two living grandfathers, and she calls them 'Pop-pop' and 'Gramps.'

"Maybe you should ask your father."

Jessie rolls her eyes. "Why? What is it? Why do you always do that? You can't *not* tell me." Jessie wonders why she never thought to ask about her father's family.

"It's..." her mom hesitates, and Jessie can't decipher her expression, "a funny story. Strange, not Ha-Ha. I should let Michael tell it."

"Let Michael tell what?" Jessie can see her father in the smaller window on the screen, a tiny figure the size of Jessie's face, standing in the doorway behind her.

"Hi Cynthia," his voice is warm, happy. Free from the tension she's heard recently when he's talking to her mom. And then he does a cartoon-worthy double-take. His head turns away and back and stares hard at the screen, moving into the room and tilting the screen so he can get a better view. "What have you done?"

She hears her mother's tinkly glass laugh but can't take her eyes off her father.

"It's a surprise. Surprise! Do you like it?"

Her father says nothing. His expression is dark.

"And please sit closer to Jessie, I can't see your face," she speaks lightly, teasingly. Jessie thinking, *you don't want to see it.*

He drops on the bed next to Jessie. "It's... well... a shock. When did you decide to do it?"

"Gregor says it takes fifteen years off," her mother repeats from earlier.

"Isn't it pretty, Dad?"

He nods slowly, without conviction, his eyes never moving from his wife, "Yes, looks great," but his voice is sad. "Is it for the play?" he asks, suddenly hopeful.

"That, and I needed a change."

"Oh." Jessie can't bear the look of sadness on his face and wonders how her mother can stay so cheery. Then it hits her. *Fifteen years off*. Before Jessie. Is this what her mother means by 'change'?

"Well. I'll leave you to your conversation," he stands and walks to the doorway then turns back. "Why were you talking about Cousin Dorothy?"

Jessie looks at him and he's staring at the picture over the bed.

"Jessie wants to know about the... about why you couldn't visit her."

Her father pulls his eyes away to look at Jessie. "Well. Okay. Why now?"

"What's the big secret? Jeez, you're making me crazy."

"All right, I'll tell you. When you get off the.... when you're done. Cynthia, I'll call you later."

"Okay, mon capitain," her mother gives a salute, earning a brief smile.

After he's gone, Jessie gets up and closes the door. She hears her mother say, "He doesn't like it." Turns and finds her mother looking sullen. There it is again, the young boy.

"You surprised him. You surprised me."

"Do you like it?"

Jessie looks at the hope in her mother's eyes. "Yeah, I do. I like it a lot."

"I miss you." It takes her by surprise. Jessie feels like she's swallowed a dry pill.

Good, she thinks. Finally. But she reaches up a hand, palm facing out, fingers splayed against the screen. Her mother does the same, aligning her fingers with Jessie's and saying "If you run away, I will run after you..."

Jessie's throat grows tight, she nods, but doesn't give the expected reply. Instead, she says, softly, "G'night Mom." Clicks on the red circle to disconnect, and her mother vanishes.

In the living room, Jessie is suddenly aware of the photos that cover the walls. She looks through dusty glass to the faded prints of people. Her people. Family she's never known.

Here's Dorothy and Jessie's grandfather again, younger than in the bedroom picture; this time Dorothy's facing him and he is looking out at Jessie. No smiles again, just a fierce possessive stare on Dorothy's part, and an almost sad expression in her eyes, which she now realizes are so much like her dad's. In another frame, a fat-faced baby frowns at the camera, bonnet string cutting into her chin, sitting in the lap of a young boy, four or six-years old, Jessie can't say. He too makes Jessie think of her father, of young photos they have hanging in her apartment back in New York. And Jessie suddenly has an image of someone, a stranger, walking through their apartment, looking at pictures of her as a child, wondering who she was, making fun of her clothes. A wave of homesickness hits her so hard she can barely stand.

"That's my dad and Dorothy." Jessie feels her father standing close behind her, his head above her shoulder at eye-level to the picture. His presence steadies her.

"As in Cousin Dorothy?"

"Yes, she was my dad's cousin, on my..." he scrunches up his face, eyes to the ceiling, "Grandma's side I think."

"What was your dad's name?"

He looks at her in surprise, "Gideon. I guess you don't know much about him, do you?"

"Gideon?" she smiles. Such an old-fashioned name, she's never met anyone named Gideon. It makes her think of the boy's name, Jared, and then of the boy, the way he looked at her when they last separated, hopeful, grateful.

"He died when I was twelve."

Jessie looks at him quickly. She knew his father died a long time ago. But twelve!

"I'm sorry."

He smiles sadly and covers her hand with his own. "Thank you."

She turns back to the picture. "What were they like? Dorothy and your dad." She realizes she's grouping them together as if they were a couple, and it's an easy mistake to make. They are in photo after photo together.

"My dad was a very fine man," her father looks proud and sad. "I didn't know Dorothy really."

"Is that your mother?" she's been looking hard for someone new, and she points at last to a young woman on the edges of a color photo of young people seated on the steps of an old classic looking building. Her father peers closely at the photo, lifting and lowering his glasses, but shakes his head. "Nope. She's not likely to be here."

"Why?"

He looks uncomfortable, and Jessie finds herself growing annoyed. Why shouldn't he be able to tell her stuff? Why hasn't he before now? After a few moments he says, "I didn't ever get the whole story from my dad, and my mom never talked about it. I don't remember asking why she wouldn't come with us. I was pretty little."

They move in unison to the couch and sit. "Dad and Dorothy were brought up together, very close." He gestures to the pictures. "As you can see."

"Where?" Jessie asks.

"Where did they live?" He repeats, frowning. Jessie watches as he goes inward, his eyes open but completely unseeing.

"As kids, as little kids," he continues, "Dorothy was probably three years old when they moved, there was still an inland settlement. You know I forgot all about it. My grandpa took me there when I was small, I can't remember the name, but by the time he showed me where they lived, it was all woods, and stone foundations. An entire town just demolished and eaten up by woods. Creepy."

Jessie's neck hair rises, and she's suddenly cold. *Angel Falls.*

"They moved into town, Dorothy's family here, my dad next door. There used to be a house just like this one, but there was a fire, long after Dad moved away." He stands and moves around the room. "I thought I saw... Yes!" He comes back with a framed photo. "Here it is."

The picture shows a trio standing in the doorway of a house much like Dorothy's. "That's Grampa Reed, and my grandmother. She died before I was born. And that's Dad." The photo was all grays and faded. The faces of the three people blurry so she can't make out their expressions.

"After college, Dad joined the Army, he fought in World War II, met my mom in England and brought her home. I think they lived in Beauport before moving to New York, but I'm not sure."

"Your mom came from England?"

"I told you that."

"No, I think I'd remember. Wow."

"Yeah. It didn't seem weird to me, until my friends would ask about her accent. To me it was just how she spoke." His eyes get that inward look again, and she can see pain there. "So, Dorothy didn't like her, and maybe the feeling was mutual, I don't know. All I know is we never talked about Beauport."

"Didn't you ask her why?"

"I was five or six, I really can't remember."

"So then what happened?"

"I don't know, honey. First Grampa passed, then my mom, a couple of years later my dad." His face ripples and becomes younger and sadder, Jessie can almost see him as a young boy, too young to deal with that kind of loss. She wants to change the subject, to pull him out of his sorrow, but can't think what to say.

She looks around the room slowly, the walls so full of items she can't tell if the walls are painted or papered. *A lifetime*, she thinks, *I'm looking at a life.*

She rises and walks to the wall nearest the kitchen. In an oval frame there is a head and shoulders portrait of a young woman, somewhat older than most of those in the pictures she's looked at so far. Dorothy could be twenty here, or thirty. There is an air of maturity stiffening a young face, determination and intelligence.

When she looks at her dad again, he's staring at the diorama.

"Here," he touches the head of a small woman. "His wife was here with the geese." He picks her up and moves her. Jessie hadn't noticed her before. Wasn't there a farmer in the yard?

"She's always with the geese." His voice sounds weird and spooky.

Jessie says, "What happened to the farmer?"

Her father makes a funny sound in his throat, and when she looks at him, he's half-smiling. "I just remembered... there was this game we played." He lifts the farmhouse and there, on his back, lies the farmer. Her father picks him up, returns the house to its place.

"Yeah, when I got up in the morning, I'd go look for him. Sometimes he was here," pointing to the bookshelf. "Sometimes one of the windowsills. One time he was right by the door." He gestures to the floor. "I'd bring him back and put him in the house before Dorothy could find him gone." His eyes were unfocussed, head tilted slightly up, as if listening for something. "If I didn't, she'd be angry with me, and pretend that she hadn't moved him."

"Some game. Maybe she was forgetful." *Or demented.*

"No," he says in that faraway voice, "it was a game." Her father places the farmer carefully outside the doorframe of the house.

Jessie gives him a little hug, then goes to the hallway leading to the bathroom. It too is lined with photographs. Couples. Dorothy and Gideon in each one. When she's finished in the bathroom, she goes inside her bedroom and notices more photos, more couples. She starts to move around the room, going from frame to frame, but the same two pairs of eyes stare at her from every photo. Every single one.

CHAPTER 14

GRAVEYARD

When Jared wakes up on Tuesday, he feels it before he opens his eyes, a raw tingling like the time he burned his wrist on a hot frying pan at Rick's, so real that he keeps checking his arm, but the skin is still smooth and unscarred.

He can still see Delany's haggard, unshaven face looming over him, singling him out from the pack. The forbidden cigarette appearing in his hand, the small quick flame, and the cloud of smoke, like a magic trick. He sees Delany lunging at him, striking like a snake. Then the pain. And that *smile*. Worse than this phantom burn is the betrayal. *Why?* What was the point?

On his way through the kitchen, Jared finds his dad asleep at the table again.

For a moment he wants to wake him up and tell him about Delany and the cigarette. What would he say? There was a time—before his mother left, before his dad had stopped working and started spending all his time covering canvasses with smears of dark stormy colors—when his dad's face would have turned red as one of his paintings, when he would have gone down to the school and let loose a storm of hard and angry words in Delany's face.

Jared pauses in the doorway and looks at his father, his head resting on one arm, a smear of dark paint on his forehead, unconscious and unaware. Right now, Jared would give anything for the father he remembers.

All day in the classroom, Jared avoids meeting Delany's gaze and keeps his eyes on the clock, waiting for it to move so *he* can move, get up and out of his desk and away from here, away from Delany. But the clock won't move, and Jared is trapped, trying not to hear Delany's slow, insinuating voice, cringing inside every time he comes near. When the bell finally rings, Jared practically knocks his chair over in his hurry to get out, and runs from the room, down the hall and outside where his bike is waiting to take him where he wants to go.

When Jared arrives at the moraine, he leans his bike against one of the big rocks and looks around for the girl. But he's the only one here, as usual. Normally, that's what he likes. It's why he comes here. But today he finds himself looking around, waiting for some sign of the girl.

He hears her before he sees her—the sound of rocks and tree branches popping under bicycle tires, then her head appearing first on the horizon of the slope like she's rising up from the ground, dirty blond hair tied back from a plain oval face flushed red and smiling when she sees him. She rides right up to him and stops, breathing a little hard from the ride. He wonders how far she had to come to get here.

"Hey," he says.

"Hey." She gets off her bike and props it against a tree near his. "We're gonna find it today."

"What?"

"The falls. You know. Angel Falls."

"Yeah, well, good luck with that," he says.

"What, you giving up or something?"

"I told you," he says, annoyed that she doesn't seem to remember or believe him. "I've been looking for it all my life."

"Not yet, you haven't," she smiles; when he gets it, he smiles back.

"Yeah. I guess not."

"So, let's go," she says, and she's off, striding down the trail five feet ahead of him.

They pass the first foundations and stone walls, the ones he's already shown her. He can tell she remembers because of the way she moves quickly past them without comment, trying to go further, deeper.

They come to a fork in the trail, and she pauses, but for no more than a heartbeat. "This way!" she yells back over her shoulder and plunges down a narrow trail to their left. It annoys him a little, the way she wants to act like she knows more than he does. This is *his* place, after all, not hers. But she's moving through the overgrown trail like she's known it all her life, and he has to do his best to keep up with her, stepping over treacherous roots, trying to avoid the branches and brambles that reach out and claw at his jeans.

"Where's the fire?" he asks, a little out of breath and trying not to let it show in his voice. Then he realizes where they are and what's just around the corner. *She'll slow down soon enough*, he thinks.

"Oh my God," she whispers, stopping. He watches her taking in the sight of dozens of old gravestones leaning at crazy angles under the trees, dark with age and mottled with moss and lichens. She stands frozen like someone who's realized they're standing in the middle of a minefield.

"Crazy, right?" he says, smiling. Enjoying this.

"Did you know this was here?" she asks. *That's a dumb question*, he thinks, but before he can say it. "Jesus, sorry, that's a dumb question," she says. Still not moving, she looks around, taking it all in—the mottled light filtering down through the tall branches high above, the old gravestones scattered around, pushing up from the earth like broken teeth. When she speaks again her voice is quieter, like she's afraid of disturbing someone or something.

"Who *are* they?"

"The people who used to live here. The town wouldn't bury them in the big cemetery there. So, they buried them here."

"Why?" She asks nervously, like she knows the answer must be something terrible.

"I don't know. I guess they just didn't want them."

"Why not?" She's still standing in the same spot, looking all around at the dark, crumbling stones.

"I don't know," he says, feeling a little impatient. "You sure ask a lot of questions."

"Aren't *you* curious?"

He had been curious, back when he'd first found this graveyard hidden deep in the woods with no roads leading in or out. He'd spent many afternoons going from stone to stone, trying to read the ancient words worn away by rain, wind, and time. But he could only make out a word or two, or a number here or there. The rest was hidden from him.

He watches her start to move, like someone coming out of a trance, stepping carefully through the brambles, pausing at the first dark, tilted slab of rock. She bends down and reads aloud:

> *Maria*
> *Daughter of Timothy Holmstead*
> *Born April 2nd, 1872*
> *Died November 11th, 1890*

"Oh my God, she was only eighteen."

When she moves on to the next stone, he steps up to look at the one she's just read from. His eyes scan the gray, cracked surface. There are no words there. Only a letter or two; an *M* and what might be a *D*, but nothing more.

While he's staring at the gravestone, she starts to read another:

> *Behold me now as you pass by*
> *As you are now, so once was I*
> *As I am now, you soon must be*
> *Prepare for Death and follow me*

"Whoa," she says, straightening up. "*That's* cheerful."

The annoyance that's been building in his chest rises up in his throat. "What are you doing?"

"What?"

He points at the first stone. "There's nothing here."

"You can't read this?" she asks, sounding puzzled, but now he's angry again, almost as angry as he was on the way here today thinking about what Delany had done to him.

"Why are you doing this?" he says, "Are you trying to be funny or something?"

The look on her face is one of genuine surprise. "What do you mean?" *Oh, she's good*, he thinks. "But ... it's right here," she says. "Can't you see it?" She points at the first stone; the sound of her voice is confused, almost pleading, but he's not buying it. She's fucking with him. He doesn't know why, but she is. Why should he be surprised? He doesn't really know her, doesn't know anything about her. Maybe where she comes from, she's the crazy girl who likes messing with people's minds, the one everyone knows to stay away from. How was he supposed to know that? Why didn't he see that from the start?

"There's nothing there," he says. "You're making it up."

"Why would I do that?"

"I don't know, why *would* you? People do some pretty fucked-up things."

"What's the *matter* with you?" she asks. He looks up and sees the beginnings of tears in her eyes. She's hurt, really hurt, and he realizes she's not fucking with him.

She's telling the truth. She's not the crazy one. He is.

Jared sits down on a log and holds his head in his hands, trying to slow down all the thoughts and pictures racing inside his skull. There's something wrong with him. He's always known it.

"I'm sorry," he says. "I...I didn't mean that. I just... there's just a lot of things going on right now."

He looks up and sees her watching him cautiously, from a distance, the hurt leaving her face slowly.

"What kind of things?" she asks.

"I don't know..." he begins, then stops. He wants to tell her but he's afraid to. What would she think? He sees Delany's bloodshot eyes looking down into his, feels the searing pain on his arm and the deeper hurt inside, the sting of betrayal.

"I just ... I don't understand why people do the things they do."

"Like what?"

"Did you ever ... did you ever know someone, someone you thought was pretty cool. You trust them, really trust them. And then they do something ... something you can't understand?"

She doesn't answer right away, and he can see her trying to think about what he's said. "Yeah. Sure. I know what you mean." But she doesn't know, he's sure of it, and the anger comes back.

"*No*. I mean ... someone who you really, really like ... does something, something that hurts you. And you can't understand why." She's looking at him harder now, a line of concern forming between her eyebrows.

"Like what?"

"*I don't know,*" he half-yells at her. It's a lie, of course, and he sees that moment again, Delany's bloodshot eyes staring into his, the cigarette and the flame, and the sudden feeling of betrayal floods his chest, choking him. He wants to tell her. He wants someone to know, to believe him, even though he can't believe it himself. That feeling fills him inside until there's no room for anything else and for a moment the world around him disappears, the trees, the rocks, the gravestones, even the girl beside him, until there's only the *want*. When the world comes back to him again, it comes back in pieces, the way it does when he wakes up after a deep dream. He sees the girl staring at him, a concerned look on her face. "Are you okay?"

"Yeah, sure," he mumbles. The words sound strange coming from his mouth. He wonders if he looks as strange as he feels, and walks away from her, rubbing his hands over his face that feels heavy and numb.

"Are you sure you're okay?" she asks again, coming over to study his face. "Because ... you were acting a little weird."

"I know. I'm sorry," he says. "It's just ..." He sees her eyes widen.

"Wait, what's that?" She looks intently at him, but not at his face.

"What?"

"That. On your arm."

Jared looks down at the place where her eyes are focused, and the whole world stops. There on the skin of his right arm is a circular burn-scar about the size of a dime, the puckered skin red and angry-looking.

It can't be there, he thinks. *It can't.* But it *is* there. Jared feels the world start to tilt on its side.

"Is that ...." The girl is still staring at him. When he thinks her eyes can't get any wider, they do. "Oh my God. That's not .... Shit, Jared, who *did* this to you?"

"It's ... it's nothing," he stammers, hearing how stupid that sounds.

"*Nothing?* That's not *nothing*," she insists, sounding angry now. "Somebody *did* that to you, didn't they? You can't just say it's *nothing*. You ..." She stops, raises a hand to her mouth. "Oh my God," she whispers. "Was it ... Jared, was it your father?"

"No! What, are you crazy? It was *not* my father, okay? My father would never do something like that!"

Jared wishes he could make this girl go away; wishes he'd never agreed to meet her. If he could act like it's no big deal, tell her he burned himself in the kitchen or something stupid like that, then maybe he could get away someplace by himself so he can figure it out. But it's too late—she's seen his face.

"Jared, please. Who did this to you?"

"It was my teacher, okay? My stupid fucking teacher."

"Your teacher?" He sees the fear in her eyes turning back to anger. "Oh my God, Jared, you've got to do something. You've got to tell somebody."

"I can't."

"Why not?"

"Because..." The words catch in his throat—how to explain this? "He didn't *do* anything."

"What do you mean he didn't do anything? What are you talking about?"

Jared rubs his hands over his face again and waits for the right words to come.

"There's this teacher, okay? Delany. Mister Delany. He ... I mean, I used to think he was really cool, but he's always sort of messing with me, with my head. So, today ... he took out a cigarette, in class, and lit it. And he touched me with it. Right here."

"Oh my God, Jared, what the hell?" Jessie says. "You've got to tell someone."

"No. You don't get it. He didn't touch me with the lit end."

"What do you mean?"

"He touched me with the part that wasn't lit. I saw him do it."

"What the hell are you talking about? Look at your arm!"

Jared looks down again at the ugly red puckered mark on his skin and his mind races. Did he see what he thinks he saw? Did Delany really touch him with the unlit end? Or did he switch it at the last second and press the burning ember into his arm?

Jared feels like crying. Not because it hurts, but because nothing makes sense. The girl is smart, but she can't explain this it to him. There's only one person who can.

He turns and starts walking back up the trail. "Wait..." she calls after him. "Where are you going? You're not going back there, are you?"

He keeps walking, hearing her pushing through the low-hanging branches behind him, knowing she's following him, but he doesn't look back. He needs to find Delany and make him explain.

CHAPTER 15

COME BACK TOMORROW

It's almost five o'clock when Jared rolls up to the school. He doesn't bother to lock his bike, but throws it against the bike rack, walks quickly to the side door of the building and pulls it open.

He senses something behind him, turns and looks, and there she is. The girl, Jessie. She's followed him all the way from Angel Falls, like he knew she would. She's standing in the grass at the edge of the parking lot like there's an invisible barrier she wants to cross but can't.

Jared looks right into those pale blue eyes he can see even from this far away, and sends the message, *don't follow me.* He knows it's impossible— she can't hear what he's thinking, but she stays where she is, so he turns and walks through the door, hearing the loud metallic *clang* as it swings shut behind him.

There's no one else in the empty hallway, and Jared's footsteps echo as he walks toward Delany's office, the emergency lights above casting their faint eerie glow. The word EXIT, lit in red, seems meant for him. *Get out*, it says, *get out now.* But the burn on his arm is throbbing, along with the blood pounding in his head. He can't turn around now.

Jared hears music echoing in the dark, thin and tinny-sounding at first, fuller and louder the closer he gets—the Irish music Delany likes, the spooky-sounding flutes, and the thin, high voices always singing about people leaving or dying. As Jared gets closer to Delany's office, the singer's voice becomes clearer. *"And if by chance you look for me, perhaps you'll not me find ...."*

The door to Delany's office is half-open, letting a wedge of light shine out across the hallway floor. The singer's voice blasts full in Jared's face, *"Sun and dark she followed him; his teeth did brightly shine..."*

Jared hesitates, raises his fist to knock, then sees the wound on his arm, and shoves the door open.

Delany is sitting at his desk behind a pile of books and papers. He looks up at Jared, a startled, angry look on his face, then reaches out and punches a button on his boom box. The music stops, and for a moment everything is silent.

"What the hell are you doing busting in here like that?"

"What did you do to me?" Jared's throat is tight the way it feels before he cries, and the words come out sounding strangled.

"What are you talking about?"

Jared steps closer and thrusts his arm out toward Delany. "This! What the hell did you do to me?"

Delany leans closer and peers at the ugly red wound on Jared's arm. His bloodshot eyes go wide. When he speaks, his voice is a hoarse whisper.

"When...when did this happen?"

"You know when it happened!"

Delany keeps staring at the mark on Jared's arm, his face a rigid mask. He leaps from behind his desk and moves past Jared, pulling the office door shut and locking it behind him. He turns and puts his back against the locked door, eyes still fixed on Jared's arm.

"What," Jared says, "Are you going to kill me now or something?"

"When did that happen?" Delany asks again.

"What do you mean, *when did it happen?* It happened when you burned me with your freaking cigarette!"

"No," Delany shakes his head. "I didn't do that. I didn't burn you. I saw your arm. So did you."

Jared remembers. The quick stabbing movement, the searing pain. Then the cold, unlit end of the cigarette held up for him to see, the skin on his arm, smooth and unmarked. It's true. Delany didn't burn him. Then he remembers the strange feeling that swept through him in the woods, the angry-looking wound appearing on his arm. A wave of confusion threatens to pull him down.

"Sit down, Jared."

Jared doesn't want to sit down. Instead, he leans against one of the bookcases and waits for his head to stop spinning, keeping his eyes on Delany.

"Jared, listen," Delany says, speaking slowly the way he does in class, "I'm going to ask you some questions. I want you to *think* before you answer, okay?"

Why the hell should I tell you? Jared thinks. *Why should I ever tell you anything again?* But he hears the familiar sound of authority in Delany's voice, and he responds to it, nodding silently.

"When did this happen?" Delany asks. "When did you first see that burn on your arm?"

"Today."

"When?"

"I don't know...maybe an hour ago."

"Where were you?"

"In the woods."

"In the woods..." Delany repeats. "What were you doing there?"

"Nothing."

"What do you mean, *nothing?* You had to be doing *something.* Think, Jared. What were you doing?"

Jared remembers the searing anger he'd had inside. Anger at Delany.

"Nothing," he mumbles, "I told you."

"Has anyone else seen it?" Delany asks. "Have you shown it to anyone else?"

"No!" His answer is too loud and he hopes Delany doesn't notice, doesn't ask him again—he doesn't want the girl involved.

"Good. Don't show it to anyone else."

"Why not?"

Delany leans across the desk, his face stern and commanding. "What would happen if you tried to tell someone else what you just told me?"

They'd think you did it. Jared remembers the look on the girl's face, her outrage, and angry words. All he has to do is tell someone what happened, show them the wound on his arm—Delany would be gone in a heartbeat. Jared pictures the cops coming into the classroom, slapping the cuffs on Delany's wrists and dragging him away.

Then he remembers—there are witnesses. It's Delany's story that would be believed, not his. He can see it now, the suspicious glances, the secret whispers behind his back. *Crazy kid. He did it to himself.* Then he would be the one taken away.

"Jared," Delany says, "I've done a lot of reading about this. About this kind of thing. I've got some books at home. I can show them to you. Meet me back here tomorrow after school, then maybe we can start to figure this thing out."

"Tomorrow? Why can't you tell me *now?*"

"I *told* you, I just need to get some things together first. Just meet me here tomorrow. Promise. Okay?"

Why should he promise Delany anything? Why should he trust anything Delany says now? Delany leans closer. "Jared, listen. You know how I always tell you that you need to figure things out on your own? Well...this is different. You're going to need help. I can do that. I can help you."

He thinks of all the other times he's sat across from Delany in this room, how many things he's struggled to understand and overcome. Maybe it's true. Maybe Delany can help him. He lets go of a deep breath and nods.

"Good." Delany unlocks the door, opens it, then turns toward Jared. "Remember. Don't tell anybody about this."

A dark twinge of alarm passes through Jared's chest. Delany's words aren't a request—they're a warning. *Don't tell anybody about this.*

Jared hurries past Delany, out into the dark hallway and past the glowing EXIT signs. He can see sunlight and green leaves through the glass doors ahead of him and he walks faster to get there, away from school, away from the smell of chalk dust and disinfectant. His mind is racing, and he needs someone to talk to. He wonders if the girl is still out there, waiting for him.

He hopes she is.

CHAPTER 16

PROMISE

Jessie's eyes ache from staring at the closed door of the school.

It seems hours have passed, but when she checks her phone, it's only been thirty minutes. *What's going on in there? What should I do? Why am I still here?* Her heart pumps faster with each question.

Different scenarios flash through her mind; dragging Jared into a police station; finding and telling his parents; marching into the main office of the school. But her mind veers off each scene when she imagines the look of horror and anger on adult faces. What if they didn't believe her? Then the door swings open and Jared steps out, looking for her, and when he finds her, she can see relief. A relaxing. *Don't relax,* she thinks. *Don't drop your guard.*

He picks up his bike and walks it quickly across the driveway towards her. "Let's get out of here." Then he mounts and rides slowly around a corner without waiting for an answer, so she does the same, following him down a side street and into a small park. They put their bikes in a rack in silence, walking past a sandbox with a couple of tiny children inside, past a bench where a tired looking woman sits, fanning herself with a paperback. Further in, Jared flops down under a sick-looking tree and rests his arms on his knees.

Jessie sits too, the dry grass scratching her legs, and says, "This..." she indicates his wound, "is sick. You have to tell–"

"No. Listen," Jared cuts her off. "You've got it wrong." He wipes a hand across his eyes, and she stares at the wound on his arm. It looks even worse than before, the edges a jagged red opening, the inside blackened and beginning to crust over. She looks away as Jared says, "Delany didn't burn me. I saw it, the other kids saw it. He saw it. There was nothing on my arm after he did it." He looks at her face. "It's true!"

"He's brainwashed you. He wants something from you."

Jared shakes his head, lips tightening. "He wants to help me."

"I waited because I thought he might hurt you again. I should have gone to the police..."

"What? No!" Jared stands up quickly. "You can't tell anyone. Please."

Jessie feels as if she's in a bad play. This boy she doesn't know is telling her to keep quiet about a thing he tells her never happened. She stands and walks back toward the bike rack.

"Listen," Jared's right behind her, "I gotta see Delany again tomorrow. Let's meet in Angel Falls Thursday. I'll tell you what he says. Just give me that."

She stares at him. "You're going back?"

"You don't know him. I do. He's going to help me. Promise me you won't tell anyone." She pulls out her bike and mounts it, and he puts his hand on her arm. It's hot, making her arm burn, but it's his eyes she can't look away from. He's so sure he's right.

She wants to shake her head but finds herself nodding. His mouth relaxes, "Thursday, same place. Okay?" The pleading in his eyes moves her, but her stomach clenches. She pulls her arm free, stands on the pedals and rides away, his words "Thursday, right? Hey Jessie..." growing softer as she puts distance between them.

When Jessie reaches the house, she slams her bike against the gate, pounds inside. She'll tell her father everything. *Dad will know what to do.*

"Dad?" Silence greets her and the emptiness of the house feels like a vacuum. She sees a note on the kitchen table in her father's handsome script.

> *Jessie, there's another public hearing at Town Hall and I have to be there. Sorry! There's still chowder in the fridge. Should be back no later than nine. Text me when you get this. Love you. Dad.*

She closes her eyes and leans against the fridge, sweat cooling on her arms and face, her heart pounding. What should she do? Call Jared's parents? She doesn't even know his last name.

But she knows the name of his teacher. Delany. She goes to her laptop, powers it on, and types in "Beauport social services." In the list of links, she reads: *Family Services, Reporting Family Abuse, Suicide Hotline*. Nothing about teachers and students. No clear way to report what happened.

What kind of person would do that? The slow, cruel torture of a burn—she can see it, fingers gripping the cigarette, its end orange, smoke curling away—then the cigarette touching flesh, the flesh blackening.

Don't follow, Jared's mouth had been closed as he'd turned to look at her before disappearing inside the school, but Jessie had heard the words. And she hadn't followed him. Instead, she'd moved to the back of the school looking through windows, dark and empty, except one, where a thick-set man was seated at a desk, his face unshaved, haggard. Then the door had burst open, and Jared was there, his mouth and body saying, "What did you do?"

It was the look she'd seen on the man's face that haunted her. A look of such longing, Jessie could hardly bear it. Jared's words kept coming back to her; *Have you ever been hurt by someone you really, really like?* She'd thought he was talking about a girl. He wasn't. He was talking about this man.

The first part of her day seemed to have happened in a former life. She'd been looking forward to being in those woods again, to the deep calm combined with an overwhelming sense of possibility. And by the time she'd ridden most of the way there she was looking forward to being with Jared, letting him show her around, looking for the waterfall together.

And now it makes her angry. She had wanted a nice day, exploring the woods, getting to know the boy, becoming friends. Maybe even more. She had wanted a good summer, a happy Jessie to show her parents— *see? this is how it's done.* Instead, she has a stranger in need. A stubborn, confused, abused boy. Yes, even that matched his name. Jared. Brooding, angry, tragic.

A flash of light pulses in the windows, and Jessie jumps up and runs to the window. A loud *BOOM* shakes the house followed by another softer one, and another flash of light. The sky was blue when she came home, wasn't it? She stares outside at roiling black clouds eliminating the late day light and turns to find the room engulfed in gloom. As she switches on lamps she wonders about the power; *are there flashlights? Candles? Where?* She goes to the kitchen where it's even darker as another great *Boom* shakes the glass in the windowpanes. And then comes the sharp *pit-pat* of rain on glass followed by a pounding deluge.

She finds a flashlight, slides the switch, nothing. One long, loud rumble begins and grows into an ear-splitting *CRASH*, and the lights go out. Jessie stands still for several moments, listening to the rain and flinching at every crash of thunder. When the lights don't come back on, she checks her phone, sees the power is at five percent.

Great, she thinks, and she texts her father quickly. Her phone dies before she gets an answer, but it isn't long before she hears a car in the drive, and there he is, bursting through the door, flashlight blazing, "Jessica?" He's brought candles too, and they light them all, then set out the rain-catching buckets.

"C'mere," her dad says, falling back against the couch and gesturing for her to join him. She curls underneath his arm, which tightens around her with every burst of thunder. They watch the flickering candles throwing shadows against the walls. Safe. It feels so safe.

Tell him, Jessie urges herself.

But Jared's voice in her head stops her:

Promise you won't tell!

CHAPTER 17

STORM

Jared looks up and sees dark, heavy storm clouds gathering overhead, rolling in from the east. The tall marsh grass across the road is already whipping back and forth in the wind, making its loud, rushing sound. Jared pedals toward home, the first few raindrops dappling his arms and face. He knows he'll be soaked by the time he gets there, but he doesn't care.

He thinks of the way the girl talked to him and his chest hurts. The look on her face, Jesus, that goddamn awful look. Not anger—anger he could deal with. But the disgust—and worse than that, the pity. It was the look of someone who'd given up.

He'd tried to make her understand, but she didn't believe him—just like Delany had warned him. And that look on her face. If he'd been on fire, the flames eating him up right in front of her, and he'd said *I'm not on fire*—the kind of look you'd give a person when you realize how crazy they are—that was the look she gave him.

Maybe she's right. Maybe he *is* crazy. *It runs in the family...* Isn't that what everyone says?

The sound of a truck horn blares behind him like an angry dinosaur, his chest vibrating with the sound. He curses as it rushes by him on the left, the sound of his voice blown away by the wind it makes.

Thursday...same place...okay? Why did he have to say it like that? So needy and weak sounding. No wonder she didn't want to have anything to do with him. But how does he know that's true? Maybe he's wrong. Maybe she'll be there at Angel Falls on Thursday, waiting for him, like none of this ever happened.

Then he pictures it—him waiting at the moraine for her to show up. The minutes passing, the sun dropping lower in the sky, the shadows growing longer. Pathetic. No. He won't let that happen. Why should he expect her to show up again for him? She doesn't even know him. And he doesn't know her.

The rain is coming down harder now, plastering his hair to his face, running into his eyes, and he pedals harder, trying to get home.

Jared hefts his bike over his shoulder and climbs the stoop to the front door, thinking the whole way up of how he wants to tell his dad. About the girl, about Delany and the mark on his arm. About everything.

Jared gets the door open and steps in out of the rain, water running from his clothes and pooling at his feet. He wipes the water from his eyes and spots a pile of mail on the hall table. Sifting through it quickly, he sees the usual envelopes from the landlord and the power company, the words URGENT and FINAL NOTICE in red ink.

No matter how many times he's seen them, they still make his guts hurt.

When Jared gets to the top of the stairs, he senses something is wrong before he opens the door. The worst thing that could happen is never far from his mind, and his hand shakes as he fits the key into the latch and turns it.

He opens the door and the smell of turpentine, linseed oil, and rotten garbage reaches out to him in the dark. "Dad?" he calls out. His hand fumbles for the light switch on the wall and a prayer flashes through his mind in the second before he turns on the light. A one-word prayer, *please*.

Light blazes in the small kitchen, illuminating everything; the glass jars bristling with paint brushes and the crumpled tubes of oil paint scattered all over the kitchen table.

"Dad?" Jared calls out again, although he knows his dad is gone; a quick look in the bedroom and bathroom confirms that.

Jared looks at the clock; almost 8 PM.

He looks around, searching for clues and finds only the usual mess. And something new, so new that Jared doesn't realize what it is at first. A huge square of wall, clean and unmarked, freshly revealed like raw tissue under a wound, an empty space where one of his dad's paintings had been.

Thunder rolls through the little apartment, rattling the brushes in their glass jars. The musty smell of rain pours in through the kitchen window, and with it a salty breath of seawater—and just like that, Jared knows where his dad is.

The rain is still pounding down when Jared gets down to the street, jumps on his bike and starts pedaling fast. It's all downhill from here to the shore but Jared can't pedal fast enough. He can see more black thunderheads rolling in and filling the horizon, lightning flickering in their dark, swollen bellies.

He hits the boardwalk, the slats rumbling under his wheels, and scans the beach, wiping the rain out of his eyes with one hand. The waves are bigger now, surging and crashing onto the rocks, the black of the sky blending with the black of the water, and there's a sense of movement, of energy gathering and releasing in the dark.

When Jared sees the figure of a man standing far down the beach, he leaves his bike on the boardwalk, jumps down into the sand, and starts walking fast, then running toward that tiny figure standing up against the surging black wall of water.

"Dad!" Jared hears his voice ripped to pieces and blown away in the strong wind. The figure ahead of him doesn't hear and raises its arms to the sea like someone conducting an orchestra. The black sky splits wide open and a bright flash illuminates the whole beach for a second. Jared sees the toothless grin and bloodshot eyes turned toward him. "Pete!" Jared yells. "Pete, what the hell? Get off the beach!"

Pete's toothless mouth moves soundlessly, the crack and roll of thunder obliterating whatever sounds he's making. The sour stink of alcohol rolls from him in waves, making Jared gag. Grabbing him by the arm, Jared pulls him away from the breakers and points toward the boardwalk. "Get off the beach! Go home! Go home!" The old man's arm feels thin and brittle in Jared's hand; he lets him go and keeps moving down the beach. Dad. He must find Dad.

The sky splits open again, and Jared sees craggy rocks ahead of him silhouetted against the flash. And in that flash, a memory from years ago. Climbing those same rocks with his dad, helping him carry his paints and easel, then playing in the sand, catching crabs in the tide pools while his dad painted. Then later, the worried look on his dad's face when the tide rose and cut off their way back, how they'd waded through the waist-high water, his dad holding the canvasses above the waves, Jared hanging on to his dad's neck as the breakers smashed them against the rock again and again...

Jared clears the top of the rocks and sees his dad standing about fifteen feet from the water, struggling to hold onto his painting that's flapping like a kite in the wind.

Jared scrambles down the other side of the rock and runs over to his dad.

"Grab it," his dad orders, like he's not surprised to see him. *"Hold on."*

Jared takes hold of one corner of the canvas and holds on tight while his dad starts rolling it from the other end. When they're done, his dad shouts, *"Come on. Tide's coming in."* The two of them walk through the crevasse in the rock like they had ten years ago, the sea surging and dragging at their legs.

When they're back on the main beach, Jared yells, "Dad, what the hell are you doing out here?"

"I just wanted to get it right," his dad says, glaring at the storm. "I almost had it." Jared sees his dad's mouth tremble for a second, and a flash of lightning lights up the rainwater streaming down his unshaven face. He looks down at Jared and his expression changes, like he's noticing him for the first time. "What are you doing out here?" he asks. "Don't you know it's dangerous to be on the beach in a thunderstorm?"

Jared stares at his dad, feeling his mouth hanging open. The laughter erupts from somewhere deep inside his body; he tries to stop it, but he can't. He puts both of his hands over his mouth, choking on the sounds coming out of him.

"What's the matter with you?" his dad asks, a concerned scowl on his face. "You're acting crazy." Laughter explodes again from deep in Jared's guts, so hard it almost hurts as the two of them stand in the rain with the sky flashing and rumbling over their heads.

The laughter finally subsides, Jared takes a deep breath and says, "Come on, Dad. Let's go home."

By the time they get back to Plymouth Street and climb the narrow stairs to their apartment, a deep weariness weighs Jared down. Rainwater runs from their clothes and pools on the kitchen floor. In silence, they peel off their wet clothes. Jared hangs his in the shower to dry. When he comes back out, his dad has dropped his wet clothes on the kitchen floor and is busy unrolling the soaked canvas and pinning it to the wall.

Jared glances at the kitchen table and sees the pile of bills scattered there among the dirty plates and sandwich wrappers, the words URGENT and FINAL NOTICE stamped in red.

Weariness hits Jared like a wave. All he wants to do is lie down. But first, he reaches down and picks up his dad's wet clothes from the kitchen floor, then walks down the hall to the bathroom and hangs them carefully next to his own. When he comes back to the kitchen, his father is still standing in the middle of the floor in his underwear, rainwater running from his hair down his back and chest.

Dad, Jared wants to say. *I'm scared. There's something happening to me, and I don't understand. I need your help. Please...*

"No..." Jared's dad mumbles. "No..." He picks up a brush, steps closer to the wall and slowly drags it across the canvas, leaving a smear of black. His eyes look like they're seeing straight though the canvas to some place a thousand miles away.

"Dad..." Jared says out loud. *Look at me.*

His father keeps muttering, dragging the brush back and forth across the canvas. Hurt rises in Jared's throat; he wants to scream and shout. Instead, he turns and walks back into his bedroom and pulls the door shut behind him.

CHAPTER 18

HOW TO HELP

Jessie tries to sleep, but the violence of the storm repeatedly startles her awake. Eventually the storm eases and she drifts off until morning. She hears her father moving around the house, clattering pans, the squeak of chair springs, click of a light. It eases her heart. Dad, a few steps away. She jumps up, dresses, and goes into the main part of the house. He looks up from his cereal bowl, spoon dripping milk, and smiles.

"Mornin' pumpkin." He looks all rumpled and undone, his shirt is wrinkled and missing a button and he hasn't shaved. She realizes he's left his glasses off. Without them his eyes are so much larger, their blue-green irises wide and deep.

"Mornin' Cinderella," she replies, thinking, *He'll know what to do.*

"Dad?" she starts, not knowing what she can say. She remembers Jared saying *Promise you won't tell anyone!* and frowns.

"Yup?" He stands, gets a bowl and spoon and sets it at her place on the table.

"Have you ever known anybody that was...," she pauses, hating the shock of the word, but unable to find a replacement, "abused?"

Her father puts down the milk carton and turns to look at her, alarmed. "Why? Do you? Is it one of your friends?" His alarm frightens her, but she tries to keep it from her face, to calm him down.

"No, no. It's... it's in a book I'm reading. The main character's friend, a boy, is being ... I dunno, messed with by his teacher. Hurt, physically... Well, emotionally too. But he won't tell anyone. So far, she hasn't done anything to help. The boy, he says it's nothing and asks her not to tell. Isn't that wrong?"

Her father studies her for a moment before opening the cabinet and taking out a box of cereal. "Cheery story. What's the name of the book?"

"You wouldn't know it. It's the girl's name. Andrea something." She wonders if the lie shows on her face.

"So," her dad says. "The boy is trying to protect his abuser?"

"Yes!"

"And he doesn't want to draw attention to himself?"

"Yeah. Exactly." Hope swells inside. "What should she do?"

Her father picks up his glasses from the table and puts them on. Then he studies Jessie closely, making her nervous. All the softness disappears. The muscles in his face tighten, and his eyes focus on her face. "Jessica. If this happens, if you ever, I mean *ever* find yourself in that situation, tell me. Tell the police."

"Jeez, it's just a story," she starts to rise from the table, but he takes her wrist, holds her there.

"I'm serious Jess. Promise me." Another promise. Why does everyone want her promise? She nods, gets up and takes a glass from the cabinet, pours herself juice. She nodded when Jared asked her to promise, too. Does it count if you don't say the words?

After breakfast, her dad proposes a hike and swim. She doesn't like the way he's watching her, that worry-furrow deepening between his brows, so she agrees, even as a part of her mind considers his words, *Tell the police. Tell me.*

They walk from the house to the end of the peninsula, past a lighthouse and onto a sea wall, taking long strides from rock to rock, watching as, singly and in concert, men and boys snap up their rods and cast their lines.

Hiking back, they stop at a beach, strip to their swimsuits and dive into the cold water, shouting as they come up, swimming hard to get warm. Lying on their towels in the sun, Jessie hooks her little finger with her father's, feeling him squeeze hers in response and takes in the sun gratefully.

What would happen if I told him? Would he make her go to the police? She sees it for a moment, the police station, something out of a movie, cops pulling them into "the box" for questioning, then a cop car pulling up outside Jared's house. Jared's eyes looking at her in betrayal.

"Come on, Pop Tart, before you become toast." Her dad is standing over her, extending a hand. She takes it and stands, grateful for the interruption.

Back at the house she watches her father emerge from the bedroom, dressed casual-nice, pressed khakis, button-down shirt. He's leaving again. "What will you do, while I'm gone?"

Get help, get help, get help. "Oh, I dunno. Read. Talk to Dyl."

Something sad washes across his face, regret or guilt, and Jessie can't bear it.

He says, "I'm sorry, kitten. It's just that I—"

"Please stop. I'm fine. See you tonight!" Jessie walks him to the door. Watches as he gets in the car, backs out onto the street. They exchange hearty waves, and she wonders if he feels the tug, the jerk, as they are separated. She stares at her bike for a moment, longing to mount it and ride... but where? She goes back into the house.

Jared. There must be something she can do. Words tumble through her brain, *My teacher ... classroom ... other kids saw it ... he didn't do it.*

Even as she struggles with that, another thought arises. *He could be at school right now.* She can go there, wait for him to come out and follow him home. She's out the door and on her bike in an instant, relief at having something to do flooding her entire body. *Follow him home. Follow him home.*

She pauses once or twice, wondering if she is going the right way, but familiar landmarks, a tiny house, a strange off-kilter intersection, and she rides confidently on.

Jessie turns the corner and the school looms up before her. She imagines him coming out the door, the way he did yesterday, looking for her. But he wouldn't look for her today; he's not expecting her. She's not supposed to let him see her...

Something's wrong. She stares and stares at the bike rack, but no bikes appear.

It's empty. Jared isn't here.

A door in the school opens and a man walks out and crosses the lot to a dusty beat-up sedan. It's Jared's teacher. He is strongly built, no more than forty, but he walks like a much older man, slowly, as if a small stone could throw him off balance. When he swings open the car door, he sits heavily, almost falling, and stays for a few minutes, his legs outside, chest heaving. She thinks of how he looked at Jared yesterday when he came in the classroom, full of hope and longing. It had made her angry, and a little sick.

Now it just seems sad.

He swings his legs in the car and closes the door.

It isn't till he's halfway down the road that she realizes she's going to follow him. She starts pedaling, slowly, wanting to keep him in view. After a few blocks she tries to tell herself how stupid and dangerous this is. *What am I doing*? But she continues. Each time he turns a corner she expects to lose him, but when she reaches it, she can still see his car.

He turns into a driveway by a small house, like the one Jessie's staying in—her father called it "Cape Ann"—shingled siding the color of wet sand.

Jessie watches him get out of the car and move with that strange heavy gait to the front door. There's a mailbox by the door, its lid propped open by a mass of envelopes, but he doesn't look at it. Puts the key in the lock, opens the door, and disappears.

Go home, she tells herself, but she's finding it hard to pull herself away. For one moment she imagines walking up to the front door and knocking. Confronting him. *I know what you've done*. The thought of it makes the hair on her arms rise.

She notices a small playground in the backyard and her mind twists. *He has kids?*

The sound of a door banging somewhere makes her jump. Then Delany walks out from behind the house with a six-pack of beer in one hand, an open can in the other.

He walks over to the swing-set, puts the six-pack down in the grass, takes a long pull from the open can, and sits in the swing. Jessie wants to leave but can't.

He finishes the first beer, drops the can and pulls another one out of the plastic ring. She can hear the *pop, sizz* as he opens it. He pushes himself slowly back, then lifts his feet and swings forward. Jessie can almost feel the gentle sway of it. When the swing has slowed and almost stopped, he pulls back, lifts his feet, and does it again.

And then he stops, drops the beer, she can see a thin yellow stream of liquid pour its way into the grass. His head drops forward. The way his shoulders move, it looks as if he's crying. And then she hears it, a low moaning sob and hitched breath, and she feels a quick stab in her heart. She turns away then, and, as quietly as she can, steps up on her pedals and rides away.

CHAPTER 19

TELL ME

It's 4 o'clock and Jared is standing outside of the door to Delany's office. He's here on time and he knows Delany is inside from the sound of Irish music playing, but he can't bring himself to knock. He looks around the hallway to make sure no one is looking, then pulls up his sleeve and looks at the mark on his arm. It's still there, ugly, red, and starting to scab. He pictures the white scar that'll be there once the scab comes off, round and pale as a little moon.

Before he can knock, the door swings open and there's Delany looking right at him with his tired, red-rimmed eyes. The stubble on his jaw looks heavier than usual, the lines on his face deeper and hard etched. Jared hesitates for a moment, then steps inside. Delany immediately shuts and locks the door behind him, then turns and grabs Jared by the arm.

"Did you do this?" he growls at Jared.

"What...?" Jared sputters.

"Did you do this?" Delany repeats, shaking Jared's arm. "Tell me the truth, because if you're fucking with me, I swear to God, I'll make you sorry. I'll make you sorrier than you've ever been in your life."

Jared pulls his arm from Delany's grip, feels a sharp pain, and looks down; the scab is torn open, pink, and raw. *"No!"* Jared shouts. *"What the hell is wrong with you?"*

Delany looks as stunned as Jared feels. He stands breathing heavily for a moment, closes his eyes and mutters, "Sorry." Jared keeps his back to the wall, watching Delany carefully. Delany opens his eyes and looks at Jared. "Alright, alright..." he scowls. "I said I was sorry. Sit down. I won't bite you."

The room is dark. That's when Jared notices that all the shades are drawn shut. Delany picks up a chair in each hand, drags them both to the center of the room and sets them down, facing each other. "Sit here," he says.

Jared sits in the chair closest to the door. Delany sits in the one across from him, his bloodshot eyes focused on Jared's arm.

"Let me see it."

Jared hesitates, then holds his right arm out toward Delany. Delany doesn't touch it, but leans closer, staring intently.

"Has anyone else seen it?"

"No," Jared lies. Only the girl. What does it matter? He'll probably never see her again anyway.

"You haven't told anyone about it?"

"No."

"Alright," Delany says. "I'm going to ask you some questions now. And I need you to think before you answer. It's important, Jared. Really important. Can you do that?" Jared nods. "Okay," Delany says. "So, tell me again, how did this happen?"

I told you already, Jared wants to say, but something in Delany's face makes him hold back his impatience.

"I...I was in the woods..."

"Where?"

"Angel Falls." At the name, Jared sees a flash of light in Delany's eyes.

"Go on. You were in Angel Falls. Then what?"

"Nothing. I just looked at my arm, and it was *there*."

"What were you doing? Right before it happened?"

"Nothing."

"What do you mean, *nothing*?" Delany's voice turns gruff again. "You had to be doing *something*. What were you thinking?"

"I don't know..." The pulse in Jared's head starts to beat louder.

"You mean you were just walking around without a thought in your head? Bullshit. Don't play stupid with me, Jared..."

"It was you!" Jared says, "I was thinking about you, okay? I was thinking about how you burned me with your freaking cigarette! That's what I was thinking!"

"I didn't burn you."

"I don't care! You lit a cigarette and pushed it into my fucking arm!" Tears rise in his eyes and he rubs them away quickly with the back of his hand. "I thought you burned me. Don't you get it? Why did you *do* that?"

When Jared looks up again, Delany pauses, starts slowly, "So. You were in the woods. At Angel Falls. You were thinking about the cigarette. You were angry. Really angry. And that's when you saw the burn…"

Delany leaps out of his chair, startling Jared, walks over to his desk and picks up a book, then walks back and hands it to Jared. On the page where Delany has opened the book, Jared sees an old black and white photo of a man's hands, ugly-looking black wounds in the center of each palm.

"What's this supposed to be?" Jared asks.

"This is what I was telling you about yesterday," Delany says. "Things like this… they've been happening to people for a long time."

Things like this? The picture is starting to make Jared feel sick, and he shuts the book. "Why are you showing this to me?"

"You know what I always say in class? That the mind is a very powerful thing? Well … some people's minds are more powerful than others." Delany lowers his voice. "I think you're one of those people."

"What are you talking about?"

"That mark on your arm. I think you made it happen."

Jared can't believe what he's hearing. "Are you fucking with me?"

"Do I *look* like I'm fucking with you?" Jared can't meet Delany's eyes. He feels dizzy.

"How…" Jared stammers. The words won't come—it feels like his brain has shut down.

"Listen, Jared. I know you don't understand. I know you're scared. People are always scared of things they don't understand."

Jared hears the confident, persuasive sound of Delany's voice and feels the pull of it. He wants to believe Delany can help him, like he's always helped him before. Maybe he can. Who else can he talk to? The girl? Jessie? She doesn't believe him.

"Okay," Jared says, "So…what do we do now?"

Delany drags his chair even closer so that their knees are almost touching, his grey eyes staring intently into Jared's.

"I want you to think of something."

"What…you mean like…mind-reading or something?"

"No, no," Delany shakes his head. "Not like that. I want you to think of something that you want."

"You mean, like…"

"No, don't tell me what it is," Delany says. "Just think of something that you really, really want. More than anything else."

Jared struggles to come up with something. *Money? A new house?* A dozen examples speed through his mind, and none of them seem right. *More than anything else in the whole world.* He glances up at the clock on the wall. He's due at Rick's for the evening shift.

"*Focus,* Jared," Delany says, the same thing he's told Jared many times before, but Jared can't focus. *More than anything else in the whole world.* What the hell does this have to do with the burn on his arm?

"Okay," Jared says, closing his eyes so it looks like he's picturing something, and so he won't have to look Delany in the eye when he lies.

"You got it?" Delany asks.

"Yeah," Jared nods. "I got it." He opens his eyes and sees Delany's face, flushed with excitement.

"Okay. Now I want you to keep that in your mind as long as you can. Think about it when you leave here, think about it when you go home, and think about it when you go to bed tonight."

"Okay, I'll try…"

"No—don't try. *Do* it. Promise me."

"Okay, okay. I promise."

"Good." Delany stands up. "Meet me here again on Monday, after class."

"What?" Jared is shocked. He can't believe this is all that's going to happen today. "That's it? I thought you were going to help me."

"I *am* trying to help you," Delany says, his voice turning harder. "Just do what I asked you to do, okay?" He unlocks the door, then turns and locks eyes with Jared.

"Remember…don't tell anyone about this. This is just between you and me. Understand?"

Jared thinks again of the girl, Jessie, and feels a quick pain in his chest. When he walks out of Delany's office and steps outside, this time she won't be waiting for him. It's true. There's no one else. It's just him now. Him and Delany, the way it's always been.

"Understand?" Delany repeats.

"Yeah," Jared nods. "I understand…"

Riding his bike to Rick's, Jared feels better with the salt breeze blowing in his face. He's trying to keep his head clear, but Delany's words keep running through his brain. *Some people's minds are more powerful than others.* Out here in the cool evening air with cars whipping past him, it sounds ridiculous and almost makes him laugh. Who is he kidding? Ten minutes from now he'll be wearing an apron, peeling potatoes and carrying big bags of smelly fish-garbage to the dumpster—how *powerful* can his mind be?

He thinks of that old photograph Delany showed him, the pale hands with those ugly black wounds. What was it Delany said? *I think you're one of those people.* Anger and repulsion surge inside Jared—he doesn't want to be *different.* He doesn't want to be singled out like some kind of freak. He has enough pressure already, trying to earn enough to keep the lights turned on, watching out for his dad every day. He wants somebody to watch out for *him,* to take care of *him* for a change. The way his dad did. Before everything went to hell.

What's the one thing you want more than anything else in the world?

Jared knows what he wants. He wants all of this to go away. The wound on his arm, the worry, the long days and nights, the clock that won't stop running. He wants all of it to go away, right now. But he knows that's not going to happen, so he leans into the wind and pedals harder until he sees the lights of Rick's shining in the distance.

Chapter 20

The Letters

"How's your father?"

It's her mom's first question in their Skype after breakfast. Why is she asking? Doesn't she talk to him herself? Is there something wrong? Jessie studies her mother's face but it's extremely still and difficult to read. Jessie remembers her saying how important it was to listen on stage to your scene partner, listen but not distract from their speech. She thinks her mother has that face now, listening but not telling.

"He's fine. A little tired, I think. You know he's at the town hall almost every day for permits or looking up records or something. Cousin Dorothy wasn't very organized."

"Yeah, he told me as much. Are you getting much dad-daughter time? Does he get outside at all?"

"Oh yeah, we go out every day." It's a small lie, but Jessie feels justified. That 'dad-daughter' line stung a little. Without her mom, it was all dad-daughter time.

"Except for today. It's raining again, big time."

Her mom makes a sour face. "I'm sorry to hear that. It's a little drizzly here too, and we—"

"Baby, where's the sugar?" A man's voice in the background interrupts.

Her mother turns her head and calls, "Cabinet under the microwave, on the right," turning back to Jessie, her mouth now relaxed.

"Who's that?" Jessie asks, suddenly cold.

"It's Sam. You know Sam, don't you?" Jessie shakes her head and doesn't answer. "He wrote the play...."

"He calls you *baby*?"

Her mother laughs. "He calls *everyone* 'baby.' There's no need to worry about Sam." Jessie wants to believe her. But her mother is alone in Jessie's home, with a strange man rummaging in Jessie's kitchen, calling her mom 'baby.'

"Don't look so miserable. If you don't stop, I'll get on the next train to Beauport and fetch you right home!"

Is that what it takes to get you here? Seeing me miserable? But Jessie doesn't want to talk anymore. "I've gotta go, Dad's calling." She closes her laptop as her mother is saying, "Jessie..."

Her phone rings immediately, and Jessie lets it go to voicemail, then turns the phone off.

She stares out the window though there's nothing much visible. It's still raining. It was raining when she woke up that morning. Jared had asked to meet her in Angel Falls today. She'd hoped it would clear up, but now, all she can see is a grey pall eating up the landscape. She can't stop looking at the rain, obstructive and endless. She pulls away from the windows, starts to wander through the house picking up objects and putting them down.

Eventually she feels hands on her shoulders, stopping her restless movement. "What *are* you doing?"

Her father brings her into Dorothy's bedroom and shows her a stack of papers and a paper shredder. "You ever operate one of these?" She shakes her head, and he demonstrates, the shredder making a soothing whirring sound as paper fingers elongate, bend, and drop into the waiting bin.

"Your mom says you hung up on her this morning."

Jessie feels a rise of anger. "Is that what she told you?"

"Yes," he sighs, "Jessie, please don't hold things in. If something's bothering you, we want you to tell us."

She thinks, *oh, like you tell me?* but tightens her lips and takes a deep breath. Grabs a few sheets and feeds them into the shredder, letting go quickly when the paper pulls her towards the machine.

"Nothing's wrong. I didn't hang up on her."

"You know this is hard on her."

Jessie stares at him. Hard on *her*?

"It's hard on all of us," he amends softly. "Call her back after dinner, please?"

She nods, but he's made her think. Her mother hadn't sounded sad. *Is* her mother finding the separation hard? She wants her to. *Miss us. Come here.*

The sound of the shredder cuts through these thoughts and helps empty her mind. She watches as it makes fine spaghetti of the paper. A few words catch her eyes here and there, business correspondence, bills, tax returns. Dull writing. The stack is high, and she has to stop from time to time to pull a staple he missed or remove a paperclip.

The stack of papers is nearly gone, and Jessie thinks she's through, when her father walks over with an armful of papers and dumps them on the bed. A small packet falls to the floor and Jessie picks it up.

It's a stack of envelopes, tied with a thin piece of yellowed lace and her name, Reed, catches her eye. The return address reads *G. Reed, 248 9th Ave, Apt 3, Brooklyn, NY*. The postmark is smeared but she can make out the year; *1972*.

"G. Reed? Is that my grandfather?" She feels a sudden excitement.

"Dammit. I thought I got rid of those." Her father takes the packet from her.

"Wait!" She reaches for them, but he's stepped back out of her reach. "*Is it your dad? Did you read them?*"

Her father's face is strange and unhappy. There's anger there, which she doesn't understand and can barely recognize; her father is so even-tempered. But then his face softens. "Yes. These are from my dad, and no I haven't read them." She can see his hand tighten on the letters, but he doesn't look at them. "He and Dorothy... they had a rift. It wasn't good. Besides, these are private."

"You were going to shred them?" she asks, amazed. He puts them down quickly on the desk, like they hurt his hands. "I should. I most definitely should." His voice is distracted, strange. Jessie can't believe he wouldn't want to read his father's letters. Her dad was so young when his father died. He must have so many questions. She opens her mouth to say it, but her dad's cell phone starts to ring.

He answers, "Hello? Oh, yes. Yes it is. Hi Ben," and then he's moving out of the room to the living room.

Alone with the letters Jessie doesn't hesitate. She picks up the packet and starts to work at the knotted lace. The knot is tight. She listens to her father's voice in the other room, trying to judge how long he'll be. She should stop.

Leave them alone. Let her father destroy them. *Private.* But the urge to see what's inside is too great.

Jessie goes to the door and looks into the living room. Her father is pacing, cell phone tucked to his head. He doesn't notice her. She puts the letters under her shirt and walks out, crosses the living room, and goes into her bedroom. The letter bundle feels hot in her hands, and she stashes them under her pillow.

The rest of the afternoon she waits for her father to notice, to question her, but he never does. After dinner and a game of rummy, Jessie says, "I'm gonna read for a while. Good night," and goes to her room. She shuts the door softly behind her, pulls out the letter bundle and patiently works at the knot till the lace falls away. She looks again at the first envelope in the stack, addressed to *Dorothy L. Hicks.* She flips the stack. The bottom letter is in a different kind of envelope, and the writing, a looser script, addressed to "Dotty 'pie-face' Hicks." This one is post-marked September 10, 1938. She opens the flap and slides out a single sheet with writing on both sides, unfolds it gently and reads:

> *Dear Dotty, I made it to the greater halls of learning! You said I wouldn't, but I fooled you. Here I am, BMOC.*

It takes her a few minutes before coming up with, Big Man on Campus, and smiles. She skims the next several paragraphs about his classes, the weather, his roommate. She stops at *be careful with your Beauport beaus. I don't want to come home to a bunch of broken hearts.*

Did Dorothy liked being teased? He's like a fond brother and Jessie thinks how nice that would be. To have a brother. She folds the paper and slides it back in its envelope. Where's the rift her father mentioned? What could have torn two good friends apart? She skips the other letters, all the years in-between, looking again at the first one, the one on top.

She opens the flap and slides out a single sheet of folded yellowed paper. There is a date in the upper left side above a short paragraph, *October 28, 1972.* There is no salutation or signature. No *Dear* anything, or *Love* or even *Sincerely.* Only a few sentences:

As you can see, I am back home. I am writing as you requested, but hope I was very clear that this would be the last. In the name of all that you value, and our good history, don't try to contact me. You made a promise. I expect you to keep it.

She puts the bundle down. The contrast between the first and last letters makes her cold. What could have happened between 1938 and 1972 to make her grandfather write that letter? Much as she wants to know, she is overwhelmed by sadness. She puts the letters in her suitcase and slides it under her bed. The past is messy, and she has enough mess of her own.

CHAPTER 21

NANEPASHEMET

At breakfast, her dad lays three brochures out on the table. "You pick." Jessie pulls out the one with an oil painting of men in a boat in a violent sea. She recognizes the artist.

"Winslow Homer," she says. "We studied him last year in art."

"He was here, in Beauport. He painted here," her father says smiling. Jessie reads the name *Nanepashemet Art Colony* and turns the brochure over to find a small map of Beauport, the circular bay with a star on its left side. "It's right down the road. We could walk!"

Her father takes the brochure, studies the map and hands it back. "Yes, you're right. Edward Hopper was here too, Childe Hassam, a lot of people."

"Child? Like a kid?"

He laughs, "Nice try. It was his name. Spelled with an 'e' on the end. American Impressionist."

Jessie reads aloud, "Nanepashemet is home to one of the oldest continuously operating art colonies in the United States. Dozens of working artists from painters, potters and textile designers to photographers and jewelry makers, display their work in Nanepashemet galleries during the summer months." She looks up. "What is a Nanepashemet?"

Her father shrugs. "*Who* is more like it. Or maybe it means 'place where great art is made.'"

"Or 'place where tourists drop big wampum.'"

Her father laughs. "Do you want to go?"

There will be no Angel Falls today. She wonders if Jared's in school right now. She remembers the man she followed, sobbing in the swing, and shakes her head to get the thought out.

"Yes. Great. Let's go!"

They start walking on deserted streets—no beach traffic, fishermen already at sea—and turn down past a small parking lot and a shale beach.

Soon they are walking by tiny, shingled shacks with big windows displaying paintings and sculpture. The first two galleries have ocean paintings, some with ships, some with seagulls; they peer in through the windows but don't enter. Then there is a modern one with fabric and clay sculptures. Jessie's dad looks at her and she nods, and they enter.

A thin young man with lots of piercings looks up from the small table where he's seated. He doesn't say anything, only stares at them as if he thinks they're going to damage something. Some of the sculptures look like gnarled people, or fabric trees. One is a mask with six eye holes, three pair stacked on top of each other. She points it out to her father with a grin, fighting the urge to try it on.

In the next gallery there are paintings, abstracts, and Jessie is drawn to a trio of large frameless canvasses covered in swathes of mostly dark paint. She doesn't have to read the small cards beside them to know they are about storms. The lightest one is on the left, simply titled *Storm #1*. There is some medium blue swirled in with the darker paint, which could be sky or sea. The second canvas is darker, the paint thicker and the impression of violence strong. This one is *Storm #2*. The third canvas is nearly black, the paint still thick and swirling, giving a sense of wind. This one is called *Night*.

The paintings make Jessie think of the wind in the woods, the way there was nothing, then sound, then the branches swaying, the leaves swirling, and then, and only then, did she feel the wind against her face, lifting her hair. They are thrilling and a little frightening. She moves closer to her father and looks at his face, smiling.

His face is sad, but when he sees her looking at him, he smiles back at her, and says, "Wow. Pretty tough, eh?"

"Tough?" She looks at *Night,* the nearly solid black canvas with only slips of gray to break up all the dark. And suddenly she is sad.

Her father's phone rings, and he silences it quickly as the girl sitting at a small table looks up with annoyance. She has hair the color of a red balloon, thickly lined eyes, and pale skin. "I've got to take this," he mumbles apologetically then steps outside and opens his umbrella.

Jessie turns back to *Storm #1* and breathes in the sense of it. It appears as if it was painted from life, but how do you paint in a storm?

"You ditched me." The voice is right behind her, she whirls around and finds Jared looking at her, smiling.

"Jared?" She stares hard at him, struggling with the image of him indoors, without a backdrop of trees, sky. "What are you doing—" realizing how stupid that sounds, cuts herself off. She tries again, "How... how are you? Are you okay?" Her eyes go to his arm, but the wound is covered by his sleeve. She looks back at his face.

"I'm fine," he says. "Listen," he lowers his voice and turns away from the girl at the table. "I have to tell you what I ...."

The door opens and a couple walks in complaining loudly about the rain. Jessie, Jared, and the red-haired girl all stare at them for a moment. The loud couple doesn't notice, and Jared says quickly, "There's a coffee shop, just down the road. Can you come?"

His eyes plead with her, and she's a little dazzled. His eyes have flecks of gold in the brown, she hadn't noticed before. She has something he wants.

"Jared," the girl at the table speaks. She sounds bored.

"Melissa," Jared mimics her tone exactly before turning to look at her. She smiles at him in a way that Jessie understands instantly. She remembers the teasing happy tone from the woman at Rick's. Girls like him. Women like him. Of course they do.

"Your father ran out with his gear just before you came," the girl's voice cuts through the air at them. "Said to tell you not to wait."

Jared's body grows rigid. He looks out the front windows where the rain is slowing, the sky a shade lighter than before, and sighs, his body relaxing slightly. "Thanks." He looks back at Jessie. "I'll buy you a cinnamon bun. Bunbury's are the best."

Before she can say anything, the door opens and Jessie's father walks in, folding the umbrella. He looks at Jared, then looks from Jessie to Jared and back to Jessie. It's comical but she doesn't laugh. Instead, she blurts, "Dad, would it be okay if I skipped the galleries and went to a coffee shop with Jared?" It comes out fast, the words running together. The silence that follows seems to go on a long time before her father speaks.

"I'm Michael, Jessie's dad. I've seen you at Rick's, haven't I?" He extends a hand which Jared takes.

Jared nods and says, "Pleased to meet you." They shake hands and Jessie looks at her father, whose eyeglasses are reflecting light so she can't see his eyes.

"Jessie didn't tell me..." her father trails off. *Tell him what?*

"I'm interrupting," Jared says, then turns to Jessie, "We can get together another—"

"No! I mean," Jessie looks at her dad, "Is it okay? Do you mind?" The light on her dad's glasses still hides his eyes.

"Actually, that call was from the contractor. There's some hitch in the repair costs... I was about to cut out on you." He turns to Jared, "So, where's this coffee shop?"

"It's by the harbor. Bunbury's."

"Okay. Bunbury's," Jessie's dad turns to her, "You'll be home by six, right?"

Jessie nods, so relieved her head feels light.

They stand there for a few moments, then Jared opens the door, standing back for Jessie, and she looks at her dad. He is studying them both like a puzzle he wants to solve. She can see his eyes now, and when he catches her looking, he gives her a big, goofy grin, and she smiles back, the relief almost overwhelming.

"Have a nice time, kitten. Don't forget your umbrella."

She digs it out of the umbrella bucket by the door, gives a little wave as she walks past Jared and into a lighter, sweeter rain, feeling him close behind her.

Chapter 22

Bunbury's

Bunbury's is packed with the usual crowd of families, young and retired couples and whiny kids grabbing a quick bite and keeping their eye on the clock for their turn to board the whale watch. Jared looks around but there are no empty tables.

"You think maybe we ought to go someplace else?" Jessie says, looking around anxiously.

"Nah," he says. "Actually, I know how to make all these people disappear. It's magic. You wanna see?"

Keeping one eye on the clock, Jared counts down the seconds till 11 AM, raises both hands in the air and says, "Three ... two ... one ... *ALAKAZAM!*"

The bell on the whale-watch boat outside starts clanging and the people all get up and hurry outside, leaving a room full of vacant tables.

"There," Jared smiles, gesturing at the empty room. "What'd I tell you?"

Jessie smiles. "*Very* impressive."

Jared leads her to a table in the back corner away from the door. He doesn't want anyone interrupting or listening in.

"I've been here before," Jessie offers. "My dad took me on the whale watch."

"Yeah? How'd you like it?"

"It was great," Jessie says, but Jared doesn't want to talk about whale watches. From the distracted look on her face, he guesses she doesn't want to, either.

The waitress brings his coffee and Jessie's coke, and the two of them sit quietly for a minute.

"Your dad seems nice," Jared says.

"Thanks," Jessie says, "He is." Then she goes quiet and Jared wonders if he's said the wrong thing. "He's ... he's working really hard right now. It's hard ... it's hard on him." Jared watches her face and knows she's not telling him everything, that there's more to it. Whatever it is, she's not ready to tell him.

"So," she starts again, "What were you doing at the gallery? Is that, like ... something you do?"

"No," Jared shakes his head. "I'm not a painter. My dad is. Those were his paintings you were looking at when I came in."

"Really?" she says, "Your dad did those? They're really good! Really scary. I mean, in a good way." He sees her catch herself, afraid she's used the wrong word. "I mean...they're powerful. Very intense. Not like a lot of the paintings you see around here."

"Yeah," he says. "I know what you mean. Like lighthouses and sailboats?" She nods. "He used to paint things like that," Jared says.

"Not anymore?"

"Nope. Not anymore." Jared waits for her to ask *why not,* tries to imagine how to explain it to her.

"What about your mom? What does she do?"

"She's not around," he says, trying to keep his voice even and matter of fact. "She left. Five years ago. We haven't seen her since then." He looks up and sees the stricken look on her face. *You asked,* he thinks. *Don't ask if you don't want to know.*

"I'm really sorry," she says in a quiet voice. He knows she means it, but that doesn't make it any better.

"How about *your* mom," he asks. "Where's she?"

"She's in New York," Jessie says.

"So," Jared says, "Your parents split up too?"

"*No,*" Jessie says, her voice not quiet anymore. "That's what Dylan always says! Why does everyone always say that?"

Dylan. Jared pictures a tall, athletic guy with white teeth and long blond hair, a Lacrosse stick over one shoulder, and his heart sinks a little.

"Sorry," Jared says. "It's just, you know, your mom's in New York, and your dad's here." Jared sees Jessie recoil, draw back into herself, and knows he's said he wrong thing.

The waitress is standing over them again. "You want some more coffee?"

"No," Jared says, "No thanks." The waitress leaves and by the time he looks back at Jessie she's sitting up straight again, chin held high. Something is different; he can sense her closing herself off, moving away from him, and he doesn't like it. "Hey," he says, "I'm sorry. I didn't mean ...."

He watches her arranging the things on the table in front of her, carefully pushing her glass aside, making a place to rest her elbows so she can lean toward him. "So," she says, her face and voice serious, "How *are* you?" He sees her eyes flicker toward the place on his arm.

"Fine," he says automatically. He wants to tell her about the things Delany said. *That burn on your arm...I think you made it happen.* He doesn't know why, but he's sure that she can help him figure it out.

"Listen," he starts. "Delany says he thinks he knows how this happened..."

"Oh my God, Jared, I can't believe..." She leans back away from him, and for a moment he's afraid she's going to stand up and walk away, but she sits with her eyes closed, pressing both hands to the sides of her head. When she looks at him again, her blue eyes are desperate. "Jared, listen, please. You can't keep going back there. He's... he's *abusing* you. It's not right."

"No, no," Jared tries to stop her, "It's not like that. You don't understand..."

"*What?*" she says, her voice getting louder. "*What* don't I understand? He burns you with a freaking cigarette? Then he makes you come see him after school?"

"Listen, I know it sounds weird..."

"*Weird?* It's not *weird*, Jared. It's *sick*. What he's doing. What he's doing to you. It's sick." She leans back and glances around self-consciously, like she's realized how loud she's getting. When she speaks again, it's in an urgent whisper. "Jared, you've got to tell somebody. Please."

"No," Jared shakes his head, "I can't do that..."

Jessie pushes her chair back angrily and stands up to walk away. He reaches out and grabs onto her wrist. "Wait!" he says. She stares down at his hand on her wrist, and he immediately lets go. "Please," he whispers. "Wait a minute, okay? Please." She keeps looking, uncertain. He sees something in her expression soften, and she sits and waits for whatever he's going to say.

"Jessie, listen. Delany ... Delany is ..." He pauses, wondering how to explain. "I know Delany seems a little ... strange. A little crazy sometimes. But he's a good guy. He's really helped me a lot."

"How?" she says, her face still unconvinced. "How has he *helped* you?"

"I have ..." Jared stops. This is the part he didn't want her to know. "I have trouble in school."

"Everybody has trouble in school."

"No. I mean ... real trouble. I can't ... I mean, I have trouble. Reading." There. He's said it. He waits for judgement, but she's still looking at him, waiting for whatever he has to say next. Jared takes a deep breath and goes on.

"Delany helped me. He worked with me. On my reading. My writing too. He really helped me. And he never, ever made me feel like I was ... you know ..." She nods quickly, still not looking away from his eyes. "And not just that. When my dad ... see, my dad, he's not well. He had to spend some time in the hospital." He looks at her, wondering if she understands the type of hospital he's talking about, hoping he won't have to say it.

She nods silently, so he goes on. "Delany really helped me then, too. He talked to me. He listened to me. He made sure I was okay." The truth of what he's telling her takes him by surprise and he has to wait for a moment before he can go on. "The point is ... I know he's a little scary sometimes. But he's helped me. He really has. And he would never, ever hurt me. Never. Not in a million years."

"Okay," she says, "Okay, so he helped you in school. But what about that burn on your arm?"

"I told you. He didn't do it."

"Jared..." she groans, closing her eyes and shaking her head.

"No, really. Jessie, I know what I saw. There was nothing there. The other kids saw it too. They were there. They all saw it. You want to ask them? You can ask them if you want. They'll tell you the same thing. *There was nothing there.*"

She stares at him for a long time, then lets out a long weary-sounding sigh.

"Okay," she says.

"Okay?"

"Okay. Maybe you're right. Maybe he didn't do it. But there's still something wrong with all this. He wants something from you. I can tell."

"I told you. He wants to help me."

She closes her eyes and lets out another long breath. She opens them and leans closer to him, her blue eyes blazing directly into his. "Just promise me something. Promise you won't let him hurt you."

"I told you. He'd never do that…"

"*Promise* me," she says again, searching his face.

"Okay," Jared says. "I promise."

Thunder rumbles through the little coffee shop, rattling the windows. Jared glances up and sees the sky turning dark, wind whipping all the little flags on the boats in the marina. Rain starts popping against the glass and the place is suddenly full of people who come crowding in through the door, shaking the rain off of their slickers and talking in loud, agitated voices. *"12 PM whale watch is cancelled,"* a man's voice calls out over the noise of the crowd. *"See the ticket office for a refund or to reschedule."*

"Wow," Jessie says, looking around at the disgruntled crowd. "Do they cancel every time it rains?"

"No," Jared says. "Only when there's a storm coming…" Then he sees it in his mind—his dad with his canvas and paints tucked under his arm, walking right into the teeth of the storm. "I'm sorry," he says, leaping to his feet, "I gotta go…"

"Why?" Jessie looks startled, "What is it? Is it the rain? My dad can give you a ride."

"No. I mean … I'm sorry. That's not it. It's my dad…." Outside there's a flash of lightning and the thunder rumbles, closer and louder this time. "Listen," he says, "Can you meet me tomorrow? Angel Falls. Twelve o'clock. Same place. Unless it's raining. Then we can meet here."

"Okay."

Jared digs deep into his pockets for loose change to pay for the coffee, but Jessie shakes her head. "No," she says, "You go. I'll see you tomorrow." He sees a smile in her eyes. It feels good, and he takes that with him through the door and into the cold wind and rain.

CHAPTER 23

THE GREAT DISAPPEARANCE

"Hey, pumpkin, how 'bout a swim?"

Jessie looks up sharply to see her dad's head peeking around her door. She nods, and he disappears, closing her door behind him. But all she can think about is Angel Falls and meeting Jared. *He would never, ever hurt me,* Jared had said, his eyes steady and calm. It hadn't changed what happened, but she'd felt something lift from her.

She calculates how much time it will take to get to the beach and back. She can make it, meet Jared on time, if she and her dad leave at once. She's dressed and standing by the door before he's even finished breakfast. "Where's the fire?"

She struggles with what to tell him, but waits until after their swim, after they're back at the house and she's changed and ready to go.

"Dad?"

"Yeah, pumpkin?"

"I told Jared I'd meet up with him. Is that okay?"

"Jared? The one you went out with yesterday?" She nods, and he says, "I guess so. Where are you going?"

His question sounds casual, but Jessie knows it's part of a bigger one.

"I told him I like history. So, he's going to show me the old stuff. You know, like buildings. In town." The lie twists in her stomach. But how can she tell him the truth? She sees the police tape in the parking lot to Angel Falls. Remembers their first night coming here, getting lost and stuck in the mud, her image of a body covered in wet leaves.

"History, eh? That'll make Ms. Whats-it happy, won't it? What was her name?"

Jessie rolls her eyes. "Ms. Kent. That was last year. I don't know my teachers yet."

"Okay then. In town. Sounds safe enough." That word, safe. That was how she'd felt until he said it. Jessie feels a chill. He continues, "Just be back by..." he looks at his watch. "Five o'clock?"

She nods and forces herself to walk casually out the door, waving at her dad and blowing a kiss. Outside she runs to her bike, mounts, and pedals hard towards Angel Falls.

When she reaches the moraine, she can see him. Standing in that same still way. The things that disappointed her before, the shabby clothes, the uncut hair, no longer bother her. He looks relieved when he sees her, even happy.

"Hey," he says, "You look nice."

Her mouth opens but there's nothing in her mind to say. She can feel her hair sticking to the sweat on her face. Thankfully, he doesn't notice her silence.

"C'mon," he says, and they walk.

Jessie asks, "Did you find your dad?"

He's silent for so long she wonders if he misunderstood. But then he says, "Yeah. He was home." He slows his pace. "I'm sorry I cut out on you. It's just...."

"It's okay. You don't have to talk about it."

He sighs, picks up the pace, moving quickly over the boulders to the trail on the other side. She's sweating and when they enter the woods she's grateful for the shade.

"Listen," he says.

She waits, thinking he's about to explain, but after a moment of silence, realizes he means something in the woods, so she turns her focus to the sounds around them. There's a light wind rustling the leaves, the repeated low warbling of some bird, something like the distant crashing of waves. Surely they can't hear the ocean from here!

"What?" she asks.

"I dunno. Everything, I guess. I love the sound of this place."

She closes her eyes and listens for a moment. "Yeah, it's quiet and then you realize there's a lot going on, lots of different sounds, almost like a choir." The roar of a distant plane breaks through and they both laugh.

They walk through the break in the wall and Jared turns left and uphill, a path she hasn't taken before. The air is cool on her arms and face, her skin dry now, and though they're walking quickly, her breath is even and deep. Her head feels beautifully clear.

"Where are we going?"

He smiles. "You'll see."

Jared's turned a corner, and the path is abruptly steep and she runs to catch up. He's standing in a break in the trees and holding up his hand. "Easy," he says as she reaches the place where he's standing and stops.

The land drops away, and far below them is rock and a pool of water. The trees start again beyond the pool, but over the tops and in the distance, she can see the ocean, small white breakers, and sparkling blue.

They stand silent for a while.

"Water?" Jared asks, taking off his backpack. He reaches inside and pulls out a bottle which he gives to her. They sit by the edge.

"This is so great," she says and instantly wishes she hadn't. *Lame,* she thinks, but Jared only nods and smiles, drinks from a second bottle. "Why is it called Nanepashemet?"

"What?" Jared seems startled.

"The art colony. What kind of Indians lived here? Do you know what it means?"

"Oh, yeah," Jared starts. "Algonquin, Iroquois, some other tribes. English settlers came here before the Revolutionary War, in the 1600's. Turns out the Indians used the land part of the year for religious rituals. Nanepashemet was a chief. He tried to explain, but the settlers didn't listen, and a war broke out." He pauses, then says, "The Indians were slaughtered."

"Yeah, I read about that. Horrible."

"Yeah. But there's more to the story. A few years after the massacre, people in the settlement started seeing one lone Indian. They see him in the woods at night, they see him at the moraine. One woman sees him standing beside her bed."

"Jesus."

"So, they called the militia in to hunt the woods. They put their wives and children inside the stockade, right in the center of Angel Falls. There's still part of the wall, I'll show you."

Jessie sits up. "They disappeared right? I read it in a book I found. Weird."

"Everybody. All the women and children, vanished."

"Did they ever find out what happened?"

"No. That's the worst part. They were just gone."

They are quiet for a while. Jessie can see it, the men marching gratefully home, it's night and there's a moon, the stockade walls are black and silent, and when they give the signal to open the gates, no one responds. They break them down, charge inside and find unmade beds, castaway toys, unwashed dishes.

"Strange things happen here. It's been going on a long time." Jared's voice is thin. She thinks he's trying to scare her.

"What things?"

"Do you remember the last time we were here," Jared says, staring out over the distant trees. "What I was saying to you about... about... Delany and..." his voice sounds choked, as if he's reliving it, becoming angry again.

"About being betrayed," she says, hoping he remains calm.

"I was..." he swallows, "I was pretty angry then. Do you remember?" She nods. "Well," he looks around, almost as if making sure that no one else is listening. "I think it happened then."

She's afraid of what he might say next and wants to stop it. Her eyes fall on his arm, on a small square bandage. "Can I see it?" He hesitates, reaches over, and peels it off.

The small circle is covered by a scab and surrounded by angry looking red skin. Parts of the scab are yellow and look soft, painful looking. Jessie's own arm has a sympathetic twinge.

"You need to let it get some air. The scab is wet." He shrugs and balls up the bandage, stuffing it in his jeans.

"Does it look like a cigarette burn?" he asks. "If I say I bumped into something in the kitchen—"

"What, so they won't think the bastard burned you?"

"He didn't. I told you!"

"Then who did?"

Jared pauses, and when he starts to speak, it's much softer. "Delany thinks I have some kind of, I don't know, greater mind power than other people. He tricked me into thinking he burned me, then I came here and kinda relived the moment, and...” he gestures to his arm.

Jessie stares at him. “*You* did it.” He nods. “Delany said *you* did it.”

“I saw my arm after he touched me with the cigarette. It was normal, not like this.” He grabs his arm and squeezes, making the wound stretch and redden.

She stands up and begins to pace. “It doesn’t make sense.”

“I know.”

“You were in class, right, with other kids there?”

“Yes, they saw it, too. If he burned me, don’t you think someone would have said something?”

Of course they would. “So, you have magical powers. And instead of, I dunno, money, a car, you give yourself a cigarette burn?”

“He told me something else.”

“What?”

“He asked me to think of the one thing I want more than anything.”

“Yeah, like have your teacher stop messing with your head!”

“I know, Jessie, listen. He asked me to think about this one thing, all day, all night, really focus on it.”

“What is it?”

“What is what?”

“The thing you want more than anything.”

Jared blinks. “I don’t know.” His hand combs through his hair.

“This is so weird,” she starts pacing again. “You *wanted* the burn to be real? Why would you want that?”

“I dunno, maybe I wanted something visible, to... to... show, you know... that he... that he hurt me.” Jared turns and stops her, holding her by the arms. “You were with me when it happened. Help me remember. What did I say, or do? Do you remember?”

She remembers thinking he was having a seizure, and then everything got quiet, he stopped shaking and looked her right in the face. That was when she’d seen the wound.

“You,” she starts, unsure of the words, “You started to ... to shake, and you, kinda... went away.”

"Then what?" His hands tighten on her arms. "It has to have been there already. It's not possible otherwise."

"Maybe it wasn't a normal cigarette. Maybe some kind of ... electronic-chemical thing, and the wound showed up later." She knows she's reaching. She remembers his red face, unfocused eyes, and the wound suddenly there.

His hands are hot on her arms and the vision of him angry is starting to rise, but she wants it gone, she doesn't want to think of that time and wishes it never happened.

"You know what *I* want?" The tears press harder, and her throat seizes before she can finish the thought aloud; *I want this never to have happened!* The words leave her mind like an arrow from a bow, and in that instant the tears recede, the anger dissipates, all that's left is clarity, cold and bracing. *Yes.* She becomes aware of a great rushing sound, she thinks it is the wind in the trees, and realizes her eyes are tightly closed and she is hugging herself and trembling. She hears Jared say her name.

"Jessie."

The tone is strange, his voice high and soft, and fear touches her heart. *Don't look, don't turn around,* and then he says her name again, a little louder, "Jessie?" She turns to him, he's staring at his arm, and when she follows his gaze, she stops breathing. The wound is gone.

She grabs his arm and turns it this way and that. "Ow!" he says trying to pull it out of her hands. She pushes him around, examines the other arm, finds nothing. She looks back at the original arm, then at his face. Now the tears come, and she doesn't bother to wipe them away.

"Jared, tell me you made it up. It was fake," she starts to sob, "Tell me you're a cruel and mean little shithead and it's all a joke," she's pulling at his arm, shaking him, "Tell me it was fake, please tell me, Jared, tell me," and he's grabbed her now, he's holding her up as her legs become jelly, and he lowers them both to the ground and rocks with her till her sobbing lets up a little. "Tell me," she says over and over, "Tell me."

"Shhh," he says, "I can't tell you that, you know I can't." She shivers, his arms grow tighter around her, and they sit in the dirt on the trail in silence. He shifts his head; she knows he's looking at his arm. "It's gone," he says, and then to her great surprise, he starts to laugh.

CHAPTER 24

READ IT

"Absence is to love what wind is to fire; it extinguishes the small, it inflames the great."

Delany's voice pierces Jared's thoughts, pulling him out of memory and back into Monday morning, the classroom, and Delany droning on about some book he's holding. He'd been thinking about the other book Delany had shown him, the photograph of the hand with the ugly dark wound at the center of its palm. *I think you're one of those people.* Jared had thought he was crazy—until he saw the smooth unmarked skin on his own arm where the burn had been a moment ago. He can still see the stunned look on Jessie's face, how her eyes grew wider when he'd started to laugh. She'd thought he was crazy. *Why are you laughing?* How could he explain it to her? The rush of amazement and relief, the thing he wasn't ready to say out loud. *Maybe it's true...*

The book snaps shut in Delany's hand, like a balloon popping. A few kids dozing at the desks around him jump a little.

"So, Johnson," Delany says, "What does that mean?"

Jared looks at Johnson and can see the boy writhe inwardly as he tries to remain cool under Delany's harsh gaze.

"What does it mean?" Johnson repeats in the voice of a grumpy child who's being dragged out of bed to go to school.

Delany flips the book open and walks slowly toward the desk where Johnson is sitting. *"Absence is to love what wind is to fire; it extinguishes the small, it inflames the great."* Delany lowers the book and stares down at Johnson. "What does that mean? Enlighten us."

"It means ..." Johnson says slowly like someone trying to decipher hieroglyphics in a dark cave, "Wind can put out fire?"

"*Wind can put out fire,*" Delany repeats, his eyebrows lifting in mock-surprise. "That's right, Mister Johnson. Wind can put out fire. Rock beats scissors. Scissors beats paper. And a bird in the hand is worth two in the bush."

Jared sees the dumb puzzlement on Johnson's face. A few stifled giggles from the back of the classroom, and Jared sees a dark shadow filling the boy's eyes, but Delany doesn't see it—he's already turned his back on Johnson and is walking away.

The hate in Johnson's eyes gives Jared a chill.

Wind, fire... He remembers the tingling in his hands before the burn disappeared, as he'd held Jessie's arms. How all the worry lines and tension on her face vanished, leaving her eyes, her mouth, her forehead smooth.

He looks up to see Delany studying him. Jared begins to pray for the bell to ring, letting out a big sigh when it finally does. He remembers Delany's face when he showed him the burn. Strange, excited. Happy even. What is he going to do now?

Delany walks past Jared's desk and says, "Meet me in my office."

Jared waits for the classroom to clear before gathering his books and walking slowly down the hall. He checks to see if anyone's around, but the hall is empty. He knocks on the office door. When no one answers, he opens the door and looks inside, but the room is empty. Jared feels his face burn. He's waited all day, all weekend for this. And now he isn't even here? He walks over to Delany's desk to see if there's a note for him, but there's just the usual piles of papers and books, the giant coffee mug that looks like it's never been washed. On the wall are dozens of quotes printed out in a large, bold font on plain white paper and pinned to the corkboard. He reads:

> *There is a space between man's imagination and man's attainment that may only be traversed by his longing.*

Jared hears a footstep behind him, turns and sees Delany looking at him from the doorway. Fear surges through him. Once Delany sees his arm, he can't go back, he can't pretend it all away. He wants to disappear.

As Delany crosses to his desk, Jared moves past him quickly and closes the office door.

"What are you doing?" Delany asks.

"I..." Jared's thought about this moment so often over the past few days, but he has no words now. Nothing to do but show him. He lifts his sleeve. Delany scowls and leans forward. Then he grabs Jared's arm and pulls it closer, peering intently at the smooth, unmarked skin. Jared sees Delany's mouth moving like he's trying to say something but can't. Finally, the words burst out:

"When did this happen?"

When? "Um...Saturday."

Delany is walking back and forth, one hand cupped over his mouth like he's trying to stop something from escaping. He stops mid-stride, presses his hand against his forehead like he's checking for a fever. A strange sound bursts from his mouth, a strangled laugh, and he quickly covers his mouth with his hand again.

"Where ..." Delany is breathing so hard he has to pause for breath between the words. "Where ... were you?"

"Angel Falls."

Jared is afraid. He's never seen Delany act this way before. Delany returns to his desk and lowers himself carefully into his chair, never taking his eyes off of the place on Jared's arm. When he finally speaks again, Jared can hear the effort he's making to keep his voice under control, the strain of it.

"Okay ... What were you doing?"

"I was just thinking."

"About what? *What* were you thinking?"

Jared searches his memory. What did he feel? Anger, like before. Confusion. Not the blazing intense light that had flared up inside him the first time when the burn had appeared. Or, if it *was* there, it was mixed up with Jessie's anger and confusion, so when he tries to remember, he can't separate one from the other.

"When it happened," Delany tries again, "Right before it happened ... were you ... did you *want* something? Was there something that you really *wanted*?"

"I ... I just wanted it to go away," Jared says.

Delany is staring at him with a look that Jared has never seen before. "And it just...went away." Delany rubs both hands over his face like he's trying to wake himself up, and a quick laugh escapes his lips. When he lowers his hands, Jared is startled to see tears in his eyes.

"This is good. This is so good." And before Jared can say *What? What's good?* he says, "Remember the last time we talked? How I asked you to think about something that you really want, more than anything else in the world? Have you been thinking about that?"

What do I want most? Jared feels it deep in his gut. To forget everything about the past few weeks. To get back to normal worries. How to get through the next few years keeping the rent paid and his dad alive. But he doesn't think this is what Delany's asking. He wishes Jessie were here. He lowers his eyes so Delany can't see he doesn't have an answer.

Finally, Delany speaks slowly and quietly like Jared is asleep and he's afraid to wake him up.

"Is there anyone...anyone you've been thinking about?" Delany's impatience crackles like electricity in the air between them. "When was the last time you thought about your mother?"

My mother? Jared stares at him. *He thinks that's what I want?* The absurdity, the insanity of it hits him. How can Delany think that, knowing what she did the last time she came back— what she did to his dad.

"Keep thinking about it, okay? The thing you want. More than anything else. Understand?"

Delany walks toward the door and puts his hand on the knob. "Come see me again on Friday, after class. If something happens between now and then, you tell me, okay? I want to hear about it right away."

"Friday!" Jared can't believe it. Bands of panic squeeze his chest and throat. "You said you were going to help me."

"That's what I'm doing."

"No. No, you're not. "You're just asking me a lot of stupid questions."

"Take it easy, kid..."

"Look," Jared says, "You've got to *tell* me. Why is this happening?"

Jared sees Delany's eyes cut back and forth quickly like he's looking for something, then come to rest on something across the room. Slowly, hesitantly, he pushes himself up to his feet, walks over to a file cabinet and opens the drawer. Delany pulls out a thick manila folder, pauses and shuts his eyes for a moment, then releases a long sigh. Walking back over to Jared, he holds the folder out toward him.

"Take it."

"What is it?"

"It's your homework."

"Homework?"

"You say you're sick of me asking you questions. Okay. Go home. Read this. Then you can ask *me* the questions. Alright?"

Jared takes the folder from Delany's hand and looks at it. It's heavy, filled with papers, and printed on the tab in black ink are the words, ANGEL FALLS.

He starts to open the folder, but Delany snaps, "No. Not here. Take it home like I told you. Meet me back here on Friday after class. We'll talk then."

Jared stares at the folder in his hand. What the hell does this have to do with the burn on his arm? How is this supposed to help? When he looks up at Delany, he starts to ask, but Delany cuts him off with a stern command.

"Read it."

As Jared rides his bike down the ocean road toward home, he's still wondering—how could Delany get it so wrong? How could he think that having his mother come back is what he wants?

Jared hasn't wanted his mother back since the last time she returned. Since the fights, the shouting and screaming late at night. Since the night when he came home and found his father passed out at the kitchen table, covered in red. He thought it was paint—Venetian Red, Terra Rosa—until he saw the razor. His mother wasn't there to help him twist the dishtowels around his dad's arms and hold them high over his head until the paramedics arrived. She wasn't there to sit by him in the hospital room while his dad slept for two days, and then, when he woke, wait for two more days until he finally spoke. She wasn't there for any of it. And since that time, Jared has never, ever wished for his mother to come back again.

Jared shuts his eyes tight, trying to force those pictures out of his head. When he opens his eyes, there's a car stopped at a red light right in front of him. Jared tries to swerve; his bike goes into a fishtail skid. Then the light turns green, the car pulls away and Jared is sitting alone at the intersection, heart hammering in his chest. What if he hadn't looked up in time? What would happen to his dad? Who would take care of him?

He pictures his dad in a state hospital, curled up on a cot, staring at nothing.

He can't let that happen.

Looking all around him, Jared pulls his bike upright and starts pedaling toward home. Carefully. Both eyes open.

CHAPTER 25

PROMISE ME

When Jared opens the door, he finds his dad sitting at the kitchen table as usual, his head face-down in his folded arms. A half-finished canvas hangs on the wall in front of him, one corner curling down where a pushpin has fallen on the floor somewhere.

"Dad?" Jared says, the same old fear squeezing his throat.

His dad lifts his head out of his arms, his eyes bleary and confused. "Hey, buddy..." His voice is dry, cracking around the edges. Jared looks at the painting again.

At least he's working. At least there's that.

"Did you eat?" Knowing the answer but asking it anyway. He pauses only long enough to put down his backpack, heavy with the folder Delany gave him. He's longing to read it, to understand, but he has to take care of his dad.

Jared goes to the kitchen cabinet and fishes out a can of bean soup, the last one. He gets a saucepan from the counter but it's full of dried-out oil paint, inky black and muddy reds, so he digs under the counter for another one, rinses the dust out and then sets it on a burner. Once it's going, he pulls a few slices of bread from the bag, but there's mold growing around the edges, so he cuts the moldy pieces off and sets them on a plate. When the soup is hot, he pours it into two coffee mugs, gets two spoons, and sets it all on the table in front of his dad.

"So, Dad. How you doing?"

"Oh, great. I'm great..." His eyes dart around like he's looking for something he's lost. He doesn't touch the soup or the bread, doesn't even appear to see it.

Jared eats his soup while his dad stares at the half-finished canvas on the wall, and a heavy silence falls over the two of them. "So...how's the painting going?"

"I don't know..." his dad says, not taking his eyes away from the canvas. His voice is even more ragged and dry sounding. He stands up from the table, slow and stiff like a man twice his age, and shuffles over to the wall where the painting is hanging.

Jared opens his mouth to say, *Dad, come eat. Please.* But he knows it's no use. He finishes his own mug of soup, then picks up his dad's and carries it back to the stove where he pours it back into the saucepan.

His dad reaches up and pushes the curled-down corner of the painting back up against the wall and then watches it fall away again when he moves his hand. It seems to confuse him, and he does it again.

Jared turns away and drags his backpack closer, unzips it and pulls out the folder marked *Angel Falls*. It's thick and heavy and makes a solid noise when he drops it on the table in front of him. There's so much of it, for a moment he feels defeated before he even begins. He thinks of Jessie. Maybe she can help him. He's seeing her tomorrow—he can show her the file, maybe ask her to read some of it, help him figure it out. The pressure starts to lift, but right behind it, resistance rises, blood burning in his face. *I have trouble... reading.* Why did he have to tell her that? He trusts her, but he doesn't want her to think he's weak. He needs her help, but he has to prove he's not helpless.

Jared opens the file and looks at the first paper on top of the thick stack. The letters look old-fashioned and strange. He realizes they must be photocopied from an old book. He starts to read, taking it one word at a time, the way Delany has taught him.

> In September 1643, Captain Gilroy Clarke led a military expedition against hostile Indian tribes, slaughtering up to "two hundred heathens and enemies of the Crown."

The slaughter of the Native Americans. He'd first heard about it in Delany's classroom. It wasn't in the textbook, but Delany had taught them about it anyway. *You can't always get the truth from a textbook,* he'd said. Jared keeps reading, turning the pages, finding more things he recognizes.

Upon their return, Clarke and his men discovered that all the English women and children left behind had vanished without a trace...

The Great Disappearance. Jared always thought it was some kind of local legend, a campfire story kids tell to scare each other, the way he'd first heard it. Seeing it here in black and white, knowing it's real, seems strange.

The words shift and swim, so Jared closes his eyes and takes a deep breath, waiting for the feeling of failure and frustration to go away. When he looks back down at the page, the story has changed.

Surviving colonists are plagued by a two-year period of disturbing and unexplained events. Roger White, a thirty-year-old carpenter, claims to have seen his wife from a great distance in the woods, but when he called her name and made to approach her, she vanished in the trees. Thomas Humphreys, a thirty-two-year-old hunter on an expedition in the deep woods north of the colony claimed to have seen a group of young children standing among the trees "with grave and silent faces." When Humphreys recognized his own son among that group of children, he cried out and made to approach them...

"What are you reading there, buddy?"

Jared jumps at the sound of his father's voice, so close, right over his shoulder.

He turns and sees his dad looking down at him, a curious frown on his face.

"Uh, nothing," Jared stammers. "Just some stuff for school..."

"Yeah? What is it, history or something?"

"Yeah. Yeah, history." Jared is confused—since when has his dad been interested in his schoolwork? In anything? But Jared's mind is filled with images—the vanishing woman, the ghostly children in the woods. He needs to know what happens next, so he takes a deep breath and goes on reading.

According to one account, a number of women who had vanished two years earlier began to return to the colony. Thomas Humphreys claims to have returned home from a hunting trip and found his wife waiting for him inside his home. This is where the surviving reports begin to offer conflicting accounts: while some colonists claim to have seen Humphreys' wife, others claim that Humphreys was "suffering from some great madness."

A shadow falls across the page in front of him. Before Jared knows it, his dad reaches down and picks up the page he was reading. Startled, Jared watches his dad scan the writing on the page, the expression on his face growing darker.

"Where did you get this?"

"One of my teachers. He gave it to me."

Jared's dad looks down at the folder full of papers, the same dark, unreadable expression on his face.

"Why? Why did he give this to you?"

Panic rises in Jared's chest. He can't tell his dad why Delany gave him this folder, about the burn on his arm appearing and disappearing, although he's wanted to, more than once.

"I don't know," Jared stalls, "It's, you know, local history or something."

"I don't want you reading this crap."

"Why not?" Jared asks. "What's wrong with it?"

His dad looks up from the page in his hand and his eyes fill with anger. He grabs the entire file from the table, his eyes darting wildly around the room. Jared leaps up from his chair. "No! Dad," Jared shouts, "That's not mine. It belongs to my teacher. I have to give it back..."

His dad looks back at him, his face flushed red, but some of the wildness has started to leave his eyes. "I don't want this in my house," he says, brandishing the file in one hand.

"But I'm supposed to read the whole thing," Jared says.

"I want it out of here. Tomorrow."

Jared starts to object again but the look on his dad's face stops him. "Okay..."

Jared picks up the folder and slips it back into his backpack where his dad won't have to see it. Then he goes to the sink and starts washing the dishes. He tries to let the clouds of hot steam relax the tension in his body and his mind the way he does at work, but it's not working. Jared isn't used to this.

His dad's presence is usually more passive, ghostly, barely there. He's often wished to have his dad back again, the way he was before. But this is not the dad he wants.

When he's through washing the dishes, Jared turns and sees his dad sitting slumped at the kitchen table, his head resting on his arms. His eyes are open, but Jared can tell he's not seeing anything in this room. Whatever storm had passed through him earlier is gone now.

"Dad," Jared asks softly. "Can I get you anything?"

No answer. Not even his eyes move or change.

"Dad, why don't you go to bed?" He waits for a response, but his dad closes his eyes and doesn't answer, so Jared leaves him there.

After he makes sure all the burners on the stove are off, Jared turns out the kitchen lights except for the one over the stove so his dad won't trip and fall if he starts walking around in the night. Then he goes into his bedroom, closing the door behind him. Jared throws his backpack on the bed, unzips it quickly, and pulls out the folder Delany gave him. He looks at the first page and sees where his dad's hands have bent the paper from gripping it so tight. Why would his dad get so upset?

He picks up the pages and keeps reading where he left off. More accounts of "the lost people" suddenly returning without explanation.

> While some gave thanks to Providence for the safe return of their loved ones, others assert that their fellow colonists were "in the grip of a great bewitchment." The divide between the two groups becomes physical as the colonists who believe their loved ones have returned and whom the other colonists deem "bewitched or mad" are driven out of the colony and forced to inhabit a region deeper in the north woods. As Reverend Roger Walters wrote in one of his surviving letters, "We are beset by a plague of angels or devils. God grant us His wisdom to discern one from the other."

The sound of a footstep outside his bedroom door makes Jared close the file quickly and look up. He sees the shadow of his dad's feet moving past the bottom of the door, blocking out the light. After a moment, he shuffles away. There's the sound of pans clattering and running water, and for a moment

Jared is twelve years old again, rising from his bed in the old house on Decatur Street, walking down the hall toward those same sounds, standing in the kitchen doorway, afraid to go in, afraid to go near the woman standing at the sink with her back turned, afraid of what he might see if she turns around. Then another image. His dad sprawled face down on the kitchen table in a widening pool of red.

A sob rises in Jared's throat, but he catches it and holds it back, clenching his teeth and digging his fingernails into the palms of his hands until the pain brings him back. *No.* He has to stay alert. Stay watchful. Keep holding it together until his dad can get better. That's all he wants. To see his dad well and happy again. To stop worrying and seeing that goddamn awful picture in his head. He has to be strong and keep going. For his dad. For his dad's sake. It's the only thing he's sure of.

CHAPTER 26

SOME HELP

Jessie peers through the plate glass of Bunbury's, scanning faces and tables, but there is no sign of Jared. People jostle her on their way inside and she steps away from the door, catching sight of her reflection; she looks like a baby, high forehead, round cheeks, large staring eyes. She turns away in dismay and considers leaving. Staying away from Angel Falls and Jared and the whole strange mess. Instead, she pushes the door open and goes inside. A large TV screen takes up the only windowless wall showing the tearstained face of a man and a woman standing in front of a house with dark shingles. The banner beneath their faces reads *UPDATE: Missing girl, Karen Holcomb, Beauport.* She's chilled to the bone. It's the first time she's seen the girl's name.

The man speaks, his voice hoarse and shaky. *"Please, if you have any information, if you've seen Karen, please..."* He breaks off and coughs, more tears leaving his eyes and running down his cheeks. *"All we want... what we want most in the world... is to see Karen again."*

Someone's moved close behind her. She smells laundry detergent, fabric softener—*Mountain Spring* the same one her father uses—and a faint undercurrent of fish. She turns and looks up into Jared's smiling face.

"Hey. I'm not late?"

"No, no, I'm early." His eyes flicker toward the TV and then hold there, his face turning serious. "That's the girl in your school? It's so sad."

"Yeah. Shit." They both watch until the parents disappear, and the news anchor's face fills the screen. "Want to sit in the back?"

They move to a table against the wall. As they sit, Jessie leans forward, grateful to be here with him, finally, to find out what he's learned. She opens her mouth, but the waitress appears.

"Hey Jared. How's it going?"

"Hey. Good. How about you?"

Jessie's fingers curl against the tabletop. *Just take our order and go away.*

"Now, what'll you two be having?"

Jared says, "Coffee for me, and do you have any cinnamon buns left?" Then to Jessie, "They're really great. Want to split one?"

Jessie nods and asks for a coke and the waitress is finally gone. She waits for Jared to say something. When he doesn't, she asks, "You saw him? What did he—"

The waitress returns, setting down a sweating glass of coke, mug of coffee and a plate with an icing covered bun, followed by a cloud of cinnamon-scented air. Jessie's mouth begins to water.

Jared cuts the bun in half, lifts one half, and pushes the plate across to Jessie.

The scent is maddening, and Jessie eagerly lifts the bun to her mouth and takes a bite. Warm and sweet, she closes her eyes in pleasure, but all at once she's in memory, back in the woods, staring at the blank place on Jared's arm. She opens her eyes quickly.

"Mmmm. I needed that," he says, pulling a napkin from the spring-loaded holder, wiping his lips. Then, "What's wrong?"

"Is it still...gone?" She's longing to see it, the place where the burn was, but his sleeve is covering it.

He makes a strangled laugh, "Uh, yeah."

"Did you show him?"

"Yeah. I did..." his eyes shift to the table, then away.

"Well? What did he do? What did he say?" She doesn't realize her jaw is clenched until she hears the way it pinches the words.

"He asked me what I was doing, where I was, who I was with..."

Her stomach squeezes tight, "You didn't tell him about me!"

"Of course not!" he says, and she relaxes slightly. "It was weird. He wasn't freaked out. It was more like ... he was happy. Like I'd done something... good."

"Does he know why it happened?" she manages to ask.

Jared's eyes shift down and away again and she doesn't like it. He opens his pack and slides out a folder. "He gave me this." He places it on the table in front of her.

She stares at it, hands in her lap. She reads the name on the tab, *Angel Falls.* "What *is* this?"

"Open it."

"What did he tell you? Have you read this?"

"Yes. Read it."

His face fills with an anxious grin, eyes excited and impatient. She looks at the folder, opens it with one finger.

"It won't bite."

She frowns. The first page is a copy of a page from an old book, the typeface is spotty, and the print is faint. She reads a series of dates followed by events. 1641 English colonists arrive. 1642 skirmishes with natives. 1643 colonists decimated local tribes. 1644 reports of a lone Indian being sighted.

She reads on and finds the story Jared told her. The women and children vanished, *The Great Disappearance,* then looks away from the pages. "What does this have to do with your arm?"

"Please," he says. "Keep reading."

She returns to the document, reluctant and confused, but now she finds something new.

> *Roger White, a thirty-year-old carpenter, claims to have seen his wife from a great distance in the woods, but when he called her name and made to approach her, she vanished in the trees.*

A chill runs down her back as she continues to read about people reappearing.

"It's creepy, but I don't understand. people disappeared and then maybe they came back. What does any of this have to do with us?"

"I don't know exactly. But this place, it's had weird shit happening forever. The Indians knew about it. They didn't even *try* to live there." Excitement enters his voice, color to his cheeks. "You can feel it, you said you could."

She remembers a good feeling of clarity while standing inside the wall at Angel Falls.

Not weird, not dangerous.

"It's- it's not the same," she sputters. "*They* lost their wives, their kids."

"They got them back."

"Did they?" Jessie, exasperated, looks for the passage and reads it aloud: *"While some 'gave thanks to Providence for the safe return of their loved ones,' others continued to assert that their fellow colonists were 'in the grip of a great bewitchment.'* It's like what happened in Salem with the witches. The, what do they call it... when a group of people all experience the same hallucination?"

"You didn't read it all. There's more."

"Jared, *what* does it have to do with us?

"*I don't know*, okay? I don't know yet." He's loud and people at the other tables look over at them. He lowers his voice, "But Delany knows something. He wants me to figure it out."

"What? He wants *you* to..."

"He's promised to help."

"Some help."

Jared pulls the file folder from under her hands, closes it and puts it in his backpack. "You wanted to know what he told me. If you don't want to read it, that's fine."

"Oh, and he's so *helpful*. Jared, what did he say when you showed him your arm? How did he explain that?"

He blinks, then splutters, "well ... he..."

"He doesn't know, does he?"

"Of course, he knows," loud again. Again, people turn their heads. "You have to drop the attitude. You don't know him at all. You don't know either of us." He pulls out some crumpled bills, throwing them on the table.

"I know you have anger issues," she mumbles, looking down at the crumpled dollars, realizing he's about to leave. She looks up.

He's not looking at her, his face flushed, jaw muscles twitching, and her heart starts to hurt. Then he cuts through the crowd and goes out the door.

She leaps up, makes it to the sidewalk and looks all around before she sees him.

He's walking fast down the street, hands thrust deep into his pockets.

"Wait!" Jessie runs after him, catching up before he crosses the street.

He stops, looking straight ahead, "My mom had anger issues."

"I'm sorry, I shouldn't have said—"

"Forget it. I think you're right. I got it from her."

"I'm sorry."

He doesn't say anything, and Jessie remembers how angry she had been right after the wound disappeared and Jared started laughing. The moment before that, right before, was so sweet, his arms tight around her, gently rocking.

"I was plenty angry at you back in Angel Falls," Jessie admits.

Jared snorts, "You sure were."

"I couldn't believe you were laughing." They start walking, side by side, Jessie starting to smile. It's like swimming, the way they work their way back to an easier place.

"You felt it, right? Like, relief?"

She nods, feeling it now, a cool, delicious easing of stress. *It's gone, it's gone.* She looks at his arm. "Can I see it?"

He snorts and gives a crooked smile. "See what?"

"*Yo. Younger.*" Two boys about Jared's age suddenly appear across the street.

Jared hisses low, "Start walking."

Jessie looks down and starts to walk fast, heart rate jumping.

"Younger, shouldn't you be in schoo-ell?" One of them says.

"Hey, introduce us to your *girl*-friend." Jessie's face grows hot, and she feels pinpricks all over her body.

"Bite me," Jared says as they pass, managing to move quickly but still appear casual.

"You wish!" is the response and Jessie ducks her head, expecting Jared to shout "Run!" and wondering if her trembling legs could respond. She looks up and recognizes the street.

"Here, this way," she tugs his sleeve and turns the corner sharply. She stops and listens.

Jared says, "They won't follow. Couple of hosebags."

"Hosebags?" Jessie starts to laugh.

"You never heard that, *city* girl?" She shakes her head, walks quickly to Dorothy's house, and stops.

"This is my house."

He looks at it, then his eyes pop. He stares from the house to her. "You're in Biddie Hick's house?"

"Biddie Hicks?"

"Yeah. This house, really?" He lowers his voice. "They say she's a witch. Did you know about that when you rented it? We used to dare each other to peek in the windows." He's standing still, staring at the house.

"Do you mean Dorothy Hicks?" Could he be mistaken? "She was my grandpa's cousin." And a witch?

"*Dorothy*?" He looks puzzled, and then, "Cousin?" Then his eyes widen, "Was? You mean she...she died? I didn't know. I'm sorry..."

"It's okay. I didn't know about her till a couple a months ago. My folks told me she died, and Dad had to come out and take care of things." It sounds so ordinary. Why doesn't it feel that way? A wave of sadness threatens to overwhelm her.

"So, city girl has some Beauport blood..." There's humor in his voice, but his eyes, when they move back to her seem glad.

"I guess so. What are you called? Beauportians?"

"Beauport-ites," he smiles and half-bows.

"Do you..." Jessie starts uncertainly, "want to come in? We've got root beer. We could make floats." She still doesn't know what Delany said. There has to be more. She imagines him saying no and closes her eyes.

"I've got maybe half an hour," he stares at the house again, "Root beer floats and the inside of Biddie Hick's house? How can I refuse?"

Jessie sighs in relief, flings open the door, and says, "É Voila. La maison de ma cousine." She goes inside and Jared follows.

"Here she is." She walks over to one of the solo portraits, Dorothy as an adult, Jessie's not sure how old, anywhere from mid-20s to 40s. She stares out of the frame as she does from them all with a look of entitlement. The confidence overrides anything that is plain or unattractive in her features, making her interesting to look at. Handsome even.

"Whoa," Jared says softly. "A handsome woman," making Jessie start. Did he read her mind? Then he looks from the portrait to Jessie and back, then back to Jessie. "She looks like you. A little. Around here." He takes his finger and traces the air around her jaw. "And here," he strokes air around her forehead. Her body reacts as if he'd touched her.

"I've thought so too." They both whirl around as Jessie's dad enters from Dorothy's bedroom.

"Hi there. It's Jared, right? How are you?" Putting his hand out.

"I'm good," Jared shakes his hand. Looking at the photo, "Sorry for your loss."

Jessie's dad looks confused for a moment. "Cousin Dorothy?" he smiles gently. "Thank you. I didn't really know her."

"So, you're from Beauport?"

"Not me. My dad, yeah. He grew up here, moved away after serving in World War II. I was brought up in Brooklyn. I only remember visiting here twice. I was very young."

"Brooklyn? The cool part of New York, right?"

Her dad laughs, "Well, we thought so. I used to write. I'm sure Jessie's told you her mom's an actor. We thought we were bohemian."

Jared looks at Jessie in surprise, "Your mom acts? What, movies, tv?"

Here it comes. The moment Jessie hates. When people realize she might be related to someone famous. She stares resolutely at the ground while saying, "Theater mostly." Then she realizes what her dad said about being bohemian in Brooklyn. "Why'd you move to Manhattan?"

He smiles at her, "You, pumpkin. Mainly. I got work at Barnard and we found the co-op. And here we are," he looks up, taking in the house, and corrects himself, "There we are. Here is somewhere else entirely." His tone is comic, but the room feels colder, the thing that's threatening Jessie's family rearing its head.

Jared laughs politely and Jessie wonders if he can feel it. The three of them fall silent. The inside of Jessie's head gets tighter and tighter until she thinks it might explode if someone doesn't speak.

"Well," says Jared, "I better get going. Gotta work."

Jessie stares at him. "But ... we, you ... you just got here." She closes her eyes at how pitiful she sounds. They haven't figured anything out about the burn. She needs more time with him.

"I could give you a ride," her dad says. "We haven't had any chowder in, what, kitten, three days? Four?" Turning to Jared, "That give you a little more time?"

"I guess. I don't have to be there till 4:30."

They stand with Dorothy looking on, not speaking, and not moving.

"Well then," her father makes an exaggerated yawn and stretches his arms above his head, "I think I'll take a walk. I've been cooped up all day." He turns to Jessie, "Why don't you get Jared something to drink? Back in half an hour." And he's out the door.

Jared watches as he leaves, then turns back into the room stifling a laugh. She smiles uncertainly. "What's funny?"

"Your dad, doing that fake stretch thing so he could get the hell outta Dodge."

"I guess we surprised him."

"He scared the shit out of me! Did you know he was home?"

"No. He's been out a lot, meeting people about the house, something called probate and Dorothy's money stuff."

"Your dad trusts you."

"What do you mean?"

Jared looks away, then says, "Leaving you alone. With me."

Her heart speeds up, "Oh, and you're *so* dangerous?"

He studies something on the wall. "He thinks I'm your boyfriend."

There is a soft roaring in her ears and Jessie is aware of two things; she wants it to happen, and Jared's stating it like this means it won't. She holds her face still and says nothing.

Jared says, "I think I'll take you up on that root beer float," so she leads him into the kitchen where they assemble them.

"Ready, set, go!" They plunge their straws past the ice cream and sip quickly as it starts to foam up over the edge of the glasses.

After a few long pulls on her straw, Jessie looks at Jared's arm.

"So," she starts. "Your teacher, Mr. Delany?" Jared nods. "You said he seemed... happy?"

Jared pauses. Nods. Something passes behind his eyes. Something dark.

"What else?" She speaks softly, hoping he won't get angry again.

He shakes his head. "He just kept saying, 'think about what you want most in the world.'"

The words are so familiar, Jessie can almost see them written in the air. *What we want most in the world,* and then she remembers. The parents of the missing girl on TV.

She shakes her head to remove the image of their crying faces.

She looks at his arm again. "Can I see it?"

He looks at her, opens his mouth like he's about to say something, then puts down his glass and rolls up his sleeve. She stares at his arm, the muscles visible beneath the tanned skin, the hair on his arm catching the light. There is no mark at all.

She looks away.

"What do *you* think happened?" she asks. It's hard to speak evenly, her throat is so tight.

He stares around the room, rolling his sleeve back to his elbow. "I think... I dunno, I felt something, you know, the first time. It hurt—I mean it hurt when he did it, and it still hurt in Angel Falls. The more I thought about it— why would he do that to me? —the more it hurt and..." He stops.

"What? And what?"

"I just sort of...blacked out, and when I came back, you were staring at my arm."

She breathes in and out, quickly at first, and then slower, trying to remain calm.

"The second time? What happened then?"

He closes his eyes, then opens them shaking his head. "I dunno. Nothing much. I wanted it gone, I know that."

"So, you made it happen. And you made it go away."

Jared shakes his head. "I don't know."

"Let's try it."

He blinks, "What?"

"You can ... make things happen, right?" she says slowly.

She can see his breathing quicken as he turns to face her fully. "I guess."

"Let's try it. Let's try it now."

He shrugs. "Okay. Like what?"

"I dunno." She looks around. "How about this," pointing to his glass. "Make more root beer. Make your glass fill up." She looks into his eyes.

"Okay," he closes his eyes. "I wish I had more root beer."

She struggles not to laugh. "No, you have to really want it. Focus."

He shifts in his chair, looks at the glass, then at her face. "Do I have to say it out loud?"

"I don't know. Try it in your head."

He looks at the glass, his hands flat on the table. His mouth twists, and after a moment he's laughing. "I'm sorry."

She tries to keep a straight face but can't. The laughter bubbles out and before they know it, both of them are rocking with laughter, tears in their eyes.

As their laughter subsides, as they look at each other, saying without speaking, *we'll figure this out,* as her father comes to take Jared away, and he says, "See you tomorrow," as the silence of the house of the witch, Biddie Hicks, falls around her, Jessie knows what it is she wants.

See you tomorrow.

CHAPTER 27

SAFE

When Jared arrives at Angel Falls, he feels like he's seeing it through different eyes. This old stone wall where he's parked his bike since he was a little boy was once Fort Clarke. He tries to imagine men, women, and children hiding behind this wall from the tribes on the other side who want to kill them; hiding from the darkness outside and what might be in it.

Jared steps through the hole in the tangle of fallen branches and briars. In a moment, he's moving through the green shadows toward the place where he told Jessie to meet him. It's cooler here; it always is, and he breathes in the thick smell of green leaves and cool, damp earth. Then he sees her, coming toward him from a long way down the trail.

Jared walks faster to reach her. She looks up and sees him now and almost breaks into a run. Her face, when she's nearer, looks pale and startled.

"Is there another cemetery?" she asks. The question surprises him.

"What? You mean ... here?"

"Yes," she speaks in a clipped, nervous voice. "The one you showed me. Is that the only one?"

"Yes," he says. "Why?" He watches her raise one hand and press it to her forehead like she's taking her own temperature, eyes squeezed shut tight.

"I don't know." A little burst of laughter escapes her, but her eyes are still a little afraid. "I was waiting for you. I went to the cemetery because ... I wanted to look at the stones, you know." She pauses, then says, "Come on," turns and heads back down the trail. Puzzled, he follows her.

The tunnel of twisted branches and briars opens up before them and there they are, all the old broken stones rising out of the earth. Jessie stands back at a distance, and he notices her hands clenched into fists at her side. "Look at them," she says in a small, tight voice.

A flush of heat floods Jared's face. Why is she doing this? Doesn't she remember? Doesn't she know he can't read them? He looks at her, the question in his face. "Go on," she says; then, softer, "Please."

The fear in her eyes and the need in her voice melt his resistance, so he steps up to the nearest stone and looks down. When he sees what's in front of him, his heart stops in his chest and then starts beating faster.

In Memory of Mrs. Mary Greene
wife of Capt. John Greene
who died Nov'r 20th 1765
in ye 21st Year of her Age

Jared straightens up quickly and looks around, trying to get his bearings. He's never been able to read any of these stones. He must have never seen this one. How had he missed it?

"Can you read it?" Jessie's nervous voice behind him.

Jared nods. "Yeah."

"Really?" Jessie sounds surprised. Jared moves closer to another big stone, split down the middle by a tree root, one he knows well and has never been able to decipher.

Once again, the letters stand out hard-edged and clear.

In Memory of Jonathan Robinson
who departed this Life April 26, 1775
In the 64th year of his age
The sweet remembrance of the Just
Shall flourish while they sleep in dust

Heart pounding harder, Jared moves from one stone to another. The letters and numbers that have always looked blurred and indistinct like melted soap now stand out hard-edged and clear in the sunlight filtering down through the leaves. Not one or two stones—all of them. A burst of delighted laughter breaks loose from somewhere inside his chest.

He turns and sees Jessie moving quickly from stone to stone, her face flushed red. "Oh my God," she says. "When I got here. I looked at them and they were all ... blurry. I couldn't tell what they said."

"And now you can," Jared finishes for her.

She looks at him and nods, the same crazy laughter bursting from her.

She lifts a hand to her mouth to hold it in. Then he sees her blue eyes grow even wider.

"Oh my God," her words sound muffled behind her hand. "You can read them too."

"I know." he says, then stifles another laugh. "Jesus, this is crazy."

"Wait, wait," she says. "Maybe, maybe it's the light or something. Maybe it's like those old ruins in England or Mexico or someplace ... you know, when the sun hits them at just the right angle."

"No," he says, "I mean ... Jessie, I've been coming here for *years*. I've been coming here my whole freaking *life*."

"Maybe..." Jessie mutters, "Maybe it's got something to do with, you know, with moisture or something ... the letters show up better when they're wet."

He turns and looks at her scowling down at the stones. She's trying so hard. She wants an explanation. One that makes sense to her.

"Come on, Jessie," he says. "It's not the sunlight. And it's not moisture."

"What is it, then?" She looks at him, her hand over her mouth again so all he can see are those wide blue eyes, looking to him for an answer.

And it comes to him. *It's you. I can see them now because of you. Because you're here.* But he doesn't say that. He can't say that, because he's afraid of how it would sound.

"Hey, you think any of those people are buried here?" he says, hoping to distract her. "You know, the ones we read about in that history."

"Yeah," she says, and together they start moving through the trees to look at more stones, eager and relieved to have something simpler to put their minds to work on.

"Hey," Jessie calls out. Jared goes over to where she's bending over a broken stone that's leaning against a tree trunk. "Humphreys. Thomas Humphreys. Isn't that one of the names in that history?" Jared looks down with her at the ancient, engraved words.

Elizabeth H.
Wife of Thomas G. Humphreys
died October 15, 1659
Aged 31 years

"1659?" Jared exclaims, "Jesus. How ... how can the writing still be so clear?"

"I don't know," Jessie says, running her finger over the edge of the numbers. The stone looks ancient, worn away and eaten up with moss and lichens, but the letters appear clear-cut and sharp. He reads the epitaph and feels a chill.

Beloved mother, friend, and wife
Twice taken from us in this life
reunited by our love
first here below and then above

"Wait a minute. *Humphreys,*" he says. "Isn't that the guy whose wife disappeared?"

"And then she came back?" He watches her lean closer to read the epitaph. *"Twice taken..."* She straightens up and takes a step backward. "That's weird. What does that mean, *twice taken?*"

"I don't know," Jared says, but again he feels that chill and the sense that somehow, he *does* know. He reads the epitaph again, running his finger along the break in the stone, feeling the cold creep into the bones of his hand, a faint vibration of something approaching from far away.

"God, it's so sad." Jessie's voice startles him, the amazement gone, replaced by a sad wonder.

"What?" He turns and sees her gazing out at all the crooked stones under the trees.

"All these people. You know...what it said in the history. How they got pushed out by the other colonists. How they banished them out here in the woods. Just because they were different."

"Yeah, well, they weren't just different," Jared says. "They were crazy. Crazy or bewitched. That's what everyone said, anyway."

Jared steps back from the gravestone he and Jessie have been reading and looks around. The light is changing, the leaves and the spaces of sky between the trunks of the trees growing dim. But the stones are growing brighter, almost glowing.

Jared thinks of the full moon high in the blue morning sky, pock-marked and sending out a pale glow. That's the way the stones now look to him. The words and numbers become darker and clearer. Jared shuts his eyes and presses his hands over his eyelids until he sees electric bursts of light.

"Jared." Jessie's voice cuts through the darkness. He opens his eyes and sees her standing over by a dead tree, looking down at a broken stone. "Jared, come here."

He walks over and looks down, expecting another mysterious epitaph, but it's the name that stops him. *Younger.*

Jared leans closer and reads.

Jeremy Younger
departed this Life November 15, 1842
in the 58th year of his age

"*Younger.* That's you," Jessie says. "I mean … that's your name, isn't it?"

Jared doesn't answer. He's fixed on the name on the stone and the strange feeling it gives him; it's a little like being cold and a little like falling.

"You okay?" Jessie asks.

"Yeah," Jared has to clear his throat to keep talking. "It's just … I don't know. It's just …"

"You've never seen your name on a gravestone before."

"No," Jared says, a sinking feeling taking over him. "It's not just that. It's…it's like you said. This is where they buried all the weird people. The ones they didn't want. You know. The crazy ones. The freaks."

Jessie looks down at the stone and then up at Jared, and he sees her eyes soften.

"Well," she says, cocking her head to one side. "*I* think it's cool."

"What?" Jared says, "You think *what's* cool?"

"You know," she says, "Weird people. Weird people are cool. They're usually the best ones, right?"

Jared looks at her and it's exactly at this moment when he understands that he loves her.

"Yeah," he manages to say. "Yeah, I guess so..."

They leave the cemetery and start climbing the trail that follows a dry creek bed uphill, stepping from stone to stone. All along the trail are the fragments of ruined walls, swallowed by briars and vines. For a while they climb without talking. It's Jessie who breaks the silence.

"It feels different here now."

"Like how?"

"It's like ... before, I knew there were people who used to live here. But then I read all that stuff about them."

They pass by another crumbling stone foundation, overgrown with moss and vines. Jessie pauses, then steps carefully over the stones into the center of where a long-gone house used to be. Jared follows her. "I mean ... this was someone's *home,*" she speaks quietly, like she's afraid of disturbing someone, or something. "They lived here, ate here, slept here. I'll bet they never thought it would end up like this."

Jared looks around and tries to picture the house that stood here, the roof that was once here above their heads. He wonders: did kids used to live here? A boy his age? Or a girl, like Jessie? Which of the headstones in the graveyard belonged to them?

Jessie's voice breaks into his thoughts. "So why do you think Delany gave you all that history? I mean, what does all that have to do with *you?* And, you know ..." she nods toward him, and he sees her eyes dart toward the place on his arm.

Jared takes a deep breath. "People disappeared...and then they came back. What if they...what if they *made* them come back?" He's afraid to look at her.

"Made them? Like how?" But before he can say anything she asks, "Have *you* ever made anybody come back?"

The question stops Jared. It's a question he's thought about before, but never told anyone. He sits down on one of the crumbling stone steps and begins.

"When my mom left...the first time," Jared says, "I was ten. I didn't know why or what was going on or anything. I just wanted her to come back. I thought about her all the time. It was all I could think about. I used to dream about it."

"So, did she? Did she come back?" Jessie asks, her voice soft and careful.

Jared nods and swallows. "Yeah. One morning I woke up and she was ... just *there*. In the kitchen, making breakfast like she used to."

"And you think ... *you* made her come back?"

Jared can't speak for a moment. It's too much. He looks at Jessie's face. There are pale freckles he's never noticed before scattered across the bridge of her nose, and what looks like flecks of gold in her wide blue eyes that are trained on his.

"I thought I wanted her to come back," he says, "I was just a kid. I didn't know. I didn't know...what it would do to my dad."

"Why?" Jessie almost whispers, "What do you mean?"

"I thought when she came back, he'd be better. And he was. Or I thought he was, for a while. Then it all started again. The fighting. The screaming. All the same stuff that was going on before. I just never realized."

"So," Jessie says, "She left? Again?"

"Yeah. And the weird thing ... right before she did, I was wondering why she was still there. If she hated my dad so much, why didn't she just leave, you know? Then one night I woke up and she was in my room, just standing there by my bed, looking down at me. It scared me because it was dark, and I couldn't see her face."

"What did she do?"

"Nothing. She just stood there for a while. Then she said, 'Let me go.'"

"Let me go?"

"Yeah."

"What else did she say?"

"Nothing. She just said that. Then she left." Jared takes a deep breath to push back the tightness in his chest. "I never saw her again."

"What about your dad?"

"He tried to kill himself."

Jared is shocked at how quickly the words came out, like they were already there inside his mouth, waiting to be said. He glances at Jessie and sees the look he knows he'll see, shock struggling to conceal itself.

"What ..." she speaks in a voice that's quieter than he thought possible. "What happened?"

"He cut his wrists."

He looks at Jessie again, and her eyes are closed, though whether it's because she's picturing what he's told her, or because she can't bear to look at him, he can't tell.

"Is that why you're always watching out for him?" she finally speaks. "Why you always have to run back home?"

"No, he's better now. He's okay," Jared says, then thinks, *why lie to her? Give it up.* And it all comes pouring out. "No, he's not okay. He hasn't worked for three years. He hasn't sold a painting or anything. I bring him food, but he doesn't eat it. I don't know when he eats. I don't know when he sleeps."

"Maybe you should get him some help."

"How? He doesn't have any insurance. He doesn't have any money. He probably wouldn't go if he did."

"But you can't do it all by yourself, Jared. It's not fair."

"He's my dad," Jared's voice shreds on the word, "He's my freaking dad, okay? What am I supposed to do?" Searing, hot pain swells inside of him, blotting out everything else, blurring his vision and clutching at his throat, choking him. And the words he'd said over and over again in that emergency room years ago when the nurses had held him back from going behind that closed door, *I want my dad, I want my dad,* come back now and fill his head until they're all he can hear.

Jared says, "I just want my dad back again." Right behind the words comes a tidal wave of yearning that washes through him, pushing every other thought and feeling out of the way. The light goes away for a moment; when it returns it's a pinprick of pale gold high above that grows brighter until it reaches down and finds him sitting on the forest floor, looking up through the leaves at the afternoon sun peeking through like a searchlight.

"What happened?" Jared asks. Jessie is kneeling next to him, a concerned look on her face.

"I don't know. You look like you fainted. Are you okay?"

Jared touches the side of his face. It's warm, like a fever, and there's the faint echo of a vibration inside his head. "Yeah," he says, "I guess so." A pang of embarrassment goes through him. "I'm sorry."

"No," she says, "Don't be. It's okay. Really."

Jared closes his eyes for a moment, then something touches his forehead. When he opens his eyes, he realizes it's Jessie's hand. The happiness it causes him is almost too much and he closes his eyes again to hide it.

"Jared, I think you're sick. You feel like you've got a fever or something."

"No, I'm okay," he says, sitting up straighter. He knows it's true. He's not sick. This has happened before. This overwhelming rush of emotion, then blindness, then light returning and the slowly fading fever. When? Then he remembers. The day he told her about Delany and the cigarette. When the anger rose up and the burn appeared.

Jared looks up through the leaves again and the sun is lower and paler now, its thin light barely reaching him. And just like that, he knows. Something has happened.

Dad...

Suddenly he's on his feet, heart pounding in his chest. "I've gotta go."

"Is it your dad?" Jessie asks.

"I just ... I just need to get back," Jared says. "I'm sorry."

"Let me go with you," she says.

He stops and looks at her. Her blue-gold eyes are serious, her mouth set firmly.

"Why?"

"Just let me go with you, okay?"

He stares at her, knowing she's trying to be kind, knowing he can't let her. Every night when he climbs those stairs and opens the door, he never knows what he's going to find. He can't risk that with her.

"No, that's okay. I'll be alright," he says, hoping he won't have to say more. He sees the disappointment hit her, her eyes downcast. "I mean," he struggles to find the right words, "Thanks, but...it's better if I do it myself."

"Alright. But...let me know. Text me. Promise."

"Okay," he says, then realizes, he doesn't have her number. Before he can ask, she has her phone out, and the two of them are standing there under the trees, exchanging numbers. Then they start down the path together, not speaking. He's grateful she's walking next to him, but his mind is on the clock, on how long it will take to ride home, how quickly he can climb the stairs, and what he will find waiting behind the door.

CHAPTER 28

DAD

Jared climbs the stairs to the apartment as quickly as he can. He puts the key in the lock, then closes his eyes for a second and says the same one-word prayer he always says before opening the door.

Please…

He turns the key, the door swings open, and he's overwhelmed by a wave of scents so intense that at first, he can't identify them. Instead, they come at him as flashes of pictures in his mind. A blinding white tile floor inches below his face with his toys scattered across it. The huge, comforting bodies of grown-ups passing back and forth above him like clouds in the sky. A giant oven as warm and radiant as the sun.

The echo of those images remains as he starts to put names to what he's breathing. Olive oil. Onions. Garlic. Oregano.

Jared glances around the room and doesn't understand what he sees. A floor swept clean. A kitchen table clear of clutter with what looks like a white tablecloth spread evenly across it, round and smooth as the surface of a bowl of milk.

Jared's first thought is that they've been evicted. He doesn't understand how new people could have moved in so fast. When he hears the soft clatter of a saucepan come from around the corner, he takes a frightened step backward, half-expecting to come face-to-face with a stranger.

Then he sees it. A single canvas pinned to the wall, freshly gessoed, a shiny rectangular field of white broken by the first strokes of the artist's brush. His dad's brush. He knows this, as sure as he recognizes the form taking shape on that white field, the quick crossed spars of what will be a sailboat like the shadow of a bird in flight.

Jared steps cautiously across the threshold and onto the clean, bright floor, the delicious aromas nearly lifting him off his feet, an answering pang of hunger gnawing in his gut.

"Dad?" He calls out softly, like he's still afraid of who might answer. He turns the corner and sees a man busy at the stove, his back turned. "Dad?"

The man at the stove turns around. A startled sound escapes Jared's throat.

His father's face is clean-shaven. His hair still long but clean and brushed back from his forehead, his green eyes clear and full of warmth.

"Hey, buddy. Come on in!" His dad's voice sounds strong and clear, cheerful. Jared wants to believe, but he doesn't trust it. His dad is cooking. Dad. Cooking.

"So, buddy," his dad says, "You hungry?" Jared tries to answer but all he can manage is a nod. "Good," his dad says, turning back to the stove. "Should be ready in a few minutes."

Jared gazes mutely at the items lined-up neatly on the kitchen counter. A tall green bottle of extra virgin olive oil, blue and red boxes of penne pasta, two fresh unopened packs of ground turkey, big cans of crushed fire-roasted tomatoes. "Dad," he finally manages to say, "How did you get all this stuff?"

"Would you believe Santa Claus?" His dad grins. "Actually, buddy, I've got some good news. I sold a painting."

"Really?" Jared can't believe it. His dad hasn't sold a painting in three years. His dad takes something out of the refrigerator, talking to Jared over his shoulder.

"Yeah! Actually, I sold three paintings. Bryce said this guy from Boston came into the gallery today, saw the big storm painting and bought it right on the spot. He asked if there were any more, Bryce showed him some in the back and he bought two more. And, you know that old seascape? The one Bryce keeps in the back of the gallery?"

"The really big one?"

"Yeah, the one I never finished. The guy told Bryce that if I finish that one, he knows a collector in New York who wants it. So, I've got a commission! It's in my bedroom now. Bryce brought it over so I could get to work on it." His dad laughs, and it startles Jared—he's not used to seeing his dad laughing. "Can you believe it?"

No, Jared thinks, *I can't*. But there it is, all the evidence, right in front of him. The food. And his dad, alert and on his feet, cooking for the two of them.

"Hey, buddy, you wanna give me a hand?" Jared sees the knife in his dad's hand, the bright blade gleaming in the kitchen light, and a cold sensation goes through him.

Then his dad turns the knife around, holding the black handle carefully toward him.

"Here, buddy. Chop this basil for me, will ya?"

Jared's dad tosses a big green bunch of fresh basil onto the cutting board. Jared stares at it, his mind spinning, the knife forgotten in his hand.

"Here, buddy," his dad's voice is practically in his ear. "Like this." His dad gently takes the knife, presses the point of it down against the wood and rocks the rest of the blade up and down over the basil. "Try it." Jared takes the knife and does what his dad has shown him. A fresh green smell rises up from the cutting board and fills his nose.

"Here," his dad says, tearing open one of the packs of ground turkey. "Help me make these meatballs. Wash your hands first, okay?" Jared moves over to the sink while his dad reaches over and turns on the water. Jared holds his hands under the warm water, feeling like he's in some kind of dream. When his dad turns off the water, Jared holds his hands in the same place for a moment, like he's not sure what to do with them.

"Okay, buddy," he hears his dad say. "Grab some of this turkey and roll it in a ball. Then roll it around in this stuff here. Like this—you remember."

Jared takes a ball of raw ground turkey and rolls it in the plate of diced onions and garlic that his dad has put in front of him. It's true. He remembers. All those Thursday nights when he helped his dad make meatballs. Before the bad time. All those years expand and collapse, stretching his mind all the way out to the edge of darkness, then snapping back to this time, this place, this moment. Standing side by side with his dad at the kitchen counter, doing this thing they know how to do.

Jared watches his dad turn on the flame under the frying pan, pour a dollop of olive oil on the black iron surface, and toss in the meatballs where they erupt in a loud racket of popping and sizzling. That good smell hits Jared right between the eyes, and for a moment he feels like his legs might give out beneath him.

A few minutes later, Jared finds himself sitting at the kitchen table with the clean white tablecloth. His dad sets a full plate of penne and meatballs in front of him with a solid-sounding *thump*. "Hold on, buddy." His dad disappears for a few seconds, then returns with a saucepan, and spoons steaming hot red sauce over the meatballs. "Takes a little longer, but it's better than that stuff you buy in a jar."

Jared's mind is still buzzing with questions, but hunger takes over and he spears a meatball with his fork, brings it to his mouth and bites down. The pan-seared meat is crispy on the outside under the sauce and bursts open, releasing dozens of flavors. He has never eaten anything this good before.

"Not bad, huh?" his dad winks at him from across the table, his own mouth full. Jared nods enthusiastically and keeps eating in blissful silence for a few minutes until he has to stop and rest. When he does, he takes the time to look at his dad, really *look* at him.

His clothes are clean and new-looking, unspotted by paint and food. His face looks naked and vulnerable without the beard, the vulnerability underscored by a few small red scars from shaving that mark his neck and jaw. But he looks more relaxed. Rested. Even younger, somehow.

"Hey, Dad. What's up with this?" Jared runs his finger along his own naked jawline.

"Oh," his dad smiles, almost shyly. "Guess I just kind of got tired of it."

"So," Jared asks, "What happened to all the other paintings that were here? Did you sell them too?"

"No. I threw them away."

"You threw them away?" The huge, dark and angry-looking paintings that have been his dad's work for the past three years, torn down and thrown away like garbage?

"Yeah," his dad shrugs, pushing a piece of Italian bread around in the red sauce left on his plate. "That guy bought all the ones he wanted. He didn't want the rest. Besides..." His dad pops the piece of bread-and-sauce in his mouth, chewing, "Bryce says he'll start selling my paintings again this season. If I do some that he likes. You know, like I used to."

"You mean like the one on the wall there?"

"Yeah," his dad leans back to regard the new canvas on the wall. "Started that one today. What do you think?"

"But I thought ..." Jared says, choosing his words carefully, "I thought you said you'd never do any more paintings like that. You know, sailboats, beach-scenes."

"Yeah, well ..." his dad's face drops its easy smile for a moment as he keeps gazing at the graceful form taking shape on the canvas. "That was then. And this is now." And suddenly his dad is laughing. "Holy crap, listen to me. *That was then and this is now.* I should paint that on coffee mugs and sell 'em, don'tcha think?" And now Jared is laughing too. Laughing with his dad, the way they used to. The joy is almost too much.

"So," his dad says, standing up from the table. "You want any more, buddy? Still hungry?"

Jared shakes his head. He's fuller than he's been for a long time. He helps his dad bring the dishes to the sink and reaches for the sponge to start washing as usual, but his dad stops him.

"That's okay, buddy. I'll wash up. Why don't you just take it easy?"

Jared starts to object, but after the big meal and the series of surprises he's had, his mind feels sleepy, his arms and legs heavy. The couch is calling to him, so he lays down, stretching out every muscle. His mind is still spinning, but the sound of his dad washing dishes, the soft clatter of plates and the steady *hush* of running water lulls him to sleep.

Jared wakes with a start, not knowing where he is. It's Thursday, and he's due at the fish market in four hours. He starts to sit up, then he feels his dad's hand on his shoulder, stopping him and gently easing him back down again.

"Whoa, take it easy, buddy. Where's the fire?"

"I gotta be at the fish market at four."

The couch sags as his dad sits next to him. His voice, when he speaks again, is soft with a note of firmness in it.

"No you don't."

At first Jared isn't sure what his dad is telling him.

"You don't need that job anymore, buddy. Working at Rick's, that's a good job for you. But you've got school. Hell, you've got a life." His dad stops talking for a moment. "I know how hard you've been working, buddy. I know how tired you are. That's gonna change. That's gonna start changing right now. Okay?"

Jared tries to say *Okay* but his throat aches, and he's afraid of what he may sound like. His dad's hand leaves his shoulder; a moment later it's gently brushing the hair back from his forehead.

Jared starts to drift off. He tries to fight it, because he doesn't want to wake up and find that this is all a dream. He wants to stay awake. He wants to stay here with this man who he remembers, this man who is sitting by his side, watching over him.

CHAPTER 29

SURPRISE

Jessie leans her bike up against the house, barely registering her dad's car in the drive. In her mind's eye, she's walking up to a different house, a different door; Jared's.

What is Jared seeing right now?

She opens her door and steps inside where it's cool and dark. She's about to call for her dad, when she's grabbed from behind and lifted off her feet. She screams.

"Happy almost-birthday!" a familiar voice shouts and Jessie is released, spins around to find Dylan, a broad grin on her face.

"Oh my God. You gave me a heart-attack," Jessie then throws her arms around her friend, heart pounding. "You're here. I can't believe it!"

"Surprised?"

She slaps Dylan's arm, "Dope." Then hugs her again. She breathes in the scent of citrus and cloves, Dylan's perfume. The same one her mom favors.

"Did Mom bring you?" She pulls away to look around the room.

Jessie's dad comes in from the kitchen, "Look what I found at the train station."

"You took a train?"

Dylan holds up two fingers. "First the Acela to Boston. That was great. Comfy seats, a food car..." No mom. Jessie bites back disappointment as Dylan drones on about her trip.

"Is she coming Sunday then?"

"No, silly. I'm taking you back. Friday. She's got something planned for Saturday," Dylan says. "And it's gonna be BIG!"

Of course, she's not coming. Her mother must have been planning this all along, to get Jessie away from Beauport, back in her territory.

"I wish you'd asked me," she tells her dad. "Why can't she do the party here?" She looks around the dusty room, trying to imagine Dylan, her mom and her other friends in this room and the picture doesn't gel. Would they even be able to come? How would they get here?

"Aren't you glad to see your friend?" Her dad's voice has an edge to it, and she snaps her head up to answer.

"Sorry. Of course!" She hugs Dylan again, and feels the pull of New York, a certain joy at the prospect of going home, sleeping in her own bed, seeing her mom. "You know what she's planning, don't you? Tell!"

"If I tell you, I will have to kill you," Dylan says.

Her dad moves toward the door. "I have to run something over to the lawyer's office. I'll pick up some chowder at Rick's for us."

Jared! *What's happened!? What did he find?* And now she's leaving Friday? She tries to picture Jared's face when she tells him. Will he be angry?

"When are we coming back?"

Her father looks surprised. "I... I have to be back Sunday night. But your mom said she'd like you to stay with her a little longer..."

"I want to come back with you," she says quickly, and when he starts to speak, interrupts, "It's my birthday isn't it?" She hears the nastiness in her tone before she sees her father blink. She forces a smile, "Yeah. Let's go to Rick's tonight."

"Okay then. That's decided." He walks through the front door then turns and tells Dylan, "Her boyfriend works there."

"Da-ad!"

He shuts the door quickly behind him while Dylan stares at Jessie.

Jessie ducks her head, "He's *not* my boyfriend. Wanna see my room?" and leads the way, Dylan on her heels.

Jessie turns and seeing Dylan in the doorway to her room—not in New York, but here—she has to grin. "I'm *so* glad you're here."

"Me too," Dylan grins back and they sit on her bed, letting their legs swing. "Do I get to see those woods you keep yakkin' about? You know *some* people come here to go to the BEACH!"

"We'll go to the beach tomorrow."

"Thank God!" Dylan rolls her eyes and makes an exaggerated sigh, then turns back to Jessie, green eyes wide and probing. "So? Tell me about Mister he's-not-my-boyfriend. Do I get to meet him? He cooks?"

"He doesn't make the food." She isn't sure this is true. She doesn't know what his job is. She remembers him carrying out the trash, the stains on his apron, his uncut hair. She starts to worry. *What will Dylan think?* But the memory is quickly replaced by Jared in close-up, the beautiful unruly hair, his eyes warm.

"I like the way he looks," she says, understanding the inadequacy of this, her cheeks growing hot as she remembers the feeling of his arms around her, the comfort of him.

Dylan scoots closer to her on the bed and takes Jessie's phone. "Show."

This hadn't occurred to her. "I don't have any pictures," she admits, and suddenly she wants one. She imagines putting her face next to his, holding up her phone, how his cheek would feel against hers. Her face grows hotter still and she stands up.

Dylan's swiping through the pictures, "What's this?"

Jessie peers over her shoulder. It's a photo of a gravestone in Angel Falls. She'd taken it while Jared wasn't looking. But she'd wanted proof. Now she peers closer trying to read the words. She grabs the phone from Dylan.

"Hey!"

She places her fingers on the screen and spreads them, zooming in, but it's no use. The words, so clear and crisp just hours ago, are completely gone.

"What's wrong?"

"Nothing," she says, "I thought it was something else." Goosebumps rise on her arms as she slides the phone in her pocket. The words were there, she'd even checked the picture after she'd taken it. How could they have disappeared? She'd like to tell Dylan. About the strange things, about the nice ones too. But how? "Jared's a friend, okay. I like him. A lot. But don't make fun. Please?"

Dylan gets up from the bed and starts rooting around in her bag, coming up with first one then another thin pink strings that reveal themselves as a bikini. "*Moi?* Make fun? What do you take me for?" Jessie thinks she sounds a little hurt.

"Dyl?"

"What?"

I think he's in trouble and I want to help him. Something really strange is going on... Her stomach tightens. "His dad's a painter, an artist, but they're having money troubles, so Jared has to work a lot. He works at Rick's."

"Does he paint?"

"I think so." She knows he said he didn't, but she doesn't believe it. Something about the way he speaks, the way he talks about the things he loves.

"Is he a good kisser?"

"Dylan!" She hits her arm, not hard, but Dylan squeals.

"Hey!"

"Sorry." And now it's in her mind. What would it feel like? She imagines his face close to hers, moving closer, and she is terrified.

She watches Dylan as she unpacks, how familiar she looks and moves, letting it lift her heart.

At the end of the night, when they've gone to bed and Jessie and Dylan are lying side by side in the narrow bed in Dorothy's spare room, she takes Dylan's hand, they lace fingers, and she says in the darkness, "I'm glad you're here."

Dylan's fingers move against hers, counting, "That's the fourth time you said that," Dylan says, then tugs Jessie's hand and kisses her cheek. "Me too."

They are silent for a few moments. Then Dylan asks, "Is Jared in trouble?"

"Wha... What do you mean?"

Dylan tugs her hand again, "C'mon girl. It's me. Don't you think I know when you're being weird?"

The weird ones are the best. Jessie's face burns.

"I don't know...Maybe. His mom... left. His dad's depressed." Oh, and there's this thing about making a burn appear and go away and letters appearing on gravestones...

Dylan waits, and the words form in Jessie's mouth. She is about to say, *there are weird things happening,* when Dylan says, "You love this guy?"

The word frightens her, even as her heart responds to it. What does it mean to love a boy? Jessie's had crushes on people, but the word love she's saved for her parents, for Dylan.

After several moments of silence, Jessie realizes by the weight of Dylan's hand in hers and the sound of her breathing that she's fallen asleep.

She waits a few more minutes to be sure, then gets out of bed, picks up her phone and slips out the door and into the bathroom. She sits on the toilet seat, legs bouncing up and down, heart racing, then opens a blank text and stares at the blinking cursor for a long time before typing.

Hi. How's your dad? and clicks 'send'.

She notices the time. 2 AM. He's not going to answer. She stands and puts her hand on the doorknob when her phone vibrates. She nearly drops it as she turns it to see what's written.

Hiya. Why are you still up?

She quickly types back, *Why are you?*

She imagines him smiling. She knows he is.

Bingo. Hour of the weirdos, right?

Her face flushes with pleasure. She wants to hear his voice. She wonders if her dad could hear her talking in the bathroom. She must have waited too long because another message appears:

He's doing okay. Thanks for asking. Better than okay. I want to tell you all about it.

She types quickly, *I'm so glad! Tell me. What happened?*

He types, *I'll tell you Friday. I can't believe it.*

Tell me now. Then deletes it, remembering she won't be here Friday. Types, *Dylan's here. We're going back to NY for the weekend. It's my birthday.* Stares at the last three words, wanting him to know, not wanting to tell him, so she deletes them and hits 'send.'

She waits for a few moments. No response. She wonders if he's upset, angry even. *Please no,* she thinks. She types *I should be back Sunday.* It seems interminable, all the days between now and seeing him again so she types, *Or I could see you tomorrow. You could meet Dylan.*

This time the answer is quick.

School.

The single word feels like a slap. She should have remembered. But he didn't have to be so short with her. Her phone vibrates again.

I gotta go. Text me when you get back.

She stares at the phone, still stung by that single word. Maybe he's not mad, maybe he simply hates school. She types; *Okay. G'night.*

Again, she rises and again she gets her hand on the doorknob before her phone vibrates.

G'night weirdo.

She smiles. "G'night weirdo," she whispers.

Chapter 30

The Woman

Jared wakes to someone's hand on his shoulder, gently squeezing.

"Hey, buddy," he hears his dad's voice. "Rise and shine."

Jared opens his eyes and doesn't know where he is for a moment. The ceiling above him is unfamiliar. Then he remembers falling asleep on the couch. The face of the man looking down at him is also startling at first until he recognizes it. The strong, clean-shaven jaw, the sharp nose, and warm green eyes. His dad, like he used to be.

"Coffee, buddy?"

Jared nods *yes,* and a moment later his dad is handing him a big white mug. Jared takes it in both hands—it's heavy. Traces of steam rise from the surface, and a strong, delicious aroma that's already waking him up before he even takes his first sip.

"*Whoa!* That's good, Dad."

"Italian roast," his dad says, taking a sip from his own mug. "You like it?"

"Yeah. It's really strong."

His dad passes his mug back and forth under his nose, takes a long, dramatic sniff and launches into a snooty-sounding British accent. "Yes, by Jove, a powerful brew indeed." They're both laughing now—where has *this* dad been for so long?

Jared watches his dad all through breakfast. He can't believe the change, even though it's right there in front of him. He remembers a few times when his dad seemed to be getting better, more talkative. Happier. Then the sudden slide downhill into crushing sadness and silence. But this time it feels different.

All day at school, Jared watches the clock with a mix of excitement and dread.

He's excited to go home, but still afraid of what he might find when he opens the door.

When Jared turns the key and walks into the apartment, he still half-expects to see the sink overflowing with dishes, oil paint smeared and dried on the table. But no—it's all bright and clean like it was last night. Jared pauses in the doorway, taking it all in again. It's like waking up from a good dream and finding that the dream is real.

"Dad?" Jared calls out. No answer. For a moment, fear starts to rise inside Jared's chest.

"Hey, buddy."

Jared turns and sees his dad coming out of the bedroom, a warm smile on his face. Jared is relieved—then he notices his dad carrying his travel-portfolio of art supplies over his shoulder. Jared tries to hide his disappointment. "Oh ... you going out?"

"Yeah," his dad says. "Actually, buddy, I thought maybe you could come with me."

Jared is startled. His dad always goes out alone to paint and draw. "Really?"

"Yeah, sure." His dad smiles. "I mean, you draw really well, buddy. I'd like to see you start doing it again."

Jared's face warms. It's true. He used to draw all the time. The expression on his dad's face is an awkward mix of embarrassment and hopefulness.

"Sure. Why not?"

A big grin breaks out across his dad's face. "Alright! Let's get going. We're losing the light."

On their way down Plymouth Street, it hits Jared—here he is, walking down the street, side-by-side with his dad. How long has it been since they've done that?

When they're in front of the corner bodega, his dad pauses. "You wanna get something to take with us? Something to drink?"

"Sure," Jared says, and they enter the store together. Grabbing a couple of bottles of water from the cooler, they approach the counter. Jared knows the man at the register, who smiles at him. Jared sees the man notice his dad and his eyes grow wide.

"*Cal?*" the man says.

Jared's dad looks down for a moment, almost shyly. Then he smiles, puts the bottles on the counter and says, "Hey, Carlos. How're you doing?"

"I'm good, I'm good," the man says, grinning and staring at his dad unabashedly. "Good to see you, Cal. You're looking good, man."

"Thanks," Jared's dad smiles, taking the bottles. "No bag, thanks."

"Okay, okay, no problem. Hey, good to see you, man!"

"Good to see you too," Jared's dad calls back over his shoulder as he pushes the door open and the two of them walk back out into the summer afternoon. Jared experiences a rush of pride and excitement. Until this moment, there was part of him that still thought this might be a dream. Now someone else has seen his dad. And Jared has seen his dad through Carlos' eyes, better, stronger. It's true. It's real.

When they reach the boardwalk, Jared's dad turns left and leads them past the vacationing families with their beach towels and umbrellas. Just ahead is a long, low ridge of black rock that extends from the sand out into the sea.

Jared's dad climbs up the rock with no trouble, turns and extends a hand down to him. "Come on, buddy," his dad says. "Grab on." Jared takes his dad's hand, feeling his firm grip, then he's pulled up and off the sand and onto the rock. He hears the smile in his dad's voice.

"Look at that."

Ahead of them the sand stretches out empty and clear. Another black ridge of rock runs straight out into the waves smashing against its sides, sending white spumes of foam into the air. At the far end of the ridge is the lighthouse, small-looking and whitewashed. A few gulls dip and wheel overhead, seeming to rise and fall with the rhythm of the waves.

His dad opens the portfolio, pulls out two big sketch pads and hands one to Jared along with a couple of pencils. Jared moves a few yards away and sits down on the rock. It's cold and hard, but the afternoon sun overhead is bright and warm. The pages of the sketchbook flutter and flap in the ocean breeze, so Jared holds them down with one hand and looks around for something to draw. He glances over at his dad who's already started, his hand moving quickly.

Jared looks back down at the paper on his lap, still white and clean as snow. Gripping the pencil tightly, he starts drawing the breakwater, sketching a straight line from the lower left corner of the paper to the upper right, but it's all wrong, it's not a breakwater, it's just a line, like something he'd draw with a ruler in geometry class, and he flips over to another sheet of paper to start again.

"How's it going, buddy?" his dad asks.

"Alright." Jared knows his dad can probably hear the frustration in his voice.

"Having trouble?"

"I don't know. I can't get it right." Jared's afraid his dad will come over and look at what he's been drawing, but he doesn't. He stays in his spot on the black rock, but his pencil stops moving and he looks up at Jared.

"Try loosening up a little, buddy. Don't try to make it perfect. Think of it like this... don't draw the thing you're looking at. Draw the way it feels inside."

The ocean breeze rattles the pages and almost pulls the sketchbook out of Jared's hands. He grabs it and holds on, then the breeze dies down and the pages lie still. Jared smooths the sheet out with one hand and holds the pencil lightly in the other—is this what his dad means by *loosen up?* He takes a deep breath, lets it out, then starts moving the pencil on the paper, looking at the dark tongue of the breakwater stretching out into the grey-green ocean. When he looks down again, he's surprised and pleased by what he sees.

"Better, right?" his dad says.

"Uh-huh," Jared answers, but he's too focused on drawing to say anything more. He almost doesn't notice when a shadow falls across the page. He looks over his shoulder and sees his dad crouched there, looking down at the drawing on Jared's knee.

"Nice, buddy," his dad smiles, nodding his head slowly. "Really nice."

"Thanks," Jared says. His dad's praise fills him with a warm glow of pride. He's right. It's good. Not perfect. But it's good.

The sun is lower in the sky now. Long shadows reach further and further across the sand, and the water is turning a metallic gray that seems to capture the light that's draining from the sky. Jared stops moving his pencil and looks over to where his dad is still sketching. He watches his dad's eyes darting quickly back and forth from the paper to the scene in front of him. Jared stands and stretches, his legs and backside a little sore from sitting on the rock, then walks over to where his dad is working. He wants to see.

"How's it going, Dad?" His dad seems to flinch, then looks up at him. The expression on his face is almost like someone who's been woken from a deep sleep.

"Hey, buddy." His dad smiles up at him, the odd startled expression on his face gone now.

"Can I see?"

The smile on his dad's face flickers for a second, then comes back. "Sure, buddy. So. What do you think?"

His dad has drawn the black breakwater reaching out into the waves, spumes of seafoam beautifully rendered with hazy strokes from the side of the pencil lead. The surface of the water is a thing of wonder, hundreds of different little currents and motions, all suggested by the slightest strokes of the pencil.

What draws Jared's eye is a figure his dad has drawn into the background, a female figure walking across the sand toward the viewer. Jared notices that the woman in the drawing isn't dressed for the beach; she wears a dark dress that appears to billow and flap in the wind from the sea. Her long hair moves in the same direction, flying almost horizontally like a dark flag. Where her face should be there is only a blank white oval. No eyes, no mouth, only an empty space, waiting.

Jared feels cold, wraps his arms around his chest and shivers a little in the wind from the ocean.

"Dad," he says, trying to keep the unease from his voice, "Who's that supposed to be?"

His dad who's gone back to drawing doesn't answer.

"Dad."

"Yeah, buddy?"

"Who is that? I mean, who is that supposed to be? There?"

Jared's dad sits back and looks at the paper in front of him, a puzzled look on his face, almost as though he hasn't seen the figure till now.

"I don't know. Just someone."

The wind coming in from the ocean is colder than before, and Jared is shivering now. His dad looks up from the drawing, a look of concern coming over his face.

"You cold, buddy?"

"Yeah." Jared doesn't want to interrupt his dad's work, but he wants to go.

"Okay, no problem. We've probably been out here long enough."

Jared helps his dad pack up their art supplies, then together they climb down from the black rock and start back over the sand toward home. A couple of times, Jared turns around to look back over his shoulder, but of course no one is there.

Chapter 31

Horseshoe Beach

Jessie dreams she's lying in the grass beside Jared, close but not touching. The day is hot, but the grass is cool and overhead the leaves flutter in a breeze they can't feel.

Beyond the leaves is a blue, blue sky. Jessie has a sudden and strong wish for Jared to put his head in her lap. The feeling is so strong, she can imagine his head there, the weight and heat of it, how the curve of his neck fits perfectly over her thigh. She lifts her hand to stroke his brow, she thinks of it with that word, 'brow,' and she feels the heat of his skin, the softness of his hair. Then she wakes, slowly returning to the room, the bed, to Dylan breathing softly beside her, light spilling on the floor from the crack in the curtains. She closes her eyes, longing to dive back into the dream. Dylan makes a sound, rolls away.

Is Jared in trouble? Dylan's words come back to her. Jessie decides to tell her about Angel Falls. Delany. Everything.

After breakfast, she and Dylan head toward the beach. Dylan's legs struggling to reach the pedals of the bike they'd borrowed from Jessie's dad. Jessie takes a detour by the harbor, hoping to see Jared there.

Jessie shouts over her shoulder, "Here's where all the fish comes in. You buy it right off the boat, it's amazing." She scans the workers but doesn't see him. He must be at school.

At the parking lot to the beach, they stow their bikes in the rack and walk up the sandy path through high beach grass. At the top, the path widens, and the sea breeze slaps them in the face. Dylan gasps.

"Whoa Nellie!"

Jessie laughs, "'Whoa Nellie?'"

"This is so beautiful!"

"This is my favorite beach. It's called Horseshoe." Jessie points to where the beach curves close to a small island. "When it's low-tide, you can walk right out."

They stand watching the waves land softly then rake the beach and bubble as they slide back into themselves. They find an empty spot near the water and spread their towels.

"Hey paleface, sunscreen first." Jessie says, and they spend the next several minutes rubbing in the lotion. They walk to the water, leaping back when it hits their feet.

"You've got to be shittin' me!" Dylan backs up out of reach, arms folded firmly across her chest.

Jessie laughs and runs in, gasping at the cold and diving through a wave. She comes up and swims hard for a few minutes before turning back, standing and waving.

"It's great. You'll get used to it."

"Like hell!" But after a few moments, Dylan shakes her head, takes a running start and splashes through the water, "Ouch...ouch...ouch...ouch!" She dives in and comes up gasping, "I will make you pay!" then starts swimming hard towards Jessie. Jessie swims away as hard as she can, but when she turns around, Dylan rears up like a sea monster and grabs at her.

They swim and splash each other, then Jessie points to a big wave, and they body surf to shore.

Lying on her towel, looking up at the different blues of the sky, Jessie tries to remember the name of the darkest shade directly overhead. *Lapis*? No, too dark. *Turquoise*? Too light, too pale. *Jared would know,* she thinks.

She remembers her vow this morning to tell Dylan everything, but the words won't come. The violent red of Jared's burn; the empty space on his arm; the gravestones blurred and then perfectly clear. Could she convince Dylan the things she saw were real? She rolls on her side and studies her friend. And she can see both things: the girl-child pudgy and adorable superimposed over this new *woman*. All the time they spent searching their bodies for signs of womanhood, and here it is, here *she* is. Has it only been a few weeks since Jessie left New York? So much has happened.

Jessie blurts, "Are you... in love... with the guitar guy?"

"I don't know." Dylan's voice is soft. "I think so. Maybe," she laughs.

"What does it feel like?"

She's silent for a moment, then says, "Crazy. He makes me crazy. I think he wants to be with me, and then he goes," she makes her voice deep, "*You're too young. You're too young.*"

"I thought you said he's a senior."

"Yeah, well, I guess he thinks he's so-o-o much older, like two years makes all the difference in world." She laughs, a harsh sound, making Jessie want to protect her.

"Is he... good to you?"

Dylan sighs, and then, in a happier voice, "Yeah. He's good to me."

"In what ways?"

"Mmmm," Dylan says, her cockiness returning, "I'm not sure *you'd* understand." And then she turns to Jessie, "Do you love this guy, Jared?"

"I don't know," she says, wondering again how to explain what's been going on, how to make Dylan believe her.

Dylan sighs again, sits up and looks Jessie in the face. "Well, you tell him from me, he better not hurt you. Okay?" And this sudden fierceness pleases Jessie, and she sits up and hugs her hard. The words *Something strange is going on,* form in her mind, and she opens her mouth, but Dylan stands and runs toward the water. "Last one in buys ice cream!"

They swim longer this time, floating on their backs, letting the movement of the ocean rock them, then body surf in.

Back on land they watch the light start to change to a pale gold. Dylan says, "Look at the tide. Do you think we can walk to the island now?" She points to the sandbar barely visible above receding waves. Jessie checks her phone for the time, then nods. "Just there and back again. I promised Dad we'd be back by seven."

They walk at the water's edge, wet sand sucking at their feet, passing other people carrying bags, chairs, umbrellas, coolers, sleeping children, and beach toys. When they reach the sandbar, they watch the water rise on either side, slamming together and shooting up in small perfect spumes.

Dylan elbows her. "Check out the artistes."

Jessie looks up and sees Jared walking on the sandbar toward them with an older man. He sees her and they stop.

The late sunlight makes his skin gold. His shirt is open, and the sight of his bare chest makes her feel strange, but his eyes are seeing her, the way they always do and that settles her.

"Hey," he says.

"Hey," she answers, aware of the sounds of surf, children shouting, gulls crying. She doesn't know where to look. She stares at the water spumes over the sand bar, then looks at Dylan, who's looking at Jared.

"Jared?" It's the older man, his voice is deep and craggy and beautiful. And then she sees the resemblance; it could be Jared in twenty years.

"This is Jared?" Dylan's whisper hisses into her ear; Jessie realizes she's surprised. Surprised and impressed.

"Sorry," Jared says. "Dad, this is Jessie." They both look at Jessie, his father starting to smile and nod, then Jared looks at Dylan. With his eyes turned away, Jessie feels unplugged, and without turning her head, sees what he sees, the abundance and beauty of Dylan's hair, the perfect heart shape of her face, and the over-abundance of flesh barely touched by the pink strings she calls a bikini. She looks down, her stomach hurting.

"This is Dylan."

"Dylan?" his voice cracks and she looks up. His eyebrows are so high he looks like a cartoon.

"Yeah, my friend from the city. I told you she was here, remember?" She can hear the sharpness in her voice, but he doesn't seem to notice, because he's looking right at Jessie and smiling broadly. He looks relieved.

"Dylan. Yes. Hi. Welcome to Beauport." Then he turns to indicate the man beside him, and says, "Jessie, this is my dad."

The older man is studying her as if trying to figure something out. She juts out a hand and says, "Pleased to meet you, Mr. Younger," feeling stupid the minute the words leave her mouth. But he takes her hand in his and shakes it gently.

"Pleasure." Before he drops her hand, she sees the dull red scar, not across his wrist, but up the inside of his forearm, and has to tear her eyes away, hoping he didn't notice.

"Caleb Younger?" The way Dylan says it makes Jessie look at her in alarm. "You're Caleb Younger? The painter?"

The name is filtering through Jessie's over-worked brain, *Caleb Younger*, she sees a painting projected on a screen in her classroom, and the words *contemporary* and *realism;* the painting was a lighthouse, the paint thick and wild like the water itself, the lighthouse rising on columns of white, blue, grey, and black, the entire picture full of motion. That hand painted it, the hand she shook. She looks into his face.

He looks at her under wild brows, the hairs go every which way, and she realizes his eyes are green, truly green and as they look from her to Dylan, the wariness in them melts into shyness then into something else. He straightens his back, and a smile starts around his eyes.

"My name is Caleb, and I paint. You ladies heard of me?"

"Last year's art class," Dylan says. "Contemporary realist painters. Your work is gorgeous!" Dylan is staring at him in wonder. Then she turns to Jessie, "Why didn't you tell me? There was something..." Dylan frowns, then says, "Yeah, they said you'd disappeared or something..."

Jessie clenches her fists. *Fuck, fuck, fuck. Shut up, Dylan. Shut up.* Jared's dad is standing right in front of her and she can feel his silence. She's afraid to look at him.

Then Jared's father says, "I guess I did, eh Jared?" and he smiles. Only his mouth at first, but then his eyes lose their wariness, crinkle up, and he starts to laugh.

She looks at Jared, who looks confused. His dad laughs harder.

The laugh is coarse, throaty, rusty sounding, coming in fits and starts, but it's genuine and contagious. Jessie joins in, then Dylan, and finally, Jared.

"Why are we laughing?" Dylan asks.

"Does it matter?" Jared's dad says, and they stop, and stand silently catching their breath. He turns to Jessie then, his eyes serious. "You've been there, haven't you?"

Although she knows exactly where he means, she says, "Been where?"

"C'mon Dad, I have to be at Rick's in half an hour." Jared takes his arm as if to pull him away from the girls, and Jessie realizes he's nervous.

Caleb doesn't move. He says, "You've been there. I can see it on you." His pupils are small, making the green an almost solid marble in the center of his eyes. What he's saying is frightening, but his eyes and face are so like Jared's she doesn't flinch or shy away.

"Yes. I have. So have you." She has no idea why she adds the last, but it seems to satisfy him, his face relaxes, and he turns to Jared and starts a little as if surprised to find him there.

"Me and my boy," the pride in that phrase fills the air between them, "must be off. Nice to meet you, Jessie. Dylan." He turns to Jared, "I'll wait for you by the snack bar," and when Jared starts to speak, "...so you can say goodbye to the ladies."

"Goodbye Mr. Younger." Dylan waves as he walks off, then looking at Jessie and Jared, says, "I'm gonna head out toward the island. If I scream, let that cute lifeguard come." And she starts walking out, her feet sinking a little in the wet sand, arms out for balance.

Jessie turns finally to Jared, feeling lightheaded. *Breathe, dammit.* She takes in a deep breath and lets it out slowly.

"Well, uh..." Jared starts.

She interrupts. "I'm sorry for what Dylan said. I... I... I didn't know and I hope your dad didn't mind."

He moves closer and she looks up. His face is calm, his eyes that incredibly warm brown she loves.

"You saw him. He *laughed*. He's been laughing a lot since yesterday."

She nods. "Yeah. That's great. What happened?"

He looks off in the direction of the parking lot. "I should go. Don't want him to wait. I'll tell you when you get back. Is it Sunday?"

She nods. "Yeah, my mom has some big plan, she does it every year, it's a surprise. Dylan knows but she won't tell me."

"Surprise for what?" Then his eyes widen. "Your birthday? It's your birthday, right?"

Jessie's face burns and she can't look him in the eye. She considers lying but knows it's too late. "Yeah, well. Um, it's Sunday, the mystery event is Saturday, but my birthday's on Sunday." She feels his hands on her arms and looks up to find his face coming closer and before she understands what he's doing, his cool lips press against her hot cheek. Her heart goes crazy, and she closes her eyes. His lips feel so sweet, she wants him to stay there, but he moves his head away and she opens her eyes. His face is flushed, and his pupils large.

"Happy Birthday, Sunday. Call me when you get back."

CHAPTER 32

SHOW ME

Before he leaves for school, Jared looks in his dad's bedroom to check on him. He peers around the bedroom door and sees his dad on his back, his face still cleanshaven and peaceful looking, his chest rising and falling in a steady rhythm. The morning sunlight falling across the big seascape painting resting against one wall. The bureau-top is covered with tubes of paint and mason jars filled with brushes, and the air is full of the smell of linseed oil warming in the sunlight.

Jared knows his dad must have been up late again, trying to finish the big painting on time. He's making good progress. This morning, the blue gray sea has spread from one side of the canvas almost all the way to the other, and clouds and gulls are starting to take shape in the half-empty sky.

He's doing okay. Better than okay. That's what he'd written to Jessie.

Why doesn't he trust it?

All day long in class, Jared is aware of the red folder waiting inside his backpack, like a secret he's been hiding. But Delany knows. Every time Jared glances at the clock and sees the ending bell getting closer, he knows Delany is waiting for it too. Waiting for everyone else to leave. Waiting to get Jared alone to himself, one more time.

Why does Delany want to see him? He'd wanted Delany to explain the strange thing that was happening to him and make it go away. Now it has. The burn on his arm is gone, like it was never there, like it never happened. Why should he keep meeting Delany afterschool like this?

Jared watches the second hand ticking toward the twelve, and just before the bell rings, he decides. *This is it. This is the last time.*

When the bell finally rings, the classroom empties. Jared watches Delany close and lock the classroom door, then walk back toward him. "So," Delany says, "Did you read it?"

"Yeah," Jared sighs.

Jared watches Delany circle behind his desk and slide into his chair. Delany leans forward and fixes his eyes on Jared's. "So, Jared. Let's have a little pop quiz. Question number one. What happened here in Beauport three hundred years ago?"

"Some people ..." Jared begins hesitantly, "Some people disappeared."

"What kind of people?"

"Women. Women and children."

"Where did they go?"

"First ... they thought the Indians took them."

"Did they?"

Jared isn't sure what Delany means. "What?"

"Did...the...Indians...take...them?" Delany says each word slowly like he's talking to a small child, and Jared's face burns with embarrassment.

"No."

"Why not?"

"Because. They were all dead. The Indians. They killed them all."

"Alright," Delany says, nodding slowly. "Then what happened to those women and children?"

"They came back."

"Show me," Delany says, thrusting one of the dog-eared documents toward Jared. "Find where it says that and read it to me. Cite your source."

Jared reluctantly takes the document from Delany's hand and flips through the pages, looking through the archaic-sounding sentences for what he remembers. He finds it, clears his throat, and starts to carefully read.

"According to one account, a number of women who ...." Here the words seem to shift on the page and Jared has to stop.

"Go on," Delany says. Jared shuts his eyes, opens them, then tries again.

"... a number of women who had vanished two years earlier in the Great Disappearance began to return to the colony. Some colonists claim to have seen these ... returnees." The unfamiliar word throws him and the phrases start to shift and rearrange themselves again. Jared's frustration starts to rise.

"Okay," Delany says. "Take a minute. Go on when you're ready."

"Some colonists claim to have seen these returnees while others say that the witnesses were 'suffering from ... from some great madness.'"

"So," Delany says, "When those people came back, some people thought it was real, some people didn't. So, those people who thought it was real … what happened to them?"

"They …" Jared starts, and now a sudden sadness has him by the throat. "They threw them out. The other people who thought they were crazy. They made them leave."

"Where did they go?"

"Into the woods," Jared says. "They settled there … made their own town."

"And what was it called?"

"Angel Falls." A chill passes through Jared.

"Okay," Delany continues, "Those people. The ones who disappeared and then came back. *Why* did they come back?"

"I don't know," Jared says.

"Yes you do," Delany glares at him. Jared's heart starts to beat faster. He thinks Delany wants to trap him, to make him say something he's not ready to say yet.

Delany asks again, "Why did they come back?"

"Because …" The words slip out. "Because the people who saw them… *wanted* them to come back."

Delany's eyes close tightly, then slowly crinkle as he smiles. "Good, good," he whispers hoarsely. Jared can hear the clock on the wall ticking loudly as he waits for Delany to start talking again. When he does, it's in a calm, deliberate voice that reminds Jared of a doctor explaining something to a patient, choosing his words carefully.

"Listen, Jared. Those people. The ones who were driven out. They weren't crazy. They were *different*. They had something … they had a gift. Those other people, they couldn't understand it. They were afraid of it. That's why they drove them out."

Jared sees the overgrown graveyard deep in the woods; the old, crooked stones, uncared for and forgotten.

"The gift those people had," Delany continues, "It had to do with their minds. With their thoughts. They could *do things* with their thoughts. That's why other people were afraid of them. It's why they drove them out. Those people are gone now. But their children, their children's children, they're still here. Jared, you're one of them. You're one of those people."

A chill like cold water rises inside him. He knows it's true. He's known it since that day in the graveyard when Jessie showed him his own name on one of the old stones. But to hear Delany say it...

"Those people back then, in Angel Falls," Delany continues. "They *wanted* their loved ones to come back. They wanted it so much, they made it happen." Delany pauses, leans back in his chair. "So, Jared," he says in a quiet voice, "What do *you* want?"

Please, Jared thinks. *Not this. Not this again.* "I don't know," he says, trying to shut out Delany's searching eyes.

"Yes, you do." Delany's voice starts to rise again. *"Yes. You do."*

Jared doesn't want to say it, but he wants Delany off his back, so the answer comes flying out of his mouth, almost a shout.

"I just want my dad to be okay...alright?"

"Oh my God...it's your *dad*?"

Delany gets up from behind his desk and paces back and forth, laughing and shaking his head. "I saw him," Delany says breathlessly, "I saw him downtown, two days ago. I almost didn't recognize him. I didn't know... Christ! This whole time, I thought it was your mother."

"My *mother*? Why would I want *her* to come back? Why would I ever want to do that again?"

Delany stops pacing and stares at Jared. There's a wild light in his eyes. "*Again*? You mean ... you *made* her?"

In two strides, Delany is standing in front of Jared, gripping him by both shoulders, a wild look in his eyes that Jared has never seen before. After a moment, Delany lets go and steps back, his eyes turned down, almost shyly. "Sorry," he whispers in a hoarse voice.

Jared rubs his shoulder where it feels like Delany's fingers have left a bruise. He watches cautiously as Delany sits behind his desk and holds his head in his hands. When he looks up Jared thinks he can see wetness glistening in his eyes.

"Jared...you don't know how... I've been reading about this thing for years. Doing research. About Angel Falls. About what happened here. I knew it was real. I knew there had to be people here. People who could *prove* it was real. There had to be. It's genetics. But I could never find anybody."

"That's why you burned me with that cigarette?" Jared says. "You were *testing* me?"

Delany slams his hand down on his desk. "That doesn't *matter!* Don't you get it? Don't you understand what a gift you have?"

And now it all comes rushing back—that moment in the woods with Jessie, the yearning rushing through him like the sound of the wind in the leaves growing louder and louder... *I want my dad back.* Then his dad's face, bright and changed, like he'd wished for. *It's true,* Jared thinks. *It's all true.* And right behind the amazement comes the fear.

"*Gift?*" Jared says, his voice rising. "You call this a gift? Every time I *think* something, being afraid it might actually *happen?* How am I supposed to live with that?"

"Jared, listen, I know you're scared..." Delany's voice is slow and measured, but it grates on Jared's nerves. This isn't what he came here for. He wants it to stop, all the confusion, all the strangeness. Now Delany is trying to pull him back in again.

"No!" Jared says, "It's *not* true. None of it. You're...you're just fucking with my mind. Like you always do."

"Don't be stupid, Jared," Delany says, his voice turning harder again. "You can't ignore something like this..."

"Bullshit! It's not true!"

"Yes it is. It doesn't matter if you want it or not, Jared. It's true."

"Alright," Jared pulls a chair out with a loud bang and sits facing Delany. "*Prove it.* Show me, right now. Or I swear to God, I'm never coming back here again."

Jared sees something change in Delany's eyes, then he comes out from behind his desk, dragging his chair behind him. He sits right in front of Jared, their knees almost touching. Delany's eyes are a few inches away from his, close enough to see the red blood vessels surrounding the pale grey irises.

"Alright," Delany says. "You're angry right now, aren't you?"

A harsh, humorless laugh bursts from Jared's mouth. "What do *you* think?"

"*How* angry?" Delany asks. "How angry do you feel right now?"

Before Jared can answer, Delany slaps his face. Shock blinds Jared for a second. Then rage.

"You want to hurt me right now, don't you?" Jared's throat tightens and he can't answer. "So do it," Delany says. "Think about hurting me. Make it happen."

Jared glares into Delany's eyes, trying to pour all of his anger into this man sitting in front of him. Delany doesn't break eye-contact and keeps staring right back into Jared's eyes, but he's not pushing back, Jared can tell; it's more like he's opening himself up to receive something. Jared shuts his eyes and thinks of the burn, then he pictures the same burn appearing on Delany's arm, then another, and another, crawling up his neck and covering his face, the skin searing and blackening. Jared opens his eyes and sees Delany staring at him, his face clear and unchanged.

"You can't do it," Delany says in a flat voice. "Alright. We'll work on it..."

"No!" Jared says. "That's it. I'm done." He gets up and walks toward the door when he hears Delany call out behind him.

"What about your dad?"

Jared stops. A cold sensation enters his back like the blade of a knife. He turns and sees Delany glaring at him.

"My dad? What about my dad?"

"Think about it. He's better now. But for how long? You changed him. You did that. But you still don't know how it works. You think you don't need me? I just gave you a chance to prove yourself. To prove you can control it. And you failed. You fucking failed. If you can't do one stupid thing like this, what makes you think you can protect your dad?"

Rage floods Jared's brain. *"Fuck you!"* he shouts and storms out of the classroom. He can hear Delany calling his name behind him, but he keeps walking, all the way down to the end of the dark hallway where he punches the door open with both hands and walks out into the late afternoon light, but he can still see Delany's face inches from his, the challenge and taunt in his red-rimmed eyes. *What makes you think you can protect your dad?* He doesn't just want to hurt Delany—he wants to erase him.

Can you feel it? —Jessie's voice—A stab of bright sunlight pierces his skull, blazing down through green leaves above...

Angel Falls.

Suddenly, Jared knows. That flash of light. The power he needs. It's all there, waiting for him. *You want to hurt me? Do it. Make it happen.* He leaps on his bike and starts toward the road, toward the old stones and deep trees, twenty minutes away.

Jared looks up and sees a figure standing in the tall grass across the road. It's a girl standing perfectly still inside a column of pale sunlight filled with swirling particles of dust. His heart leaps. *Jessie?* The sunlight transforms her hair into a disheveled halo of light, but her face is a blank shadow. Then her head turns slightly and light spills onto her features. The cold rises in Jared's guts, because now he can see who it is. It's the missing girl, the one who disappeared a month ago. Karen Holcomb.

She stands in the tall grass, staring at him, expressionless. A sound like the roar of some gigantic animal and a blast of wind hits him in the face—a big truck blasts between them, making Jared cough and wipe his eyes. Before the dust clears, the girl is gone. But that's not what brings the cold feeling in his guts all the way up to his throat. It's what he saw the moment before the truck passed between them. For one split second, the girl standing across the road had no face.

CHAPTER 33

NEW YORK

At 11 a.m., Jessie, her dad and Dylan pull out of the driveway and make their way through Beauport to the Cape highway. She looks up to see the facade of Benjamin Franklin High School, and she squints her eyes in an effort to see Jared's classroom in the back. It's shadowed by trees, and they turn the corner before she's identified which window is his. She wonders if he's there, with Delany. The thought of Delany telling Jared something new and strange——stranger than what they already know—gives her chills.

"A/C too high?" her father reaches for the knob, turns it down. "Or just excited?"

She pulls her thoughts from Jared, tries to look enthusiastic. "Oh, yeah!"

They enter the traffic circle, passing the exit that leads to Angel Falls, and how wrong it feels to pass it by. She turns in her seat to look out the back window, but it's only road and trees. They merge onto a bigger road, and after a few miles they get on the Interstate, shopping malls with identical brand name stores; DSW, Macy's, Target, rise up and fall away. The landscape between them, a mix of greens and browns, is indistinguishable from any other park with trees, making Beauport and Angel Falls seem further away, less possible somehow.

She thinks about New York, about her mom, and suddenly she misses her, purely, simply. Gone is the anger, the fear, the yearning to have her come to Beauport. All she wants is to see her mother's face.

Jessie's going home.

She wonders what's she planning this year. Jessie imagines her mom's hands covering her eyes, making her wait to see... what?

"What's she planning?" And when Dylan refuses to answer, she pinches her.

"Ouch!" Dylan says, scooting away.

"What if I kidnap Rusty, would you tell me then?" She pulls a stuffed golden retriever from Dylan's backpack.

"Really?" she rolls her eyes. "You'd stoop to kidnapping?"

"Deliver the goods or the dog gets it," Jessie intones with a Brooklyn accent shaking Rusty by his neck.

"I'd like to see you try." Dylan grabs at Rusty and they both pull.

"Girls!" Her dad's voice is raised, but not angry. "Jessica, your mother wants to surprise you. You know what that means to her."

"Yeah. I know." And she lets go of Rusty and leans back into her seat. The urge to see her mother growing stronger by the second.

The drive takes forever. They leave Massachusetts and Jessie thinks, *almost home, almost.* But Connecticut is a long road of trees, dappled sunlight, the occasional body of water, and more trees. By the time they cross into New York, there's traffic, more buildings, morphing into familiar landmarks, New Roc Center rising up beside the highway, Coop City apartment buildings clustered in their landfilled swamp. Until finally they turn the corner on a raised highway and there it is: Manhattan, laid out before her with its jewel-like bridges, skyscrapers interspersed with spiderlike cranes, thousands and thousands of windows catching light, rooms, people, excitement, and noise, and there, inside one building, her mother is waiting.

The rush hour traffic forces them to crawl over the bridge, down the highway and through the busy crosstown streets till finally they are on her block, pulling up in front of her building. She jumps out and runs to the door.

Dylan's right behind her, and she hears her dad saying, "Tell your mom I'm parking," before the front door closes and they're inside. The lobby's plain except for a carved wooden structure her mother calls a prayer grille. It covers the wall next to the stairs with knights in armor, ladies with tall, pointed hats and round bellies, dogs and pheasants, cooked birds on platters, goblets of drink. Jessie's loved this piece her entire life and moves straight to it now to put her hand in a lion's mouth. Dylan growls and chomps her teeth together the way she always does, and they laugh.

They both run to the elevator, Jessie beating Dylan by a small fraction, her finger on the button first, Dylan's smashing it with her own. With a "Ping" the elevator doors slide open. Jessie's stomach falls.

"C'mon," Dylan pushes her softly, then pulls her by the hand until she steps awkwardly into the small carriage.

"Do I look different?"

"If you mean stupid, then no. You always look stupid."

"C'mon. Tell me."

Dylan studies her for a few minutes, then the elevator makes the ping sound again, and the doors slide open. "Maybe. Let's go."

Her mom is standing in the hall. Jessie eyes blur and she runs straight into her arms, knocking her backwards a few steps. Her mother's arms are strong, and she squeezes Jessie hard. "Welcome home, welcome home!" her mother says over and over as they rock together.

Jessie blinks away tears and straightens to look at her mother. She's standing at eye level, and this shocks her. Did she grow in the few weeks away?

"You're so tall!" her mother exclaims, "And so brown! Are you using...?"

"Yeah, Mom, I sunscreen all the time. You look wonderful." In person her mother's haircut is even better. Accentuating the angle of her jaw, making her eyes look enormous. She's wearing a loosely fitted linen dress and smells wonderful.

"Hi Mom," Dylan squeezes between them for a quick hug, then steps back and salutes. "Your daughter has been retrieved as ordered, SIR!"

"At ease, officer. Root beer floats anyone?"

Jessie hesitates at the front door. The hallway pegs contain the usual assortment of scarves and summer sweaters, and the late day light is spilling onto the red rug. As she enters and walks among the familiar things, she's surprised and glad that it hasn't changed.

They enter the kitchen and put together the floats. Her mother makes a small one for herself, and on the count of three, they put the straws in and gulp as the foam climbs up and over the sides of the glasses.

They are laughing and slurping up liquid when Jessie's dad comes in.

"Hi Michael." Her mother looks up with the smile still on her face. Jessie looks at her dad, catches a certain cautious frown before it's wiped away by a happy grin. She closes her eyes and thinks *please make it right*.

"Cynthia. You look great."

"Thank you. You're brown. Beauport agrees with you."

Dylan stands and takes her glass to the sink. "I gotta run. My folks *said* they'd be home for dinner." She gives Jessie a squeeze saying, "See you in the morning!" and she grabs her backpack and is gone.

"So," her father says, "now that you've spoiled your appetites, what would you like for dinner?" Jessie looks at him quickly, but he's still smiling. She checks her mom, and she's smiling too. The dread she's been carrying around about the two of them lifts and dissipates.

Jessie falls into being home so easily it surprises her. Dinner conversation is mostly around the play and she's happy to watch the light flickering across her mother's face as she describes rehearsal, the director, changes to the script. "So, Sam walked out, can you believe it?"

"Like a bad movie." Jessie says.

"Exactly!" Her mother chimes in. "Tossing down the script and leaving in a huff. I just laughed. He came back of course, and the changes were brilliant."

After dinner, her mom pulls her onto the couch beside her, squeezing her and kissing her cheek. "I can't believe you're here. I missed you so much."

Jessie settles her head against her mother's shoulder, smiling while her dad sits in his armchair, snapping open the New York Times. "You need a pipe," Jessie laughs.

"Over my dead body," her mother says, but her father mimes one beautifully, a hand holding the bowl, his lips puckered around an imaginary stem from which he takes a puff.

"Now you just behave yourself young lady," he waggles the pipestem in her direction so convincingly she can almost see it. Then he flips the paper back up covering his face.

Her phone chimes several times that evening, birthday wishes from friends, a couple that say *r u excited?* from Dylan.

"What are we doing tomorrow, Mom?"

Her mother pokes her head out of the kitchen, pretends to zip her lips, locking them with a twist of her fingers, and tosses the invisible key over her shoulder.

"I'm fifteen, you don't have to treat me like a kid."

"Not yet, you're not. Not till Sunday. And when have I ever spoiled the surprise?"

Another *ding* from her phone. *Hey Sunday. I miss you. Give me a call.* Jared. Her face warms and her heartbeat becomes erratic. She reads the text again. 'I miss you'? Instantly she feels guilt and then longing. She hadn't missed him, she'd been so enthralled by coming home; by normality. She starts typing *I miss you too* but stops to read his text, again. *Give me a call.*

Is something wrong? She wonders. He's seen Delany. Now the longing's mixed with fear and a hint of resentment. She'd been so happy.

She types, *how about tomorrow morning, around 9?*

His answer is immediate. *Can't. Going out to draw with my dad.* So, maybe nothing bad has happened. A chime sounds. She looks at her phone.

How about the afternoon?

"Mom?" she calls to her mother in the kitchen now. "When are we going back tomorrow?"

Her mom steps back into the room and mimes zipped lips again.

"Really?" Jessie's face twists, but her mother smiles and returns to the kitchen.

Mom's not telling me when we're back. Birthday surprise stuff. Tomorrow night? Might be late.

He doesn't answer, so she puts down her phone and goes into the kitchen to do her usual chore of putting away the dishes.

"Who are you texting?" her mother's voice is soft, unassuming, but Jessie doesn't fall for it.

"Nobody," she says, knowing even as the words exit her mouth that it's a mistake.

"Oh, really?" Her mom's mouth twists in and out of smile. "Is 'nobody' the boy from the fish shop?"

Jessie stares at her mother, then shuts her eyes and drops her head back. "I'm gonna kill him," she whispers.

"Your father is simply keeping me informed. Don't kill him, please," her mother closes a cabinet, and moves back toward the living room.

"It isn't a fish shop. It's Rick's Chowder, and it's the best seafood place on the Cape." Jessie can't stop herself. She feels ridiculous.

"Glad to hear that," she says, and after a moment adds, "'Nobody' just answered."

Jessie runs out to her phone and picks it up.

OK. I guess. Call me whenever. Can't wait to talk to you. This place is creepy without you.

She falls on the couch and stares at the words, smiling and reading them over and over, ignoring her parents as each of them enter the room and stare silently down at their happy child.

Saturday is a whirlwind of motion and delight, and Jessie forgets about everything except the challenges of a treasure hunt designed by her mom and the pure joy of discovering every spot in Manhattan the clues reveal. By the end of the day, she falls back in her bed feeling as if she is still moving, riding subways, cabs, walking the sidewalks and finally a boat ride in the harbor. Something nags at the edge of her mind, something she's supposed to do, but before she can remember, the rocking motion of the remembered boat drags her into a dreamless sleep.

Chapter 34

Stay

Sunday morning following her birthday party, Jessie goes to the kitchen to find the table set with flowers, three small, wrapped boxes, and the remains of her birthday cake.

"Happy birthday, Fifteen!" her mother hugs her from behind. "Eggs or pancakes?"

Jessie eyes the cake, slides it to her place and grins. "I'll have this."

When they've finished eating, after she's opened her presents, her father rises from the table. "Well, we better get a move on."

Jessie and her mother stand, Jessie's stomach beginning to twist. She isn't ready.

Her mother pulls her into a tight embrace, resting her chin on the top of Jessie's head and facing her father. It feels good in her mother's arms, cheek against her mother's throat, a gentle pulse there ticking against her face. She can't pull herself away. "Let me have her for the week. I can bring her up on Saturday."

Her father starts to speak, but only makes a sound, "Uh..."

A week! Part of her leans into the idea with relief. Just stay. Maybe her dad could stay too?

"Pumpkin? Is that okay with you?" Her dad's voice is calm, even cavalier. As if it doesn't matter what she does. She pulls away from her mother and looks at her father's face. He's smiling, but the creases around his eyes don't match. His eyelids droop slightly. She turns to face her mother, ready to say *I want to go back with Dad,* but the words evaporate. Her mother's face is so hopeful, the eyes so much bigger, doe-like, beautiful as always, but also strange. Her skin, with no makeup, is papery and thin. Jessie notices the faint blue tracings of veins at her temples and running down her cheeks.

"Okay," Jessie says slowly, "But when you bring me back, stay for a while." Her mother shakes her head.

"I can't, sweetheart. My play..." her mother waves her hand as if the four walls of their apartment included the other actors, the director, the stage. "This week's rehearsal schedule is light, so I can spend lots of time with you."

"Then come back with us now..." Jessie starts, but her mother is already shaking her head.

"I *have* rehearsal, just not every day."

"Are you coming at the end of August like you said?" her voice is petulant. She turns to her father. "Can you stay here? Then we can all go back together. For the weekend. Go on a whale watch..."

But her father is shaking his head. She is afraid to look at her mom. "I can't, pumpkin. I've got meetings and there's so much work to get the house ready..."

She pictures her father standing by the sink, eating out of a take-out container. One of those round containers from Rick's. *Jared!*

She'd forgotten to call him last night! She feels a rush of heat, followed by cold across the skin of her face and arms. She looks at her mother, at her raised eyebrows, expectant eyes. Then at her father's kind half-smile. If she goes back now, she'll hurt her mom. And the pull of home is strong, it feels so good here. If she stays, she'll hurt her dad. She hates the thought of him alone in that house. And then of course there's Jared. What has he learned from Delany? The need to contact Jared burns in her stomach; he may already be angry with her. Would he even speak with her?

She turns to her mom. "Could you take me back tomorrow?"

Her mother looks at her in surprise, frowning slightly. Jessie steels herself against that disappointment, against her own. Eventually her mother sighs, "Okay. Tomorrow. That okay with you, Michael?"

Her dad smiles now, clearly relieved. Jessie hugs him hard. "See you tomorrow?"

And he nods, moving gently from her arms to the door and is gone.

"I'll just put this away," Jessie indicates her suitcase, takes it back to her room and gently closes the door.

She quickly brings out her phone, types a text to Jared, *Hi. Sorry I didn't call. Fell asleep!* She adds an emoji face-palm and pauses. She types, *Change of plans. Coming back tomorrow. Don't shoot me!!*

She puts her phone on the bed and opens her bag when there's a soft *ping.*

Can't shoot you if you're not here. Everyone okay?

Is he angry? *Everything's fine. Mom wanted me to stay for a week!*

A week? You've got to be kidding.

He is angry. She quickly types, *she's bringing me back tomorrow. It's just one day.*

Maybe you should stay there.

She stares at the words, confused, and hurt. She types: *Maybe I will.* It makes her breathless. Another soft ping makes her look at her phone.

I could make you come back.

Her body turns to ice. She can hear wind in the tops of trees, and she knows they're both thinking of Angel Falls.

Another ping.

Sorry! I'm an idiot, I take it back. Please, please, Jessie...

The text trails off, and Jessie knows what the *please please* is for. The icy feeling starts to wane, though her muscles are stiff, her thumbs slow as she types: *I'll be back tomorrow.*

Call me later, please? I have a lot to tell you.

She types *K,* and *Later.*

Jessie drops the phone and falls back onto her bed. She shivers. Looking around her room, she lets the familiar objects comfort her; stuffed animals on the dresser, toe shoes hanging from the floor lamp, her bookshelf with the ballerina music box open but still. She crosses to it, turns it over and winds it up. The tiny ballerina turns slowly as the music plays and Jessie sees another small figure; the farmer's wife, hand extended as if feeding the geese. Dorothy's house. She should be there. No, not there. In Angel Falls, helping Jared understand what's going on.

She grabs her bag in anger, turns it over, dumping the contents on the bed. A small packet thuds to the floor.

She picks it up. Her grandfather's letters to Dorothy. A chill ripples through her as she sits back on the bed.

"Honey, are you okay?" her mom's soft voice is right at the door.

Jessie freezes, manages to say, "Fine. Just putting my stuff away. I'll be out in a few," then lets out her breath when she hears her mother move back into the living room. She glances back at the letters. She knows she shouldn't have kept them, shouldn't read them. But she's tired of grownups keeping secrets from her.

She pulls one side of the lace bow, and it opens easily, letters fanning out across her legs. She studies the envelopes. The first several letters bear the return address of Boston University. Then she sees one from Camp Edwards dated July 29, 1942, and pulls out the sheet and reads:

Dear Dottie,

Here I am, enlisted man! Hope you're proud of your cuz. I'm building up to carrying the 40 pound packs and guns they have us lugging across the beach every day. Ocean breezes make it so we don't pass out from the heat, makes me think they'll send us to Africa, but I'm hoping for Europe. Guess we'll find out soon. I sure do miss your cobbler. The food is okay, but bland. They say 'chow.' So next time you're sitting down to a nice lobster stew, think of me and my plate of white potatoes and corned beef.
Yum!

She imagines a young man with short-cropped hair, face red from the sun and effort, jogging on a beach in a green uniform, or did they have camouflage? She looks at the date again, 1942. That would be World War II! Images of black and white film scroll behind her eyes, heavy-looking planes dropping bombs, men in helmets struggling out of the water and up beaches, skeletal humans in pajamas lined up against a barbed wire fence.

She folds the sheet and returns it to its envelope. Picks up the next one. It has a much later date; the return address including *England*. The envelope is made of a paper so thin she wonders how it travelled across an ocean, how it survived the years. Inside, pages also thin, covered with loopy blue ink.

September 17, 1943

Well, your wish to get me out of danger worked. Unless you meant to protect me from a pair of beautiful green eyes, and a voice like heaven. But I'm telling it out of order. Guess I didn't want you to think anything bad had happened. It did. But not too bad. Sorry, guess my brains are still rattled from the fall. Broke my leg in two places, cracked my skull. But the doc says I'll be right as rain in a couple of months. They want to send me home, but college came in handy. Seems they need some help analyzing data to help with maps, so the minute I get out of here, I'll be at a desk helping our boys behind the scenes. Not as good as the front, but still part of the team. The war has got to end soon. And with any luck, I won't be coming home alone. Send more good wishes my way.

He was wounded! Jessie looks at the paper again, turning it over and over. Where are the details? How did it happen and what did he mean by 'cracked my skull?' And whose green eyes and beautiful voice? She looks at the next one, postmarked Brooklyn:

July 14, 1945

Father told me you have been ill. I am sorry to hear it, but understand you are on the mend. May this letter find you completely well. If, as I believe, your last letter was written under the influence of a sick and weakened mind, I hope both of us can forget its contents and move on. It's difficult for me to be completely happy (and I am so very happy, Dotty, believe me!) when you are clearly not. So please, congratulate us. As soon as you are completely well, I'll bring her to meet you. You will love Lily, I promise. Everybody does.

Green eyes and beautiful voice? Lily is her grandmother.

May 7, 1946

I was so very sorry to hear about Uncle Nathan. I got your letter the day of the funeral. I wish you'd sent a telegram. You know I would've liked to be there. To say goodbye. To comfort you. I'll try to make a trip soon. It's hard to get away, the firm is getting more work than we can handle. Lily's been unwell, but the doctors say she's getting better. It just takes time.

She pictures a woman in a bed, dark hair fanned out across a pillow, pale cheeks, but still lovely. Her grandmother. Jessie turns to the next letter dated October 29, 1951. It starts out talking about a baseball game on TV. She skims through and then reads:

You keep asking me why I don't come and visit and I'm not sure how to answer. In your letters you make it plain that you want to see me, but when we visit, you are cold and unaccountably busy. I hope I'm wrong about the reason for this. Father enjoys coming to see us in New York, so other than visiting you, I cannot justify taking the time and expense to visit Beauport. And I have no intention of coming there without Lily. I hope these words are not painful for you to read. Give my love to the neighborhood. And to your own self, Dottie. You'll be fine. You'll see.

Jessie has the feeling of the room growing dark, like a cloud covering the sun. *I hope I'm wrong about the reason for this.* She quickly opens another letter. There's a photo inside of a newborn baby.

November 10, 1959

Wanted to share our happy news. Introducing your first cousin once removed (I believe that's the correct term) Michael Theodore Reed, born a strapping 8 pounds 12 ounces. We're hoping to show him off in person by the holidays. I won't hide from you our desire to have Father move down here with us. I don't much care for that fact that he's all alone since the stroke. But he's stubborn. So, for the time being, we'll just have to come to him. We will certainly make time to visit you as well.

Jessie studies the newborn face, looking for her father in it, for herself. But it is the same barely-human look of all newborns, fur-like hair, bleary eyes. A nubby blanket swaddles him tightly so she can't see the tiny hands. Back to the envelopes, and the longest gap so far. Ten years.

July 31, 1969

Thank you for your condolences. I am sorry to be so late in responding, and I hope you will forgive me. Lily's sister must leave by the end of the month. We've been busy looking for a housekeeper, Michael is too old for a babysitter but too young to be completely on his own, and I am an abominable cook. Thank you for your offer, but I'm sure you understand my job, my life is here. I cannot take a leave of absence, nor tear my boy away from everything he's known. We'll be fine, I hope, given time that heals all wounds. Or so they say. I can't imagine this wound will ever close completely.

Her grandmother's death. What did she die of? She hasn't asked it, can't risk the look of pain across her father's face. But now she wants to, needs to know. *Lily's sister.*

Is she still alive?

Jessie reads the next two letters quickly.

January 23, 1971

Thank you for the kind offer to take us in. I thought I was clear in my last letter that we were transitioning to double bachelorhood quite well. Not to mention how New York is our home, the only home Michael knows. But thank you for the offer.

November 2, 1971

Dorothy, I'm sure you have our best interest at heart, but I must ask you to stop. The tone of your letters is unseemly. You may not realize it, but your insistence we suffer 'more than you know' is insulting and insensitive. That we suffer is both inevitable and private. Please do not speak of it again. You are welcome to visit here any time you like, but I do not see us visiting Beauport any time soon. As for the other topic, your 'confession' as you call it, comes not from a valid mind, but from some confusion on your part regarding our long association and deep affection. I am quite sure on further examination you will be as appalled at what you wrote as I was to read it. I will not mention it again.

Jessie's heart is racing. All those pictures in the house of the two of them. Is that why she never married? She looks at the second to the last letter in her lap; it's thin, almost as light as the airmail letter from England. The softness of the paper makes Jessie think it's been handled more than the others. The address is barely legible as if he wrote it during an illness or in a great hurry. She pulls the single sheet out slowly, afraid it will tear, afraid of what she'll find.

May 17, 1972

I relent. Dear Dottie, I give in. I have arranged for Michael to spend the summer in England with his aunt. My partner at the firm seems dismayed but they have agreed to this hiatus. They see the toll your letters have taken on me but know only my continued grief at Lily's passing. I have no more will to fight you. You say, 'Come home,' and I find that I must. My arrival will follow this letter by only a matter of days.

The hair on her arm is standing up and a band of ice circles her chest. There is only one letter left, one she's already read. Postmarked Brooklyn. Dated five months later.

October 28, 1972

As you can see, I am back home. I am writing as you requested, but hope I was very clear that this would be the last. In the name of all that you value, and our good history, don't try to contact me. You made a promise. I expect you to keep it.

"Whatcha reading?"

Jessie looks up, heart in throat. She hadn't heard the door, no footsteps, her mother just appeared and is now sitting on the bed and looking at the letters in her lap.

Too quickly for Jessie to hide them or come up with a lie.

"I found them in Dorothy's house. They're from my grandfather." She sticks her chin out. *My grandfather.* As if being possessive will keep her mother from taking them from her.

"Your grandfather?" her mother looks at the letters frowning. "Does your father know about these?" She reaches for them, and Jessie holds them down in her lap.

"Yes." So far, she hasn't had to lie.

"Have you read them all?"

Jessie frowns, nods. "Did you know about these? Have *you* read them?"

"No! Of course not. How could I?" her mother's expression is difficult to read. Jessie would say she looks nervous, but it makes no sense. Then, as if she knows how carefully Jessie is studying her, her mother's face goes smooth. "Anything interesting there?" It's spoken so casually anyone else would think her mother was only being polite.

Jessie knows otherwise. The questions spill out.

"What happened? Do you know? Why didn't I know about Dorothy, that my grandmother is from England? Do I have other relatives I've never met?"

Her mother bites her lip, looking off into the distance, clearly choosing words.

Jessie's chest tightens.

"What did your father tell you?" she asks without looking at Jessie.

"He told me his father and Dorothy had a... a rift. I think that's what he said. He didn't say why. Do you know?"

"Not much more than that, I'm afraid." Her mother frowns and finally looks at her. "So, Michael gave them to you?" She nods toward the envelopes in Jessie's lap.

Caught, Jessie looks down at the letters, saying nothing.

"Jessie?" her mother draws out her name, in warning.

"He wanted me to put them in the shredder, so I took them. He doesn't know."

"Oh Jessie."

"You won't tell him!? Please?"

Her mother studies her for a moment before gently taking the bundle from Jessie's lap, tugging a little to get them free from her hands. "*1972*," she reads from the final letter. "Your dad was what, twelve? Thirteen?" She frowns for a moment and then her face clears, her lips growing thin and determined.

"Did your father read them?"

"I don't think so."

"Come with me." She stands and walks to the door.

"Where?" Afraid her mother's going to the phone to call her father.

"Just come," spoken softly but with such command, Jessie obeys.

They walk through the living room and out the front door. Jessie realizes where they are headed, before her mother stops in front of the door to the garbage chute. She turns to Jessie and gives her the letters.

"You should do this."

"Mom, no! They're all I have..."

She grabs the thick black handle and jerks open the angled door; the scent of rotten food rises out of its depths.

"Please. I want to keep them!" Jessie knows it's no use. Her mother's face is too calm. It is her actor face, her ability to draw in energy from everything around her, becoming stronger than all the rest, immovable.

She studies the envelopes in her hands, the writing from her grandfather, the paper thin and worn by Cousin Dorothy's touch. Pleading with her eyes, she looks at her mother's face again. She doesn't expect her to say anything, but then she speaks.

"These letters represent a difficult time in your father's life. He doesn't want or need to be reminded of that. I think just being there," her voice is tinged with distaste, "in Beauport, has been hard on him." She gives Jessie a probing look, "Have you noticed anything? Does he act strange or sad? Do you feel anything unusual in that house?" She remembers the way her father stared blank-eyed at the diorama. Then she sees his face as he took the letters from her hand, sad and confused, as if their continued existence surprised him. Jessie's mind is reeling and she's grateful when a door opens across the hall and a neighbor appears, turning to lock the door before greeting them.

"Cynthia, I see the missing chick has returned to the nest."

"Hello Mrs. Bernstein. How are you?"

They chat for a few moments, and Jessie realizes her hands are perspiring, fingers sticking to the letters, leaving marks.

"You be good to your mother, now," Mrs. Bernstein says, looking sternly at Jessie. "She's been awfully lonely without you around." Even before the pang of guilt hits, the woman is smiling at her mother and saying, "Ta-ta," and disappearing down the hall.

Jessie and her mother stand staring after her until they hear the *ping* of the elevator. Her mother looks first at Jessie's face, then the letters, then back to her face.

"You said Michael wanted to destroy these?" Jessie nods, frowning. "Then we should honor that, don't you think?" Tilting her head toward the open chute.

Slowly she raises the letters to the dark hole in front of her, wishing she'd shredded them at first sight, without reading them herself, without opening a door to a world she doesn't understand and which both parents are unwilling to share. They fall from her hands, one of the envelopes sticking for a moment to the wall before detaching and disappearing soundlessly into the dark. The door slams shut making Jessie flinch. "I'm sorry," she says, shuffling back to the apartment, feeling her mom's arm snaking around her waist.

"Me too."

CHAPTER 35

COME BACK

Jared's sitting on the edge of his bed, staring at his phone, waiting for Jessie to call. It's past eleven o'clock, and for every minute that ticks by, his heart beats a little faster, a little wilder. He doesn't want to be the one to call first, because he's afraid of what it will feel like if she doesn't pick up. He hates the thought of interrupting her family celebration, of being an *interruption*. She's in a whole other world now, *her* world, the one he's not part of.

He glances at the time again—almost 11:30. The little screen suddenly lights up with her name, and the phone begins vibrating in his hand, louder and harder than seems possible. He clears his throat and pushes the little button that stops the buzzing and opens up the path across the miles between them. The silence he hears on the other end seems alive—the sound of Jessie waiting.

"Hey," he says, then waits.

"Hey," he hears her voice, cautious and gentle. Already, he feels better.

"So," he says, "How was your big city birthday?" He instantly regrets his choice of words, hopes it doesn't sound angry.

"It was great," she says, and he can hear the happiness in her voice. "It was a big day. Crazy good. Every year Mom tries to top the last one, doing something wild for me, and she did it again."

"Yeah? Like what?"

"A treasure hunt! A real New York City treasure hunt."

A series of ridiculous pictures flash across Jared's mind—Jessie and her friends wearing cardboard pirate hats, a Jolly Roger skull-and-crossbones flag flying over the birthday cake. "A treasure hunt? Really? Where do you bury treasure in the city? Don't tell me you got chocolate gold doubloons or something..."

She laughs. "No, not like that. I mean she gave me clues, each one leading to one of my favorite places; the Cloisters, The Mad Ha... "

"Cloisters? You mean like where nuns live? You got a thing for nuns or something?"

"No!" she laughs again, "*The* Cloisters. Way up at the top of Manhattan? It's a museum, a restoration I guess, of a real building they brought here from Europe. You never heard of it?"

Her question stings. *No, city-girl, I've never heard of it.* He takes a deep breath and changes the subject. "Where else?"

"The Mad Hatter—it's a bakery, they have the *best* cupcakes—then Hans Christian Andersen—Dumbo..."

"Hans Christian Andersen? The fairy tale guy? You *do* know he's dead, right?"

"No, silly. The statue? You know, in Central Park?"

The sting returns—doesn't she realize he's kidding? She can't really think he's that dumb, can she? "Okay, if you say so."

"Oh. It's sweet. A little bigger than life-size, he's sitting down with an open book on his knee, and there's a duck on the ground looking up at him."

"A real duck? So—you like nuns and ducks. What else don't I know about you?"

She laughs long and loud—he loves the sound of it, loves making her laugh like this. *Come back,* he wants to say.

"The last clue took us to South Street Seaport, and we went on a sunset cruise! It was so beautiful..." She pauses for a moment like she's picturing it. He tries to picture it too—Jessie standing at the railing of a schooner, her hair flying like a flag in the harbor breeze, warm sunset colors lighting up her face.

"Sounds nice."

"It was," she says. "So...what have you been up to?"

Jared's head spins, thinking of all the answers to her question. There are so many, too many. He wants to get to all of them, so he picks one and starts...

"I spent the day with Dad."

"Yeah? How is he? He looked so good at the beach. So, what happened? You were going to tell me..."

"He sold some paintings. Got a commission. It's crazy. I mean, I came home the other night. Jeez, was it only Wednesday? And he was cooking! And he cleaned up the apartment, everything. Like he used to."

"Jared, that's wonderful!" her voice full of happiness for him, "I'm glad. Really glad."

"Me too." The happiness slips away as he says it.

"What?" she asks, and he thinks she must hear it in his voice. "What is it?"

"I saw Delany after school..." then he can't say any more. He wants to tell her, and he doesn't.

"What. You're making me nervous. Spit it out."

"Delany told me...he thinks I'm one of them. One of those people from Angel Falls. Like in the history. All that stuff about them bringing their loved ones back. He says it really happened, that they had this *power*... And I'm one of them."

She doesn't speak for a moment. *Say something,* he thinks. *For Christ's sake, say something.* When she does finally speak, her voice is soft and cautious.

"What do *you* think?"

"What do *I* think? I think he's fucking nuts." Another pause—he wishes he could see her face. When she speaks again, her voice sounds even more cautious than before.

"What else did he say?"

"He...he says he thinks I made my dad better." He waits for her to say *that's crazy.* When she doesn't, he goes on, alone. "He's nuts. I mean, my dad sold some paintings, that's all. He made a lot of money and the guy at the gallery wants him to have a show. I mean that's enough to make anyone feel better, isn't it?" Silence again. *Say something, damn it.* "Jess? Hey Jess, are you there?"

"Yeah, I'm here..." Her voice sounds worried, distracted. "Jared...*did* you wish for your dad to get better?"

"Of course I did. I wished that all the time. That doesn't mean I'm *magic* or something."

"What about your arm?" Her voice is quiet but deliberate—she's not backing down on this, he can tell, and the anger flares up again.

"Jesus, Jessie, it's not the same thing!"

"I know, I know," she says. "It's just...do you remember that last time we were in Angel Falls. When you told me about your dad... you know? And you sort of blacked out or something. Is that what you did then? Wish for your dad to get better?"

Jared knows the answer, but he can't say it.

"Jared?"

"Yeah. Yeah, I'm here..."

"Did you? Wish for your dad to get better?

Yes. Yes, I did.

"So what if I did? That doesn't mean anything. He sold some paintings, for Christ's sake..."

"You *did*, didn't you? You wished for your dad to get better. You blacked out. And when you went back home, he *was*."

It closes around him, the certainty he hears in Jessie's voice.

"It's true, isn't it?" Jessie says.

"No! Why are you saying that? You know how crazy that is?"

"Jared, calm down..."

"No! You think I *want* this?"

"I'm not sure you have a choice."

"Jesus, that's what Delany said! You think I want to be some kind of goddamn freak...?"

"Jared, listen...have you ever stopped to think...maybe you're not the only one?"

"What do you mean?"

"I mean...think about it. All those people from Angel Falls, the ones who got driven out of Beauport because people thought they were bewitched or possessed or something...how many of them do you think there were? A hundred? Maybe a couple of hundred? Those people had children, right? And those children had children too..."

"Okay, I get it," Jared says, "My last name on that tombstone...I saw it too, Jessie. I was there."

"Yeah? Did you see all the *other* names? All those tombstones, Jared. They're *families*. They're children and grandchildren and great grandchildren."

"But..." Jared stammers, "How come I never heard of anyone?"

"Would you tell anyone? If you didn't have to?"

Jared tries to wrap his mind around what Jessie is saying. All those names on the tombstones, the faces of all the other kids in his classroom, of all the men, women, and children he's seen all his life walking right past him in the stores and restaurants and on the street, how many of them are carrying a secret like his?

"Jared?" her voice breaks into his thoughts. "I...I know this is going to sound weird...Just listen, okay?"

"Okay..."

"I found these letters. They're from my grandfather. He wrote them to his cousin Dorothy..."

"You mean Biddy Hicks?"

"Yeah. I think she was in love with him. I mean, you can tell from some things he says in the letters. But he wasn't in love with her. She kept trying to get him to leave New York and come back to Beauport. To be with her. He kept saying no. Then..."

"Then *what?*"

"I think she made him come back."

"What do you mean, she *made* him come back?"

"You know what I mean."

Jared pauses, letting what she's saying sink in. "How do you know?"

"It's the things he says, the way he says them. First he says no, then he sort of gives in and comes back. He says he doesn't have *the will* to fight her anymore. You can just tell...there's something *not normal* about it. My dad doesn't want to talk about it. And my mom...she found me reading the letters...and she made me throw them away."

"Jesus."

"Jared, I think Cousin Dorothy was one of those people. You know, like in the history."

"But...she wasn't from Angel Falls."

"Yes she *was.* She moved to Beauport when she was like two or something. I'm telling you, Jared, I think she was *one of them.*" She pauses—when she speaks again, her voice is quieter, almost hesitant. "That means I could be one of them too."

"Are you serious?"

"Think about it, Jared. The scar on your arm going away. The deer. What if *I* did all that?"

We did it, Jared thinks. *You and me.* He's known this and has felt it for a while. Now that she's said it aloud, it feels like a wall falling down inside of him.

"Yeah. Yeah. I do." He hears a strange, soft sound and thinks she's crying. "Jess, don't. I'm sorry..." The sound she's making grows louder and clearer, and he realizes with a shock that she's laughing.

"I'm sorry..." she says, catching her breath. "I guess it's just...it's just the relief or something, you know? When you said you believe me. It's like, I'm not crazy."

"*We're* not crazy," he says, and a smile he didn't expect takes over his face—he hopes she can hear it.

"No," she answers, the smile in her voice coming through loud and clear. "We're not crazy."

Just like that, the distance between them closes until it's as if she's with him. Neither one of them speak for a while—he thinks she must feel it too.

"Jared..." she says after a while, and it's as if her cheek is resting on his shoulder.

"Yeah?"

"Will you help me do something?"

"Yeah, sure," he says, sinking back into the pillow and the comforting sound of her voice.

"Help me make a wish. Go to Angel Falls with me so I can wish for something."

A pang of alarm shoots through his chest. He sits upright. *"What?"*

"When I get back. There's a wish I want to make. I want to try it."

"No! Jess, listen, you don't want to fool around with this stuff."

"I'm not talking about fooling around! I'm serious."

Then it comes to him. "It's your mother, right? It's about her." Her silence tells him he's right. "You want to make her come here, like she promised. Jesus, Jessie, why don't you just *ask* her?"

"You think I haven't?" He can hear the grief and anger in her voice. "I *have* asked her! I'm *tired* of asking!"

"So now you're going to *make* her come." It sounds like a judgement, he knows. But she needs to hear it. "Jessie, listen. This stuff...it's dangerous. It really is. When I was with Delany the last time, I was so angry at him, I wanted to kill him. And I almost did it. I mean...I tried to make it happen."

"But he *didn't*, right? He didn't die."

"No. But he *could* have."

"But...this is different—me wanting my mom to come here. That's a *good* thing, right? How could that be bad?"

"I don't know..."

"Please, Jared. I just want to try. Maybe I *am* crazy, I don't know. Maybe we're both crazy. I just want to find out. Please?"

"I don't know..."

"Jared, please...I can't do it by myself. Please."

Jared closes his eyes, takes a deep breath, and lets it out slowly, feeling the last trace of resistance melt away. *You've got a lot more power than you think.*

"Okay," he sighs.

"Okay?"

"Yeah, sure. I mean, it's your birthday, right?"

A small, choked sound comes over the phone. He's not sure if it's a sob or laughter. When she speaks again, he can hear her smiling.

"Thanks. That's sweet."

"Yeah," he says, "That's me, alright. Sweet."

"So, three o'clock, Monday, Angel Falls?"

"Sure. Three o'clock, Monday."

"Good," he can still hear her smiling, can see it in his mind. "See you there, okay?"

"Okay."

"Okay. Good night..."

"Good night."

Jared hears the phone go dead. Now that the warm sound of her voice is gone, panic starts to rise in his chest. Why did he agree to what she asked? He'd tried to tell her it was dangerous. Like wanting Delany dead.

Then he remembers the girl, Karen Holcomb, the way she stood watching him from across the road, more motionless than a living thing should be. He'd wanted to tell Jessie. He knows it should be a good thing, a missing girl returning. Why didn't he tell her? Because of what he saw or thought he saw in that flicker of an instant before the truck passed between them? How her face seemed to vanish a split-second before the rest of her did? How could he ever explain *that?*

CHAPTER 36

ONE WRONG MOVE

Monday morning, Jared wakes up to the smell of coffee and bagels toasting in the kitchen. He's still not used to this, to being taken care of, and the surprise and joy of it hits him all over again, like the first time.

He walks into the kitchen and sees his dad standing at the counter, stirring eggs in a bowl. Jared knows his dad was up late last night working on the big painting; the deadline is coming up, and the rich guy from New York will be here soon to collect what he's paid for.

His dad looks over his shoulder and smiles. "Hey, buddy. How'd you sleep?"

"Pretty good," Jared says. "You?"

"Oh, you know. No rest for the wicked," his dad smiles. He looks so happy, so together, and ready for anything, Jared decides he's going to tell his dad everything.

About Delany, about Angel Falls. All of it.

His dad turns around and pours the eggs into the pan where they crackle and sizzle. "Grab yourself some coffee, buddy."

Jared shuffles over to the thermos, pours himself a big mug of French Roast, stirs in a couple of spoons of sugar, then goes into his dad's bedroom to look at the big painting that's propped against the far wall. It's taking shape; all the white gessoed canvas is gone now, covered with sand, sky, and water. The ocean is a vast whirlwind of brushstrokes, thousands of them, grey, blue, green, and white, and the lighthouse standing up against the sky looks so real Jared feels like he could walk around it.

Something in the corner catches his eye. It's the same dark figure he recognizes from the pencil sketch his dad did when they were at the beach together. A lone woman in the background, walking across the sand, the same dark dress and long dark hair whipped by the wind. Like before, the figure has no face. At first Jared assumes that his dad hasn't gotten around to painting the face yet. But there's something wrong about it.

Jared looks closer and sees the careful brushstrokes of shading and light, giving the face contour and dimension. He realizes with a cold feeling in his gut is that his dad hasn't neglected to paint the face—it's a face with no features, only faint shadows where the eyes and mouth should be, like hollow places grown over with thin pale skin.

"You like it?" he hears his dad's voice behind him.

Jared doesn't know what to say. "Yeah. It's good..." He follows his dad out to the kitchen table where they sit and eat in silence for a moment. *I can't do it,* Jared thinks. *I can't just not say anything.*

"Hey, Dad. That woman, in the painting. Who is she?"

His dad stops chewing and looks up. Jared notices that his dad hasn't shaved, and the dark circles under his eyes are starting to return.

"Who *is* she?" his dad repeats in a dazed-sounding voice.

"Yeah," Jared says. "Who is she?"

Jared's dad keeps staring at him. His mouth hangs open a little, and Jared can see the half-chewed bagel inside. Jared can hear the clock ticking on the wall, loud as a hammer. "I don't know," his dad says. "It's just ... somebody. Just somebody."

Jared studies his dad's face and for a moment he sees a glimpse of the old dad, the one who never slept and then slept for days, the one who couldn't go outside or put two words together or even make a meal for himself. It's a glimmer, a flash, like a flickering light bulb that's loose in its socket. But Jared has seen it.

The clock on the wall is hammering even harder; Jared looks up at it and realizes it's time to leave for school. He looks back at his dad who's still staring into space; he looks smaller, lost in his chair, like a child.

Jared hasn't been afraid to leave his dad alone for ... how many days has it been? How many days since he's been able to stop being afraid like that?

"Dad," he says, "You okay?"

"Sure, buddy," his dad says. His smile is back, his eyes normal again. "Why?"

"Nothing," Jared says, "No reason. See you later..." Jared closes the door without looking back.

Down on the street, Jared climbs onto his bike and lets gravity pull him down the hill, faster and faster. *"Fuck!"* he shouts into the wind. *"Fuck—Fuck—Fuck!"* His voice shreds on the last one, tears blur his vision, and he rubs them away with the back of one arm. *This can't be happening,* he thinks. But he knows it can. He saw the empty, haunted look on his dad's face. And now he can't un-see it.

Delany's words come back to him. *You changed him. You did that.* What made him think it would last?

As soon as he walks inside the school, Jared feels assaulted by the usual cacophony of loud voices, senseless shouting, and pointless laughter. He hates it, hates this place, can't wait for it to end. Six hours of this before he can go to Angel Falls, before he can see Jessie again. Is she back from New York? He wants to see her, to hear her voice in person, not trapped in a cell phone, squeezed down to something smaller than she is.

He thinks of what she told him, *it's more dangerous if you pretend it isn't real,* and resentment flares inside him. Why shouldn't he ignore it? All those talks with Delany, all those stupid stories from the past. What good has any of it ever done him?

He waits outside the classroom, letting it fill up before he goes in—he doesn't want to risk being alone in the room with Delany. Then he looks up and sees Delany walking down the hall, coming right toward him. Jared starts to go inside but Delany is quicker and slips between him and the door.

"So," Delany says in a low voice, "See you after school today. Right?"

Jared tries to slip past, but Delany lowers his arm and blocks him. "Right?" Delany says again. When Jared tries to slip under Delany's arm, Delany takes hold of his shoulder, and Jared pulls away.

"Don't touch me again," Jared hisses, "or I swear to God, I'm gonna call the security guards."

Delany's face goes slack. He looks stunned. He stares at Jared for a moment, then lets his arm drop, and Jared quickly slips past him into the classroom and into his seat, taking deeps breaths to slow down the beating of his heart.

Delany walks to the front of the classroom, pauses in front of the dry erase board and stares at it, even though there's nothing written on it. For a moment, he looks like he can't remember what he's supposed to be doing. It reminds Jared of his dad standing in front of one of his paintings, looking helpless and lost.

Delany turns to the bookcase, scowls at the books for a moment, then pulls one out, flips it open and starts walking up and down the front of the classroom, thumbing through its pages. He stops, stares intently at the page open in front of him, then begins to read.

> *"The feelings that hurt most, the emotions that sting most, are those that are absurd. The longing for impossible things, precisely because they are impossible; nostalgia for what never was; the desire for what could have been; regret over not being someone else; dissatisfaction with the world's existence. All these half-tones of the soul's consciousness create in us a painful landscape, an eternal sunset of what we are."*

The words sear into Jared's chest and burn. He hears Delany snap the book shut, then his voice, hard as iron. "Who can tell me what that means?"

Jared hears the familiar uneasy shuffling from the desks and chairs around him, one or two nervous sighs.

"Jared?"

Jared doesn't answer. He keeps his eyes trained on a spot in the corner of the room.

"Jared…" Jared thinks he hears a softening in Delany's voice, almost like a plea, and it pierces his chest like a knife. He takes a deep breath and lets it out, turns away from Delany and looks out the window at the green leaves outside.

There's a silence in the classroom, deeper than before. Jared hears something in the middle of all that silence, a harsh, labored sound; the hair on Jared's neck stands up; it's Delany's breathing getting louder.

"Anybody?" Delany raises his voice this time. "None of you geniuses can figure this one out?" Another wave of nervous noises ripples through the classroom. "Alright," Delany says, "How about this? Everybody here gets three hours detention." A roar of outrage rises up around him, and Delany has to shout to be heard above it. "I want a five-hundred-word essay on what I just read. And the winner gets *one* hour detention." The room explodes with angry groans and curses. Jared sits as still as he can, letting the waves of noise rise and break over him.

"This is bullshit!" Johnson yells. Delany's eyes swing toward the angry boy and lock onto him.

"You know what's bullshit, Johnson?" Delany shouts, his face turning red. "I'll tell you what's bullshit. Someone who doesn't respect their own mind. Someone who has a brain, and a heart, and a mind, and is too stupid to use it. And when they get the chance to use it, when someone hands it to them on a silver platter, they piss on it. *That's* bullshit!"

Jared digs his fingers into the edge of his desk, trying to remain invisible.

"Three hours detention is bullshit," Johnson yells. "You can't do that! I didn't do anything!"

"That's right, Johnson," Delany says. "You never do anything. Except take up space."

"This is abuse!"

"You want abuse?" Delany's voice sounds thicker, dangerous. "You don't know what abuse is."

"You want to abuse kids?" Johnson hurls the words at Delany. "Why don't you go home and abuse your own."

Delany's face turns dark red. Then he grabs the boy by his shirt and hauls him up onto his feet. Kids shout and scream, surging away as Delany and Johnson start grappling and punching at each other. They fall to the ground, and the crowd of shouting kids close in around them, blocking Jared's view. Jared knows he should do something, but he can't make himself get up from his desk.

A uniformed security guard rushes through the doorway and wades into the bodies, then disappears into them like a diver. A few moments later he reappears with Johnson locked in his arms, the boy's lip bloodied and swollen. The guard pushes Johnson toward a teacher waiting outside the door, then drags Delany to his feet. Delany is breathing heavily, and his teeth are red, smeared with blood. The guard puts his hand on Delany's arm and Delany knocks it away angrily, then lowers his head and walks out of the classroom with the guard following close behind.

The rest of the day seems to move in a blur of slow-motion—Coach Harrison coming in to growl at everyone to calm down, police officers in the hallway with their radios spitting static, Principal Hawkins talking with the officers in a hushed voice. Then, like a flock of blackbirds all bursting from a tree at the same time, the police move away together, the statics bursts of their radios growing farther and farther away with them.

When the bell finally rings at three o'clock and everyone gets up to leave, the kids are talking in low voices, quieter than usual. Jared stays in his seat and waits until the room is empty. The image of Delany being taken from the classroom, bloodied, and bowed, still in his head.

He looks around at the empty desks, at Delany's book still lying on the floor where he'd dropped it. *The feelings that hurt most...* Jared doesn't want to think about the rest. His stomach clenches as he realizes—he'll never hear Delany read again.

Jared rises to his feet, picks up his book bag, then moves through the door and down the hall toward the afternoon sunlight. Saying the words in his head, over and over.

It's not my fault. It's not my fault...

CHAPTER 37

A NEW PATH

Jessie's on her bike pedaling hard towards Angel Falls. It had been a quick ride from New York, helping her mom run lines, talking, and laughing. But always, in the back of her mind she was thinking of the woods, of Jared, of her wish.

"Fuck!" It's a man's voice. Jessie looks up to see a car stopped in the middle of the road, the driver's head barely visible above the hood of the car as he curses and struggles with something. She slows her bike, not wanting to see what it is.

The man groans, and she can hear the sound of something being dragged. There's no one else around. This stretch of road has never felt so deserted. If she hurries, she can keep the car between them and maybe he won't notice her.

She stands on the pedals and pumps hard, the bike gaining speed as she starts to pass the car. She can make out tan fur, red-splattered white legs. A deer!

Jessie keeps going, eyes on the road, hoping the man won't see her, won't say anything to her.

On the incline, she has to pedal hard to move at all, so she hasn't gone far when she hears an engine revving, tires spitting gravel and the car speeds past, hot air whipping her hair against her face. *Still speeding!* She thinks, *Asshole.*

She stops and looks back at the spot where he dragged the deer. She can see the rise of a pale belly, one leg at an angle. Tears fill her eyes.

Then the leg twitches.

"Oh my god," she says aloud, turning her bike and pedaling back. He left it alive?

The head lifts slowly, and Jessie stops. Its eyes are black and huge, and the doe lunges with her head, struggling to rise.

"Don't!" she drops her bike and walks towards it, hands extended.

The deer scrabbles in the dirt, causing clouds of dust, then rocks forward, getting her hind legs under her. She rocks back and she is up on three legs.

The doe shakes all over, stares at Jessie for one cold moment, then hobbles away, one back leg dragging. And where that leg meets the body, she sees a familiar long white scar.

Jessie starts to shake. She is in bright hot sunlight, yet her body is freezing. The deer disappears into the dense foliage lining the road.

She walks the bike on shaky legs to the next level bit of road, then rides it into the park, onto the path and finally to the moraine.

Jared is standing there smiling until she gets closer.

"What's wrong?" And he's taking her bike from her, leaning it against the tree, pulling her to a rock and making her sit.

"There was a deer. A car hit it. The man was pulling it off the road…" She's shaking now and holds her arms tight trying to make it stop.

His places his hand on her back. "Did he say something to you? What happened?"

"No, no, he left. And then…" She sees the eyes of the deer so clearly, dark, and full of something - what? - pain? - accusation? "She got up." She looks at Jared. "How did she do that?"

He shakes his head, "I dunno. Maybe she was just stunned."

"No, no, no! You don't understand. I saw the scar. It was the same deer!"

Jared looks confused, and then his eyes widen. "You mean…the one we saw before? The one with the limp?"

"I fixed her, remember? I did that! It was me. And now this happened. Shit."

"You don't know that."

"Yes I do! I wanted her to be well. I wished it, just like when you wanted your burn to go away. Everything got still and clear. Then we saw her again, and she wasn't limping anymore. And now this!" She puts her head in her hands. "Her leg… it was mangled, I don't know how she got up and walked away. It was horrible."

She feels Jared's arm come around her as he sits beside her. "It'll be okay," he says. "I'm sorry. We'll be okay."

She remembers this is supposed to be their reunion. She can still hear Jared saying *come home,* how warm it made her feel. She'd hoped he would kiss her. Then they'd walk hand-in-hand deep inside Angel Falls and she would make her wish. All ruined.

"Delany hit a kid in class today."

Her eyes pop open and she sits up. "He hit a kid? Why?"

"I don't know." He's staring at the ground looking miserable. "Delany was riding this kid, Johnson, riding him and riding him. I felt bad for him.... And then they were on the floor punching each other. The security guard took Delany out of the building."

"Why would he do something like that?"

Jared head drops. "Maybe... maybe I said something."

"What?"

"I told him I was finished. Not going to meet with him after school anymore."

"You told him that? What did he say?"

"Nothing. I just went into class, and he started acting weird."

"But what about the boy? What did *he* do? He must have said something."

"He did. He...he said something about Delany hitting his own kids. That's when Delany went ballistic."

She remembers Delany's house, the swing set. "*Does* he have kids?"

"I don't know. He never said."

"What did you do? When it happened?"

Jared drops his eyes, turns away from her. "I didn't do anything. I just watched."

She wants to comfort him but doesn't know what to say. She puts her hand on his shoulder, squeezes gently. After a moment, he looks into her eyes and says, "There's something... else. I think I saw Karen Holcomb."

There's a pleading look in his eyes, like he's asking for something, and it takes a second to recognize the name. "The missing girl?" He nods. "You *think* you saw her?"

"Something's wrong with her. I mean it was her face."

Jessie wants to be relieved. The girl's alive! She flashes on the parents crying on TV, wishing their daughter safely home. Now she imagines the tight embrace of parents and child, tears again, but happy ones. Except Jared's face is saying something different.

"Did you talk to her?" she presses him. "What did she say?"

He shakes his head without speaking, looking at the moraine. He jumps to his feet.

"C'mon!" And he leaps onto the nearest boulder and then he's running, leaping across the moraine.

"Jared! Wait!" She has to move fast to keep up. When they pass through the gap in the low stone wall and enter Angel Falls, Jessie stands still and closes her eyes. The clarity runs up through the soles of her feet and throughout her body.

When she opens her eyes, Jared is standing still, waiting for her. She runs to catch up and they walk in silence for a while.

"Where does that go?" Jessie points to a trail they haven't taken before.

"I don't remember this one." He walks forward, pushes aside a tall dangling weed. He turns back to her. "Wanna see where it goes?"

"Will we get lost?"

"Maybe. Are you a-skeered?"

She smiles. "Nope. Let's do it."

This path is darker, the trees closer together, the canopy covered over almost completely. There is light, but it is a green light and shadows are everywhere. The path, narrower than the ones they are used to, twists and rises alongside a brook they can hear but have trouble making out through the brush. As they walk, the scent of honeysuckle rises and falls, and though Jessie looks for it, she can't see any pale-yellow flowers. Beside the trail, clouds of red dots lead them to raspberry bushes, and they stop to pick some, popping them into their mouths and letting the warm fruit burst into juice on their tongues. They walk in silence for a few steps, shoulders brushing, then she feels his hand slide into hers.

Suddenly, she can't see, or hear, or breathe. She doesn't know if they are walking, if he is talking, all she knows is *Jared's hand*. Her heart stutters, she feels it thumping against her chest. And yet there's something natural about it too, like his hand has been in hers all along. She closes her eyes for a moment, letting the warmth of his hand soothe her, quiet her trembling.

Jared says, "How's your mom? Was she okay about you coming back today?"

And there it is. Jessie can't believe she's forgotten one of the reasons she was coming here. "Jared," she stops and turns to him, keeping hold of his hand. "I want to make a wish. I want you to help me. You have to say yes. You have to."

He looks at the ground, "Jessie, I want to. I really do, but there's something..."

"What?"

"It's my dad. I'm worried."

"Your dad? What happened?"

He starts to walk again, and she steps quickly beside him. "I dunno. Maybe it's nothing. But ... His face ... It was for just a minute, the one he used to have, blank. Like he's a million miles away. Like *he's* gone." He's walking ahead of her a little so she can't see his face, but his voice is uneven, a little hoarse.

"You said it was just a minute. How is he the rest of the time?"

"I guess he's good," Jared says. "I mean in comparison. Great really. He talks to me like he used to, still cooking and stuff, painting..." he trails off.

Jessie opens her mouth to offer encouragement, but the words aren't there. And then she hears rushing water, not a brook, something faster, bigger.

"Jared, listen."

"What?"

"The Falls! Can you hear it? I bet we're close..."

"I told you. I looked everywhere..."

"Not here. You told me you didn't know this path!" She starts walking ahead. "I bet it's here!" and then she starts running.

"Jessie, wait!" She hears Jared behind her, but doesn't stop, she hears the water over the sound of their pounding feet and for a few moments all the other things fall away. She is running, and it feels good.

"Stop! Jessie, it's getting further away," Jared's voice is close behind her, she doesn't want to, but she stops to listen. And he's right. She turns to him.

"Don't move!"

She freezes, watching Jared as he stares at her shoulder, then something touches her skin, lightly. A bug! "Oh! Get it off get it off!" she says softly, somehow without moving, and Jared smiles. "Not funny, get it off!"

"Just turn your eyes and look."

"I don't want to!"

"Just look, Jessie." His words are so tender, she obeys, turns her eyes, and catches a moving wing, bright orange and black, turns a little more till she can see it all, a butterfly resting on her shoulder, and then it lifts off and flutters away.

They both follow it with their eyes, Jessie dropping hers first to find Jared still staring, his face open and relaxed, eyes wide. She feels her heart jerk.

"You hungry? Let's sit over there." Jared doesn't wait for her, he's pushing his way through low bushes, and under tree branches and she has to hurry to catch up.

The woods open up to a small meadow with a grassy mound.

"Ye olde burial ground," Jared intones in a deep voice, swinging off his pack and plopping on the grass.

She hesitates, not sure if he's joking. The mound seems too perfectly centered; the trees look like a circle of tall frozen men. She kneels down and sits on her heels.

"Jared," she says after a moment, "I think I'm ready."

"For what?"

"To make my wish."

"Your mom, right?" And when she nods. "Jessie, I don't... I mean, it's not a good idea."

"You said you would."

"I know, but..."

"Please!" The need in her rises like a cold fist in her chest, "You don't know what it's like. I feel I'm losing her."

"I bet she feels the same." He says it softly, but it stings.

"What do you mean?"

"I'm pretty sure it was you who left New York for Beauport." Jessie's certainty cracks, and it hurts. She'd been so sure what needed to be done, and now... He's right. Jessie was the one who left.

She has an image of her mother sitting in their apartment, a candle on a table, holding hands with Gregor, wishing Jessie home. She wants to laugh but the image chills her.

She looks at Jared. "Do you really think this power is a bad thing?"

Jared pauses, gazing off in the distance. "Yes. I guess. I don't know. I gave myself a fucking burn. I brought my mom back and that was a mistake."

"But what about your dad? You made him better, right?"

"I... I guess. I don't know. What do you want me to say?"

"I want you to say it's okay for me to make my wish."

"Jessie..."

"My parents are tearing apart. If Mom could just come here, be with us for a while, she'd change, I know she would, I..." the tears are there before she can prevent them, the lump filling her throat, so she stops, squeezes her eyes tight, breathes deeply to get under control.

"Jared, listen, please. Maybe it's not a curse at all. Maybe we can do good."

"You wanna be a superhero? Did you ever notice superheroes have no lives?"

She stares at the grim line of his mouth, the determined eyes in disbelief. He promised her he'd help.

She wonders if she needs him. Maybe he has to be here with her, but what if she doesn't need him to do anything? Maybe all she needs, right here, right now, is to wish her mother to come to Beauport and stay the summer. For her to fall in love with the village, the house, her dad, and for them to be happy, all three of them, together, always. She feels it starting, it's cool and sure and powerful, a slow surge from her feet upwards.

"Jessie, stop!"

She opens her eyes, not knowing when she closed them. Jared's face is close, the crease between his eyebrows deep.

"You were doing it, weren't you?"

Her eyes jerk away from his. She wants to lie but can't.

"Jesus, Jessie." She looks back and he's shaking his head. "I want you to promise me something. Don't ever try it without me. Do you promise?"

She doesn't want to. She's sure he'll tell her no, but she nods.

"Don't ever make a wish here unless we agree. Will you promise me that?"

"But Jared, I need…"

"Because this thing is so big… we don't know how big… and you're smart, I know that… but alone? It's so fuckin' easy to make a mistake. And what if we do that? Make a mistake we can't fix? I can't be responsible for that."

She feels the stiffness in her face and realizes she's folded her arms. A stubborn child. She looks at Jared, sees the certainty there, on top of fear, as if the fear were making it possible. As if he believes he can keep them both safe. She wants that so much.

"Alright, what are we supposed to do?"

"Agree. Work together. You're smart. You say I am too, so trust me here. We need each other. So, please. Don't do it alone."

He's not going to let her do it. She frowns and bites her lip so it doesn't shake. She looks at him, and her determination weakens.

"Okay," she says finally. "What now?"

He runs his hand through the tall grass beside them, tugging gently at one long blade. She can almost hear his thoughts, struggling for ways to let her down easily, to tell her no. But then he lifts his head and looks her in the eye.

"You can make the wish…"

Jessie claps her hands, "Yes!"

"But…." she lowers her hands and looks at him. "You need to be very clear, okay? And it can't be just for you. The wish needs to help your mom too. What if she really doesn't want to be with your dad anymore?"

"But you didn't see them this weekend. They were so friendly together, happy even."

He keeps looking at her, eyes steady. "That's great." But she can tell he doesn't believe it.

"Okay, then. So, I should think; 'Can Mom come here to be with Dad and me if it makes her happy?'"

He nods. "Just keep everyone in mind, your dad, your mom, not just you."

Jessie starts to close her eyes, but then she looks at Jared, smiles a little. "Thank you." He blinks, then smiles back, nodding once, and so she closes her eyes. Instantly a picture of her mother comes, lovely and independent, walking into the house in Beauport.

The dream mother is clear in her mind, smiling and beautiful, her face full of love. She comes first to Jessie to embrace her; it feels so real, she can smell her delicious perfume. She then goes to Jessie's father who looks like he's under a powerful spell, stunned and happy. They kiss on the mouth, and Jessie feels it in her own skin; not the kiss, but the heat it generates. And then they're taking her hands and walking on the beach, it's Horseshoe Beach, the island is outlined sharply against the sky, the sun is setting and her parents' faces glow orange to gold. "Jessie," her mother says softly, then more urgently, and then it's not her voice at all and everything goes dark.

"Jessie."

Her eyes fly open. Her skin is tingling everywhere. She is lying on the grassy mound and Jared leaning over her, face full of worry.

"What?" She sits up, dizzy and slightly nauseated.

"You ... went away. What did you wish?" He sounds frightened.

"I saw my mother come in the door. At Beauport. She was happy, Jared." She sees it like a movie that keeps going, they are at the dinner table in Cousin Dorothy's house, playing a board game and laughing. "It was perfect, Jared, really."

"How do you feel?"

The movie stops. Jared's face comes into focus. "Weird. Fine. A little weird."

"Well then. Weird it is." And Jared stands, extends a hand to her, and pulls her to her feet, and they walk out of the clearing to the path.

"I felt something," he says.

Jessie is still seeing the images, not new ones, but the first ones, Mom walking in and kissing her dad. She can't remember ever seeing them kiss on the mouth.

Jared speaks again. "I felt something. While you were... wishing."

She turns and stares at him. "What? Felt what?"

"I don't know, it's like... I *saw* it. The three of you in your cousin's house. It was nice. You looked ... happy. Then I opened my eyes, and you were...you know, out of it."

"You saw it?" Jessie's still seeing it herself, stunned at how real it seemed. Could he see it too?

There's a crashing in the trees as something large makes its way towards them. Jared places himself in front of Jessie as a doe staggers onto the path. *The doe*, Jessie thinks, seeing its back leg dragging, the familiar white scar. Nothing about her shape is right, the crooked dangly leg, her torso flattened in one part, something poking under the skin, Jessie thinks it must be a broken bone. There is blood dripping from her mouth, and pain and fear in her eyes.

"Oh my god. Is that the deer?" Jared asks her, his arms slightly raised as if the deer might charge them.

Jessie eyes fill and tears start running down her cheeks. The deer's eyes are enormous, wet, and they stare and stare. "We have to do something. What can we do?"

Jared shakes his head, staring hard at the deer who should not be standing, how can she still stand? The deer staggers a few steps, falls to her knees, struggles up, falls again.

She's crying harder now, can barely speak, but manages, "Is she dying?"

Jared's eyes haven't moved from the deer since she entered the path. He shakes his head slowly, "I don't think she can."

"Don't think she *can*?"

The deer has struggled to her feet again, the lopsided torso undulating with the effort. The deer makes an awful sound, something like a barking moan.

Jessie can't watch. "What do we do?"

"We have to wish it."

"What?" She doesn't want to understand what he's saying.

"We have to help her out of this. Help her... go."

"You want to kill her?"

"She's dead already. Look!"

"No."

"Wish it! We have to."

"No we don't," Jessie starts crying hard.

Jared takes both hands in his and shakes them till she looks into his face. "Think of her. Think of how much better off she'll be."

An image starts to form in her mind, the deer rising, leaping freely, whole! Jared shakes her.

"Not that! Let her go."

A new image forms. The deer lying in the grass, her eyes closed, her body at peace. Asleep! She looks so peaceful, Jessie falls into the image, tans and whites and greens blur together and grow brighter. She wants to lie down in the shining grass beside the deer, but Jared's talking to her, saying her name.

"Jessie. It's done."

She opens her eyes, looks around Jared to the body of the deer, lying still in the grass, its eyes still open but foggy looking, dull.

"No!" the word flies up and spits through her clogged throat. She runs over to the deer, kneels beside her. "No! No! No!" Pounding her fists in the grass. "We killed her! We're murderers!"

His face is pained, "No, we let her die."

She puts her hands to her eyes, surprised to find them dry. Then she reaches for the deer.

"Jessie, don't..."

"I'm not going to wish anything," she hisses the words at him, can see him flinch, then completes her move, placing one hand on the deer's cheek. The fur is warm, the bones beneath are firm. She strokes its head gently, then touches the eyelid, moving it down until the eye is closed. Now the deer looks like the image in Jessie's mind.

Jared helps her to her feet, and she brushes off grass, dirt, picking at small pebbles that stick to her skin.

"It was you, wasn't it? That image of her sleeping?" she asks.

"You saw that?"

"You saw mine."

"Yeah, I guess I did."

"You tricked me."

He frowns and color floods his face. "I wished her at peace."

Exhaustion washes over her, like weights on her limbs, her eyelids. "I'm tired. Can we go home now?"

Chapter 38

Is This What You Wanted?

The door slams behind her in a house that seems empty, and she moves with heavy steps, feeling so tired, straight toward her bedroom, flinging herself on the dusty quilt and kicking off her shoes.

If you change your mind about coming home... Her mother had planted it firmly in her mind, hugging her tightly, whispering it once again, then pulled away before Jessie could respond.

She opens the compartment of her backpack and pulls out her phone, pressing a button and waiting for it to light. Nothing. She presses the 'on' button. Still nothing. The first frisson of alarm hits. How long has it been dead?

She reaches for the charger, then stops. Her mom is driving to New York. When did she leave? She wouldn't be home yet, would she? What if her wish worked? What if her mom turned around, is coming back to Beauport?

She plugs in her phone and waits for it to power on, nothing but the small apple with the whirling disk for a long time, then finally her wallpaper, the photo of the harbor lighthouse in Beauport. Lighthouse equals hope. She closes then opens her eyes.

There are several texts from her dad, starting with: *Your phone is off or dead. Call me the minute you get this.* The following ones repeat: *Call me when you get this. Call me Jessie. Call me!*

Then a voicemail too; "I don't know why but your phone must be off. I hope you turn it on soon. Please call me." The sound of her dad's voice makes her cold.

Jessie presses the word *Dad* on her screen, and he picks up on the first ring.

"Jessie! Thank God, where are you?"

"I'm home." She feels annoyance mix with the fear. "I just noticed my phone died, I'm sorry. Where are you?"

His silence scares her more than anything. "Dad?"

"Your mom was in an accident."

"Oh my god, oh my god..."

"She's going to be fine. She broke her leg, her jaw, her face is banged up, some cuts, bruising everywhere... We're at St. Catherine's hospital. They're wiring her jaw, and they're waiting on the results of a CAT scan. She hit her head on the windshield..." he trails off. Fear and anxiety collide in her, and suddenly she's crying.

"Jessica. Hush. It'll be okay."

"I should have been there. I'm sorry. I'm so sorry." Anguish clutches at her chest, but she has to speak, she breathes, gulps back sobs. "How did it happen?" She's not sure she wants to know. And yet without that knowledge, her part in it is incomplete.

She must hear this.

"She ran off the road into a garbage dumpster. She doesn't remember much. Listen, I'll bring her home as soon as we talk to the doctor. Just sit tight."

"Home? New York?"

"No. Dorothy's house. Shouldn't be more than an hour. I'll call you if it's longer."

"I want to come."

"We'll be home soon."

"I could ride my bike."

"No! Stay off the roads!" His tone is sharp, she feels the pain of it in her chest. "I'm sorry," his voice softer, hoarse. "It's all been so...." He clears his throat, then says, "Why don't you see what we have to make smoothies? And if there's soup. It's all your mother can have for a while. Make a list for me, I'll go back out after she's settled in."

She nods and whispers, "Okay," and "Bye," and lets the phone drop to the bed.

Mom. That beautiful face mangled with cuts and bruises? Her knees curl to her chest and she wraps herself around them tightly, making herself small so all the hurt can be contained. She thinks of the bubblegum pink Zipcar her mother rented to drive them back this morning. A crumpled hulk of pink metal rises in her mind, and she squeezes her eyes as if to block it out.

Will her mom need plastic surgery? What about the play? How long does it take a broken leg to heal? Her mind loops around and around and she opens her eyes to slow it down. She sees her phone and she thinks of Jared.

My mom's been in an accident. Imagining saying those words makes it all real and she can't bear it. And then she imagines his response, can hear him saying, as clearly as if he is in the room, *is this what you wanted?*

"NO!" she cries and the word echoes in the empty house, "No...no...no" and the image of the deer rises in her mind, lifeless, misshapen, someone's mother.

"STOP!" She pounds the heels of her hands against her temples. She has to pull herself together. They'll be home soon. What was it her dad asked her? Grateful for a task, she goes down the hall to make the list her dad requested.

On her way out of the kitchen, the diorama catches her eye. The farmer's wife is missing. She is no longer feeding her geese, the geese themselves are huddled in their gaggle as if discussing her disappearance. But then Jessie sees her in the doorway of the house, her back to Jessie. *Why does it keep changing?* Jessie grabs the base of the diorama, jerking it upwards, and the farmhouse and all the figures topple, the fences pile up like pick-up sticks, and the farmer's wife is pinned beneath the house. It looks like the aftermath of a natural disaster. *Good,* Jessie thinks.

The sound of crunching gravel makes her jump. She runs to the door. *I won't cry. I won't,* she tells herself. Her father's car door is open and he's swinging out his legs. For a moment she doesn't recognize him, his face haggard. She can see the old man in him, the one waiting twenty or thirty years down the road. He sees her, smiles weakly, stands, and opens his arms. She's in them instantly, tears flowing. Behind him she glimpses her mother, seat reclined, face bandaged.

"Help me get her inside." They walk to the passenger door, open it, and Jessie gets her first full look. One piece of gauze is taped across her forehead, and there's a bandage on her nose. Her jaw is swollen and her eyes bloodshot. Her leg is in a cast from her foot up past her knee, it barely fits with the seat pushed back all the way. "Mmm-kll," her mother's voice is hoarse, thick, her father's name mumbled through swollen lips and clenched teeth. She's starting to lift the cast, but he is there, gently lifting it until it clears the door ledge, then setting it down while she puts her other leg out and turns in the seat, looking directly at Jessie. "J'ssca," she holds out her arms, and Jessie's crying again, but she leans in and kisses her on an unmarked stretch of cheek, then, helps her stand.

With one on each side, they walk her slowly down the path to the front door which hangs open. Inside they take her to the couch, helping her sit, pulling a hassock close, collecting pillows for her leg.

"Jessie, take care of Mom. I'm going to the pharmacy and the store. Did you make a list?"

Jessie hands it to him, and watches as he leaves the house. Then she turns to her mother, trying to act normal, though it's hard to look at her. "Can I get you something? Water, ice, Tylenol?" Her mother shakes her head. She pats the couch beside her, and Jessie sits close and curls under her arm.

"Ths m' grl," and she squeezes her daughter tight. There's a strong odor of something medical, maybe rubbing alcohol, or that orange stuff they spread on wounds, she can't remember its name. The smell is 'hospital' and unpleasant. She snuggles closer, despite the smell, and she can just make out her mother's perfume.

"J'ss-ca," she says again, grimacing and swallowing, then grimacing again.

"I don't think you're supposed to talk much," Jessie says.

She looks at Jessie, one eyebrow raised in warning and frustration. Then, as if it pained her, closes her eyes, and lays her head back against the couch. "L..l..l..pt...mp," comes out.

"Lips... something? Do you want Chapstick?"

She sits up, opens her eyes, and mimes opening something and moves her fingers up and down on her empty lap.

"Laptop!" Jessie stands up, then stops and turns back. "Shouldn't maybe you just rest now?"

Again, she is fixed with those red-laced eyes, their blue-green stark in contrast, knows there is no arguing with them. She fetches her laptop from her room, returns to the couch, opens it, and powers it on.

"What do you want to do?" she asks as it hums to life, the light washing up her mother's face, making her eyes hollow and her skin pale blue.

"Erd," comes out and Jessie clicks on the icon for MS Word, a blank page floating up, and starts to understand.

Her mother takes the keyboard, and types, *Thank you, sweetheart.*

226

Jessie nods, waiting for the next words.

I have to email some people about... and then she lifts her hand from the keyboard, sweeps it across her face and indicates her leg, then continues, *Sam, Robert, he's the director, my agent.* She pauses and frowns, *Zipcar, your dad did something with the insurance, but I think I have to...*

Jessie puts her hand on her mom's, mostly to stop the fear rising inside, the horror image of mangled pink metal. "Dad will handle that. Don't think about it."

Her mom nods, and with one hand pulls Jessie's head close, presses her lips against her forehead.

"Well, this is cool. You can type to us till your jaw is better. Or I could get you a slate to wear around your neck, remember that movie? They tapped letters on a slate, they didn't even write anything..."

Her mother laughs, and grimaces, a soft moan escaping the clenched jaw.

Types: *It only hurts when I laugh.* And then, *Sweetie, I need to write these emails, okay?*

Jessie nods, but doesn't leave the couch, leaning her head on her mom's shoulder and closing her eyes. The soft 'whuf, whuf, whuf' of her typing is calming and so normal, she can almost believe she dreamed everything, that she'll wake and find her mother in New York and whole, her father fixing dinner. *In New York,* she repeats in her mind. *She should be in New York,* and her thoughts break apart in a shower of sparks, a tangle of things she wants and doesn't want, and she is grateful when she hears the car pull in, and sees her father open the front door.

Later, her dad turns to her and says, "Mind switching rooms? The bed in Dorothy's room is too high for your mom."

Jessie jumps up to move her things into Dorothy's room, and then they settle her mom into Jessie's bed. By the time they've gathered all the extra pillows they can find and made her comfortable in a half-prone position, her mother's eyes are drooping, so they leave her to sleep, a pewter dinner bell from Dorothy's china cabinet by her side.

"Where will you sleep?" Jessie asks her father as they fall onto the sofa, his arm around her.

"You're sitting on it," he answers, and she sees a pile of sheets and a pillow on the chair.

"What did the doctor say? What's going to happen now?"

Her father pauses, squeezing her close. "She's going to be right as rain." Jessie remembers reading that phrase recently. Her grandfather's letter! *The doc says I'll be right as rain.*

"That's a funny phrase," her dad continues. "What's right about rain? Anyway, the jaw and the leg are broken, but not badly, not as badly as they could have been. No surgery, thank God, and she'll have some physical therapy when the cast comes off, but otherwise..."

"What happens now?" She sees them leaving Beauport, going home to New York while her mother recovers. And how long would that be?

"What?" Her father sounds far away. She looks up to find him looking at the diorama.

"I said, what happens now?" She doesn't want to say it. What happens to me, to this house, will we ever come back?

"Oh. Well. I'm not sure. Honey, this has been so hard. A couple of hours ago I got a call saying, 'your wife has been in an accident.'" He pauses and trembles visibly. And *she* wasn't with him. *Stupid, stupid phone.*

"We'll figure it out tomorrow." He rises and walks across the room examining the diorama. "What happened here?"

Jessie stays on the couch and curls her knees to her chest, holding her breath.

But her father begins putting things back the way they were, calm and unaffected by the disarray. "Musta been a twister," he says, and when Jessie lets out a single barking laugh, looks at her with a frown. "Was that funny?" Then turns to finish making it right. Right as rain.

Jessie climbs onto Dorothy's bed, which smells like sunscreen and her father's aftershave and something else, something herbal and strange. Not lavender, Jessie knows that smell, nor roses, some other flower or herb dried and kept with the sheets. She rolls on her back, clawing the sheets not to jump up and check her phone. She wants to talk to Jared more than anything but can't imagine getting words out without crying. He's texted her several times, each subsequent text more worried than the last. She hopes his dad is okay. She hopes Jared will forgive her. She can't face it. Telling him will make it bigger, and it already fills the room, the house, everything. *What have I done?*

Despite these thoughts, she falls asleep quickly, deeply, till early morning when the dreams come.

She is riding her bike on the road to Angel Falls, and car after car pass her, as deer after deer jump across the road, colliding with each car and being tossed off the road. It's like the nightmare version of counting sheep; one-deer SLAM, two-deer SLAM, she tries to close her eyes, but her bike is wobbling, the road is full of holes, and she can't stop watching cars hitting deer, over and over.

She is lying on her back in a high bed in the dark, although she knows it's morning, she can hear the birds. If she opens her eyes she sees no change, a reddish-brown veil with dark spots that run away when she tries to focus on them. "Jessie."

It's her father's voice, but she can't see him. "Jessie, get up. I have bad news."

Though she feels like her body weighs a thousand pounds, she sits up slowly, dizzily, imagining a quick rise, but barely manages to stay upright.

"What?" The darkness grows and whirls, and a dim roar fills her ears and turns into music; a song she knows but can't name, as she feels herself sliding down into the sheets.

Jared's hand slips into hers and her body is alight. She can see it, twinkly lights up and down her arms, her legs, wrapped around her torso, a halo around her head. She squeezes his, she needs him to know she hasn't left yet, she loves him. "It's okay, Jared. I promise. Everything will be okay." She squeezes again, but her hand is empty.

Someone is speaking quietly somewhere. A man's voice, low and insistent. It sounds like a phone call, he speaks, pauses, speaks again, pauses again. Jessie opens her eyes and this time she can see. The windows are shuttered, but light squeezes through gaps in the slats making thin white lines against the dark rug. Jessie doesn't know where she is, the light is strange, wrong somehow, and the rug with the thin white lines is unfamiliar.

She recognizes her father's voice, imagines him on the phone with her mom, until the events of yesterday pour into her mind, an avalanche of horror, and even though it's hot in the room, she throws the covers over her head, closes her eyes and tries to fall back to sleep. The last dream, the sensation of Jared's hand, returns to her and she feels herself drifting into comfort and delight when a loud *whirring* jolts her, boring into her head as if the machine was on her pillow instead of in the kitchen. It's the blender. Her father's making breakfast for her mom, that small domestic chore confirming everything that happened. Her mother is here, in Beauport. *Is this what you wanted?*

Her mother is on the couch, propped up much the same way as last night. She looks up and smiles, then grimaces in pain. Her face is mottled with blue, bruising around the still swollen jaw, and her eyes have black semicircles underneath, with blue across her eyelids. The whites of her eyes have returned, however, no longer bloodshot. Jessie hopes she slept.

"Good morning, Mom," she says, sliding beneath her beckoning arm and curling against her. The arm comes round her shoulders, squeezing her tight. The strength in it reassures her.

"How did you sleep?"

The laptop is open so Jessie watches as her mother keys; *Not too bad. How about you?*

"Like a log."

Her dad enters with a dark pink concoction and bendy straw. "Strawberry peach pear. It's really good. Want one?" the last is directed to Jessie. She watches her mother take the glass, bend the straw, and slip it between the nearly clenched teeth. She finds herself grinding her teeth in a clench, imitating her mother.

"Yes please," she tells him and he's back in an instant with a second glass. "Did I take yours?" she asks him.

"I'll make more, don't worry. You keep your mom company."

She glances over to her mother, watching her drink. Her eyes drift to the laptop, to words further up the page; *You're right. I'm tired, and ache all over. But when I go, I'm taking Jessie.* Her mother quickly opens a blank document, covering the words.

Jessie slurps her smoothie directly from the glass, the thick mix coating the space above her upper lip. Her mother laughs, groans, laughs again.

"Stop it. You'll hurt yourself," but it's good to see her laughing.

I love to laugh. Her mother types. And Jessie hears the song from "Mary Poppins" sees the floating tables and chairs, the rising children, looks up to

Dorothy's cobweb ridden ceiling, too low to accommodate an aerial tea party. *I'm taking Jessie.*

The words can't be unread. She's taking her home, to New York, sometime soon.

The blender whirs loudly then stops, and her father comes in with a glass of his own. "Cheers!" he chinks glasses with her mother's, then hers, then sits in the armchair.

"So, I'm going home to fetch some things for your mom. I'll probably spend the night, be back here tomorrow morning. Do you think you can take care of her?"

Jessie's mind can't process his words, *go home to fetch things*. He's leaving her alone with her mom?

"What if something happens? What if she needs to see the doctor?" Jessie finally says, hearing the panic in her voice. Her mother's hand squeezes hers reassuringly. Why is she making her mother comfort her? Shouldn't it be the other way around?

"She grew up in a city and can't think of a car service?" There's a smile in his voice, and she sees him addressing her mom. He looks at Jessie now, speaking kindly, leaning forward as if to take her hand too. "Nothing's going to happen. She needs to keep from moving around too much, and from being bored to death. Do you think you can handle that? You'll have to help her, but Ms. Independence here is insisting on using the crutches, and I've got a guy coming in to install a bar in the bathroom later this afternoon, so you won't need to worry about that."

Jessie hadn't considered helping her mom to the bathroom. She looks at her now, unable to keep the alarm off her features, but her mother winks. She removes her hand to type in: *No worries. I'll be getting around on my own.*

Her father tips back his glass letting the last of the smoothie slide into his mouth.

"I'd better get going. Jessie, do you have any questions?"

"What's going to happen?" She can't help herself. The words slip out and her mother shifts beside her.

Her father doesn't frown exactly, but the openness goes away and the skin around his eyes tightens.

"Your mother... is going to stay here a few days." He stops and looks at her mother, so Jessie looks too. Her eyes are wide, and she nods once, slowly, as if urging him to continue.

"After that, I'll bring you both home."

There it is. They are leaving Beauport. It's real. And it's way too soon.

"I'll come back, of course, to finish getting the house ready to sell." He doesn't sound happy, but Jessie refuses to look at him.

You brought her here, a voice whispers in her ear, *you can make her stay*. The promise of the words draws Jessie like light, but she remembers the force of her wish, her imagining; how happy her parents were together. She looks at her father, who is studying her, waiting for Jessie to release him, to say goodbye. Why isn't he looking at her mom? Why isn't she looking at him? She remembers the kiss she'd imagined so clearly. What happened to that?

Jessie opens her mouth, pauses, then says, "Okay, I guess. Drive safe."

There's an awkward pause as Jessie realizes what she said, closing her eyes in dismay so that she misses the moment her dad turns away, opens the door. She opens her eyes in time to see the door shut behind him.

CHAPTER 39
WHERE R U

In Jared's dream, the deer is wounded, but it's worse, much worse. The brown fur and flesh are split along the jaw and peeling back, revealing the white jawbone and grinning teeth. The mutilated creature takes awkward, shuddering steps toward them and the terrible sound of bone grinding against bone grates on Jared's ears. With each step it takes, more wounds split open, growing wider like seams unraveling. There is something coming through the openings in the deer's body, a dangerous light pouring from another world into this one. Jared realizes the deer is growing larger, even as it's disintegrating and falling apart before their eyes. They have to stop it. He and Jessie. They have to stop it before it's too late. He opens his mouth to say the words that will make this happen, but they stick in his throat. He strains and strains to speak, but all that comes out is a strangled, bleating sound.

Jared wakes up with a shout, the echo of it still hanging in the air, fading now. He looks around his bedroom, sees the stripe of sunlight on the wall, exactly where it should be at this hour of the morning. Seven-fifty. Ten more minutes before his alarm will ring. He closes his eyes and pictures Jessie's face, that moment when she made her wish. The way her face grew still, how her features almost began to blur before his eyes.

It's true. She's one of them. Like he is. But what if there is no "them"? No one else out there who knows and feels what he and Jessie know and feel. No secret tribe for them to seek out and rejoin. In a way, Jared thinks, it's like he and Jessie are the last two people on earth.

Where is she? He hasn't heard from her since yesterday afternoon. He grabs for his phone and checks it. No messages or texts from Jessie. After yesterday, after everything that happened, how can she go silent like that? He types a quick message under the ten he's already sent, *R U OK?* And presses SEND. He waits a few moments—no answer. Then he slips the phone into his shirt pocket so he can feel it vibrate during the ride to school, but it stays silent the whole way.

At school, it's the same chaos of kids milling around, the same smell of ink and disinfectant. But one thing isn't the same—Delany is gone. Before Jared gets to the classroom, he senses it; a missing presence, like a blank white space in one of his dad's paintings.

When he walks in the classroom Jared quickly looks around at the other kids, and yes, it seems they sense it too. The absence. The wrongness. He can tell from the tentativeness of their movements, from the nervous edge in their too-loud laughter. He turns all the way around to look at the back of the classroom and yes, Johnson is there, his lip still swollen, the bruise an ugly purple now.

As soon as school is out, Jared pulls out his phone and checks it. Still no messages.

Jared starts typing, *Where r u? What the hell is going on?* Then he pushes the delete arrow, erases the last sentence, and starts over. *Now I'm worried. Coming over to see you now.*

Jared pushes SEND, gets on his bike, and pedals toward Jessie's house. He's only halfway down the block when he feels the buzz against his ribs, stops his bike by the side of the road, pulls out his phone and opens the message.

Don't come. Can't see you now. I'll explain later.

Jared stares at the letters on the screen. *Don't come. Can't see you now.* Something's wrong. He knows it, and it kills him that she won't tell him. How can he help her if she won't tell him?

For a moment he almost starts pedaling fast as he can to Jessie's house. Then he pictures himself banging on her door and calling her name like a character in a bad movie, and he shakes that picture out of his head—he knows that would only make it worse. He puts the phone back in his pocket and starts pedaling toward Rick's.

Customers are lined up two or three deep at the counter with Kate calling out orders and Jeff and José hustling to fill them. Jared is back at the sink again, elbow deep in hot soapy water, trying to clear away enough dishes before Jeff brings another load, but his mind isn't on the job. *Don't come. Can't see you now....*

"Yo, Jared, what the hell?" Jared looks up and sees Jeff holding another heavy rubber bin piled high with dirty dishes.

"Sorry," Jared says, "I'm going fast as I can." Jared isn't sorry. He wants Jeff to drop the dishes and go away.

"Bullshit. Stop screwing off." Jeff dumps the bin full of dishes into the sink before Jared can clear room for them. Soapy water sloshes over Jared's shoes and a dish slips from the pile, onto the floor, and shatters. "Nice job, dickhead," Jeff grins as he walks away.

For a moment, Jared almost goes after him. He wants to grab Jeff by his scrawny shoulder, spin him around and punch him right in his stupid, smirking face—but he doesn't want what would come afterward. He pictures Delany's face, bruised and bloodied, the uniformed guard's hand on his arm, leading him away...

Jared twists the hot water tap so high that it nearly scalds his hands, but the heat and steam rising into his face and the rushing sound of the water begin to soothe him the way they always do.

"Jared."

Jared turns and sees Kate leaning around the door, a sweaty strand of hair plastered across her forehead.

"Somebody out here wants to see you."

Jessie.

Jared, turns off the water, dries his hands on a dishtowel, combs his fingers quickly through his straggly hair, and walks out front, his heart already beating faster.

Jared runs his eyes over the faces on the other side of the counter, but he doesn't see Jessie. One face, one set of eyes, nervous and impatient, is looking directly into his. Scruffy white whiskers over full, red-veined drinker's cheeks, nervous blue eyes behind square hipster frames.

As soon as the man speaks his name, "Jared?" he remembers. It's Bryce Beecham, the gallery owner. Jared knows him from openings he's attended with his dad, a big, jovial presence moving through the small crowd of tourists and art-lovers. "Hi," Jared says, wiping his hands on his apron, then holding out his right hand.

Beecham reaches across the counter and gives Jared's hand a quick, firm shake.

"How are you, Jared?" Jared wonders why Beecham's smile looks so strained.

Then it hits him like ice in his gut. Something's happened to his dad.

"Uh ... can we talk outside for a minute?" Beecham asks.

Jared's chest tightens and he tells himself to breathe. He follows the man through the screen door and a few steps out into the parking lot where Beecham turns around and nervously clears his throat. "Have you seen your dad today?"

"Yeah. Just this morning. What happened?"

"Your dad and I were supposed to see each other this afternoon." Jared can see anger struggling with embarrassment in Beecham's face. "He was supposed to show me the painting. The one he's been working on."

"Maybe..." Jared says, his mind still racing, "Maybe he forgot."

"He was supposed to see me Friday. Then yesterday. No one answered then, either." Jared's mind starts to relax—maybe his dad isn't in danger. Maybe he's avoiding Beecham. But why?

"I'll tell him ..." Jared starts to offer, "I'll tell him you're looking for him."

"I think he knows that," Beecham says. He looks across the road at the marsh grass bending in the breeze, but Jared can tell he's not seeing it. "Uh ... when do you get off work?" Beecham asks.

"Ten. Why?"

"How about I meet you there? At your place, I mean. A little after ten." Jared feels something like a fist tightening inside of him. He doesn't know why his dad is hiding from Beecham, but he knows he doesn't want to help this man track him down and find him. It feels like a betrayal.

"Jared!"

Jared turns and sees Rick leaning out the kitchen door, glaring at him.

"I gotta go," Jared mumbles, turning to leave. Beecham's hand touches his arm. It's a light touch, but it makes him want to shake it off.

"So, I'll see you at ten. Okay?"

Jared doesn't answer. He keeps walking all the way across the parking lot, past Rick and in through the screen door. It all comes flooding back, all those days when he'd come home from school and find the landlord waiting at the bottom of the stairs, or the mailman holding a certified letter demanding that some bill be paid. All those adult faces looking down at him with irritation, shame, and pity.

When Jared gets back to the sink, he stops and stares. There's a new mountain of dishes that have piled up and spilled over the edge, broken pieces lying on the floor.

He senses Jeff standing behind him before he hears him.

"Enjoy your break, dickhead?"

Anger surges up through Jared's spine and into his arms as he turns and grabs Jeff by his shirt and shoves him into a cabinet, knocking over pots and pans that go clattering to the floor while he and Jeff thrash and twist—then Rick's big hands are on him, pulling him back, holding them apart. Rick's face is flushed red, his eyes hot with anger and a disappointed sadness Jared can't stand to look at.

"Go home, Jared!" Rick says. Jared stares at him, his mind still spinning, not comprehending, and Rick says it again, even louder. "I said *go home!*"

The spell breaks, Jared turns and pushes the screen door open and he's out in the parking lot, the cool summer night air all around him, his head still hot and pounding like a drum. Home. He has to get home.

He walks up to his bike and suddenly hates the sight of it, leaning against the back wall of the building. It's a kid's bike, a child's toy. But it's all he has. He mounts it and starts pedaling.

Fuck, fuck, fuck, he thinks, riding hard into the oncoming Tuesday night traffic. *What the hell did I do?* Is he fired now? He thinks of the disappointment in Rick's eyes and feels a fresh stab of pain in his chest.

Why is this happening, Jared thinks. *What did I do wrong?* All he wanted was for his dad to be okay again, to be the way he used to be. Was he wrong to wish for that? How could that be wrong?

Looking up, Jared is startled to see his house rising in front of him, faded white and stark against the blue summer night. He turns the key and opens the door and there's his dad, sitting at the kitchen table, staring down into his coffee mug.

"Hey Dad." Jared's voice sounds tighter, more nervous than he wanted it to.

It takes him a moment to answer. Jared thinks of astronauts talking with people back on earth, the long delay while their words reach across all those miles. Something is wrong.

"Hey, buddy."

"Dad. That guy from the gallery. Beecham. I saw him at Rick's. He says he's been looking for you."

At the name *Beecham*, Jared's dad closes his eyes, no expression on his face.

"He says he's coming here tonight. At ten." No response. "Dad ... what's going on?"

Jared's dad raises one hand to his face and rubs it back and forth across his eyes, hard, like there's a stain he's trying to wipe away. When he finally speaks, his voice sounds small and weak. "I wish I could tell you, buddy."

"Why is he looking for you, Dad? What does he want?"

"The painting," his dad says in a voice so faint Jared can barely understand.

"So? Give him the painting."

"I can't."

"Why not?"

His dad won't answer. A chill cut through Jared's stomach because he suddenly knows the reason. It appears in his mind, walking across the sand toward him—the woman in his dad's painting, the one with no face.

"Is it...is it because of her?" Jared asks. "That woman in the painting?"

Jared's dad closes his eyes and nods once.

"Dad," Jared says, "Is that Mom? I mean, is that supposed to be Mom? In the picture?"

"No, buddy," Jared's dad shakes his head slowly. "It's not."

"Who is it, then? Who's it supposed to be?"

His dad shuts his eyes and shakes his head again. "I can't tell you, buddy."

"You can't tell me? Or you don't want to?"

His dad looks up at him. Jared is alarmed to see wetness shining in his eyes. "You'll think I'm crazy." A bitter laugh burst from his lips. "Hell, you already know that, right?" His dad takes a deep breath, holds it in, then lets it out and begins, slowly.

"You remember that time you were really sick? You were five, maybe six. You had a fever for two days. A hundred and three. You'd start screaming in the middle of the night. You said you thought your mom was in the room with you. But she wasn't. You kept saying there was someone in your room, and they had their hand on your chest. And you couldn't breathe. Remember that?"

Jared thinks, and the memory slowly rises to the surface, the feeling of suffocating, and of not being alone in the dark. He nods slowly, and his dad tells him.

"That's who it was. That was her."

A wave of cold passes through Jared's body, and with it, a memory of being very young and standing under the trees at Angel Falls, wind roaring loud as a waterfall in the leaves above, and the feeling of being watched. A faraway figure standing on the ridge against the sky, motionless as the trees around it, an empty white blur where its face should be.

His dad nods toward the other chair. "Want to sit down?" Jared nods numbly and lowers himself into the chair. His dad waits for him, then continues.

"Remember when I came home from the hospital? After ..." his dad's eyes waver, can't meet his. Jared nods and manages to speak, to help his dad finish.

"Yeah."

"Remember how I stayed in bed? How I wouldn't get out of bed? For two weeks?"

"Four," Jared says. "Four weeks."

Jared sees his dad flinch, shocked, then swallow it back. "Four weeks. I stayed in bed. And you stayed with me." His dad stops, takes a deep breath. "She was there too. Every time you left. To go to school. To go to work. She was there. Every time I tried to get up, she wouldn't let me. I *wanted* to get up. But I could feel her hand on my chest." Jared watches his dad lift his hand and put it over his own heart. "Right here. Like this. And I couldn't get up. I couldn't move."

"What happened?" Jared asks.

"She went away."

"But ... now she's back?"

Jared's dad lowers his face into his hands and doesn't answer.

"But she's not *real*. You don't think she's real, do you?" Jared looks closely at his dad's face, looking for a sign. His dad stares at the wall, a lost look in his eyes.

"I don't know, buddy..."

I saw her too, is what Jared wants to say.

"I thought she was gone," his dad is saying, "Now every time I try to paint or draw, she gets in. She keeps getting in. I try to keep her out. But I can't." His dad rubs his hands across his face, his eyes weary and red.

Jared looks at his dad's bedroom door. It's half ajar, a vertical slit of darkness showing. He stands up, walks into his dad's bedroom, and turns on the light.

The painting is in shreds, ripped and torn away in drooping pieces. Some cuts look clean and straight like they were made with a knife; others are more ragged with loose fibers sprouting from the edges like someone has torn them apart with their bare hands.

Jared goes back out into the kitchen where his dad is sitting with his face in his hands. "Oh my God, Dad... Why the hell did you *do* that?"

"I had to," his dad mutters into his hands. "I can't keep her out. She keeps coming back."

"But ... you *sold* it! To those people. Beecham ... he gave you money for it, didn't he? That's why he's coming here! What are you gonna tell him?"

His dad sits with one hand on his face, not looking at Jared.

Jared stammers, "Just tell him you'll do another one. Tell him you'll do another painting. Same as that one."

Jared's dad shakes his head slowly. "No," he says, his voice barely audible.

"*No?* What do you mean, no?"

"I can't."

A loud banging on the door makes Jared's heart leap into his throat. He looks at the clock. 9:50. Beecham is early.

"Dad."

"I know who it is," Jared's dad says in a quiet voice.

"What should we do?"

"Let him in," his dad says. "And Jared, don't come back up for a while, okay? I don't want you to ... Just come back in an hour, okay?"

Jared stands up, feeling numb, slowly walks down the stairs, unlocks the door, and opens it. The stairwell light hits Beecham's face and makes him blink like some kind of nocturnal creature. "Hey, Jared," he says, peering nervously around him.

Be good to him, Jared wants to say. *Please don't hurt him.* Instead, he mutters, "He's up there," then squeezes around Beecham and runs down the stoop onto the cracked sidewalk.

When Jared gets far enough away, he turns and looks back up at the lighted window of their kitchen. He watches for silhouettes moving back and forth, arms waving, voices raised in anger. But he sees nothing, hears nothing. He turns his back on the house and looks up over the rooftops at the steeple of Saint Peters rising against the stars. He thinks of all the other people out there sleeping peacefully, the ones whose lives aren't falling apart.

His phone vibrates. Jared digs it out of his pocket and sees a text from Jessie, the one he's been waiting for all day.

I'm sorry I haven't written or called. I'm sorry. My mom was in a car accident. She broke her leg, her jaw. She's here in Beauport for now. I guess I got my wish.

It happened yesterday afternoon. Yeah, right then I think. Right fucking then. Shit. This is so hard. You know how I always cry around you? That's another reason I can't call. It's too hard.

So, get this, do you know why she had the accident? Oh Jared, I can't write it! Maybe we need to meet up. If I can get away. She needs help, and Dad went to New York to get some stuff for her.

Oh shit. You should be glad you're not here. You'd just have to mop me off the floor. I'm useless.

Jared. It was a deer. Oh God. Help.

CHAPTER 40

BREAKING AND ENTERING

When Jared gets to Jessie's house, the windows are dark. He knocks anyway, quiet enough to not wake anyone, but loud enough for someone waiting on the other side to hear. He's about to knock again when the door swings open halfway. He catches a half-second glimpse of Jessie silhouetted in the doorway, then she's wrapped around him. Her arms locked around his neck are stronger than he imagined. All the anxious thoughts he's been carrying inside dissolve in the feeling of her body pressed against his and the summer-smell of her hair. She lets go and steps back to look at him, and for a moment he feels like he might fall down.

"Are you okay?" she asks.

"Yeah," he says. "You..?"

She nods quickly. "You wanna come in?"

He looks over her shoulder into the dim front room, a lamp glowing in one corner by the couch that looks deep and inviting. She's turns and walks back into the house, and he follows her inside. The smell of ancient, mildewed wood and old furniture envelopes him.

"Your mom..?" he says, looking around.

"It's okay," she says, "She's asleep now."

"I'm sorry," he says, knowing how small and weak his words are, "I'm sorry that happened to her.." but now Jessie is weeping, a quiet, shocking sound that pierces his heart.

"She's so beautiful," Jessie says, "And now, her face ... God, it's so awful."

"It's okay."

"*No!* It's not okay! I *did* that to her."

"No. It's not your fault," Jared says. "You didn't cause that wreck."

"*Yes I did.* It's just like in those stupid letters, Dorothy's letters. I *wished* for her to come here. And look what happened."

"You don't know that."

"Jared, it was a *deer!* It was a freaking *deer*, okay?"

Jared doesn't know what else to say. She's right. He knows she is.

"You made the wish too," she says sadly. "We both did it." *We're both guilty.* That's what he hears. And what he feels.

"I'm sorry," she finally says. "Your dad. Is he okay?"

"No. He's not."

"What?" she whispers, her hand coming to rest on his arm. "What happened?"

"His painting. The one I told you about, the big one he was working on. He ripped it up. Tore it to pieces. The people he sold it to...They already gave him money for it. A lot of money. They're coming to pick it up. The gallery owner came by tonight. He wanted to see it."

"Oh my God, why did he do that? Why would he destroy his own painting?"

Jared hesitates. If he tells her, what will she think?

"There's this woman. In the painting. She's...she's not supposed to be there. Dad says he didn't want to put her in the painting, but he couldn't help it. He kept trying to take her out, but he says she kept coming back."

"Coming back? You mean...by herself?"

He dares a look at Jessie and sees her holding her hand over her mouth, her eyes wide and frightened. It makes it hard for him to go on and tell her the rest of it—but now that he's started, he has to finish it.

"I saw her too. When I was a kid. In the woods at Angel Falls. I saw someone standing on the hill, looking at me. I told myself there wasn't anyone there..." Jared pauses, swallows hard before he can go on. "I think it was her."

Jessie takes her hand away from her mouth, never taking her eyes off of his.

"You...you think she's real?"

"I don't know," Jared says, "But...there was this other time. The day my mom came back. I woke up and she was standing in the kitchen. She turned around and ... right before she turned around, I got this feeling like it wasn't really her. Like it was somebody else."

"But...but it *was* her, right? It was your mom."

"I don't know...it looked like her. But there was something wrong about it, you know? I wanted her to come back. And she did. Then...then I wanted her to go away." He looks at Jessie again. "That's crazy, isn't it?"

Jessie puts a hand on his arm, the warmth of it on his skin makes him want to cry.

"I just wanted my dad to get better," Jared struggles to get the words out. "I just wanted him to be the way he was before."

"But he *is* better," Jessie says.

"He *was* better. I really thought he was. Jesus, what did I do wrong? What did I do?" The tears come, and he turns to hide them from her.

"We'll figure it out," she says.

"How? How are we gonna figure it out?"

They stand close together, not speaking. The dim light of the room seems to wrap itself around them. Jared hears the sharp intake of Jessie's breath and her grip on his arm tightens.

"Those papers," she says. "The ones Delany let you see about Angel Falls, about all that stuff that happened. Are they still there? At school?"

"I don't know. Maybe. But we read those."

"Maybe we missed something. Maybe there's something in there we didn't see. Because...you know, we didn't really understand it yet." He knows what she means. *Because we're different now. Because it's real.*

The sound of a bell ringing from somewhere in the house makes Jared's heart skip a beat. "It's my mom," Jessie says, her eyes wide and sad. He knows he should let her go, but he doesn't want to.

"Should I wait here..?"

A smile breaks out across Jessie's face that beautiful to see, even in the dark.

"No. You need to get back to your dad, right?"

He nods, silently. She looks up at him, her blue eyes so large, for a moment he can't remember what it is they were talking about a moment ago.

"The papers...," he says. "I'll have to go back after school to get them."

"Can you do that? I mean, could you get in trouble?"

He thinks. "Well, it's not really breaking and entering if I don't break in, right?"

She nods and smiles. "I guess ..." she says, then, "I want to go with you."

"No. That's ... I don't think that's a good idea."

"Why not? I thought you said it wasn't dangerous."

"I didn't say that. I said it wasn't illegal."

"What can they do to you if you get caught?"

"Nothing. I mean ... I'm not gonna get caught."

The bell rings again.

"I gotta go," Jessie says, looking around anxiously. "Text me from school tomorrow when you're going to do it. Okay?"

"Okay," he says, then waits, super-conscious of his own body standing there like a tree rooted to the ground. Then she leans over quickly to give him a quick kiss on the cheek, and now she's moving away from him, back deeper into the house.

"Thanks," she smiles. "I gotta go. I hope your dad's better."

"Thanks," he says, walking backwards out the door so he can keep watching her moving away from him toward the sound of the ringing bell— then she turns a corner and is gone.

It's past eleven when Jared climbs the stairs to his apartment and unlocks the door. He half-expects to find his dad passed out at the kitchen table like before, but he's not there. Jared looks inside his dad's bedroom and finds him curled up on the bed, the ruined painting still leaning on the wall next to him. He waits until he's sure he can hear the sound of his dad breathing, then he goes back to the kitchen and pours himself a glass of milk. His mind is racing, he knows he can't sleep for a while, so he sits on the sofa and turns on the TV, making sure the sound is low, so it won't disturb his dad.

He takes a drink of milk, half-watching a dull commercial for a local furniture store, then another one for an injury attorney in a cheap-looking brown suit. *If you've been hurt, call me....*

Then the news returns, the whole screen filled with a girl's smiling face, and he almost drops the glass of milk. It's Karen Holcomb. The missing girl. It's the same photo in all the posters and TV spots. He tries to match this smiling face with the one he saw watching from across the road that day, the one with the vacant eyes.

The picture changes to a man and woman standing in front of a small wooden house, a dozen microphones aimed at them. Their faces are haggard and pale but smiling. The man is talking. Jared grabs the remote and turns the sound up so he can hear.

"We just want to thank everyone who helped look for Karen…everyone who supported us through all of this…" The man falters for words, and the woman speaks for him. "We're just so grateful to have our little girl back again." Jared studies the picture and wonders, where is she? Inside that house in the background, staring out through the window at all the people gathered there?

The next morning, Jared wakes up on the couch, the TV still on. There's no breakfast cooking, no French Roast, and he's late for school.

"I'm sorry buddy. I overslept." Jared jumps at the sound of his dad's voice and turns around. He's standing in the doorway to his room, rubbing his face. "Let me make you something."

"I gotta run. I'm late." Jared grabs his bag, makes it halfway to the door and stops. He walks back and throws his arm around his dad for a quick hug. "Love you. See you later." And then he's out the door.

When he walks into the classroom, he senses something is different. One look around and he knows what it is. Karen Holcomb's desk is still empty but the air around it is charged. The desks closest to hers looks like they've been moved a few inches away, as if the other kids don't want to be too close. Coach Hargove turns out the lights and the title "American History" flashes on the screen, but Jared can't concentrate on the movie. He remembers what he saw, or what he thought he saw—the girl in the shadows with no face.

When the dismissal bell rings, Jared joins the throng of kids swarming for the exit, then breaks away and slips into the boys' room. He stands behind the stalls where no one who comes in can see him, pulls out his phone and types a message:

The Eagle has landed. A moment later his phone buzzes.

That was fast. You got it already?

No. Still in the bathroom.

The door to the boys' room bursts open with a loud, echoing bang. Jared flattens himself against the wall, trying to remain unseen—realizing how strange he'd look if someone found him like this. Trying to keep his breathing quiet, he hears the trickling sound of someone pissing, then the flush, the door swinging open and banging shut— then silence.

Jared doesn't realize he's been holding his breath until he lets it go, his heartbeat drumming in his ears. *This is stupid,* he thinks. What's he got to be afraid of?

The phone buzzes again against his leg and he jumps, curses under his breath, then reads her message:

You're confusing me. Why are you still in the bathroom? What's going on?

Someone came in ... he starts to type, then deletes it. He doesn't want to make her nervous. *Just waiting till the coast is clear. No worries.*

His phone buzzes again, almost immediately. *I saw everybody leave twenty minutes ago. A lot of students. Teachers too. Who's left?*

He stares at her message, then types back. *Where are you? Did you follow me?*

Right outside. In the parking lot. You didn't expect me to stay home and wait, did you?

"Jesus," he says, then types, *Stay out there, OK? I'll be out fast as I can.*

Jared eases the door open a few inches and looks up and down the hall. It's empty. The lights are already off, only the red exit signs are on, throwing their faint red light. He can see the door to Delany's classroom at the right on the far end of the hall.

Jared steps out into the dark hallway and starts walking. His footsteps echo from the walls, louder than they should.

He finally gets to the door, reaches out for the doorknob. It won't turn. *Shit.* Why didn't he think of this? All those times he came before, Delany was here, waiting for him. Now he's gone and the door is locked.

Jared looks around, expecting someone to turn the corner any moment. Then he remembers—the window. Was it open today?

He walks quickly to the nearest exit sign, pushes the metal door open and finds himself at the back of the school, surrounded by garbage bins and chain link fence.

Scanning the row of windows that stretch out in front of him, he tries to get his bearings. They all look the same—except for one at the far end of the building, halfway open. Jared moves close to the window and peers inside. He can see Delany's posters on the wall, and his own empty desk.

One quick look around to make sure no one is watching; Jared pushes the window open a few more inches and climbs inside. He looks at the empty desks, feeling the strange quiet all around him. *Okay,* he thinks. *Now it's breaking and entering.*

He knows he's alone but feels like there's someone in the room with him. It's Delany. All those days in class. All those long talks after school. They're all still here somehow, in invisible layers, like the dust covering the floor and walls.

Moving quickly, Jared goes over to the file cabinet and opens the drawer. He half-expects to find it empty but the drawer drags open heavily, still stuffed with folders full of dog-eared papers. Jared flips through the tabs until he sees the words, *Angel Falls.* He pulls the folder out and yes; it's the one Delany gave him before. Then he sees another tab behind where the first one was, *Angel Falls 2.* Jared pulls it out and opens it. Photocopies of newspaper articles and other documents, headlines with the words *Angel Falls.* He starts to read—then his phone buzzes against his leg. He closes the file and opens his phone.

Where are you? What's taking so long? Are you ok?

Jared types back: *Had a little trouble. AOK now. I got it.*

The answer comes back right away: *What kind of trouble? I'm coming in. Where are you?*

"No!" He says it out loud, then types as fast as he can: *No. Don't come in. Stay there. I'll be out in a minute.*

Jared shuts the file drawer, grabs both folders and walks toward the window, then stops. Voices are floating in from outside. He looks out the window and sees three guys from the school maintenance crew standing about ten feet away, talking and smoking.

"*Shit!*" Jared hisses. What the hell is he going to do now? He looks back toward the door. Only one thing he *can* do—walk out the front way.

There's no one in the hall when Jared looks outside. He locks the classroom door and shuts it behind him, then starts walking toward the main door. The afternoon sunlight streaming through is dimmer now, and he walks as quickly as he can.

"*HEY!*" a voice booms out behind him, ricocheting off the walls. Jared's heart freezes in his chest. He turns around and sees one of the school security guards staring at him. "What are you doing in here?"

"I ..." Jared stammers, "I forgot something."

The guard peers at the folders under Jared's arm. "What are you doing with that?"

Jared is trying to think of an answer when a loud scream erupts in the dark hallway, a girl's scream. There's a figure standing at the end of the hallway in front of the main door, silhouetted against the daylight.

"Oh my God, help! There's a kid ... a kid just got hit by a car! Hurry!"

The guard breaks into a run, clawing at the radio on his belt. He blows past the girl and out the front door. Then Jessie is running right toward Jared, straight as a gunshot. She grabs his wrist and says, "Come on!" Then they're both running toward the red exit sign glowing at the other end of the hallway. They hit the doors hard with their outstretched arms and an alarm goes off, clanging in their ears, and they don't stop running until they can't hear it anymore.

Jessie's laughing and gasping for breath, her face flushed red and shining. "You got it," she says, nodding toward the two folders. He can't believe they're still there under his left arm.

"You *stole* something," she says in a funny sing-song voice, a wicked glint in her eyes. "What's it like to be a criminal?"

"You helped," Jared smiles. "That makes you ... what? An accessory. How's it feel to be an accessory?"

Jessie grins, still catching her breath. "Kind of awesome."

Jared thinks of how they must look to the people passing by, a boy and a girl standing on a normal street corner in the normal afternoon light, letting their minds catch up with what they've done. He feels the folder under his arm, the weight of it, and wonders—what has Delany been hiding from him?

What if we're not the only ones?

CHAPTER 41

NOT THE ONLY ONES

"I have to check on Dad," Jared says.

Jessie's exhilaration at their escape vanishes. *His dad...* They have to make sure his dad is still alive. She sees her mother's face as she had left her, sleeping awkwardly on the couch, her mouth crooked and wet.

"Your mom?"

She looks up, startled. Did he see the image in her mind?

"Do you want to go see her? We can meet back here in half an hour–"

She pulls her phone out, but there are no messages. She shakes her head.

"Dad's with her. They're not expecting me till dinner."

"Wanna come with me?"

A wave of fear courses through her, but she holds her face still, hoping Jared won't see. *He's better, he's better, he's better,* she repeats as if saying the words will make it true. And Jared wants her there. Of course she'll come. She nods once and Jared leads the way.

The house is a two-story building, white painted clapboard, weathered but neat. They climb a long set of noisy stairs to his apartment. "Wait here," he says, and when she starts to speak, raises his hand, "Please?" And she nods.

He opens the door enough to slip inside. She hears him calling, "Dad?" before he shuts the door, leaving her alone on the landing. In an instant he is back, frowning slightly. "He's not here," he says and lets her in. The smell of paint, linseed oil and turpentine assault her, and she's imagining easels and wall hangings, but there are no paintings anywhere. Everything is clean and tidy. Her eyes fall on a table between kitchen and living room, and in the middle, there is a folded paper with Jared's name on it. Jessie starts to point but Jared is already there, grabbing it up and reading.

She holds her breath, but he says, "It's okay," and hands the note to her.

Buddy, going out to paint. Tomorrow I'll start another large one. I should be able to finish it in a week or two. Beecham knows. I love you. See you at 8.

"That's good," she says hopefully. Then, "Buddy?"

Jared smiles with his whole face and drops his backpack on the table before disappearing around a half wall near the kitchen sink. She hears the soft suction of a refrigerator door opening.

"Thirsty? We have orange juice, water, and..." he pulls his head around the wall and holds up a can, "Your favorite, if I remember right."

It's root beer, and Jessie smiles. Several notches of worry fall away.

He pours two glasses, sets them on the table, pulls a chair out and sits, so Jessie sits too.

Jared pulls out the folder and places it on the table. "So, how do we do this? We could each read some, then talk about anything good..." Jared reaches into his backpack again.

Jessie studies him, trying to remember him as he was, what, only a month ago? The first time she saw him. Now he looks like the kids her dad teaches, college kids, or one of the fishermen in the harbor, a grown-up. Has he always looked this way?

He pull out a second folder down on the table. "Check this out," he holds it up so she can read the tab *A.F. 2.* "He was holding out on me." He pulls a stack of papers out and hands them to her.

Jessie looks at the first article as Jared pulls a chair out and sits beside her, looking at his own stack.

"This is 2005!" she says, and then starts reading.

Beauport Daily Times, March 22, 2005. Gerald and Zoe Jones of Beauport reported daughter, Amy, 16 years old, missing as of Saturday night, March 19. She was last seen on the grounds of Benjamin Franklin High School around 9 pm. She was wearing jeans, black boots, and white down jacket. Amy is 5' 4" about 110 lbs., blonde hair and hazel eyes. If you have seen her, or have any information please call Beauport PD at....

There is a photo in the article, not a school picture but a candid shot of a pretty girl, laughing, her head at an angle, hair swinging, clear sky behind. She has perfect teeth, a dimple in her left cheek. She could be Dylan, or a prettier version of Jessie. Only one year older. It makes her sad and a little frightened.

When she lifts the paper she finds it's clipped to another article, dated a year and a half later.

> *Amy Jones, 17, of Beauport, reported missing by her parents Gerald and Zoe Jones in March 2005, unexpectedly reappeared at her parents' home this morning after a year-long absence. According to doctors, she has no memory of the intervening year since she disappeared and seems in good health.*
>
> *"We're just glad she's home," her parents say.*

Jessie looks at Jared, bent over his own set of clippings. His lips move slowly, she can almost see the words there.

"Hey, she says. "This one's from 2005. A teenager disappears, then reappears a year later like nothing happened."

"2005?" He looks down at the papers in his pile, "This stuff is older. Same thing though." He reads, "*1918, Jonas Pyle disappears.* A couple of years later there's a church bulletin of his wedding."

They continue reading, Jessie's excitement builds with each new example of a disappearance followed by a mysterious return. Jessie gets through four more accounts when the name *Younger* leaps off the page.

> *Eleanor Younger, 35, wife of famous local artist Caleb Younger, missing since February 28, 2007, told her husband she was going walking and never returned home. Her husband notified police later that evening. A manhunt with dogs in the parks surrounding Angel Falls came up with nothing. There are over 4,000 acres of woods and rocky ground in the middle of the Cape.*
>
> *Hikers are frequently lost on the untended, poorly marked trails. Last fall a family of five went missing for over a week*

*before being recovered, hungry and dehydrated, by another
set of hikers with working GPS...*

The article is accompanied not by a photo of the woman, but of Caleb. A publicity shot with Caleb posed on a stool, the serious artist, in front of large seascape. She flicks her eyes up at Jared without moving her head. He's absorbed in his own clippings. Jessie starts to speak but there's something wrong with her throat, and there's another clipping attached. Her fingers tremble as she flips the first clipping behind and starts reading.

*The missing persons investigation into the disappearance of
Beauport resident Eleanor Younger was closed today when
Mrs. Younger returned home after an absence of nearly a
year. No reasons were given regarding her absence, and the
family has stated a request for privacy. She is the wife of Caleb
Younger, famous local artist, and mother of a young son.*

Jessie struggles to remember everything she's been told, but the information is slim, ghostlike, compared to the solid dark print of the articles she's read. Didn't Jared say his mother left them? If she walked out on them, why did Jared's dad report her missing? Didn't Jared know about the investigation?

She steals a look at Jared. His face is bent over the yellowed paper, eyes wide and moving across the page and back again, lips relaxed and parted, perfect skin marred by a single erupting pimple on his forehead. The contrast between his beauty and that pimple makes her stomach twist.

He says, eyes never leaving the papers in front of him, "This stuff is crazy. Listen. Eugenia Dorris, age 49, walked into the funeral of her husband, Samuel after being missing for five years..." He shakes his head, then looks at Jessie. "What?" he frowns.

She manages not to look down and tries to flip the articles over before he can see them. But it's too late. He's staring at the picture of his father. He grabs the paper from her.

She blurts, "You said she left. You never said she disappeared."

"Stop!" His hand is in the air, he's still reading, and his face is dark red.

"Jared, you told me.... "

"I know what I told you." His voice is choked, harsh.

"Did... didn't you know?"

He lets the clippings fall to the table and leans forward on his elbows, raking his fingers through his hair. "Did I know the police were looking for her? That they thought my dad..." She feels her insides begin to shred.

"I'm sorry," she says quickly. "It was a shock. To read it." She reaches out, afraid to touch him, but needing to. His head is still bent, so she touches that, the soft curl of his hair, his hot cheek. He jerks, but not away. He looks up at her, then turns his face into her palm, taking her hand and holding it there for an instant. Jessie barely has time to register the feel of his lips, his nose, before he lets her go, and she lets her hand fall. She leaves it on the table next to him, close enough to take if he needs to.

Jared rubs hard at his eyes, and her stomach clenches—is he crying? But when he takes his hands away, his eyes are dry.

"Why is it here?" he indicates the pile of papers, the folders. "What did he want with it?"

"It was before you were in his class, right? It's just a coincidence." But that doesn't feel right. And then she realizes something's missing from the stories. "Is there anything later? I mean after they return? Is there anything in yours that shows what happened then?"

Jared looks back at his clippings. "I don't think so. Just that they came back."

"So," she looks down at the clippings, "from these articles, it's all good news. People disappear, then they come back, right?"

Jared frowns a little and nods.

"But..." She can see the deer, staggering, staring into her eyes, accusing her. Her mother's bruised and swollen face. "Why is it going so wrong for us?"

"Wait a minute..." Jared reaches for her clippings. "These people... they're not much older than we are. Maybe they're still around. This girl, Amy, she'll be, what, 26, 27? And her folks? Maybe they're still here, in Beauport."

She can tell he's excited, but the thought of seeing these people, the fact of their existence gives her chills.

"These guys have it too." His color is high, his eyes glittery and strange. "Maybe they made it work." His words both attract and repel her. *Made it work?*

He stands up and starts to pace. "Let's Google 'em. Find out where they are."

Yes. No! She shakes her head, breathless. "Then what?"

He stops moving. "Well, we could..." he pauses, then says, "Maybe we tell them we're journalists, doing a report for school, something."

Maybe they made it work.

"Okay. Or..." she ponders a moment, "Genealogy! That's big. Half my English class was doing it last year."

"I wish I didn't have to work."

"I'll start tonight, or whenever Mom doesn't need me." Jessie glances at the clock. "I better go."

They walk out quickly, Jared locking the door behind them, then down the stairs to the street where they left their bikes.

Jared's still carrying the folders, so he hands them to her. One of folders flops open and an article flutters out. Jared picks it up and glances at it before dropping it in the open folder. Then he turns back to it and stares. Jessie looks at it and sees the headline:

Son of Local Teacher Missing

She looks up at Jared who looks scared. They turn back to the article:

Beauport Daily Times, April 17, 2000. Griffin Delany, age 6, son of Christopher and Janet Delany of Beauport was reported missing as of 7 a.m. Friday morning. Griffin's parents called police shortly after going in to wake him for breakfast and finding his bed empty. His mother reported checking on him when she got up at 6. Griffin was wearing pajamas with SpongeBob SquarePants on them. Anyone with information should call Beauport police immediately.

Jessie says, "He had a son?" but Jared isn't listening, he's rummaging through the folder. His face flushed and mouth grim.

"What are you doing?"

"Motherfucker," Jared says through gritted teeth. "God damn him! Where's the article?"

"Jared!" Jessie puts a hand on his arm, "Why are you—" She sees tears in his eyes, and that frightens her more than anything. "Stop, please."

"He did it." His voice breaks. "He knew. All along. Bastard!"

Then it hits her. "Jared...Stop. it's not there."

"What are you—"

She gently pulls the file from his hands. "He didn't bring him back. He couldn't. Don't you see? That's why he wants you."

She sees the change in his face and realizes she said something wrong. The anger and redness vanish, he sways and his skin turns sickly pale beneath his tan.

She puts a hand on his arm to steady him, but he brushes her off, turns and mounts his bike.

"Wait!"

But he stands on the pedals and pumps hard riding away from her, shoulders curled inward, head down. She looks down at the folders in her hands. Why did she have to say it?

That's why he wants you.

CHAPTER 42

SORRY

That's why he wants you.

The words stick in Jared's mind all day long, and he can't get them out. And the images—Delany hunched over a table with a pair of scissors, the pile of newspaper clippings in front of him, Jared's father's face, his name, Jared's name, *snip-snip,* on top of the pile, then *snip-snip,* buried under another one.

And the other image—Delany holding the hand of a small boy whose face is just a white blur that Jared tries to fill it in with Delany's mouth, Delany's chin, Delany's eyes.

The clearer the boy's face becomes, the more Jared feels himself fading away.

That's why he wanted you. All day in school, Jared holds onto those words until they start to burn. He needs the anger to remind himself of what's real, and what's not.

At three o'clock, Jared walks to the bike rack and pulls his bike out from all the others. The moment he puts his weight on it, he knows something is wrong. The whole thing sinks lower to the ground and rolls forward awkwardly, reluctantly, like it's caught in quicksand. One glance down at the tires tells him what's wrong—they're flat, both of them.

Cursing, Jared checks for slashes or puncture marks and finds none. Then he sees—both valve covers have been removed. He looks around angrily at all the other kids leaving school. One kid is laughing; Jared wants to grab him and throw him to the ground until he realizes the kid isn't looking at him, isn't even aware of him.

Jessie's house, he has to get to Jessie's house. Jared knows he can get there in twenty minutes, ten if he takes the shortcut through the woods.

Lifting the bike, Jared rests the crossbar on his shoulder and starts walking past the empty basketball courts and the green garbage bins to the dirt path that leads into the trees. He never rides through here—too many big tree roots, and he steps over them now carefully.

The sound of kids laughing and yelling fades behind him as the path leads down deeper into the trees. Soon he's enveloped in the patchwork green light and shade, empty bags of chips and plastic soda bottles littering the trail around him.

A man steps out of the trees about twenty feet ahead and stands in the middle of the trail, facing him. Jared stops and wonders—did the birds stop chirping?

"Hi, Jared." The man's scruffy beard and dirty clothes aren't familiar. But the low, hard voice and bloodshot brown eyes are. Jared opens his mouth to speak but nothing comes out.

Delany steps closer. His face looks gaunt and hollow, his eyes hungry.

"Can I talk to you?" Delany says. "Just for a minute? Please."

Jared is about to walk away, but that one word, *please*, startles him. He lifts his bike off of his shoulder and sets it down on the ground—then it hits him.

"Why did you do this?" Jared gestures toward his bike's flattened tires. Delany's eyes go narrow. *Don't lie to me,* Jared thinks. *If you lie to me about this, I swear to God, I'll walk away, and you'll never see me again.*

Delany looks at Jared's bike as if he's seeing it for the first time. Then he sighs wearily. "Would you have stopped? If you saw me? Would you have stopped and talked to me?"

"Okay," Jared finally says, "What do you want?"

Delany steps closer. "Listen, Jared. I think we should start meeting again. Like before. I think I can help."

"I know about your son." The words are out of Jared's mouth before he realizes. Jared watches the color drain from Delany's skin while his eyes fill with a pain Jared has never seen in them before. "Why didn't you tell me?"

"What was I supposed to say?" Delany asks. "How old are you, Jared? Sixteen? Sixteen fucking years old? What do you know about ..." Delany stops himself, raises his fists and presses them hard into his eyes. When he speaks again, his voice is quieter but ragged. "Okay, okay, sorry. Listen, let's start over, okay?"

We can't, Jared thinks.

"That's what all this was about, wasn't it?" Jared says. "You want your son back. You think I can do it. You want me to bring him back. That's it, isn't it?"

"Okay," Delany says. "You're right."

The ground sways under Jared's feet, and he clutches the handlebars of his bike to steady himself. He's known this, ever since he first learned about Delany's son, but he didn't believe it—not until he heard Delany say it.

"It *started* that way," Delany says, "I thought you could help me. But ... I thought I could help you too. I *did* want to help you. You know that, right?"

I don't know anything anymore, Jared thinks.

"But you've gotta know why I couldn't just come right out and tell you everything all at once. I mean, it was too much. You never would have believed it. You would have thought I was crazy. But you believe it now. Right?"

Of course I do, Jared wants to say. *I don't have any choice—you made sure of that.*

"Listen," Delany says, "I know you feel like ... like I misled you or something. Maybe I did, I don't know." Delany stares down at the ground like he's looking for the answer to something. When he looks back up, his eyes are bright and hard. "But you still need me."

"No. I don't."

"Jared," Delany says, "I know your dad's in trouble. I can help you."

"*How?* What are you gonna do? Are you gonna do card tricks? Cut my brain open?"

Delany raises his hands, palms outward, like he's trying to slow down the blood that's pounding in Jared's head. "Just come to my place tonight..."

"No."

"Listen. Just ..."

"It only works at Angel Falls!" Jared spits out the words with disdain. *Big fucking teacher,* Jared thinks, *think you know so much.*

Delany stares at Jared, surprise and understanding filling his eyes, then his look darkens.

"You think you know more about this than I do?" Delany says, his voice turning hard and dangerous. "How long has it been, Jared? A month? Four weeks? I've been studying this thing for *fifteen years*, Jared. *Fifteen years.*"

"Yeah? And what good did *that* do? How's that working out for you?" *Did it get your son back?* It's right on the tip of Jared's tongue.

"Jared, you're a kid. You're a fucking kid, okay? You don't know what you're doing. You think you do, but you don't. I'm trying to help you out, here."

"You *lied* to me! I trusted you! I trusted you and you fucking lied to me!"

"I did *not* lie to you! I kept things from you. Things I didn't think you could handle. But I never lied to you. It's not the same thing."

"Bullshit! How do you know what I can handle? What gives you the right to decide that?"

"Fuck, Jared. That's the way it is. That's what teachers *do*." Delany pauses to collect himself, and when he speaks again his voice is quieter. "That's what fathers do."

Fathers...?? The word hangs suspended in the air for a moment, before it explodes in Jared's head—then he's pushing past Delany, his brain flooded with rage.

"Jared ..." Delany reaches out with one hand, but Jared shoves it away.

"Go to hell!" Jared shouts. He swings one leg over his bike, stands up on the pedals and starts pumping as hard as he can, the flat tires rumbling and wobbling crazily under him. He can hear Delany's voice behind him, calling his name, but he keeps riding as hard and fast as he can until he can't hear it anymore.

CHAPTER 43

THEY SLEEP IN DUST

Jared's shoulder aches from carrying his useless bike, and his shirt is soaked with sweat as he approaches the door of Jessie's house. Before he can knock, it swings open. Jessie's standing there, clutching the red folder under her right arm, her face strained and pale.

Without a word, she takes him by the arm and leads him away from the door and off of the porch. He follows her through the narrow space between the houses into a small patch of yard surrounded by high brick walls and completely overshadowed by a single oak tree. At the foot of the tree there's an antique iron bench curled around the trunk. She brings him to the bench and then sits down heavily, her eyes exhausted.

"Those people, in the file," she begins in a quiet, nervous voice. "The ones we read about yesterday ..."

Jared nods. Jessie swallows and continues.

"I went online to see if I could find them." She stops and Jared is startled to see tears at the corners of her eyes. "It's not good," she says, shaking her head. "It's *really* not good."

"What? What do you mean?"

Jessie takes a deep breath and starts. "Remember the family with the girl who came back?"

"The teenage girl? Yeah."

"Amy Jones. Back in 2007. They're dead."

"Who? Her parents?"

Jessie shakes her head. "All of them. The girl, her parents, her two kid brothers. They're all dead."

"What happened?"

"There was a car wreck. The car burned. They all died."

"Jesus, that's terrible."

Jessie shuts her eyes and shakes her head. "That's not all. The girl. The one who disappeared and came back. When they did the autopsy, her dental records matched, but the DNA didn't. The medical examiner said there was something *wrong* with it."

"So ... it *wasn't* her?"

Jessie shakes her head. "I don't know. It's almost like it *was* her, but it *wasn't*."

A loud *bang* makes Jared's heart explode in his chest. He looks toward the house and sees Jessie's father leaning out of the back door, the old wooden screen door still shuddering where it struck the side of the house.

"Hey, sweetie," Jessie's dad calls out. "*There* you are. Everything alright?"

"Yeah, Dad, everything's fine," Jessie calls back. She even manages a weak smile.

"Hey, Jared," Jessie's dad calls out, raising one hand. He's smiling, but Jared thinks he can see a trace of worry on his face.

"Hey," Jared says, raising his hand in the air. Jessie's dad closes the door and for a moment Jared can see him standing behind the screen, still looking at them, then he moves out of the frame.

Jared turns back to Jessie. The distracted, worried look is still on her face. "But ... there were other people in that file, right? Other people who came back. What about them? Did you find anything about them?"

Jessie nods. "You know the guy who disappeared in 1957? And then came back? Marsden? Harold Marsden?"

"Yeah...you mean the guy whose wife got remarried and everything?"

"I Googled his name and found some more stuff. The new husband started telling everyone that the guy who came back was an imposter, that he wasn't really Harold Marsden at all. But his wife said it *was* him."

"How do you know all this?"

"Court records. The second husband tried to get a restraining order. But he couldn't 'cause the court said there was no proof that the guy who came back was a threat. Then ... the wife and the first husband, Marsden. They disappeared. Everyone thought the second husband did it. You know—went crazy, got rid of them both."

"And he did?"

"Nobody knows. I mean, he got arrested. Held under suspicion. The whole time he kept saying that the guy who came back wasn't his wife's first husband, that he'd tricked her and stole her away from him. Anyway, they couldn't prove anything, so they let him go. Then he kind of went crazy. Spent the next nine years in the Danvers Lunatic Asylum."

"Jesus." Jared thinks hard, trying to do the math, but the numbers swim around in his head. "Do you think he's still around?"

"I don't know," Jessie frowns. "I couldn't find that. He *could* be. He'd be almost eighty now." Her eyes brighten. "Wait a minute. His sister. He had a younger sister. She's the one who got him out of the asylum. *She* might know something." Jessie flips through the pages. "Hettie Gardner."

"*Gardner?* Are you serious? Her brother ... is his name Pete?"

Jessie quickly scans the page in her hand. "Peter. Peter Gardner."

"Oh my God!" Jared shouts. "That's *Pete!* That's old Pete! *You* know ... the old guy who scared you, in the parking lot."

Jessie's eyes go wide. "Oh my God, that's *him?*"

"It's gotta be! We can talk to him, find out what he knows!" Jared looks at Jessie and sees fear in her wide blue eyes. "What's the matter?" he asks. "Isn't that what you *want* to do?"

"I don't know," she says. "I'm scared."

"Don't be," he says as quietly and calmly as he can. If he lets her see that he's scared too, they'll never go, never find out, and nothing will ever change.

"Okay," she finally says, rising to her feet. "Let's go."

Jessie leads them around to the front of the house—then Jared sees his ruined bike and curses. *"Shit!"*

"Jesus. How did *that* happen?"

"It was Delany. He did it, let the air out of my tires when I was in school..."

"What?" Jessie's face is a cartoon of shocked disbelief. "What the hell..?"

"He wanted to talk to me. He was afraid I wouldn't stop if I saw him."

"He didn't do anything, did he? He didn't try to hurt you..?"

"I told him I knew about his son."

"Oh my God..." Eyes wide and fearful, she stammers, "What...what did he say?"

"He admitted it. He said that's why he wanted me..." Jared can't finish it.

"It's true..." Jessie's voice sounds small and fragile. "He really wants you to bring back ..."

Jared sees Jessie start to tremble as if she's cold. "Jesus, Jess," he says, it's not that bad, okay?" He starts to pull her close, then stops, realizing his shirt is soaked with sweat. "Sorry...I guess I'm sort of disgusting, right?"

She laughs a little, shakes her head. He's glad he can still make her laugh. It's going to be okay. All they need to do now is find Pete. Go find Pete and talk to him. Maybe then they can learn how to control this thing. Keep his dad safe. Jessie's mom, too.

"Alright," he says. "Let's go."

"Shit!" Jared curses, seeing his bike's ruined tires. "My bike..."

"Don't be stupid. You can ride my dad's."

Chapter 44

It's Not There

"Wait here." Jessie leaves Jared standing in the yard, open-mouthed, and runs inside, past her mother on the couch, straight to her father at the kitchen table. He looks up from his documents.

"You okay, pumpkin?"

"Jared and I wanna go for a ride. Can he borrow your bike?"

"Juh- rddd?" She turns to see her mother is beckoning, pointing to the back door, then gesturing toward the room.

"We can't right now. I'll bring him in another time, 'kay?" Then to her father, "Can we have the bike, please?" She sounds like a whiny kid.

"Uh, well.. yeah. Sure. When will you be back?"

She runs over and kisses him on the top of his head. "Seven at the latest. Thanks!" She runs to her mother and kisses her cheek. "Don't talk too much!" She walks outside, past Jared and to the shed.

"He said it's fine. I told you." She pulls out her father's bike.

Jared takes it from her. "Whoa! How many gears does this thing have?"

"I dunno, 18? 21? I never ride it."

"Jesus. Where's the shifter?"

Jessie shows him all the controls, and then they adjust the seat.

Jared straddles the bike, "All right then. Let's go."

It takes him a couple of blocks to get the shifting down, but once he does he's off like a shot. Jessie has to pump hard to keep him in sight, and even so, he has to stop from time to time so she can catch up.

Soon they turn down the narrow road leading to the Neck, and then turn off onto a one block street, lined with single-story shingled cottages with wide windows. Many of them have flower boxes overflowing with red petunias.

"How do you know where he lives?" Jessie asks.

"I help him home sometimes."

He leans the bike against the fence with care and marches up the walk. A vision of Pete's squinty face rises up in her mind. "Wait! What will we say?"

"We'll ask him what he knows about Angel Falls."

"Just like that?"

"Yeah. Unless you have a better idea."

She wants to have a better idea, another option, but her mind feels stuck, like a broken gear has ground it to a halt. She shakes her head.

"Okay then. Follow me."

Jessie wants to stop him, but his hand is already raised and he's knocking.

The door opens. A thin woman with sharp features and bright blue eyes peers out at them with a suspicious frown. Then the lines in her face rearrange upwards into a broad grin, and her eyes sparkle.

"Jared Younger. Why, what a surprise! And you brought a friend. Please, come in. Come in."

"Hey, Miss Gardner. Is Pete here?"

"Yes, he's here. Introduce me to the young lady."

Jessie steps forward and smiles, though her cheeks feel frozen. "I'm Jessie Reed."

"Like Jesse James!" Miss Gardner claps her hands. "Pleasure to meet you. Come on in. Would you like some tea?"

Jessie gives Jared a long look, not knowing what to do. He gives Miss Gardner a brilliant smile.

"Thank you, but no. We don't want to trouble you. Just want to ask Pete a couple of questions."

"He isn't in trouble, is he?" Miss Gardner's eyes turn dull and wary. "You know, I don't think he *is* here after all," and she backs in the doorway and starts to close the door.

"No trouble, Miss Gardner. I promise. I told Jessie he has some good stories about the old days. Fisherman stories, you know? She asked to come meet him." Again, that brilliant smile. It makes Jessie's insides warm. She's sure no one can resist it, and she's right.

"Oh. Well then, come on inside. I'll fix the tea." And after they cross the threshold, she whispers, "Just don't get him going too long. If he gets agitated, you just stop and go away. You hear me, Jared? You just stop."

"Yes ma'am."

After a short, crowded entryway full of coats on hooks and framed prints, photos and embroidery samplers covering every square inch of wall, the room opens into a larger space. In the center of the room, beneath chandelier of perforated tin, is a round table, topped with an embroidered cloth, a bowl in the center overflowing with flowers.

Pete is seated at the table, a blue-glazed earthenware mug in his hands. He studies them all with a look of amazement, as if they'd materialized out of thin air instead of walking noisily through the front door, boards creaking and groaning with every step.

Jared walks right up to him, puts out his hand. "Hey Pete. How ya doin'?"

Pete's face cracks into a smile, his right eye squeezing closed while his left becomes a perfect upside 'u.' "Jared! Jared. Good to see you!" he takes Jared's hand and shakes it hard. "How's your father? I saw him on the beach today."

Jared's face falls and the skin around his eyes grows tight. "Where? Was he in the cove? Did he have his paints?" Jessie puts her hand on his arm.

"No. Maybe. I don't remember," Pete rubs his eyes and looks directly at Jessie for the first time.

"I know you. You were in a car. I thought you were my Hettie here," he makes a swipe as if to grab his sister, but she sidles out of reach and leaves the room.

"Yes," Jessie swallows, "I'm Jessie Reed."

"Reed? Reed... I knew a George Reed. Lived over on Granville Road. By Biddie Hicks. I think they were cousins."

"That's my grandfather," Jessie says, amazed. "You knew him?"

Pete's right eye closes. At first Jessie thinks he's winking, but after a moment, when it doesn't open again, she realizes he can't control it. His left eye is wandering meanwhile, until it lands on Jessie's sneakers.

"Pink sneakers. I never."

Jared leans forward, "Pete, can we ask you something? About the past. About Angel Falls?"

Pete's right eye pulls open with effort, and both eyes burn into Jared with a fierceness that's startling. "Don't go there. You can't ever go there. She went there and she never came back."

"Who did Pete?" Jared asks. "Who went there?"

"You don't want to know. None of your business," he looks at his mug, takes a drink. Jessie gets a whiff of alcohol.

"Why shouldn't we go to Angel Falls?" Jared continues, gently.

Pete looks at Jared, a sudden clarity, almost peace coming to his face. "The dark lady lives there."

Jared looks at Jessie, his eyes wide and vulnerable. Jessie wants to reassure him, but he's looking back at Pete, swallowing hard and saying, "Does she have a face?"

Pete looks frightened now, his right eye starting to close, "You've seen her? She took my Deirdre away."

An image of a faceless woman dragging Pete's young wife away starts to form, and Jessie squeezes it out. She sits across from Pete and resting her arms on the table, leans towards him, hands inches from his. "Deirdre? Was that your wife? I'm so sorry." Her voice is low and gentle. Pete stares at their hands for a moment, then looks up at her gratefully.

"You've been there too."

"Please. We need to know. What happened to your wife?"

Pete curls up, head low on his chest. "Have you seen her?"

Jessie looks up at Jared who shakes his head. He sits next to Pete. "No, Pete. Can you tell us what happened?"

Pete's head drops forward. Jessie gasps. For a minute she thinks he's dead, but then he starts speaking, it's hard to make out what he's saying.

"She married me for the baby. Wanted him to have a father. I loved her so I didn't care. I didn't know what she was doing. 'I need some air,' she'd say. 'I'm going to pick berries,' but she wasn't, she didn't. She was summoning him."

"Harold?" Jessie says.

Pete looks at her through his open eye. "You know Harold? The bastard died but he wouldn't stay that way."

"She... Deirdre brought him back?" Jared prompts.

Now Pete sits up, pops open the lazy eye and looks at Jared with clear pure hate. "No she did not, sir. She did not bring back Harold. What she brought back wasn't him."

Jessie looks at Jared but he's focused on Pete. He says, "Yes, we know. Then what happened?"

Pete stands up, banging the table with his legs, his mug tips and thick black liquid oozes onto the white embroidered cloth, a jagged stain growing, a black hole threatening to swallow them all.

"DEEDEE!" the scream comes from deep inside, tearing from his throat.

His sister runs out from the back, a towel in her hands which she drops to take her brother in her arms.

"What have you done?" she hisses to Jared and Jessie before murmuring, "It's okay, it's all right. She's not here, dear. You're safe now."

"Deedee!" he moans, so much weaker this time, now looking into his sister's face and repeating, "not here?" in a tone that breaks Jessie's heart. His sister leads him out of the room, talking to him in a high voice as if to a child.

"Your show is almost on. Let's go watch it, shall we?"

Jared turns tragic eyes on Jessie, jerks his head toward the door. They get through the front door and onto the walk when they hear Pete's sister.

"Children," she calls, making them stop and turn. "Come back, please."

She is standing behind the screen, in shadow; Jessie can't see her eyes. "Tell me why you came. Why you torture him with these old things."

Jared mumbles, "I'm sorry. I'm so sorry, Miss Gardner. We didn't want to hurt him."

"Then what? Why bring it up at all? Where did you hear of this? Why are you here?" She's ticking off a list of question, but something doesn't sound true to Jessie. *She knows why we're here,* she thinks.

"I ... we..." Jared fumbles for words, staring at his shoes.

Jessie looks directly into the old woman's eyes. "We want to know how it works." She feels Jared staring at her but doesn't take her eyes off the woman. "You know, don't you? You know what I mean."

Jared touches her arm so she'll look at him. His eyes are big with warning.

"You've done it, haven't you? You've brought someone... some *thing* back, and now you want to make it go away," Hettie's tone is edged with disgust, her mouth twisting. "I've got to get back to Pete. He's all I have, do you understand?" The woman looks over her shoulder into the house, then back to them. "You want my advice? Keep out of that place. Whatever you thought you wanted, it's not there." She starts to shut the door. Jared puts his hand up, his face is twisted, and his eyes look wet.

"Please, Miss Gardner, it's my dad. You don't know! I have to help him..." his voice is unrecognizable, so ragged and filled with grief, Jessie can't bear it.

The woman pauses, opens the door, puts her hand out and reaches for Jared's face. Jessie's back stiffens and she wants to shout *Don't touch*, but it's too late. The white hand, fingers twisted with age, knuckles thick, cups Jared's chin, the thumb wiping away a tear.

Her voice comes softer now. "You listen here. Caleb messed where he shouldn't have. I'm sorry about your mother. But Caleb brought it on himself. Like they always do. Keep out of that place, you hear me?" And she drops her hand and shuts the door.

They turn and walk slowly to their bikes. Jessie's limbs feel stiff and heavy, her mind slow. She keeps her eyes forward, afraid to look at Jared's face.

At the corner of where the Neck meets the mainland is a shale beach. The sun is low, and clouds are lit from beneath, pink, and orange and grey. The colors reflect in the water as it sucks out to sea. Without speaking, they drop their bikes and climb down the seawall onto the pebbled sand. After a while Jessie notices a puff of mist rising from a small hole in the sand. She blinks and waits to see if it recurs, and after another moment or two, it does, and then there's another one, a few feet away.

"Clams," Jared says, and she turns to see him staring at the puffs of mist rising at different intervals across the beach. She remembers the other things he's shown her, the boulders engraved with sayings, the graveyard, the cellar holes, all in Angel Falls.

She's crying before the full weight of loss hits her, and feels Jared wrap his arms around her, pulling her close.

"Shhh," he says, "It's okay," he whispers.

"We can't go back," she says, her voice strained and strange. "We can never go back." All that loveliness, the mystery, the magic, all gone. She pushes Jared away hard, almost making him fall.

"Hey!"

She marches up the ramp off the sand to where the bikes are lying and jerks hers off the ground.

"Jessie, where are you..."

"I hate this place. I wish I never came. I want to go home." She mounts her bike and stands on the pedals ready to pump but Jared stands in her way.

"Okay," he pauses, his voice calm, despite the effort to hold her bike still. "I'll bring your dad's bike back tonight when I get off work. We'll talk then." He's staring right at her, like her father does when he's telling her to do chores. He's telling her, not asking, and it makes her want to scream.

"Let... me... *Go*!" She sees a man and his dog stopping across from them, looking at them. Jared turns his head, loosens his grip a little. She pushes down on the pedal hard, the rear wheel slipping a little, then gripping, flinging her forward through Jared's arms, his body arching backward, almost falling. She hears him calling, "Jessie! Wait!" She pedals harder.

CHAPTER 45

THE CALL

It's getting dark when Jared rides up to Rick's. He leans the bike—Jessie's dad's bike—carefully against the side of the building, then hesitates. It's all too much, all too strange, Rick's forgiving phone call, Jessie's harsh words when they parted. *I hate this place. I wish I never came here.* It hurts, the thought that this place that she now hates includes him.

Rick is there waiting for Jared when he walks into the kitchen.

"How are you, Jared?" Rick peers down at him like a doctor looks at a patient.

"I'm okay," Jared says. He tries to slip inside, unnoticed, but Rick doesn't move out of the way, so Jared has to stand there on the threshold, waiting for whatever Rick has to say next.

"What happened here Friday night, I can't have that here. Understand?"

Jared nods, feeling heat rise to his face. *Just let me in*, he thinks. *Stop talking at me and let me in.*

Rick steps aside and for a moment Jared wonders, *Did I just make that happen?*

But he knows it wasn't him, because he's not in Angel Falls. And the sadness hits him, like it hit Jessie before—not because he can never go back, but because he can never go back there with her.

He can't imagine it. Angel Falls without Jessie. He thinks of the first time he stumbled upon her at the moraine, sitting on her bike and looking around at the giant rocks and thick green vines. He remembers what it felt like to find her there, in *his* place. She was a trespasser. An invader. And then she wasn't. He'd shown her things, seeing the place through her eyes. And then she'd shown him things. And everything was new.

Jared plunges his hands into the hot soapy water and scrubs the dirty plates, not seeing them, not feeling them. What fills his mind is the look of disappointment and fear in Jessie's face. Disappointment in him. She'd deny it, but he feels it the same. He'd led them both there, to Pete's house, and she'd followed him, trusted him, like she'd done all along. And he'd failed. Failed her. Failed his father too. Failed them all.

You can't fix this. The words come to him clearly as if someone is standing at his shoulder, whispering them into his ear, and for a moment he almost turns around to see who's standing behind him. *You can't fix this.* There's almost comfort in that thought. *You can't fix this. Stop trying. Stop running around from one place to another looking for answers. Because there aren't any. Or, if there are, you will never find them. Give up. Give up.* He feels something in his body like dark water, a rising flood that extinguishes every light it touches; it isn't relief. It's numbness, and he thinks he understands what his father was trying to do when he picked up the razor blade that night.

"*NO!*" The word explodes from Jared's lips. He looks up to see Kate standing in the kitchen doorway, staring at him wide-eyed.

"Jared," she says in a voice that strains to sound normal, "Phone for you."

Jared wipes his hands on the dishtowel hanging nearby and walks to the old black phone on the wall near the kitchen door. He puts one finger over his right ear to block out the sound of shouted orders and clattering plates.

"Yeah?" he shouts into the receiver. The voice on the other end is muffled and scratchy and he can't recognize or understand it. "Wait. Wait a minute," he says, and tries to move as far away from the door and the noisy counter as he can, until the cord to the receiver is stretched tight. Pressing his finger even harder over his other ear, he says again, "Yeah? Hello?"

The scratchy sounds on the other end come together into syllables, words. A voice. "Jared..."

"Yeah," Jared says, and in the second before the voice speaks again, Jared knows who it is.

"I've got your dad."

The words whirl around in Jared's head, refusing to come into focus. "What?"

"*Your dad,*" Delany's voice rises a little in pitch. *I've got your dad.* The words start to slow down and come into focus.

"What do you mean?" Jared says. "What's going on? Is he okay? Where are you?"

"Angel Falls," Delany's voice measures the words out slowly. "Meet me at Pulpit Rock."

"What ... is he hurt? How did you ..."

"You better get here now." Then the line goes dead.

Jared leans against the wall with the receiver still in his hand, his mind racing. Angel Falls? Where his dad swore he'd never go again? It's not right. Not right. And Delany...

Jared pulls out his cell phone and sees the power drained, almost dead. He hits the speed dial button for his dad. If his dad's okay, he'll pick up. He listens to it ring once, twice, three times... The power warning message pops up onscreen. Five rings, six... *Pick up, pick up*...Then, finally, the click, followed by his dad's awkward sounding recorded greeting. "This is Caleb Younger...Leave a message and I..." The loud beep stabs Jared's ear and the phone goes dead and dark in his hand.

Pulling the apron off from around his waist, Jared steps out of the kitchen and behind the counter where Rick is ringing up a customer. "Rick," he says, knowing this is the end of his job, not caring. Rick turns and frowns at him, at the wet apron trailing from his hand. "Rick, I'm sorry. I gotta go. It's my dad. Something's wrong."

Rick's frown immediately changes to a look of concern. "Go."

The summer air is hot and thick as Jared pedals hard, standing up and pumping his legs as fast as he can. Car drivers honk and hit their breaks as he blasts through the red light at the corner of Plymouth, but he doesn't stop or slow down.

When he finally gets past the town where there are no more cars, he tries to think clearly, figure it out. *What happened? What was his dad doing at Angel Falls? What was Delany doing there?* If his dad was hurt—if he'd tripped and fallen on the rocks, or worse—why hadn't Delany called 911? Why call him? No ... there's something wrong about it; none of the pictures fit. But he can't stop. It's his dad, and he rises up from the seat and pedals faster into the growing darkness ahead.

CHAPTER 46

THE DARKEST EVENING OF THE YEAR

By the time Jessie reaches her house, her face is dry, the skin stiff with salt and her jaw hurts from clenching her teeth.

Maybe they can leave Beauport tomorrow. Maybe she can put the whole thing behind her forever.

As she pulls her bike into the backyard, she sees her dad beside the grill, piling up charcoal.

"Hi Pumpkin," he says. "Burgers or dogs?"

The thought of food makes her nauseated, she clenches her teeth and swallows hard. But she doesn't want the interrogation that follows the words *I'm not hungry.*

"Um... burger I guess." She stows the bike and goes to the back door.

"What happened to Jared?"

Happened? "Wha... what do you mean?" she says, her throat tight.

"You left together...with my bike..." he gestures with the spatula.

"Oh." She exhales sharply, before saying in a rush, "He's at work, he'll bring the bike back later. I hope that's okay," and she goes inside the house.

She notices flickering images on the TV screen, but there's no sound. Her mom isn't watching. Instead, she's pulled up a chair close to the diorama, and studies the figures by the farmhouse. Jessie wants to pull her away from it, tip the base again and make the figures fly. Instead, she touches her mother's shoulder.

"Mom?"

Her mom turns to her, and Jessie tries not to flinch. Her face looks worse than when Jessie left—only an hour ago or two? —more bruising, the jaw lopsided. There is a patch of wet from the opening in her clenched jaw to the edge of her chin, and as Jessie watches, it forms into a drop and then a thin stream of drool. Jessie has to look away.

"I...I think I'll help Dad with dinner," she says.

"Wait," her mother stands, grabs her crutches and hobbles to the couch, gesturing for Jessie to follow.

"Is Jared outside?" Her words, still pressed through teeth are a little clearer now, but Jessie sees the strain in her cheeks.

"He had to go to work." Jessie sits, keeping her face turned away. She can still hear his desperate, *Jessie, wait!*

She feels her hair being lifted from her neck, gently tugged. "What's the matter, cupcake?" The last word is particularly crushed *k-k-k-p kehk.*

"I want to go home." Jessie leans her head onto her mother's shoulder, her lips start to tremble. She closes her eyes and lets her mother's body comfort her. "Did you have a fight?"

Jessie's eyes fly open.

"We didn't fight." She's suddenly back by that shale beach, Jared holding her bike, so beautiful, so calm, despite all they'd learned. She stifles a sob.

"Shhhh. It's okay. You'll see. Hush, now." The words are tortured and strange, *Y'll sheee, Shhhh, no,* but the voice, low and musical, is still her mom's voice, and it comforts her.

A loud bang from the back door and her dad comes in carrying two plates with burgers and potato salad. "Dinner is almost served. Smoothie's on its way."

Jessie's mom sits up, reaches for the TV remote, and the room is filled with the sound of crackling flames. Jessie stares at the screen.

Flumes of water shoot from hoses into towering yellow-orange flames. Firefighters race between trucks. The camera zooms in on a single black wall, flames shooting from the open frame of a window. Jessie can see the sky behind the fire. A photo fills the screen, high school yearbook picture of a girl, Jessie's age. Just as she realizes who it is, the words shoot across the screen in a wide banner:

Karen Holcomb, missing girl, dead in fire.

The scene returns to the smoldering charred building, and firefighters manning hoses. A news reporter stands in front of it all holding a microphone, but Jessie only catches a few of her words; "unbelievable tragedy...home burned to the ground... entire family dead."

Jessie turns it off, her brain dull with shock.

"That girl," her mom says. "The one who disappeared. It's so sad."

"My God!" Her dad's voice behind them. Jessie swivels around. He's standing in the kitchen doorway. "They just got her back. Last week, right? They just..." he trails off, stares out the window.

Jared! She needs to tell him. "I'll be right back." She jumps up and goes to the bathroom. Pulls out her phone and texts:

Karen Holcomb's dead. Her family, too. A fire.

She waits for a few moments, remembering he's at work, he probably won't get the message for a while. Texts again:

I'm sorry. About earlier. Text me please.

Back in the living room she finds her dad sitting on the couch next to her mom reading something on the laptop.

"We could leave on Saturday." Her father says, looking at her mom's face. She looks relieved and lays her head back against the sofa cushion.

Saturday! She is paralyzed in the doorway. Four days. In four days she'll leave Beauport, Angel Falls, Jared! forever? *I want to go home.* She'd just said it to her mom. She'd said it to Jared.

It's too soon. She's not ready.

The minutes crawl by, and Jessie wants to throw her phone out the window for its silence. Finally, it's 9 o'clock. And then 9:05. By 9:10 she can't bear it; she goes to her room and calls Jared. It goes straight to voicemail.

She paces around her room before getting up the courage to call Rick's. A woman picks up, "This is Rick's, hold please." An electric guitar squeals a solo of a song she doesn't recognize. The woman comes back on half-shouting over the noise of clattering dishes, "Can I help you?"

"Is Jared there? Could I speak with him please?" She has to repeat it twice before the woman can hear her.

"Nah, he's gone."

"How long ago? He was... supposed to come..." she trails off.

"I don't know honey. He got a call and left early. Try his cellphone."

"I *did* try his cell. It's dead, I..." she realizes the woman hung up.

And then it hits her; why would he leave work early? Something's wrong.

She walks into the living room and grabs her shoes. Her parents look up. "Is it okay if I go over to Jared's? It isn't far. I won't be long." She can see the surprise on their faces, knows they're about to say 'no'. So she says, "He's... his phone is dead. I'm worried. His dad's been... sick and..."

To her surprise, her father stands up, "I'll drive you."

"No!" It's too firm, so she tries to cover, "Thanks. I'd rather walk. Is it okay?"

Her mother looks intently at her father for several moments, then she reaches out. Jessie goes to her, takes her hand. Her mother nods. "Call us when you find him."

She pulls her close and kisses her cheek. "Be back here by 10:30 latest!"

Jessie flies out the door on a breathless, "Thanks!," the night air hitting her in the face, hot and wet. She walks quickly up the hill, over several blocks, the streets looking strange in the late dusk. Finally, Jared's building rises up in front of her. The lights are on in the upstairs apartment, and she runs the last block.

At the top of the stairs, she hesitates. What if nothing's wrong? What if she's interrupting them? She pictures Jared's face, annoyed, *why are you here?* Her limbs are so stiff it's hard to lift her arm, but she knocks, and the door swings open.

"D'you forget your keys, buddy? I made your fave...." the voice trails off.

Jared's dad is in the doorway, looking at her with surprise. She smells paint, notices splotches of gray and blue paint on his arms. The surprise changes to a friendly smile. "Jessie, isn't it? Well, what a nice surprise. Come in, come in. Are you hungry?"

She's having trouble connecting what she sees to what she expected. There's no ambulance, blood, despair. Instead, Caleb is standing here, clear-eyed and smiling. She has to clear her throat as her face grows almost unbearably hot.

"I'm sorry to bother you. Is Jared here?"

Caleb is pressed against the wall, waiting for her to enter, so she does. "He's probably right behind you," he says. "Come in and wait for him. Have you eaten?" Something smells good. Her stomach growls, reminding her she hasn't eaten. Along one side of the room there is a canvas pinned to the wall, light strokes outlining a beautiful cove bordered by a breakwater. Then she remembers why she came.

"I called Rick's and they said he left early, got called away. I thought..." She stops, looks down and catches a glimpse of the scars before he folds his arms across his chest, hands disappearing under his armpits.

"They said Jared left early?"

"Yeah," Jessie says quietly, embarrassed.

"It wasn't me. But I guess you figured that out."

"He didn't call you?" she asks him.

"No... well... I don't think so..." he moves around the room, searching till he comes up with a phone, looks at the screen. "I'll be damned," spoken softly, a frown forming. "He did call. Damn ringer is off, I'm always forgetting..."

Jessie runs to his side, peers at the phone. "What did he say?"

"No message," he's pressing buttons slowly, checking to see if there's a message he missed, or a text, Jessie has to restrain herself from pulling the phone from his hands.

"What time was it?" They both bend over the phone.

"Over an hour ago. He should be here by now," his dad says, frowning. He presses something on the phone and holds it to his ear. She can hear Jared's voice, tiny, higher pitched, the word *Hey,* and it's enough to give her hope. He's okay. But then it's only the rest of a recording: *Time and tide wait for no man. So what's up?* and then the beep.

"Hey, it's your dad. Give me a call. Jessie's here. You're worrying me, buddy." *We're wasting time,* she thinks. But she doesn't know what to do.

"Jessie. What's going on?" Caleb is watching her with friendly concern. He seems completely unafraid. But Jessie knows, by a sudden sharp pain behind her eye, that Jared is in trouble – and then she thinks she knows who called him.

"Mr. Younger, can you check call records? You know, online?"

The kindness on his face disappears. "You want me to spy on my son?"

"Mr. Younger. Please. I think he's in trouble."

His eyes narrow and his voice goes hard. "What kind of trouble?"

Jessie freezes. There's no way to answer without sounding crazy.

"Listen Jessie," Caleb moves to the kitchen, adjusts the flame under a pot, "I don't know what happened, but I'm sure he'll call me back when he sees the message..."

"His phone is off. He's not getting messages. He's over an hour late. Don't you think something's wrong?" She can hear panic in her voice, sees how closely Caleb is studying her. *Does he think she's crazy, a strange psychotic girl?* "Please," her voice wavers and she clears her throat, digging her fingernails into her palms. "Please, can you check the call?"

He frowns, but nods once, moving toward another room. She follows, finding herself in a room covered with posters of metal bands.

Caleb is in front of a massive ancient-looking computer terminal, pale yellowed plastic on all sides. There's a grinding noise, then a 'whir' then the entire screen clicks and turns blue. She moves over to watch as he opens a browser and starts to log in to his account. It takes a few tries, but finally it works, but then he stops, squinting at the screen. *Just let me do it,* she almost says. Instead, she leans over to point at the icon with Jared's phone number. "Click here," and when he does, she points to the words, *usage,* and *calls.* "Now this, and this," and a list of numbers appear, the last call five minutes ago. "Is that your number?" she asks. When he nods, she looks at the next one. "That one's mine," she tells him, points to the next one, "Do you recognize this one?"

"No. Looks like it's in Beauport."

"Put it into Google."

Instead of cutting and pasting, he searches for a pen and paper, writes the number down, opens a new screen, types in the numbers carefully. Jessie wants to scream; it's all taking so long. But finally a name appears, complete with address, and the bottom of her stomach falls away.

"Chris Delany?" Jared's father says. "Why would he call Jared?"

"Oh my God," Jessie feels the air leave the room, but her legs know what to do and she's out of the bedroom and almost to the front door before Caleb stops her.

"What's going on?"

"Please. I have to go. We can't waste time..."

"*Tell* me what's going on."

I can't! she wants to say, knowing how useless it is. She takes a deep breath, "Delany's crazy. He got kicked out of school for punching a kid, and…" she hesitates before the lie, but pushes on, "…he burned Jared with a cigarette."

"What?" Caleb's eyes move quickly from amazement to anger. "Why is he calling Jared? Is he threatening him?"

"Yes," she nods quickly; it's the easiest thing to say.

"Bastard!" and then he's grabbing keys, phone. He disappears into Jared's room and returns with a slip of paper. "His house is ten minutes away, let's go!"

Everything looks different by streetlight, but Jessie recognizes the turn and within minutes they are pulling up to Delany's house. A single light glows in an upstairs window, but the driveway is empty. And no sign of the borrowed bike.

"Place looks empty," Caleb pulls out his phone and stares at the screen. "Still nothing. Where else would he take him?"

Jessie tries to think. "The school?" But she knows it's wrong; why would Delany risk that? And then it comes to her, stomach dropping. "They're in Angel Falls. We have to go now!"

But Caleb doesn't move. He's not listening. He looks frozen.

"What are you waiting for? Let's go!"

"But why… there? Why Angel Falls?"

"Because that's where it works! Please, we have to go! Jesus!" and she starts to cry, realizing all the things he doesn't know, all the things she can't tell him.

"I can't. I'm sorry. I just …" His hands grip the steering wheel, knuckles pale in the darkness. "I promised I would never go back."

The words make no sense. "What?"

"You don't understand. I can't." He raises his face to look at her, his eyes lit by the dashboard, his mouth a shadowy grimace. "That place is evil."

He knows?

She can't think of anything else to say, so the truth comes spilling out.

"Delany's son disappeared several years ago. He thinks Jared has the power to bring him back. Please, I don't know what he'll do to Jared if he can't make it happen."

She expects surprise, disbelief, but what she sees on Caleb's face is a weary grief.

There's fear there as well, and she watches it transform into grim determination.

"Alright," he says, "Let's go."

CHAPTER 47

PULPIT ROCK

The trail to Pulpit Rock is long, winding up the steep ridge in switchback patterns, but Jared has no time to waste so he takes the short cut through the woods, even though he hasn't brought a light. The moon is nearly full, and patches of pale light filter down through the branches, but where the trees are thick, the light is choked-off and Jared crashes blindly through the blackness. Briars and thorns catch and pull at his clothes, scratch his arms and hands, but he keeps going.

Pulpit Rock. A place he'd never shown to Jessie. A place he rarely went himself. An outcropping of stone like the broken jaw of a whale that thrust out from the lip of the highest cliff. Like a lightning rod, it drew stories to itself—about the crazy preacher who'd howled his sermons about the fire at the end of the world from that rock a hundred years ago. And hundreds of years before that, the Native Americans who'd made sacrifices there. He'd re-enacted some of those sacrifices with his friends back when they were twelve, bored and crazy for something to do, first with beetles and worms, then with frogs, grinding them into dark stains on the shale.

Why was his dad at Pulpit Rock? Or anywhere near Angel Falls? *Never again,* he'd sworn. Like Jared and Jessie were going to have to swear. *Never again.* And now here he is, maybe for the last time, climbing toward the darkest heart of it.

The trees part and Jared is in the clearing before he realizes it, blue moonlight reflecting from the wide slope of slate under his feet, which rises like a ramp toward the jagged outcropping.

He looks around for Delany, for his dad, but sees no one. No sign that anyone was here at all. He looks at the whale-jaw of stone thrust out over the edge of the cliff and imagines walking over to the edge and looking down. He doesn't want to see what might be down there. But he has to. Heart pumping wildly, a feeling of sickness rising in his throat, he steps carefully to the end of the ledge, the yawning gulf below pulling at him, and looks down—nothing but blackness.

"He's not down there."

The voice behind him is so close that Jared feels like he's been pushed, and he grabs the rock to steady himself before he turns. Delany is standing in the blue light on the rock slope, looking even thinner than before. For a moment Jared almost thinks he can see the moonlight shining through him. "Where is he?" Jared asks. "Where's my dad?"

"I've got him," Delany says.

"Where is he?" Jared says again, looking around.

"I said I've got him. I didn't say he was here."

Jared stares at Delany for a moment, letting what he's said sink in, then the strength drains from his legs, and he crumples, first to his knees, then all the way down until he's sitting on the cool rock floor, looking up at Delany towering over him.

"Oh, have I got your attention now?"

Jared looks up at Delany, his mind reeling. "Where is he? What did you do to him?"

"What do you care?" Delany spits the words at him. "Seriously, why should you give a shit about where he is?" Before Jared can answer, Delany steps closer, reaches down and grabs Jared by the wrist.

"Okay, show me," Delany says. "Show me the place where I burned you."

Jared pulls his arm away and moves a little further away from the ledge, keeping his eyes on Delany. "That's right," Delany says. "You can't. You can't because it's not there. You made it go away, remember? Now look at this."

Jared watches Delany pull up his left sleeve. High above the elbow there's a long white scar, old and healed but still angry looking. "See that? I can't make that go away like you can, Jared. You know how it got there? I did it. I did it the day after the cops told me they were going to stop looking for my son. I did it because I didn't have someone like you there to save me, like you saved your dad. I had to save myself. You know what I did? I tied a fucking extension cord around my arm and drove myself to the hospital. I was bleeding all over the fucking car and I almost blacked out twice, but I did it. You know why? Because I knew if I stayed on that kitchen floor, I'd never see my son again. Even though everybody told me that was never going to happen, I came back anyway. I came back. I haven't done much with my life, Jared. Wasted twenty years teaching a bunch of brain-dead shit-head kids. But I did that. I came back for my son, and I never stopped looking for him. Never."

"Where's my dad?" Jared shouts. "What did you do to him?"

"You think he gives a fuck about you? My son was gone. But I came back for him. Your dad still *had* you. You were right there with him. And he tried to check out anyway. Remember when you came back to school—you had his blood on your shoes. Your own dad's fucking blood on your shoes. What kind of asshole does that to his own kid?"

"Shut up!" Jared screams. "You tell me where my dad is right now!"

"Or what? What are you gonna do, Jared? Kill me? You wanna kill me? Alright ..." Jared watches Delany move around him and stand with his back to Pulpit Rock. "I'll stand right here on the edge, like this. You wanna push me? That's what you want? Go ahead." Jared's blood is hammering so loud in his head he can hardly think, and for a moment, that's exactly what he wants, to run straight at Delany and drive both hands into his chest, hard enough to hear his ribs crack, and watch him disappear.

"This is where you thought your dad would be, right?" Delany says. "Standing right here on the edge like this ... just waiting for you to come along and pull him back, one more time? What about you, Jared? You know who was there to pull you back? Me. I was. All that time your dad was in the hospital, I stayed with you after school. When everybody else wanted to make you talk about it, I left you alone, I let you be quiet. And when you started talking about it, I let you talk. And I listened. Didn't I? I helped you, Jared. Why won't you help me?"

And now it hits Jared, like the hard ground at the bottom of a long fall—why Delany has brought him here.

"I can't bring your son back." The surge of regret and pity these words drag up takes him by surprise, and his throat swells shut.

"Yes you can," Delany's voice starts to shred. "I know you can. You know it too. Why won't you do it? Jesus, why do you hate me so much?"

I don't hate you, Jared wants to say, but he can't push the words past the ache in his throat. He takes a deep breath, swallows hard. "I'm sorry. I'm really sorry ... but it's not going to be the way you think it is. You think it's going to be a good thing. That's what everyone thinks. That's what I thought too. But it's not. It's bad. It's really, really bad."

Jared can't say the rest. He doesn't know how. He and Delany stand looking at each other in silence. Then a loud noise starts to rise up from the hills all around, a sound like rushing water, an invisible force moving through the leaves and setting them into motion. When Delany speaks again, his voice is low but harder, with an edge to it that sets Jared's nerves on fire.

"I thought you were different. But you're not. You were so worried about that. Remember what you said to me? I don't want to be different? Well, guess what. You're not. You want so fucking much to be normal? Congratulations. You are. You're just as stupid and self-centered as the rest of these shitheads around here. How's it feel, Jared? How's it feel to be just like everyone else?"

The noise in the trees is deafening now, louder than Jared has ever heard. He starts to walk past Delany, not knowing where he's going, not caring, then finds himself flat on his face, hands burning and forehead aching from where the rocky ground has scraped them. He rolls over and sees Delany standing over him, a looming silhouette against the thrashing leaves.

"Don't walk away from me, Jared. Don't you ever walk away from me again."

Jared can't believe what has happened. Delany has never put his hands on him like that. He's ashamed to feel tears burning his eyes, and he wipes them away angrily.

"Alright," Delany says, "I'll make this simple. You want to see your dad? Then bring my son back. Now."

"No. You don't understand."

"No, *you* don't understand! You don't get to say no anymore, Jared. Not anymore."

"Listen, please, listen to me.." Jared says, shouting to be heard over the thrashing sound of the trees. "It's not like you think. What comes back ... it won't be your son. It's something else."

"Shut up!" Delany shouts, taking a step closer to Jared. "You want your dad? Bring my son back! Do it! Now!"

Jared searches for more words to say, but there are none. All he knows now is that he has no choice. Not anymore. His dad ....

Jared closes his eyes, squeezing them shut, and tries to figure out how to do this. It's Delany's wish, not his, and he can't get a grip on it, can't make it real. He shuts his eyes tighter and looks for that little spark inside, a glimmer in the dark. But there's nothing there. Of course not. He can't do it alone. He needs Jessie.

"I can't do it."

"Yes you can," Delany shouts at him. "Do it! Do it now!"

Helplessness overwhelm him. He can't do it. It's over. Then the fear. What will happen to his dad now? *No...* He has to try. Jared holds his breath until the blood is pounding in his ears, digging deep into the darkness behind his eyes for something, anything.

Another noise begins. Jared can hear it from far away, rising up from the hills and valleys beyond the ridge, a long harsh sound like something being torn away, a rip opening in the fabric of the world. The sudden pop and release of pressure as the world rushes in. Leaves. He sees leaves moving, or he is moving through them, or someone else is. Moving fast, then the image breaks apart, like a momentary reflection on the surface of rough water, coming together, breaking apart, then coming together again. A glimpse, a glimmer, but it's enough, and he knows that he's not alone.

Jessie.

CHAPTER 48

A PLAGUE OF ANGELS

Jared! A wave, an uprush of the earth, the sound of wind in leaves increasing to a roar, then silence. *He's here. He knows I'm here. Everything is going to be okay.*

"Where do we go now?"

The voice is like Jared's but not; she knows it's his father talking, but Jessie can't see him. What she sees is a part of Angel Falls where she's never been. Great stone rising against the moonlit sky. She's longing to see Jared but knows she's looking through his eyes. *Pulpit* comes to her, and she speaks the word.

"Pulpit rock? That's where they are? Come on!" Caleb's face comes into view and he's gesturing to follow him. They start to run.

Her mind fills again with the clarity, the surge of power, that sense of being completely sure, and she realizes he's doing it, he's wishing.

Jared, don't!

I have to. I'm sorry.

The image he's sending, so unclear, more words than image, *boy* and *come,* and Jessie thinks it's not too late.

Stop. Now. It's okay. We're coming.

But Jessie can imagine the boy, and the suggestion of him brings his name, Griffin, the picture in the paper, the *SpongeBob* pajamas, and there it is, there he is. *JESSIE!*

It's almost a scream, what does he see? *Blank-blank-blank, make your mind blank!* Jessie tells herself even as a terrible image appears next to that surging rock.

"NO! GO AWAY!" It's Caleb shouting and for a moment Jessie thinks she can see inside his mind too, it's all swirling and dark, like his storm paintings, but something in the darkness is starting to form, taking the shape of a woman.

Suddenly, she's airborne. Flying. *No.* Falling! *NO!* Her leg unable to come forward to catch her forward-moving body, and she's going down, slowly, oh so slowly, knowing, long before her knee hits the rock, before the skin of her hands is raked by debris on the trail she is screaming, *NO ... NO ... NO ... NO ... NO.* And then she's down and rolling over, the shock of it, the pain in her knee obliterating all else, until: *Jessie?*

Jessie!

It's like he's there, beside her, and she realizes it's stopped. The image stopped, and the pain in her knee is fading. Jared's father is squatting beside her, taking her bleeding hands in his, looking at her with despair in his eyes.

"S'okay. I'm fine," she says, her voice harsh. "Help me up." She doesn't want to see the damage, knows only that she has to continue, has to make it to that clearing, to Jared, to end this night once and for all.

She leans slowly onto her injured leg and a sharp jolt of pain and nausea rises up, making her grab at Caleb, letting him hold her up as she swallows hard, tries to will it away. Again she hears Jared's voice, his concern. *Jessie?*

I'm fine, it comes out testy, and she can feel a loosening in her mind, as if Jared was close to smiling.

This time when she puts weight on the leg, the pain is bearable, but she knows she can't run.

"You go," she says to Caleb. "I'll follow as best I can."

"I'm not going to leave you." The words are so familiar. In that voice so close to Jared's. And then she remembers, after their first meeting, after he did leave her, how he had looked at her and said those words. Yet she had left him. At the beach on the Neck, she sees his face as she shoved her bike past him, the deep unhappiness there.

"You have to go..." Jessie says, then Caleb disappears and she's in Jared's mind. She can see Delany for the first time. He's leaning over her, his face distorted and horrifying. It comes closer and she can feel his hands as he grabs Jared's shoulders, starts to shake him. *"Keep going! I saw him, I saw him, and you stopped, you fucking bastard. Keep going!"* She feels her neck snap as he pulls Jared up, shaking him, sees the hand rise and pull back...

"NO!" She screams, but the blow never falls.

"What is it? What's happening?" Caleb's hands are on her arms and his face in front of hers. Fathers and sons. Caleb wants his son. That's what Delany wants. Something's happening in her head, some knowledge, an image; fathers and sons. Jared's voice, when did he say this? *He was like a father to me.*

"Is he okay?" Caleb's voice is raked with pain, his eyes full of fear. He's seeing something else, that woman maybe; Jessie doesn't want to know.

"He's crying." Jessie sees Delany curled up, face in his hands, shoulders heaving, and tears come to her eyes.

"Jared?"

"No. Jared's okay. It's Delany."

Now she sees a small barefoot boy, at the base of the rock. It's clearer and clearer, and then she sees the strange light around him, sees the featureless face, like a mirage, one moment it's Griffin, then blank, then Griffin.

There's a flash, and then a *BOOM* so loud it takes several moments for her to realize it's thunder. Caleb grabs her arm and pulls her. "Come on!"

Her knee screams and burns, but she continues to hobble along holding Caleb's arm.

The wind in the trees is violent, leaves and branches fall around them as they hurry forward. Pressure is building inside her skull, the rain coming, and then it's there. Sheets of rain, filtering through the leaves and slapping them as they run, soaking their clothes, and filling their eyes.

Think of what he really wants. Jessie sends to Jared, and immediately receives, *He wants his son back.*

No, Jessie thinks. *He wants to stop hurting.*

She can see Griffin standing by the rock, every flash of lightning bringing out more details. His feet are bare, his hair is uneven on one side as if he's been sleeping on it. It burns an afterimage, strange child-like glow behind her eyelids. *What he wants... Think of something else. What does he want?*

Image of Griffin in a burst of lightning.

No, Jared. He wants a son. He wants you!

She sees again the weeping Delany, Jared's hand reaching out but not touching him. *Yes!*

All of a sudden she's indoors. Delany's hand reaches toward her, landing heavy and warm on her shoulder, all that comfort, security, acceptance. Now she's sitting at a desk, book open in front of her, Delany's seated in front, reading, simply being there, allowing her to be there too. "You can stay here as long as you like," Delany's voice, calm and practical. Then she's back in the woods, sees Jared's hand getting closer to Delany's back.

Son. He needs a son. She focusses on the hand, the weeping man, *touch him, go on.*

Something hard, like rock against rock, and Jared's hand stops. *He's got my dad.*

The fingers curl into a fist.

No! Jessie's thrown out of Jared's mind and sees Caleb's anguished eyes and wet face. He's mouthing words she can just make out, *Leave him alone!* Then she's back at Pulpit Rock, looking at the image of Griffin and something else, a figure rising behind him, or from him--*a woman.*

Jared stop! But the image continues to grow. And then she hears a voice outside her mind, a short distance up the path.

"Daddy?"

The voice is clear and horrible. Jessie and Caleb stop and look at each other for one horrifying moment as Jessie's every nerve-ending screams to run the other way.

"Jared! I'm coming!" Caleb shouts and he's running ahead. She follows, breaking into the clearing and there is Jared, hand extended but not quite reaching Delany, and there is Delany, water running down his face looking toward the rock, and there's the child-thing. It speaks again, and Jessie covers her ears.

"Daddy?"

Delany stands, starts walking towards the thing by the rock. "Griffin?"

"No! Stop!" Jessie cries, but he doesn't hear. Jared stands to follow, but the other figure, the horrible one, female, faceless, rises up behind and above Griffin; slowly she extends her arms.

Jessie shuts her eyes, and for a moment imagines her mother gesturing *come*, feels the warmth and softness of her, the firm grip she has when she holds Jessie, and she wants it so badly, she feels the beginning of a new wish. *No, Jessie!* Her eyes fly open.

Delany's kneeling on the ground, arms around the boy, she can see its arms around his neck, its head pressed against Delany's, and above them more arms, hungry and old, reaching and surrounding them both.

"Where's my dad?" Jared shouts, and the images by the rock ripple.

Delany turns, looks at Jared, and then his face contorts, mouth open in surprise and pain and he's clutching his arm, going down, falling slowly and Jared runs to catch him as the images behind begin to grow and swirl surrounding them both in a mist, and when it starts to dissipate, the child is gone. The woman's gone. There is only Jared kneeling beside his teacher's still body.

"We killed him, Jessie! Fuck. We killed him."

Caleb reaches him first, and then, as Jared turns to him in surprise, pulls him to his feet and into his arms. "I've got you, buddy. I've got you. It's over."

Chapter 49

Time and Tide

The sunlight is warm on Jared's face and arms. He tries to remember the last time he felt it—how many days since that night on Pulpit Rock? Five? Six? He's lost count, lost track of time in the dark haze that followed. It's like a blur to him, the sirens and flashing lights, the doctors, police, and psychologists, their questions and concerned faces, images from a dream he can't quite remember. The only thing that seems real from these past few days is his dad's presence, sure and steady by his side through all of it.

The tidal pools are full and still as glass, reflecting big pieces of the sky, flat mirrors full of clouds and light at their feet. Jared walks close to one of them and looks down, trying to see through the reflection of what's above to what's below. He sees a slight movement, something small scuttling or flickering away from the long shadow he's thrown across the surface of the water.

"See anything?" his dad asks.

"Yeah. I think so."

"You have to hold still," his dad says. "It takes a while, sometimes."

Jared tries to stand as still as he can, watching for signs of movement in the shallow water at his feet. It reminds him of something, and he suddenly feels the cold, hard surface of Pulpit Rock under his knees, his eyes shut tight, searching his mind for a glimmer of something hiding just out of sight.

His dad breaks the silence. "How long have you known, buddy?" Jared's heartbeat races. His dad doesn't explain what he means, but he doesn't have to.

"When Mom came back. That day you and I were at Angel Falls, and I said I wished Mom would come back. And the next day ... she was. I always felt like *I* did that, like I brought her back."

"*We* did, buddy. We both did that." Startled, Jared looks at his dad's face, haggard and tired, but his green eyes are clear. "I wanted her to come back too. We both did. That's how it happened. Anything that strong takes two people."

"Dad, was that really her? Was it Mom?"

"It was her," his dad says. "But ..." Jared's dad looks down at the sand at their feet, trying to come up with the words he needs. "We wanted her to come back. You did. And I did. But *she* didn't. She didn't want that." His dad squints out at the horizon where red clouds have started to gather. "Her heart wasn't there. So *she* wasn't there."

A gull caws overhead. Jared looks up and sees it flying across the dimming sky. *Trying to get home before dark,* he thinks. Jared watches his dad walk along the shoreline, his face lifted to catch the breeze from the ocean, drinking it in. It's been days since either of them have seen the sun or the sky, and he thinks of how their roles have been reversed over the past few days. Lying in bed in his darkened room, the heavy weight of guilt and grief pressing down on his chest, his dad always nearby, watching over him, watching and waiting for the darkness to lift.

"Dad," Jared says. "When did *you* know? I mean, about..."

"When I was twelve," his dad says, looking out over the waves. "My grandma was in the hospital. She had cancer. She was in a lot of pain. But I didn't want her to die. She was really great. I wish you could've known her. One day, my dad and I were at Angel Falls, and I told him I didn't want grandma to die. He said he didn't want her to die either." Another gull cries overhead. His dad peers up at it and takes a deep breath.

"So...she didn't. Not for a long, long time."

"How long?"

"A year. Almost two. The doctors didn't understand it. But I knew. We both knew."

"But ... she did die?"

"Yeah, buddy. She died."

"Did you ... did you *wish* for her to die?"

"No," his dad shakes his head. "She just kept getting worse and worse. It got really bad. We were just out at Angel Falls one day, my dad and me. He said he wished she wouldn't suffer any more. I said I wished that too. By the time we got back to the house, she was gone."

The weight of his dad's words presses down on him, each one heavier than the last. A sob rises in Jared's throat. He feels his dad's two strong hands on his shoulders.

"Listen to me, buddy. Listen. You did *not* kill that man. Do you hear me? You *did not* do that."

"But ... but you said ..."

"I said I wished my grandma would stop suffering. Don't you think she was wishing the same thing? A long time before I ever thought of it?" His dad grips his shoulders tighter, looking closely into Jared's face. "Delany had to *want* what happened. Somewhere inside, he had to want it. It's not because of you. Anything that big takes more than one person. Remember that."

Jared looks up at his dad's face, at the serious green eyes searching his. "He died of a heart attack, buddy, like the medical examiner said. That's what happened. You don't have anything to feel guilty about. Understand?"

"Why didn't you tell me?" Jared asks. "Why didn't you ever tell me about any of this?"

"I'm sorry, buddy. I should have. I guess...I guess I was just kind of hoping that maybe it would...pass you by. You know, skip a generation or something. Then you wouldn't have to deal with it."

"What about your dad?" Jared asks. "Didn't he ever talk to you about this stuff?"

Jared's dad nods. "Yeah. He did. He told me to stay away from Angel Falls, that I was probably too young to handle it. I asked him how old I had to be. He said, *Nobody's ever old enough.*"

"Is that all he said?"

"No. He told me you can want something, really want something with all your heart, and that still doesn't mean it's *right*. It took me a long time to figure that out." His dad shakes his head, staring down at the sand. When he speaks again, his voice is low and unsteady. "I'm sorry, buddy. I should have told you. Maybe then you would have been prepared."

"But no one's ever *prepared* for it, right?" Jared says quickly. "Isn't that what your dad meant? *No one's ever old enough?*"

Jared's dad looks up at him, his tired eyes glistening. "Yeah. Yeah, I guess you're right." Jared sees a smile beginning at the corner of his dad's mouth. It's not much of a smile yet, but it fills Jared with relief and happiness, knowing he can lift some of his dad's pain with a few words. He realizes that this is the only power he wants, the only power worth having.

A sudden warmth touches Jared's face. He looks up and sees the sun has set the ocean on fire. The two of them stand there for a while, not talking, watching the colors spread into each other.

"So," his dad says, "School starts in a couple of weeks, right?"

At those words, a sharp pain enters Jared's chest. *Jessie. Jessie's going back to New York.* He hasn't been able to think about it, can't bring himself to think about it now.

"Yeah." It's all he can manage to say.

"You can make her stay, you know," his dad says casually. Jared looks up, shocked. His dad is standing with his hands in his pockets, looking out to sea.

"*No,*" Jared stammers, heat rising to his face. "No, I'd never ..."

"I know you wouldn't, buddy," his dad smiles, looking at him now. "I know you'd never do that. No matter how much you might want to." Jared's dad looks down, idly turns a seashell over with the toe of his shoe. "Just like I could keep you here with me. In a lot of ways, that'd be the easiest thing in the whole world for me to do."

Jared stares at his dad—he can't believe what he's heard. *I could make you come back.* He remembers the anger he'd felt when he said those words to Jessie, the shame afterward, the ugliness of it all. Then he sees a smile break out on his dad's face.

"Don't worry, buddy. I'd never do that. It's like my dad told me. No matter how much you might want something, that doesn't make it right." Jared watches his dad peering out at the horizon and notices the wrinkles have grown deeper around the corner of his eyes.

"You don't have to wish for that," Jared says. "I'm not going to leave."

"Oh, sure you will," his dad's voice is calm and even. "One day, you will. And that's okay. That's how it's supposed to be."

The two of them look out over the ocean. The sun is making a trail of blazing light across the water, all the way from the horizon to the spot where they are standing. Jared's father steps closer to him and gently rests an arm over his shoulder. He smells a trace of the menthol shaving cream on his dad's neck, the good animal smell of dried sweat in his old blue shirt. After a few minutes, his dad speaks.

"You ready?"

Ready? Jared doesn't feel ready for anything. Not for going back to Rick's. Not for starting school in a couple of weeks. And he's not ready for Jessie's leaving.

His dad's arm lifts from his shoulder, so he nods, turns his back on that fiery trail across the water, and together they head for home.

Chapter 50

Let Me Go

Jessie and her mom hobble around the kitchen making cookies, Jessie in her knee-brace and her mother in her cast. Her father stands in the doorway. "How're my favorite gimps?"

Jessie smiles, "The cookies aren't done."

"I'm gonna do some work in the library, to avoid the maddening smell. I'll be back in a couple of hours. Don't eat them all!"

Jessie makes a face at him, "No promises," following him to the front door. He kisses her on the top of her head and leaves.

Her phone vibrates against her thigh. She pulls it from her pocket and sees a message from Jared. *Hey. Are you okay?*

She types, *Getting there. How about you?*

Getting there.

It's the same exchange every day since the night at Pulpit Rock. And though it's brief and the words never change, it comforts her.

When the cookies are done, she and her mother take a plateful and two glasses of milk to the backyard. The weather is perfect, not too hot. A slight breeze lifts Jessie's hair off her neck, blows it around her face. Leaves flutter down, although the trees are almost all still green. She looks down and finds a leaf in her lap. When she looks up, her mother is holding one, looking at it with such confusion that Jessie starts to laugh. Her mother joins her, and it feels so good, laughing with her mom, outside in the sun, she wants it to go on and on. But school starts in less than two weeks, and no one has said anything about leaving.

"When are we going home?" Jessie asks.

The last of the laughter is wiped from her mother's face. It's frightening how fast her expression changes, and Jessie can't read the new one, her brow furrowed, and her jaw clenched tight.

"I can't leave."

Jessie stares at her mother.

"What?"

"I can't leave," her mother repeats. Jessie's heart skips and stutters. She feels her mother's hand on her leg. The palm is hot.

"Let me go." Every hair on Jessie's arms stands up. Her mother continues, "I know what you did."

Jessie's fingers start to curl into her hands, nails driving into the palms. She has the sensation that all the leaves from all the trees are letting go, falling down, striking Jessie with their sharp edges.

"I know you wanted me and Michael to be happy together. But...You can't force it. You can't fix this. Not this way."

Her mother knows. Somehow she knows. Jessie whispers, "How...how do you..."

Her mother wipes her face, and Jessie realizes she is crying. "I was here. Once. Before you were born." She pauses, looking around the garden. "Cousin Dorothy had a health scare, wanted to make amends, so she invited us here. When Michael was out on an errand... maybe she sent him on purpose, I don't remember, but once we were alone she told me about Angel Falls. She talked about the history, the legends. Then she told me it was true. She told me how she brought your grandfather back."

Jessie's having trouble parsing the sentences. Certain phrases echo in her mind; *make amends ... she told me ... it was true.* And all Jessie can think is: *She knows.*

"Was that what you read in your grandfather's letters?" her mother asks. "Could you tell what happened?" Jessie nods, remembering her mother's face, clear of purpose but wiped of emotion, while she stood waiting for Jessie to put the letters in the garbage chute and let go.

Her mother continues, "Dorothy told me what a mistake it was. Things went very wrong."

Jessie thinks about the wounded deer, struggling to its feet. She can't look at her mother. "Why do you...," Jessie takes a breath, "why can't you leave?"

"I just... can't." Her mother looks up at the trees, follows the course of a falling leaf. "The morning after the accident, I started making plans to go home..." she's staring at the leaf on the ground, Jessie almost expects it to rise up again. Later, I... I don't know. I stopped thinking about it. I'd start planning to go home and get distracted." She turns to look at her daughter. Her eyes are wide, piercing.

"It kept happening every day. I didn't understand. Then you went looking for Jared, ended up in Angel Falls, and I knew... It happened again this morning. It happened just now when you asked me when we're leaving. I can't leave. Not until you let me go."

I can't! It's on the tip of her tongue even as she imagines doing it; being in Angel Falls, feeling that surge of power.

"What if I made you *want* to stay?" Jessie knows the answer and hot tears press behind her eyes.

"Is that what you want, to *make* me stay? Please Jessie. Please."

The word *please* pushes into Jessie's chest like a dull knife, it hurts and shames her, her fists so tight her knuckles ache. She nods slowly as tears run down her face, and mouths the word, "Okay," her voice completely gone.

Her mother angles her body as close as her cast allows, leans over, and takes Jessie's hands. "Sweetheart..." she starts, and Jessie can hear tears in her mother's voice. "Your father and I have problems. I know you've seen the way we are together. And I'm sorry. So sorry for it..." Jessie doesn't want to hear this, but she can't help noticing how beautiful her mother looks. "This summer was...I'm sure you guessed, a trial separation."

She feels the milk that coats her mouth, cloying, the cookies in her stomach want to rise back. The words *trial separation* make her start to shake. But a part of her is relieved – it's out at last, what she's felt and known for a while.

Her mother hops up on her good leg, pulling Jessie up too. Pulls her into her arms, rocking her, this great love easing the pain. And this is how her father finds them.

Jessie senses him in the air behind her, standing there. She gently disengages from her mother, moving into the tight circle of her father's arms.

CHAPTER 51

PROMISES TO KEEP

Jared stands by the moraine exactly as he did the day she first saw him here. Tall and still, he looks so normal, the tension she's carried here drifts away, dropping from her fingertips, exiting through the soles of her feet. He smiles at her, broad and warm. If there's anxiety in him, Jessie can't find it. Not like in Bunbury's two days' ago when she'd told him what her mother asked her to do.

His eyes had met hers in horror. *No, no, no. I promised my dad...* But eventually he'd agreed.

He had seemed so scared and angry at the thought of returning, to find him smiling now is both a delightful surprise and somehow exactly right. She leans her bike against a rock and walks up to him.

"Hey," he says.

"Hey. Thank you."

"For what?"

"This," she gestures to the woods and the path. "Coming here."

"Oh, sure. Are you okay?"

She nods. "You?"

He looks over the moraine, to the woods beyond, then back to Jessie and nods.

"It's funny. I thought I'd be sad or scared..."

"Me too."

"Are you?"

She shakes her head. "Not at all. I mean, I could be, if I wanted to."

"Yeah. Exactly." It makes her smile. "Come on. I have something to show you."

He leaps on the rocks, agile as ever, turns back to help her up, then moves ahead slowly, careful of her own slower progress. Her mother had made her wait till her knee was better, and she's glad of it now, every twinge reminding her of her helplessness that night. She can't fall now, not on her last day here.

He stands with his hand ready to help her down, like the first time. She remembers how she'd ignored his hand then, even as she's letting him help her now, with gratitude, leaning a little against his shoulder as she jumps gingerly off the rock.

"This way," he says, and they start to walk on a path Jessie doesn't remember.

"Where are we—"

"Just wait," he interrupts. "You'll see," and they walk in silence for a long way. At one point she realizes they are holding hands, though she doesn't remember it happening. It feels so natural, their hands, like magnets coming together without either of them giving it thought.

After a while, Jared says, "I found my mom."

It's spoken so casually, Jessie almost misses it, "What?"

He looks away, up the path, his face calm, then he looks down and kicks a rock.

They both watch it make a perfect arc, before disappearing into the brush. "She wrote me, a couple of months ago. Dad didn't think I ... well, he didn't tell me. A few days ago she called him. He said she sounded... normal. Better. So he gave me the letter."

Jessie watches him closely, looking for anger or grief, but his face is calm. His hand in hers is still, fingers relaxed. "What did she say?"

"That she had...," he sighs, "problems. She's taking care of them. Therapy, medication, I don't know exactly. 'In treatment' is what she said. She wants to see me."

"What are you going to do?"

"I don't know," he pauses. "She lives in Worcester. There's a bus I could take from Boston."

Jessie feels dizzy. Jared's voice is so casual. He's had time to absorb it, while she is only hearing it now for the first time. She opens her mouth to say something, but all that comes out is, "Wow."

He looks at her, smiling, and suddenly she wants him to kiss her. A longing so powerful it almost overwhelms her. She starts to close her eyes and feels a familiar sense of clarity, of power, the beginnings of a wish rushing up from the ground.

No! she opens her eyes, jerking forward, arms out to catch herself, but she isn't falling. She's standing quietly beside Jared who hasn't noticed anything.

Then she remembers why they're here.

"I'd like to do it now," she says. He nods, waiting. "I'm scared," she says, the words moving something small and cold in her stomach right up into a fist at her heart.

He squeezes her fingers. "It's okay. Let's do it." He's so sure, and she loves him for it. She squeezes his hand back, then closes her eyes.

She hears a bird nearby, endlessly repeating a five-note phrase. Her mind won't settle. She still feels guilty from almost wishing Jared to kiss her. She breathes deeply and slowly, and an image rises up. It's the one she'd made in her original wish; her mother coming in the door, her dad embracing her, Jessie and her parents smiling in Dorothy's living room. Suddenly she's looking at the diorama. She sees both farmer and wife inside the farmhouse looking out. A girl figure stands in the yard looking back at them.

Jared shifts his weight, brings her back to the woods, the smell of pine, the sound of the pointed five-note bird. She takes another deep breath and returns to the image of her mother in Dorothy's house. She forces herself to picture her mother walking out the door. A sharp pain crosses her chest.

Jared makes a sound, a sharp expulsion of air, but Jessie continues the vision.

Outside Dorothy's house she hugs her mother tight, then opens her arms and lets her go. The pain hits her heart again, but softer this time as her mother smiles, kisses her forehead and whispers, *thank you*. There is a soft sound of something being ripped slowly, and she feels her heart separate from her mother's, snap back into itself. The soreness slowly dissipates, until all she feels is her own heart's steady beating.

When she opens her eyes, Jared is studying her closely. "You all right?"

And when she nods, he says, "Come on."

They walk in silence. Jessie hears leaves rustling, birds chirping, breathes in the scent of damp earth, green grass, sun-warmed cedar. Her senses are a bunch of greedy hands, taking in everything and storing it for the time after today, when she can no longer come and see and smell and hear these things and has to rely on memory alone. And Jared walking next to her, his hand in hers; this too will end. If she doesn't burn this into her memory now, she'll have nothing.

He stops. "There's something I have to do. If you don't want to come, that's fine."

Jessie frowns, "What is it?"

"At Pulpit Rock. It's just there," he points through dense brush, and she looks away, afraid of what might still be lingering there.

"Why do you want to..." but then she understands. He's looking at her like he needs help, and even though the thought of walking into that space again terrifies her, she says. "I'd like to come."

They walk through the brush, and now Jessie can see the path, and then the clearing. Everything looks different. It's beautiful in the sunlight. Even the erupting jaw of rock is majestic, no longer frightening. Jared takes off his backpack, opens it and takes out a small book.

"What is that?" He shows it to her, and she reads, "*Collected Poems of Robert Frost.*"

"He gave it to me. I couldn't read it."

"And you can now."

He nods. He turns toward the space at the foot of the rocks. She can see evidence of all the trampling from that night, a larger flattened space where she knows Delany died, although the grass is already beginning to recover, to unbend. When Jared moves to the flattened grass, Jessie turns away to give him privacy.

She hears rustling, thinks he's kneeling to place the book on the ground. He's quiet for a long time, then more rustling and now he's standing behind her. She turns and finds him wiping his eyes with the heels of his hands like a young boy. Jessie walks over to a grove of tall blue flowers and gathers some. She carries them to the spot where the book lies and places the flowers beside it, thinking *peace. Peace.* And then she stands and walks quickly to Jared, and they exit the clearing, hands coming together again, fingers lacing.

Their path grows steeper, Jessie's knee starts to ache, so she slows down, and Jared keeps pace with her.

"Listen," his voice cuts into her thoughts, and for a moment she thinks he's about to tell her something. But then she hears it. The sound of running water.

"Is that...? Oh Jared! How did you..."

"Dad told me. We're very close.."

Her nose suddenly fills with the scent of water, and the air is damp and then they break out of the heavy woods and there it is – water cascading off a cliff thirty feet above, pummeling the pool below.

She looks at Jared's face, his proud bright eyes taking in the beauty of the waterfall. *Just one more wish,* she thinks. *Just this one.* And then Jared turns and sees her looking at him. For a moment he looks surprised, then he leans his face into hers, and their lips meet. The kiss is like riding her bike downhill as fast as she can go; it's the thundering Falls in her pounding heart, and it's Jared, of course, her Jared. She has to break away to breathe, to look at him, touching his face the way she's wanted to for so long.

"Like riding a bike?" he asks, and they both laugh.

Jessie remembers her wish. "Did I make you?"

Jared smiles and shakes his head, "No," and they kiss again, and this time it's more like falling. Falling without fear, wrapped tightly in each other's arms. When they stop, they remain pressed together, Jessie resting her head on Jared's shoulder, Jared's cheek against her hair. He whispers, "Jessie..."

After a while she says, "Remember when you didn't know my name?"

She feels him laughing, his chest moving against hers, shoulder rising and falling under her cheek. "Jesse James. *Pshoo-pshoo.*"

I never want to leave you, she thinks.

She can hear him answer, *I don't want you to go.*

And they hold on a little tighter before Jared suddenly stands back. "Beecham scheduled Dad's show. The opening is October 10th. Do you think, maybe, you could come?" He looks worried and hopeful at the same time. Jessie has to smile.

"Yes. Yes! Of course."

Then he wraps his arm around her back, hand settling at the curve of her waist, and leads her back onto the path. She tentatively snakes her own arm around him, finding the bony ridge of his hip and how perfectly if fits her hand.

They reach a path she recognizes, and far too quickly, she can see the old stone wall that separates this place from the world outside. They stop before the gap.

"I guess we should say goodbye." Jared says softly.

Jessie's heart drops. "Here? I thought we'd go out together... go home..." She's blinking hard, but the tears come anyway.

"I'm sorry, I didn't mean us," he laughs softly, putting one hand on her face. "I mean goodbye to..." he gestures back the way they came. "Here."

Jessie nods sharply, watching Jared's face as he turns his back to the opening in the wall and faces Angel Falls. She knows this must be harder for him than for her, this letting go. She looks back at the path, the leaves on the trees beginning to change color, a moss-covered boulder marking the bend in the path.

Jared turns, gestures to the gap in the stone wall, "Shall we?"

He doesn't look sad. He looks okay. So she nods, takes his hand, and together they pass through the wall and out of Angel Falls for the last time.

243-16608303

ACKNOWLEDGMENTS

Writing can be a lonely act. One spends years creating a world and characters with very little, if any, acknowledgment from anyone. That was not the case with this book. As partners and best friends who happen to live together, we created the characters and world of Angel Falls together, week by week, trading chapters and discussing the story on long walks through appropriately spooky woods. We acknowledge the great gift of collaboration; writers helping writers.

Many thanks to our beta readers, Linda Surface, Beth Rust, and Katy Wood. Your feedback and encouragement were (and are) greatly appreciated. Thanks to the good folks at Haverhill House Publishing, especially John McIlveen, for believing in our book and bringing it into the world. Thanks to Tony Tremblay, Christopher Golden, and James A. Moore for their kindness and support in welcoming us to the Haverhill House community. Crafting this novel was guided by Mary Carroll Moore's excellent advice in *Your Book Starts Here.* We also thank Irene Rocha, whose Sky Island Cottage provided much-needed writing retreats. Thanks to public libraries and librarians everywhere.

Having a writer as a parent can be a challenge, so we're both incredibly fortunate and grateful for the patience and encouragement of our amazing children, Matthew, Cailey, Peter, Katy, and Tim. Thanks also to Beth and Mary Hall for outstanding sibling support.

Two locations served as models and inspiration for Angel Falls; Dogtown in Gloucester, Massachusetts, and Doodletown by Bear Mountain, New York. Many thanks to Dogtown Preservation Commission, NYS DEC Doodletown Wildlife Management Area, and Bear Mountain State Park for creating and maintaining these sites for public use. May the beauty of nature and the mystery of abandoned places continue to inspire writers and artists for many generations to come.

9 781949 140330